Black HEARTS

A. M. DARLING

11 AM Publishing
An imprint of 11 AM Publishing LLC
its11am.com

Copyright © 2025 by A.M. Darling

First paperback edition May 2025
Book design by A. M. Darling

ISBN: 979-8-9877914-2-4

Dedicated to anyone who has ever lost a soulmate.

And to my soul sister, Tierra, thank you for being my biggest cheerleader and my greatest friend. Rest in paradise, sweet angel of mine.

PLAYLIST

Hours- Josh Makazo

1216- Echos

Certain Things- James Arthur feat. Chasing Grace

Me & Who- Mack Lorén

Suranna- Ty

Heartbeat- Honeyy

Striptease- FKA twigs

Passion- Kidd Phantomm and Kendra Williams

Body Loud- SWIM and Limi

Control- BURY

Alarms- Mellina Tey

Pitty Pitty (Get You Right Back)- BRIDGE

In Cold Light- Vanbur

Guilty- BOBI ANDONOV

 Important Note

Please be advised that this book contains themes and references that may be sensitive to certain audiences such as death, domestic violence, child abuse, gun violence, assault, murder, suicidal thoughts and ideations, miscarriage, sadism and masochism, stalking, kidnapping and explicit language.

Prologue

Journal,

The unfortunate truth about goodbye is that no one ever takes it seriously enough, until they realize goodbye could be forever. Until the end of a journey has arrived and the absence of what was is felt. And when that ending is with someone you love with everything in you, goodbyes are the most nightmarish thing in the world. Though somehow, despite such great dread, I found the strength to leave my Alexander.

This has shattered me.

I must have watched him for hours this morning, committing everything about him to memory. How he sleeps, the little lock of hair that fell across his brow, his steady breathing, the subtle curve of his lips. I imagined what sweet dream he could have dreamt and hoped with all hope that it wasn't about us, because he didn't deserve what he'd wake up to.

My heart aches for him. He had no idea that when we made love last night, it was for the last time. No idea that as he was drifting to sleep and

I told him I loved him, and he said, "I love you too, my sweet Aralyn," that it was, in fact, our farewell. Farewell to over three years of happiness. Farewell to the future we had spoken about. The future with the only white dress I'd ever wear, the adventures we'd take around the world and the children who'd have his bright smile and profound aspirations.

I had already prepared two suitcases of my most personal belongings and kept them in the trunk of my car for two weeks. It's taken me two whole weeks to walk away and, for a moment, I wasn't sure if I'd be able to do it. But as I watched him in his peaceful slumber, I knew. I knew it was then or never. Alexander is my everything; I love him more than life itself. It seems fitting that my last memory of the man I adore is the image of him in a state of bliss.

It tears me apart to know how gutted I'm certain he was, waking up to my absence along with a note that read, "You'll never know how sorry I am that it's ended this way. Just please know, it's for the best. Goodbye, Alex."

Something simple and to the point. Void of any true emotion in fear that he'd come after me to find out what's wrong and fix it. He can't fix this. No one can.

Once he moves past the shock, he'll hate me, I'm sure of it. But I'd rather he hates me than mourns me. And perhaps that's twisted. Perhaps I'm insane for thinking this is the way. But I know in my soul that to give him the best chance at happiness with another, he needs to feel like he can be happier with them than he could have ever been with me. I truly believe that to do so, he needs to feel bitter. I just hope and pray he won't let this keep his heart closed forever. That is my greatest fear with all of *this. But I have crafted a plan. I know what I must do as I embark on the journey toward another end, the end of my story.*

My sole mission now is to align him with the new love of his life.

I have to find him a different happy ending.

Alex, if for some reason you ever read this, forgive me, my love. If things could be different... Oh how I wish things could be different. This may be my last and greatest act of love. I hope you'll feel every bit of it

1

The smell of sex and sweat permeates the air accompanied by the sounds of moaning and lustful breathing. One would think the orgy happening on the bed in front of me would capture my full attention. But instead, I watch intently as the second hand of the clock on the wall ticks by, second by second, until another minute passes. My awareness is keenly focused on the fact that I'm choosing to spend each precious moment frozen in observation of the time I'm wasting. It feels haunting, taunting me to move, to act, to make decisions, and I hate it. But I can't seem to pull myself away.

Here I am, feeling as though I'm on the precipice of insanity, within the walls of an underground kink club in the heart of Paris. Five months ago, I wouldn't have even thought to set foot in a place like this. But that was before my world was spun out of orbit. That was a different life. Some might even argue a different dimension. The woman I was before is gone now, and I'm still on a mission to understand the woman I've become. I feel like I know her some days. On other days, like today, I feel detached and a bit confused, lost in the woods without a map or a compass to guide me.

One of the women on the bed, who's wearing nothing but a silver thong, traces the length of my arm with her fingers. "Join us," she insists in French as she gently grabs me. A second later, I'm being dragged down onto the mattress, landing on my back.

I stare at the ceiling, still in a daze, my senses muted. I'm barely here. I hardly notice the kisses along my neck or the unhooking of my red corset.

A man's face, hidden behind a silver skull mask, comes into view and he brushes aside strands of my hair stuck to my glossy lips and scattered like vines across my cheeks. His eyes bore into mine and I can feel the rough skin of his hand as he cups one of my breasts, tugging gently at my nipple. I softly gasp as my body reacts instantly, sending a flash flood of arousal through me from head to toe causing my back to arch. My mind gives into this as well, grateful for the distraction as the feeling of failure looms over me like the angel of death, ready to kill off the last bit of hope I've carried. The hope that my choice to not travel to London and chase after the man I care so much for was the right one.

I allow my eyelids to close, and behind them waits a different face, the only face that truly matters to me: Alexander's. His smile is radiant, and I can smell the phantom scent of his cologne. I get pulled into his captivating gray eyes framed perfectly beneath long lashes. I see the dimples in his cheeks, so deep they could cradle the earth. And I can practically hear his deep, enchanting voice telling me how beautiful I am and how sweet I taste.

This is how it should be: me and him giving the middle finger to time as we are suspended in a world where nothing is given notice except our connection to each other. I've never wanted anything more than to be *his*. Never yearned to be intwined with anyone's life as much as this. For a split second I allow myself to believe this is my true reality, and the life in which we are apart does not exist.

His lips fall upon my own, kissing me firmly … but something about this feels off, foreign and strange. My eyes fly open at the awareness of my mouth being overtaken by the previously masked stranger. I immediately scoot my head to the side and then bolt upright. Some of the others in the group look at me inquisitively. My corset is almost completely undone, hanging at my waist. The girl who had asked me to join is in between my legs kissing my thigh. She stops and asks if I'm okay. "I'm sorry. I-I can't," I mutter frantically and dash off the bed and out of the room.

Music continues to thump and blue lights pulsate sporadically as I move through the hall of the dark club. Feeling nauseous and panicky, I take a moment to lean against a wall and catch my breath. I've got to pull myself together and get out of here. I call my driver to let him know I'm ready, then rush to the bathroom while trying to redo the clasps of my bodice.

As soon as I enter, I grab paper towels and wet them with cold water before dabbing them across my neck and collar bone. I stare at myself in the mirror, my brown eyes wide and the rosy hue of embarrassment on my cheeks standing out against my ivory skin. My hand trembles as my fingertips lightly brush my rouge lips, still slightly damp from where the man kissed me. Shame is now added to the slurry of emotion swirling within my chest, giving rise to a greater sense of anxiety.

The door to the bathroom opens and in walks the woman who gave me a quick tour of the club earlier. Concern is written across her face and she rushes over to me. "Madame Rivers! Que s'est-il passé? Are you alright?"

"I'm fine."

She ignores my response. "You don't look very well."

"I haven't gotten much sleep. I think the exhaustion is catching up with me." The lie tastes bitter on my tongue, but all I want to do is to make an escape with as little socialization as possible. "I'm going home. Perhaps I can try this again some other time."

She peers at me like she knows I'm not telling her what's really happening. But she doesn't make a fuss, and for that I am grateful. "We'll be happy to have you again, madame, anytime. Get some rest. Is there anyone to drive you home?" I assure her there is and that gives her enough comfort to say goodbye and take her leave.

I don't know why my decision to not track down Alex and attempt to get him back has been haunting me so much recently. I'm just doing what he asked, after all, giving him the space he requested. *But you made a promise,* my consciousness reminds me. I can't evade the nagging feeling urging me to not let this one go, especially when it was made to a dying woman. Even that reminder doubles the shame. I'm not here to kiss strangers and allow myself to get carried away with self-pity. I need to get it together, and fast.

I change back into the knee-length blue dress I came in and then head out, collecting my jacket from the coat desk before making my way toward the exit. I am delighted to see my chauffeur, Jean-Philippe, waiting for me at the curb.

"Bonjour, Mademoiselle Rivers! The car is ready."

"Merci! You're a lifesaver." He walks out ahead of me and unfurls an umbrella, holding it up to shield me from the torrential summer downpour.

I wrap my gray coat a little tighter around me and we hurry out to the car. Water begins to seep into my blue pumps and the wind whips my hair. I climb in as soon as he opens the door. "I collected your clothing from the cleaners as requested earlier." The kind man holds up the small bag I brought with me for my lingerie. "I'll place this in the back with them." I give him a warm smile and he closes me in.

I examine my disheveled hair in the rear-view mirror. It had grown to a few inches past my shoulder since my makeover months ago. The growth is something I'm quite proud of, remembering how Alexander had liked the length of it before the big chop. I've continued to dye it black, however, having become attached to the color on me.

Besides the wind, the moisture in the air today has made my hair a bit frizzy, starting to bring back some of my natural waves. I run my fingers through it, hoping to make it appear a bit tidier. But when that does little to satisfy me, I take the hair tie off my wrist and pull it up into a ponytail. Of course, that doesn't quite satisfy me either. Very little does these days, it seems. I surrender, breathing out a long sigh of disappointment, and let my head fall back against the headrest.

Jean-Philippe gets in and starts the car. "Home, mademoiselle?"

"Oui, Jean. Merci." It's strange to have Aralyn's chauffeur as my own. Very strange. It wasn't my idea to hire him. In fact, I insisted against it. But at a certain feisty, ice-blonde Madame's demand, he's part of the deal. A deal I'm still on the fence about. Because ever since Madame Chérot walked into my home to deliver her shocking proposal to take me on as her new protégé, I've been completely thrust into the life of Aralyn De la Rue, quite literally.

My mind drifts to the memory of that day. I can still recall the entirety of our conversation as though it happened yesterday. Madame Chérot, in all her imperious and down-to-business demeanor, stood at my kitchen island and told me she was looking for a new protégé due to Aralyn's resignation. I was stupefied when she offered the position. What would have given her the idea that I, out of all the people she could select, would be the person to take Aralyn's place?

My response to her was, "Um, with all due respect, there's no way I can do that. For starters, I have a whole career! One that I'm quite happy with, by the way."

She folded her arms. "And?"

"And I'm far too busy to learn the ropes of helping you oversee a fetish empire!"

"C'est n'importe quoi!" she declared, basically calling out what I said as bullshit.

"Pardon me?"

"Your excuses bore me. You forget that you are talking to a woman who owns a vast number of salons across Europe, not to mention the additional locations in Canada, while also overseeing construction of a new salon in the States. None of that has stopped me from being the head of the largest fetish den franchise in Europe. There is no such thing as being too busy to do something. When you truly understand the value of time, you prioritize, organize, you *make* time. Just as I have made time out of my extremely busy schedule to come to you about this today."

"But why? Why pick me? It doesn't make any sense."

"Trust me, I would never have dreamed of choosing you for this position if my Aralyn did not beg me to take you on. She sees something in you. I don't know what just yet, but I hope to figure that out soon enough. At least you have proven you can keep things confidential, and for that I'm impressed. I'm sure you recall that I had my doubts. So, it's a start." She sighed dramatically and eyed me with heavy skepticism. "We shall see whether you are actually capable of the position."

It irritated me greatly that she asked me to take on a role she didn't even want me to have. I mean, honestly, so what if it was Aralyn's wish? Why would I want to be somewhere I'm not wanted? "The fact that you're proposing this to me is absolutely absurd."

The sound of her heels against the wood floor echoed through the room as she walked my way. "And yet," she said, coming to a stop inches in front of me, "you have not said no."

"Okay then. NO."

She stared me down, smirking. "I see the spark of curiosity that shines in your eyes, mademoiselle." Her tongue clicked. "You don't realize it, but though you have indeed made up your mind, the answer is not the one you just gave."

"Oh my God, you're serious. HA! You really think I'm just going to say 'Oh, oui, madame! Whatever you wish!' and show up ready to be whipped into your perfect, obedient little assistant?"

"Oh, I know you will." She turned and walked back to the kitchen island. "That look in your eyes is also the look of a woman with many questions. Many questions that you know your inquisitive little mind will never move on from until you get the answers. That, my dear, is the look of a woman determined to know that which she does not yet understand, and it is that very urge you carry within that will move you to accept my offer."

I huffed and stormed over to the front entrance. "Madame, I'm afraid the time you took to show up here today has been wasted." I swung the door wide open. "As I said, the answer is no." How incredibly presumptuous of her, thinking she could stroll into my home and speak for me!

Taking the hint, she moved toward the door, but paused just before exiting to examine my face. "Now, this look … this look right here, is of a woman who cannot stand to be wrong." She cocked her head. "What chaos that must stir within you."

I could feel my cheeks grow hot with anger, though I did my best not to give her the satisfaction of knowing she got under my skin. "Have a nice day, Madame Chérot."

She donned her sunglasses and her smug smile turned into a wide, mischievous grin. Then she took a card from her pocketbook and gave it a quick wave. "For when you become honest with yourself." She set it down on the small entry table. "Bonne soirée, Jess." And with that, she walked out.

I truly wanted to believe everything she saw in me that day was dead wrong. But within days, curiosity was indeed eating me alive, literally keeping me up at night! At first, I couldn't stop thinking about what I might miss, passing up the opportunity. Turning her offer down could mean losing the chance at an inside scoop on a whole fascinating, taboo world, one that Alex had introduced me to. I then realized that, although Alex gave me a taste of that world, he left me with an insatiable thirst for more. A door was opened that simply couldn't be shut.

It became difficult to focus that entire week. Memories of my wrists being bound in leather straps, being spanked, and ordered onto my knees repeatedly drifted through my conscious.

I gravitated to books, articles, movies, even toys to satisfy my mind and satiate my body, but they only made the craving worse. I found myself unable to stop thinking about what I could learn, and even more, what of these erotic lifestyles I could explore.

Going deeper down a rabbit hole of thought, as I do, triggered an epiphany that I was going to need to accept I could not go back to the sex life I had before Alex, and at the same time, there was so much I needed to explore about the sex life I wanted. I had reached a pivotal moment of my life, a new era, a sexual awakening. And if I wished to discover more about this new woman I transformed into, a woman who had become vastly intrigued by the allure of kink, what better way to do it than to take the opportunity to become a madam myself?

So, eight days after our conversation, I stared at Madame Chérot's business card for over an hour. And while enjoying a glass or two of wine, I wrestled with the temptation of giving her the *yes* she claimed she saw. But, in the end, no matter how much I wanted to stay firm in my *no*, I ultimately gave in and sent her a text to let her know I was interested in discussing the position further.

"We have arrived, mademoiselle." My chauffeur's voice echoes through the hold of my memory, guiding me back to the present.

"Oh, um, merci."

Jean-Philippe makes his way around to open my door and I step out, but only make it three steps before coming to a stop. I stand frozen, stunned at who I see waiting on my stoop. My breath hitches and my heart races as emotion quickly swells within me.

Sweet heavens. It's been way too long…

2

armyn Calloway waves sweetly as I approach. I gawk at Alexander's assistant in disbelief, and she addresses me as I climb the steps. "Ms. Rivers, hello!" I can't begin to describe how good it is to see her again.

I flash an enormous smile. "Oh my god, Carmyn, hi!" I fling my arms around her in a hug to confirm to myself that she is, in fact, really here before me. She laughs, taken aback, and wraps her arms around me too.

Unexpectedly, my eyes well with emotion. She pulls back and looks at me with such tenderness. Then, with a gentle sweep of her thumb, she wipes away the lone tear that spills over. "Oh no, Jess darling, I didn't intend for my presence to sadden you."

"Exactly the opposite! I'm so incredibly happy to see you, you have no idea." Besides missing her, her presence is the closest I've come to Alex in almost half a year and my soul is beyond pleased.

She looks gorgeous as ever in a short-sleeved lavender blouse that perfectly complements her dark complexion, along with a white knee-length pencil skirt and umbrella hooked around her arm that matches her outfit perfectly. It just now hits me that the last time I saw her was when she was keeping banquet guests from discovering the chaos of Arthur and Alexander's tussle. Though, it wasn't much of a tussle. Arthur was nearly out before he was in.

"Well, it's marvelous to see you too! I'm so happy I caught you just in time. I'd no way of knowing if you'd be home." She gives me a once over, "You look *really* good." I catch the subtle surprise in her voice. It's almost as though she thought I'd be in an abysmal state. I've done my best not to appear that way on the outside. Inside, however, I can't say that notion would be far from true.

Suddenly, a glimmer of sadness springs to her hazel eyes. The cool, damp evening wind blows dark curls across her face. She brushes them back. "Erm, sorry to say, Mr. Marc is not here with me. He's taken a holiday to visit family in Florence."

"Oh, it's alright." I can't ignore the slight sting of disappointment. "That's good! I'm glad he's taken some time away to enjoy the company of loved ones. How's he been?" I'm unable to keep the question from escaping, coming from an instinctual need to know.

I can see Carmyn's hesitation, cautiously calculating in her mind exactly what she should say. She's clearly on edge about it and I don't blame her. She had asked me not to break Alexander's heart, and I fear I did exactly that when he discovered that I did not disclose to him my agenda with Aralyn. Although, I'm unsure if she actually knows that.

She responds, "He's been as well as could be expected, I think. He's doing what he can to cope and, as I'm sure you can imagine, coping for him involves work, so that's where his head is at, currently." I understand what she means. I'd come to know Alex as a man who believes he needs control in order to function. So, when the events that occurred the night of the charity banquet flung his world out of orbit, it makes sense that he'd gravitate heavily toward the thing he could manage most.

"Truthfully, I'm concerned about him," she continues, "The man constantly tries to act like he's alright, but I know he's not. He's more distant and his demeanor is rigid. I've never seen him like this, putting forth so much effort to keep everything tightly held together, not even when he went through his breakup with Ms. De la Rue. Back then, he was mostly just frustrated all the time." My heart aches at this news. "It's clear he's conflicted. Perhaps constantly being at war with his own emotions has taken a greater toll this time around." She sighs, "I just want my boss back."

For Carmyn, though she is poised and professional as ever, I know this is deeper than wanting her boss back. She wants her *friend* back. Or as she described him before, her family. I may not ever hear her say it again, but I know it's true.

"Which brings me to why I'm here. I rarely ever meddle in his personal affairs, but I care about him too much to not try and do something to help him in his current state. If you are open to it, I'd like to attempt to arrange a meeting for the both of you. I suppose I'm praying that if you two talk things through, it will bring him a modicum of peace."

This has to be a sign from the heavens, a gift even, literally placed on my doorstep. I have no excuses now! To decline would be to surrender to my fear of rejection, which could very much be a real possibility. But this is a chance, a true chance, to fulfill my promise to Aralyn and reclaim happiness for myself, and potentially Alexander, too, if he takes this chance with me.

"Wow, okay. Okay, yes, if you can arrange it, I'd be happy to speak with him."

Her smile is bright. "Marvelous. It just so happens that next week he will be making a quick stop here in Paris. He has an order he personally wants to ensure is handled correctly. He'll only be here for the day, but he will be here. Keep in mind I can't make any promises, but I'll speak with him."

No promise necessary. I'm overjoyed just knowing that Alex is coming to Paris, and I may have the opportunity to see him. Despite my doubts about us pulling this off, my heart beams. "When exactly is he supposed to arrive next week?"

"Wednesday." Five days from now. "He has a small window of time at eleven that morning. It's right after his meet up with the project manager and a couple hours before his flight home."

"Alright. Well, if we want to give this the best chance of success, I think we should present it from an angle that will put the least amount of pressure on him to meet. Alex should feel like the choice is really up to him. I say leave the ball in his court. Just tell him that I spoke to you and said that I have no expectations, but if he'd like to meet with me, I'll be at Bouilloire Sifflante Café between eleven and noon on Wednesday."

She nods. "I will. Thank you."

I grin. "Carmyn, did you really fly down here just to talk with me about this? You could have called or emailed me, you know."

"Yes, well, I've always believed some things are best spoken about in person. It's been quite some time, and I wanted to ensure you knew the sincerity of my desire to help the two of you."

A sense of guilt washes over me again. "I have so much to apologize to him for."

"It's nothing you haven't apologized to him about before, I'm sure." I gaze at her questioningly and she answers, "He told Tommy about what happened. Naturally, Tommy then talked with me about it."

"I really am the worst."

She chuckles, "Well, it's not as though you acted alone. And though I can't speak for him, I don't believe Mr. Marc has any ill feelings toward you. Understand that his choice to part ways with you that night was largely due to his need for space and time to process. I imagine being confronted with the dramatic events and harsh truths from that night was incredibly difficult. The biggest shock was likely Ms. De la Rue popping in on him like she did after so long, and with such heavy news." She sighs. "That alone would be a lot for anyone to handle in his position."

"I just feel so awful for the way it all went down. And if I'm being honest, though I miss him greatly, a part of me is upset with him for leaving me high and dry. I do understand the need for space, I do. But I personally feel as though he—I don't know— gave up, I guess. He couldn't even tell me whether or not he'd ever contact me again. So, how much do I really mean to him, you know?"

"All perfectly valid feelings. Let's pray we can get you both together so he can address them."

Hope shares a seat with dread on the bench of my heart. Everything is very much up in the air. There are several directions the future could go, and I'm hoping with all hope that Alexander and I can head in a great one, the most ideal one, if possible. But, what if the chance of that is such an immense gamble? What if the probability is higher that our future together has no continuation at all? He could ultimately choose to stay clear of any communication with me.

"How rude of me. Would you like to come inside? I can make us some tea, or we could have a glass of wine."

"That's very kind, but I should go. My flight home departs in a couple of hours and I'd like to be timely to the airport."

"Of course. Thank you, Carmyn. This is the best news I've received in a while. And I know you aren't doing this for me, or making any promises, but I want you to know how much I appreciate you for even trying. I've been on the fence for months about reaching out to him. Each time I chose against it, determining that it's best to respect his wishes."

It begins to drizzle again. Carmyn puts on fashionable white gloves and unfurls her umbrella. Then she reaches out and hugs me. This time I'm the one caught off guard by the act, but I quickly return the warmth, delighted.

"Here's my ride." I follow her gaze to a black car that pulls up, and the driver steps out to open the passenger door. Carmyn starts down the steps and turns to me when she reaches the bottom. "Best of luck, Ms. Rivers. I'm rooting for you. I'm rooting for you both. May we see each other again soon." I give her an appreciative smile and watch as she makes her way to the car.

Longing. That is what is currently in my heart. Longing for what I once had. Even if it was short lived, it was oh so sweet. Carmyn represents much of what I'm longing for, what I miss with everything in me, what I yearn for again. It's nice to know she's in our corner, praying that we can set things right.

I truly pray so too.

❤

*T*oday is moving day. I'm almost finished packing the last of the boxes in my living room. I look around at the almost empty space, a bit sad. This flat has been my home since I moved to Paris six years ago. It's strange leaving it. So many changes have happened in such a short time, and this move is absolutely one of the biggest, even if I'm only moving a few miles away.

As I pack the books on my bookshelf, I come across Aralyn's journals. I could have read all of them by now, several times over, but every time I sat down to crack one open, I was racked with guilt. It didn't feel right to indulge when I hadn't made any forward momentum toward achieving her final wish. However, throughout all this time, I have been mulling over what I might do with her story.

I have decided that I will attempt to write a biography. Big emphasis on 'attempt.' I never dreamed I'd ever write a book. Articles have always been my place of comfort. Though, when I really think about it, simply keeping to articles was a limitation I placed upon myself.

I haven't a clue what will be in the pages of these journals, but I have a strong feeling that Aralyn De la Rue's story—her sacrifices, her triumphs and tragedies—is deserving of more than a short piece in a magazine or newspaper that will likely be discarded and not thought much of again. A book seems more fitting. And though it will certainly challenge me to breach my self-imposed limitations, it's a challenge I'm willing to take.

I have some time before the movers arrive. Might I now be bold enough to open the first journal and dive in? Seeing Carmyn alleviated some of my anxiety over not reaching out to Alex. There's a plan in place now. It's *something*. It's perhaps even the best thing, the best way to bring ourselves back into alignment with each other's path.

Hmm, yes, I think I will. I take a seat on my couch and flip to page one, finally allowing myself to relax into exploring the depths of Aralyn's world.

Journal,

I don't have anyone to share my most intimate thoughts with, so a journal seems like a good idea. We shall see how long it lasts. Nothing around this home seems to stay secret for long, unless Papa wants it to. I suppose if he gets a hold of this I'll be in a world of trouble. Thing is, I don't really care anymore.

Where do I even begin?

Well, Paris bores me. Everything and everyone bores me. I've come to think there's no longer anything in my life worth taking an interest in. I no longer allow myself to have interests because what is the point when the only thing I get in return for my desires and curiosity is betrayal and disappointment?

I was told not to go to the art festival this weekend after being given the same reason I am given every year, that it's stupid to spend time gawking at art when I could be home putting more time into my studies. My whole world, it seems, revolves around school work and rules. Any freedom to explore interests of my own has always been stripped from me.

I tried to connect to my passions secretly. At night, when everyone was asleep, I would take my paper pad and paint set from inside a hidden cubby I created in my dresser, and I'd get lost in the colors and brush strokes. But my Nanny found them and told on me. She was the one person I thought might have some sympathy for my lack of opportunity to be who I am. There's always a look of pity on her face whenever I'm reprimanded for the stupidest of reasons. But tonight, I learned that she's just like everyone else and the pain of the welts on my thighs and back won't soon let me forget it.

There's no one left in my small, sheltered world whom I can trust. I was a girl who once had hope that she could live whatever life she wanted. But she is gone, long since departed. I am now just the shell she left behind.

Happiness? What is that? I have not known happiness in years, and even when I did, I questioned its authenticity. My pretty smiles hide troubles and fears. That's my truth. That's my life, to move through each day as though everything is okay when it's far from it. I have no idea who I am outside of who they want me to be and that's terrifying. Because if I'm not living for me, then why is this fake, boring, tragic existence worth living at all?

They toy with me, use me, make decisions for me. And I no longer put up a fight because why should I? Why care? What would be the point when there's nothing I can really do about any of it? Why try to use a voice that has long since been silenced when I know that to try would be futile?

So, you see, boredom has become all I know, all I feel. Boredom is my cage. Boredom is the only thing you're allowed to truly express as a girl who's to be seen but never to be heard, to be intellectual but never permitted to think for herself.

Who am I to challenge it?

3

My eyes flutter open, adjusting to the morning light pouring in from the window. I get a good stretch in but instantly want to curl back under the covers. The movers didn't finish till late, and I stayed up till almost 2:00 trying to get at least some of my belongings organized. Unfortunately, my alarm is intent on reminding me that I have a job to forsake sleep for this morning. How I wish I could just stay home.

Hmm, home. I smile wryly as I look around the bedroom and realize how far from home I actually feel. Never in a million years did I think I'd end up here.

I reach over to shut off the secondary alarm and then proceed to stare at the ceiling, reflecting on how I ended up in this house to begin with. "It all goes back to you, Aralyn," I whisper. "It always seems to go back to you."

When I accepted Madame Chérot's offer, I had anticipated that I'd start training with her immediately. To my astonishment she was gracious enough to give me a couple months to settle myself after all my major life shifts.

The first time I had heard from her since accepting her offer was about a month ago. She asked me to meet her at an address she sent and, when I looked it up, I saw the location was a townhome. She wouldn't tell me a single thing about it even when I met with her at the front door. It wasn't till we walked in that I realized it was far from an ordinary house, regardless of how plain Jane the exterior looked. It was gorgeous—completely decked out with a burlesque-meets-high-fashion aesthetic.

Every wall was painted white, and red sofas and chairs were gathered in conversational clusters in nearly every room. Stunning crystal chandeliers hung from the ceilings, and the black marble of the floors was echoed in the steps of the elegant staircase, which was flanked by black banisters made of elaborate scrollwork. Sensual up-close, black and white photographs of various areas of the human anatomy hung on the walls, some male, some female, some couples—male and female or same sex—in one shot. I gazed around in awe. "Wow, I didn't realize you were so into red and black as well. What is this place? Is this the den where the magic happens?" I asked, jokingly, waggling my eyebrows. She didn't even crack a smile. What a tough woman to get through to.

"This was Aralyn's home," she replied.

My eyes grew large. I didn't know why I was so shocked; it was the reigning queen of such a color palette we were talking about. "Wow, yeah. Got it. Makes sense. She seems to have always been intensely devoted to her aesthetic in the most fashionable way."

"It is your turn to be devoted now. She's leaving the home to you."

"I'm sorry, what?" My brow furrowed in confusion. "You're being serious. Why on earth would she do that?"

"Oui, I've asked the same question. But she seems to think you somehow deserve it." I could tell Madame Chérot herself certainly didn't think so. Could I blame her? Aralyn barely knew me, and yet she trusted me to cherish the heart of her ex-boyfriend, somehow convinced her superior to offer me her position, and on top of that was signing over her home to me. If I were the Madame, I would be unenthusiastic and highly suspicious too.

She sauntered over to me and dropped a set of keys into my hand. Then, with a bitter tone she said, "Congratulations. Don't fuck it up."

I stared at the keys in astonishment. "Look, I-I-I don't know about this. Moving in here would be too weird and strange."

"Mademoiselle, this whole thing is strange. But what's done is done." She pointed to the coffee table in the middle of the living room, where a large white envelope sat. "She left you a copy of her deed to look over. The deed won't officially be in your name until she has passed and her will is read. However, I've been asked to inform you that as far as she is concerned, you can move in today if you wish."

I wasn't sure what I wished at all. I was horribly perplexed. Surely, I should have been grateful to be gifted a home, but I didn't understand why it was gifted to me, nor did I know if I was comfortable living in it, with all her possessions and the looming possibility that I'll always wonder what memories she had here, particularly with Alexander. It didn't seem right.

She continued, "All utilities will be managed until the house is in your name. Hopefully, by that time you will have learned all that's necessary to be a fitting head of house at the den, and you'll be earning more than enough for the upkeep." It sounded like the perfect set up, but I was racked with nerves and unbridled doubt.

"The location is very beneficial. Aralyn didn't want to be far from headquarters in case she was needed in a hurry at any hour, so the den happens to be a few blocks away. Six, in fact. It's a quiet neighborhood with plenty of lovely parks, boutiques, and restaurants in the area. Come. I'll show you upstairs."

I followed her to the second floor where there were two bedrooms. She explained that one was a guest room and the other was the master. We walked into the master, which was as regal as the rest of the home. The sunshine streaming in from the windows glowed on the white walls and bounced off the red crystal chandelier hanging in the middle of the ceiling, dispersing ruby-colored speckles across the room.

The Madame opened the doors to an impressive walk-in closet full of all manner of outfits and shoes, in Aralyn's signature colors, of course. "Oh, my God." I mouthed, struggling to register it all.

"I'm not sure how many of these will fit you. You have a bit more bust than Aralyn, but they are all yours too."

"She didn't want to take any of these things with her?" It seemed unusual, knowing what I did about her, that she'd leave them all behind, even knowing she wouldn't have much need for them soon. She seemed to have cared about what she wore a great deal, no matter what her state of health was.

"She took most of her wardrobe with her. This is, apparently, what was left. Oh, and this." She opened yet another door almost obscured behind a rack of dresses, and my eyes widened in shock! Toys! So many damn toys, organized on every wall in a space the size of a small bedroom. Whips, paddles, anal plugs, dildos, feathers, chains, you name it this woman had it!

"Holy fuck." Aralyn was *truly* living the lifestyle. I mean, I knew, but I didn't *know*, not the extent, anyhow. I don't even think the knowledge that she was next in line to take over a fetish empire prepared me for just how in it she was. Hell, even the awareness that she was with Alex didn't prepare me.

"Um, what exactly did Aralyn do at the den?" I then wondered why I didn't ask for details about the job before I took it. Where on earth was my sense?

"She took on many roles before she was protégé, but she preferred being a dominatrix." A dominatrix? How did she go from kink den dominatrix to Alexander's submissive?

I blew out a long breath, overwhelmed. "Wow, this… This is all so much."

"Oui, well, as I said, it is yours. Move into it. Don't move into it. It matters little to me. But whatever you do with this home, respect it and don't sell it. If she wanted it sold, she would have done so. Clearly, that was not her wish." I was mulling over the woman's words, and then she piled on even more words that made my head spin. "I take exceptional care of all my managing staff. What I offered you is a highly paid position and an equally high honor. As my protégé you will be provided with a chauffeur to take you wherever you need to be." At that point I could feel my brain turning to mush as I tried desperately to process everything as quickly as it was coming at me.

"You will meet your chauffeur tomorrow. His name is Jean-Philippe."

"Wait, the same man who chauffeured Aralyn?"

"Exactement."

"Jean-Philippe is great, but is a personal driver really necessary? I mean, I have a car. I'm perfectly capable of driving myself wherever I need to be."

She pretended not to hear me. "You will also be provided an assistant to help you organize and manage schedules, handle client and staff communication, and ensure all necessary paperwork has been properly documented and filed."

"Um, right … okay. Anything else?" As if I could actually handle more than the mountain of information she just bombed me with.

"That is all for now. I must be going. I'll give you a couple weeks to figure out how you'd like to proceed with everything here, and then we will talk business. Bonne chance."

Four weeks later here I am, settling in while unsettled, deeply questioning my decision to move in here. It's not like I'm tight on money. My career has really started to flourish since the article on Alex. I could have easily kept this place and continued to live in my flat. But I didn't, and instead of worrying, I try to keep in mind my whys.

For one, I have this stirring need to feel close to Aralyn in order to understand her better. I figured the best way to accomplish that would be to literally be in her space, the place where she thought, felt, dreamt and loved. I want the opportunity to immerse myself in the totality of who she is to hopefully get a grasp on why she's made certain life decisions.

Second, it was absolutely the journalist in me that gave the stamp of approval on this choice. I simply found it too hard to resist the thirst I had for uncovering a more in-depth story by way of this venture. That same drive is also partially responsible for my acceptance of the Madame's offer to be shown the ropes as her protégé.

This will indeed be a hell of an experience and an adjustment. In a way, though, I prefer the unknown aspect of all this to the "normal" life I was living prior to having met Aralyn. I've become hooked on it, entrapped by the alluring potential of more adventure and intrigue. Yet at the same time, such a driving pursuit has been a struggle to accept, for it is that same preference for the unknown that led me to some heartbreaking scenarios.

After more than enough time lost in thought and memory, I drag myself from the comfort of the bed and start preparing for the day. All my belongings are in Aralyn's room, but last night I crashed in the guest room, unable to bring myself to sleep in her bed. It just felt too weird; this all does. But her room, I don't know if I'm ready for that yet. It seems like it would be a complete takeover, and I'm already trying hard to not feel like I'm becoming her replacement in every sense of the word.

I finish getting dressed when suddenly I'm caught off guard by the sound of voices coming from downstairs. I've got to be hearing things. But as I walk to the bedroom door to listen, my suspicions are confirmed. The tone is low, but it sounds as if there is some sort of an argument. This is freaking me out. There shouldn't be anyone in here!

With a fire poker in hand from the bedroom fireplace, I creep down the staircase to see what's going on, then carefully peek over the banister. I spot Madame Chérot arguing in hushed tones with a man I've never seen before. His back is to me so I can't quite see his face, but I take notice of long wavy black hair cascading down the back of his black leather jacket to the middle of his shoulder blades. He's tall. Definitely over six feet.

I lay the poker on a step, then slowly proceed the rest of the way to the first landing and lightly clear my throat. The Madame looks past the man's shoulder, eyeing me with disapproval as though I've made the huge mistake of interrupting. "Bonjour, madame. I'm surprised to see you here. I wasn't expecting you today." How did she get in here anyway?

The man turns at the sound of my voice, and I'm stunned. His straight nose with a prominent bridge, high sharp cheek bones, and chiseled jawline are straight off a romance novel cover. His mustache and full beard are neatly groomed and his lips, though pulled tight with frustration, are full. Far from marring his beauty, the jagged scar that runs a few inches across his cheek, slightly below his left eye only makes it more interesting. His eyes are what grabbed my attention first; they're an intense bluish-green, like the ocean in the Caribbean, with a hint of amber sparkling in their depths. Those eyes seem so familiar … and they peer at me with intense scrutiny.

Madame Chérot speaks up, "Jess, this is Luca, Luca De la Rue."

My eyebrows lift, my interest piqued more than before. "De la Rue? He's a relative of Aralyn's?"

"Oui. Luca is Aralyn's brother. He's come to retrieve one of her belongings." Oh! I knew Aralyn had family, but even in the journal I've been reading from her late teens, she hasn't mentioned a brother, so far. Good looks obviously run in their genes.

"Wow! Pleasure to meet you." I step toward him and extend my hand. He takes it but he's doing a horrible job of keeping the irritated scowl off his face, if he's even attempting it. "Um, however I can be of help, I'm happy to assist. I haven't moved much around. Most of her things are still where she had them."

"Where is her vanity?" His clipped tone is laced with a Spanish accent, which I find rather curious. I know Aralyn is half Spanish, but her accent was definitely more French. I find it interesting that her brother's differs so drastically, though I don't dwell on it.

"In her bathroom, which is in the master bedroom. Up the stairs and to the right." I didn't even finish my sentence before he breezed by me, heading for the second floor. I gaze at Madame Chérot, wondering if I missed something that would explain his demeanor.

She answers my silent question, "He does not like the fact that you've moved into this house."

"Did you tell him this was Aralyn's idea?"

"Of course. But he does not care." She sighs. "The point is, whether it was your idea or not, you are here. He's always been very protective of Aralyn, perhaps overly so. Personally, I believe it's part of the reason she could never keep many friends; if Luca did not approve, they were run off. There are quite a few things she does that he does not approve of, I've noticed."

Geez, I mean I grew up an only child, but that seems a little odd. Who has to be *that* protective of their sibling? "And Aralyn let him have that much impact on her life? Doesn't seem like her."

"What does she say in the journals about her upbringing?"

"I haven't gotten too far into them yet, but most of the entries talked about how troubled her life was. So far, she hasn't mentioned Luca, but I recall she wrote a lot about her father, how she didn't think she'd ever be enough for him. Nothing she did was enough to please him."

"Well, I suspect their upbringing has something to do with why she chose the path she did, and why Luca is how he is with her. Keep reading. You're bound to learn more."

She's right, I need to dive deeper into this. Seeing that I'm writing a biography of Aralyn's life, knowing her origins, especially if they contributed to her life decisions, is important. And Luca, I now see, is the missing link to understanding that portion of her existence.

"It's also possible it could just be a twin thing," she adds.

"What?"

"Why he's so protective of her. He's her twin brother." I'm learning so much, and it's only been five minutes. Things are growing more intriguing by the second. "You know how twins are, a bond like no other."

"Right…" I trail off as Luca bounds down the stairs with empty hands. Without so much as a look at either of us, he walks right between us, then straight out the door.

"I guess he found what he was looking for," she says.

"How do you know?"

"Trust me. If he didn't, we'd be hearing about it." How bizarre. "How was your first night?"

"It was fine. Though I will probably now be on edge, having discovered that I'm not the only one with a key. Please tell me that letting yourself in here whenever you wish will not be a regular thing. As a matter of fact, why didn't you hand over your key when you gave me my set?"

She doesn't respond right away, making me think she really doesn't have a good answer. "Must have slipped my mind. I've had a key since Aralyn first moved here. She felt comfortable knowing that if anything happened, I could check on her. I'm a creature of habit. I got so used to the accessibility of this home that I didn't think much about giving you the key."

"Why would she think anything would happen?"

"She simply took precautions."

I cross my arms over my chest. "Okay, well, were you also not thinking about it when you let yourself AND Luca in here?"

Her eye twitches slightly and her lips purse in that way I discovered they do when she's either annoyed or trying to quell her emotions. "As I said"—she holds up the key—"creature of habit." I reach out and she drops it in my palm, turns on her heels, and heads for the door. "Oh, before I forget. I have arranged a couple play sessions for you to observe next week. It will give you some more insight into the BDSM world and the various lifestyles. I'll have the details sent to you soon. Au revoir."

Well, so far, this whole morning has done nothing but give me more anxiety. And on top of once again reanalyzing my choice to move here, I'm really starting to reconsider my decision to go through with this underground lifestyle the Madame is involved in. Will it satisfy my curiosity? Certainly. But at what cost?

I fidget with the black key in my hand. First order of business is to get the locks changed. For all I know she could have made copies. I don't know her like Aralyn does and I sure as hell don't feel comfortable with her having access to my private space.

Remember, Jess, always be two steps ahead. Right, because that's my new plan to make it through this venture as unscathed as possible. If I always aim to be two steps ahead, I can potentially avoid a shit load of issues.

As for the Madame, she will soon come to realize that no matter what she's accustomed to, she has no control over my life. She has no access to it that I don't personally grant her, and depending on how things progress, she may come to find that whatever access I do grant will be quite limited indeed.

I'm not fucking around this time. This is my fresh start. The upper hand will always be mine.

I proceed to the kitchen to make myself some coffee. It's far too early for all this. I need energy, and fast.

Just as the brewer finishes up, there's a knock at the door. "Ugh, what now?" Aralyn's brother back for another item?

I open it to find a bright-eyed Jovana standing there with an envelope in hand. "Bonjour, Jess!"

"Hey—Oh my god, I totally forgot you were coming by today! I've been so distracted."

"Ah, maybe I come by anther time?"

"No, no, that's okay. I was going to go down to the news station today to talk to one of the editors, but I'll just check in with him after lunch." I totally spaced that I had asked her to come over to help me pick an outfit for when I, hopefully, go to meet Alex in a few days. Even after helping me with the whole alter-ego scheme, Jovana has continued to be such a help with style and makeup. In exchange, I've been helping her with her English and she's made great improvement.

"Come on in, I just made some coffee. You like two sugars, no cream, right?"

"Hahaha, oui. Oh! Here. A man gave me this when I was coming to the door. Said it is for you."

She hands over the small white envelope she was holding. "Uh, okay, strange. I wasn't expecting anything." Sure enough, it has my name on the front. I open it and the solid black card it encloses. Written in white font are the words:

Stay away from Alexander Marc.

What the actual hell? I rush past her, out the door and down the steps, frantically looking both ways down the street and across it. "Jovana," I call back, "What did the man look like who gave you this note?"

"I do not know. He wore a big shirt with the hood and uh, *lunettes de soleil.*" Sunglasses. The sensation of a knot forms in my throat as quickly as the fear that's manifesting in my mind.

"Is everything okay?"

God, do I hope so, because if not, my fresh start might turn into nothing more than a rotten extension of my past.

4

I walk through the door of La Peep Café, instantly greeted by the aroma of freshly ground coffee and the overpowering sense of nostalgia. This place continues to be my favorite little spot. Sometimes I find myself watching the doors, hoping Aralyn might walk through at any moment. A pang of sadness always follows when I remember that she'll never do so again.

I wave to the Benoît, the barista I've come to know over the years, and he waves back. Then I grab a seat at my usual table, happy to see it hasn't moved since their recent expansion and renovations. To me, it's always the best seat in the café, even for today. It's not too close to the door that I'd appear desperate to catch a glimpse of Alex coming in, but not too far from it that he would have trouble spotting me, should he show. However, it doesn't look like spotting me should be an issue, due to the surprising lack of patrons. From where I'm sitting, there's no one else here except for a customer placing an order at the bar. I've never seen La Peep so empty, especially on such a lovely summer's day, but I'm not complaining in the slightest. The added bonus of privacy will surely work in my favor.

I pull out a small handheld mirror from my purse and check my makeup and my hair, which I have pulled back into a stylish low bun with some hair left out in the front, framing my face. Jovana's expertise has really come in handy. Soon, I might become a style pro myself. Even she was impressed when I picked out the cute, form-fitting violet dress I'm wearing today.

After a short time, Benoît walks up to me just as I overhear the other barista inform a woman who enters that they are only accepting to go orders. "Pardon, Benoît! I didn't know the seating areas were closed off today."

"You are fine, Jess." He sweetly replies as he places a cup of café au lait in front of me with an intricate design in the foam.

"Oh! Um, I haven't ordered anything. This isn't mine."

His smile is kind as he says, "Compliments of Monsieur Marc." It isn't till he strolls away that I fully register what he said. Could it really be?

I immediately get up and walk a few paces to the door, my eyes scouring every visible inch of this place in the hopes of finding … *him*… the man seated on the far front side of the café, obscured by the bar. He's at a table next to a large window, in a beautifully tailored navy-blue suit, similar to the one he wore when I first met him. His hair hasn't changed much. He still sports dark brown curls. His piercing gray eyes shine silver in the streaming light while he stares right at me, a tender smile pulling at the corners of his lips, and I instantly feel myself flush as joy swells within my chest.

I approach him slowly, afraid to blink, as though he could be a mirage that will simply disappear if I do. I clasp my trembling hands in front of me. My breath hitches and, for a length of time I'm unable to measure, I struggle to breathe properly.

He rises from his seat just as I come to a stop a few feet away. "Hi, Brown Eyes." The sound of his voice makes my heart flutter. It's as though I haven't heard it in years.

A shy grin blooms on my face. "You're early." Ugh, it's the only thing I could think to say and I'm mentally kicking myself for it. I had prepared for many weeks, reciting my speech for when I laid my eyes upon him again, but I remember none of it now. My chest tightens from the weight of sudden emotion. It's so damn good to see him, and at the same time it's hard to believe he's here in front of me. He's resided only in my dreams for five months that felt like ten. I honestly wasn't sure I'd ever be in his presence again.

He chuckles, amused by my greeting. "Yes, well, you know me; I thoroughly enjoy utilizing the element of surprise." His expression becomes more serious. "That, and I couldn't bear the thought of you coming here to wait on me. Didn't seem proper." He walks forward till he's standing a single step shy of my rattled frame. His hand reaches toward my cheek. Then, at the last second, in an act of great hesitation, he pulls it back, and I ache with a mixture of need and heavy disappointment.

He clears his throat, straightens his suit jacket, and gestures toward the empty chair across from him. "Join me?"

As soon as I'm seated, Benoît sneaks up and places my gifted drink in front of me along with my belongings. I'm amused by my momentary lapse of awareness; I had left everything behind.

I thank him and then return my attention to the man before me. "Did you have them close down the seating area just for us to meet?"

"I wasn't sure I was going to at first, however, I liked the idea of it being only the two of us. And the staff was more than happy to oblige, not just for the money, either. You seem to be quite popular here." How funny it is that he hasn't a clue that *here* is where it all began. That this very place is where I met Aralyn.

"I'm definitely a regular. A lot of the time this is my office."

"That doesn't surprise me in the least. Seems very you."

I raise my brow. "I can't tell if you see that as a good thing or a strange thing."

His dimples are on full display as he flashes a breathtaking smile. "I always see you fondly." There's a slight pause before he continues, "You look beautiful, Jess."

I blush, "Thank you. You still look … very handsome." Sexy as hell, actually, but it may not be appropriate to say that at this time. I have no idea where the boundaries are with him anymore, and it's a scary realization. How much is too much? Am I perhaps doing too little? I tell myself to just follow his lead. Seems like the safest choice.

The joy his presence gives me makes me giddy, but soon, I quickly bounce back to a more serious demeanor. This is all great, but it's time for me to get my act together and display some self-control. Best to not get too excited, especially when there is still so much that could go wrong.

He takes notice of this energetic shift and looks at me questioningly, though he does not verbally question it. "Right. Well, I won't beat around the bush, love. I know that there is a lot to discuss, things to sort out in regard to what happened with us. I'll be honest, I wasn't sure if I would show up today, but I owe you a conversation. It didn't feel right how we left off. I'd like to try and talk about it. You're welcome to start, as I'm certain you must have quite a few things you wish to say."

"Thank you. I do." I take a moment to collect my thoughts as the speech I had prepared finally returns to memory. "I want to express my gratitude to you for showing up. I would have understood if you weren't ready for this but, well, it really is so good to see you, Alex."

His eyes light up as he smiles tenderly, though he continues to allow me the floor to speak. "I do want to talk about what happened between us, but first, there's something else I'd like to discuss. Since that night I've tried hard to piece things together on my own and move on but it hasn't been easy. I have some questions about you and Aralyn. I'm hoping you'll do me the kindness of answering them."

He leans back in his seat, hands clasped in front of him. "Of course." He didn't hesitate with his response, but I sense he may be a bit worried about what I might ask.

"I did have that talk with her that you recommended. She's discussed her version of events with me regarding your connection to each other. However, I'd really like to hear your side." Unbeknownst to him, the reason I'm inquiring about his relationship with Aralyn isn't just because I'm genuinely curious; I want to gauge his energy. I want to make sure he's in a good enough headspace to even address the coming discussion about the two of us. Sure, he said he wants to talk, but does he really, or is he saying so because he feels he owes me this?

Alex squirms in his seat. It's a tell of his discomfort, though he tries to hide it in his expression. "What would you like to know?"

This is where I get to be my most journalistic self and I intend to take full advantage. "I've scoured the internet in search of photos or any mention of you and Aralyn. Nothing. I recall you telling me you two were in a relationship for three years. How was there never any mention of her? How is it that you were not seen with her in public?"

"You know as well as anyone that I'm a private man." I detect the slightest hint of defensive energy.

"And yet, you had no issue being seen and even photographed with me at your event after only knowing me for a short time."

He clears his throat and briefly looks away before responding. "I kept my relationship with Aralyn hidden from the public to keep her out of the spotlight."

Interesting. "How come?"

"Because there were people who didn't want us together. It took a lot of convincing to even get her to date me, let alone enter a relationship with me. She's… Let's just say if certain people saw us in public together, it would have caused a lot of trouble for her, and potentially for me as well."

"What, is she tied to a Mafia or something?" My question is meant as a joke, but I ponder whether it could be true. Whatever trouble he mentions sounds dangerous.

The last time he kept someone "out of the spotlight," it was his mother, protecting her from the media's snooping and intrusive questioning surrounding his father's murder. I'm starting to think that Alex is a protector of secrets, a safety deposit box for issues that are not his own. All you need is his love, and he'll make sure you're always safeguarded like Fort Knox. Which I'm sure is fantastic for everyone else, but it's difficult to fathom the amount of pressure and stress that must put on him.

"I think right now, it's best that you don't know," he replies. "I truly don't want you to get roped into anything."

"Me? Roped in? Never!" My sarcastic remark has him grinning from ear to ear.

I am secretly disappointed that he will not tell me. I suppose I should be used to it, being that I've been in this situation before with his silent refusal to provide me with the answers I seek. It's clear he believes that by withholding this information, he's keeping me safe. But the journalist in me doesn't want protection, I want answers. So, to obtain them, I'll have to be more tactical in my approach, and it's going to require some patience on my part, and taking a chance that he'll be more open to providing me with answers down the road, assuming there will be another opportunity for us to speak. God, I hope so.

I move on. "When she left you, were you not able to find her or something? I mean, you hired private investigators to uncover Ritter's dirty secrets. Surely, finding Aralyn wouldn't have been as difficult."

"You'd be surprised. I attempted to track her down on numerous occasions. And yes, I hired a couple professionals, but the search came up with nothing. There oddly wasn't any trace of her. I took it upon myself to go to her place of business several times, but they said she had quit and refused to tell me where she was, no matter how much I implored them. And because we kept our relationship hidden, I didn't know enough people who knew her that could point me in the direction of her whereabouts. So, after about seven months, I gave up. It had become quite obvious that she didn't want to be found. I believe she knew I'd do whatever it took to find her, and so she made sure to make that impossible for me.

"I was incredibly disheartened by it, especially because I did not know nor understand why she would have left, other than, perhaps, someone who didn't want us together had threatened her. However, even then, I thought it odd that she couldn't just tell me that. The whole thing took a toll, to the point where it started to affect my work and home life, so, for the sake of my mental health, I had to let her go."

"So, I'm guessing that means when you came to Paris for your charity banquet, you didn't stop by the salon or the den and try again?"

"Correct. I didn't bother. In fact, I did my best not to think about her at all. It had been nearly a year. And I had already solidified the decision within myself to move on." He suddenly smirks and there is a twinkle in his eye. "What do you know about the den, Brown Eyes?"

I grin, "I think you'd be shocked by a lot of what I know now." Hell, he'd definitely be floored by what I agreed to.

His index finger runs along his lower lip. "Care to enlighten me?"

Using his own words, I respond with, "I think right now, it's best that you don't know."

"Mm. Still bloody cheeky, I see." His voice has taken on a sensual tone, and it seems like he's taking the lead in a flirtatious direction.

I test my theory, hoping I'm not crossing any invisible boundaries while doing so. "I bet you'd like to do something about that."

The seductive fire in his eyes intensifies. "I get the feeling you'd very much like me to, Ms. Rivers."

I squeeze my thighs together. Oh, how I've missed this sensation, this ache, this pure, feral need growing stronger with each passing second. After a pause for effect, he says, "Don't get too distracted, darling. You might not get those answers you're looking for if you don't focus." Damn, that look is terribly sinful. He knows exactly what he's doing, and I both hate it and love it.

Suddenly, he blinks and drops his gaze, the heated glow on his face extinguishes, and his expression turns reflective. "If I may, I'd like to shift our conversation away from Aralyn, just for a bit, to have that conversation about us. I'm sure you'd agree that's the real purpose of our meeting here today."

It's a relief to hear him say it, and at the same time, I'm stricken with anxiety. Despite it all, my head nods in agreement and he continues, "What happened that night after the banquet was jarring in many ways. And I made the grave error of believing that I could do what I do every other time things become overwhelming, divert all my focus into something I know is within my ability to control. But my focus constantly wavered, because no matter what I did, I couldn't get you out of my head, Jess. From the moment we parted, you have followed me everywhere." He chuckles lightly, "Especially when all I wanted was to be alone. Anytime I tried to shut out the world, you were there, your image, the memories, the longing, all there, tormenting me. And I wasn't sure if it was from guilt or desire."

I remain quiet, pondering how best to respond, or if I even should. Right now, it seems like my time to just listen. "There's a war within me," he continues. "I am battling between what I want, which is to continue what I started with you, and what I fear. And what I fear is screaming at me to walk away before I place myself in a position where I may have to watch you depart in tears again."

"I don't understand."

"I get the sense that you want something from me that I'm not sure I'll be able to provide you."

"Which is?"

"My heart, Jess." His words bring to mind the conversation we had before our first kiss, when he told me that he wasn't sure he was ready to give his heart to another again. I can see how what happened the night of the banquet shut him down even more. But he doesn't understand that this truly isn't about that. I have to get him to see the bigger picture.

"Have I hoped for your heart? Yes! I'd be lying if I said I didn't. But right now, do you know what I want more? I want you to fight, Alex. I want you to fight like hell for what we had between us because I truly believe that with proper time, patience, and openness, we could really be something phenomenal! Tell me I'm not the only one who sees that."

"Jess, I don't think you quite understand what I'm telling you. I may never be able to show up for you the way you need me to."

"I don't believe you." I shake my head violently in protest. "You can, because you've done it before. It's a choice. Showing up for someone is a choice. Showing up for *me* is a choice. And sure, you don't have to choose it, but I hope to god that you will." He studies me as if trying hard to comprehend why I am so adamant. "You know, Aralyn had told me that if I didn't have this conversation with you soon, you might retreat so far into yourself again that you'd never come back out. It's regrettably been several months," I pause to allow him a moment to digest my words. "Am I too late?"

He lightly huffs and his features soften as he considers what I've asked, carefully crafting his response. "There isn't a day that's gone by, since I watched you drive away, heartbroken, that I have not been haunted by an intense urge to get you back. Not a single day."

Tears well up in my eyes, brimming in sync with the burning anticipation rising in my chest. He stands and walks around the table to me, then leans down till his face is level with mine. He grasps the back of my chair and gently hooks a finger under my chin, then tilts my head up so that my eyes meet his. "But baby, you do not deserve me in this state."

My voice cracks under the weight of my emotions. "What state is that?"

"Broken, Jess." I realize I'm holding my breath, and the trembling release of it is laced with sadness for his mourning heart and mine. It hurts to see a man who is worthy of the best kind of love run from it because of the looming burden of heartache.

He squats down in front of me. "When you asked me, back at the estate, if I still loved Aralyn, if you recall, I couldn't give you a straight answer. I wasn't sure. I've come to realize that the truth is I have never stopped loving her. I just hid that love under a blanket of anger and disappointment. The gravity of such truth didn't hit me till I returned to London.

"It's been difficult to shuffle through my thoughts and feelings surrounding everything that's transpired. I've had to face the reality that the woman I had envisioned spending my life with, the woman who never stopped loving me, either, is going to depart this world soon. And in knowing that, there's a chance part of me will be buried with her." The more he speaks, the more it feels as though there's a vice gripping my heart. Emotions swell inside me, each heavier than the last. "So, you see," he continues, "I could give you the world, my love, but my heart… I truly don't know if I could ever give you that."

There it is, then. The answer to the question I now wish I never asked. I've replayed this possibility a thousand times in my head and still I was not prepared for it.

"I don't care." My own utterance shocks me as much as it does him.

"Jess—"

"I don't care. You don't know if you can, but you could, right?"

He fumbles for his words. "Jess, I just—"

"Answer me this: Can you at least see yourself loving me?"

He stands and places his hands in his pockets, looking away while he ponders. "Potentially." He sighs in surrender to his internal truth. "Yes."

"Then we have a chance. Even if it's small, it's a chance. To me, that's worth the uncertainty."

"I fear it's more complicated than that."

I rise to my feet too, and gaze at the beautiful man towering over me. "At some point in our lives we are all broken, Alex. Hell, I'm still picking up my own shattered pieces. Look, I'm not trying to force myself on you; I know you need more time to heal and process. All I'm asking is that you don't shut me out completely. Just leave the door open a crack."

He's trying hard to suppress the yearning in his eyes, but he can't hide it from me. I had committed that look to memory. "You told me once that you love a challenge. So, take this challenge with me. We can move at whatever pace you'd like. I just want to be a part of your world, to know you and cherish you and be here for you. I'd like to think that, regardless of what has happened, and your current uncertainty around the potential to love again, you want the same with me too."

He sighs again, softly, rubbing a hand across the back of his neck, but then his lips curl into a subtle smile. "Your determination is admirable."

"I'm not giving up on you, Alexander Marc. Please … don't give up on me." With a single step, he closes the small gap between us, cups my face with his hands, and plants a sweet kiss on my forehead. Then he wraps his arms around me like the most comforting blanket. I allow my body to soften in his embrace, reveling in his intoxicating scent and heavenly energy, appreciating this closeness after so many painful months of tremendous distance.

We stay like this for a time, within this quaint café on a corner of a bustling and charming Paris street; my head rests perfectly against his chest and I hear the beating of his heart. I give it a silent promise that I will protect it, cherish it, love it. I let it know that it's okay to be afraid, that I'm afraid too, but we can make it. We can.

As if relaying his heart's response, Alexander rests his chin atop my head and says, "Okay, Brown Eyes. Okay. Challenge accepted. I won't shut you out. We're in this together."

Journal,

There's this boy who's been coming to my window every evening at seven for the past month, just waiting for a glimpse of me whenever I go to shut my drapes. I've seen him many times before. He's the chauffeur's son, Pierre. He must have discovered a profound confidence to pursue me, knowing who my father is.

He's brave. I admire that. He's incredibly good looking too!

Every other night I've stood at the window for a few moments, smiling at him before closing the curtains. But tonight, I decided to be brave too and waved. He blew me a kiss. And for the first time in forever, I felt like one of those giddy, blushing schoolgirls people talk about.

Seventeen, and I've never had a crush before. Being homeschooled and confined to strict curfews and supervision does not give a girl a lot of opportunity to interact with boys. How exciting that tonight could be different.

I've been lying in bed for a solid hour, thinking about him. About what kind of life we could have, what our children would look like. I'd be known in the community as the popular local artist with my own little studio in town and he'd own one of the most luxurious and trusted chauffeur service companies in all of Europe. Together we'd be the envy of France.

But, I feel silly. Such a grand dream. So grand it would be nearly impossible. That type of life is meant for someone untouchable. For someone who's not just a puppet on a string.

Though maybe, just for tonight, I'll allow myself this chance to dream big and hard and freely. Maybe, just for tonight, shackles and strings can wait.

Journal,

I kissed him! I kissed Pierre! Well, it was more like he kissed me. It was so romantic!

Papa was holding a dinner tonight for himself and some other very wealthy friends whose names I've never cared to memorize. Just as I went downstairs to go to the dining room, he came from around the corner, grabbed my wrist and pulled me behind the staircase. All we did after that was look at each other for what felt like a blissful eternity. It was like he was speaking to me with only his eyes, telling me how much he'd longed for my presence, excited to finally be with me.

I had no idea what to do or say or if I should do or say anything at all. God, I'm so inexperienced with boys. All I could think to say was, "You can kiss me if you'd like." I was immediately embarrassed, but to my surprise, he did not hesitate to take me up on my offer.

His lips were so warm and soft. The kiss was everything I had dreamed even though it was quick. I shocked myself by grabbing his face and kissing him again, longer, and I swear it was my first taste of heaven. Then I heard the maid call out for me down the hall so I told him I had to go, but that we'd meet again soon, and we kissed one last time.

There was freedom on his lips. I sampled it and I fell head over heels for it.

Is this love? Is this the kind of love everyone talks about being the most magical, beautiful thing you could ever experience in life? Has it finally crossed my path? Is it mine to keep forever?

5

"*We're in this together.*" Alexander's words float through my thoughts as I walk home, going over everything we discussed. Our conversation has become like a record I've had on repeat in my mind for the last three days. In true Jess Rivers fashion, I push the boundaries of overthinking every time. I can sense myself toppling into the black hole of self-examination, wondering if I could have hurt our chances of getting back together by insisting we try reconnecting right now, no matter the pace.

There's a possibility he could have said what he did simply to appease me, but in reality I may not hear from him again. I shake my head to declutter my mind. *NO. Stop this.* Alex wouldn't have said anything he didn't mean, and to top it off, he has always proven himself to be a man of his word. If he says he'll reach out to me soon, he will. I just have to be patient.

I shift my focus to my surroundings, taking in my new quaint neighborhood with its many trees, chirping birds, and friendly passersby. Madame Chérot was right, the house really is in a perfect location. Everything I need is close by, and because it's such a lovely day out, I opted to walk to and from the store. Paper bag full of groceries in hand, I'm excited to get home and continue work on my newest assignment. It's one I've been anticipating being chosen for, and I was delighted to discover I had been. I'm nearly finished with it too, and love how the story has been shaping up so far.

Business has been booming since the release of my article on Alex. Many top companies reach out to me for assignments so I no longer need to do too much reaching out on my end, hoping enough publishers will be interested in what I have to write. Little ol' me is now one of the most highly sought-after freelance journalists in Europe. Just last month, the same company that published my article on Alex contracted me for an assignment that had me traveling to Portugal, and another to Germany. It was a busy month.

Funnily enough, even after everything that went down with my old boss, Dante Ritter, my job has become the one solid planet of joy that I orbit around. Its gravity has been keeping me semi-stable while I sift through the chaos that swirls everywhere else. I'm grateful.

Besides work, I should also focus on getting ready for Genevieve's arrival. Though she's been my best friend since high school, we haven't talked as much as either of us would have liked the last couple years. But ever since I called her that one night, when I had been so confused by my feelings for Alex, and after learning of Arthur and Ritter's betrayal, we talk constantly. Shockingly, she recently made the decision to travel beyond the borders of Nebraska for the very first time to come visit me. In her words, *"Your life is far too adventurous for me to miss out on."* So here she comes.

I remember when I first met her. We were six and she lived across the street from me. Her parents had just adopted her from Japan and wanted her to have a friend to help her acclimate to the new environment. Gen didn't speak much English at the time, but despite the language barrier we hit it off immediately once I showed her my Barbie collection.

Until I moved to Paris, there was hardly a day that went by that we didn't see each other, college days included. One of my biggest regrets was neglecting our connection while building my new life. But now that she'll be here in Paris with me, even if for a short time, I can move beyond that and make up a little for what was lost.

I walk through the front door, set my groceries and keys down, then take in my surroundings. This place is definitely going to take some getting used to. Granted, I've only spent a week here, so it's expected that I wouldn't feel a normal level of connection to it just yet, but I believe it's deeper than that. Much deeper. I didn't find this home; it found me. And even if I was in search of one, this would never have been my pick. The décor alone, though luxuriously dramatic and attractive, is so far from who I am. And sure, I can do a complete redesign, but somehow, it would feel wrong to change anything. Aralyn hasn't even transitioned from this world yet. It seems disrespectful to replace so much of the personality she left behind here.

Perhaps it's not the worry of being disrespectful. Perhaps, similar to Alex, I'm really just afraid to let go too. Unfortunately, that's not something I'm ready to unpack and sort through at this time. There's already more than enough on my plate. I'm full and I need to digest before another helping.

I ascend the stairs, preparing my mind for the task of settling into Arlayn's room. I decided the other day to suck it up and purchase a brand-new bed for the master bedroom. If I'm going to get used to living here for a while, I might as well start restructuring the space that I feel the least comfortable occupying.

As I'm reaching the last few steps, I hear the sound of running water. It's puzzling, and swift panic swells inside me. Shit! Did I somehow forget to turn off the shower this morning? I must have. Aralyn may be paying the bills for now, but it's certainly not my intention to run them up.

I book it into the master bedroom and throw open the bathroom door. I let out a terrified shriek and back out several paces at the sight of a man in my shower. My breathing is rapid as I strain to see who it is through the steamy glass. I soon realize it's not a stranger—not exactly, anyway. "Luca?"

Luca De la Rue smiles as he leans his head back to finish washing the soap from his hair. "I see La Princesa has returned to the castle."

"What the hell are you doing in my shower? Actually, screw the shower, what are you doing in my house?"

He cuts the water off and opens the shower door; steam billows out and then dissipates, revealing him in all his naked glory. In shock and embarrassment, I turn my head, but it's too late. The vision of his blessed package, wet and swinging between his legs, is going to be hard to erase from my memory. Not that it's all that bad a memory to have.

Focus, Jess! He's in the wrong here! Get your shit together and demand answers!

"To answer your first question, the water pressure is much better here than the shower in the guest bedroom. In response to your second, well, this isn't actually your house, now, is it?"

I hear the rustling of a towel and I wait a few seconds for him to wrap it around himself. Then I peek back quickly to make sure he's tucked away before I glare at him. "You must have missed the memo that the deed is being signed over to me."

He strolls to the sink, drying his hair off with a second towel. His back, now turned to me, is covered in a large, highly detailed tattoo of an angel and a demon at war with one another. It's unclear which is winning. The inked image extends over his shoulders and fades into many others that run down his right arm like a sleeve. The man has an incredibly muscular physique, and not to the point where it's over the top. I had no idea he was hiding all that under his jacket the other day.

"Yes, I am aware she's leaving it to you. However," he says as he turns to face me, leaning back against the counter, long locks of wet, wavy black hair cascading over his shoulders, "my sister is not yet dead."

"Madame Chérot didn't say anything to me about your sister needing to have passed in order for me to move in here; in fact she insisted I did."

"True. It's Aralyn's wish that you feel free to live in this home if and when you so desire. But make no mistake." He slowly strides up to me. I crane my neck to stare him down and catch his eyes doing a quick sweep over my body. "You are still a guest in my family's home." His arm brushes mine as he walks out.

"You can't be serious. I don't imagine your sister would take too kindly to you inviting yourself into her space unannounced, knowing full well I reside here!"

"Imagine whatever you'd like. While you're busy doing that, I'm going to finish setting up in the guest room."

"I beg your fucking pardon?"

He turns around. "You've got quite a naughty mouth on you." A wide grin spreads across his face. "Love it. We might actually get along. MIGHT." Then he continues across the hall.

"There's no way you're staying here!"

"Sorry to tell you, but I am."

"I'll call the police!"

He stops and leans against the doorframe. "Before you do that, I suggest you consider what I told you. You know, about being a *guest*. You legally have no authority to kick me out."

"You legally have no authority to be here! Your name is not attached to this place!"

"You're right. Looks like I'm my sister's guest too. Now, are you finished?"

"How did you even get in here? I had the locks changed earlier this week!"

"Climbed up the guest room balcony and got in through the window. That thing I needed the other day was an excuse to unlock it." He winks and I feel the heat of anger bringing a glow to my face. The absolute gall of breaking in and helping himself to a room is mind blowing. First Madame Chérot entering the house whenever she pleased, and now him? For what purpose other than to torture me?

"I'm calling the Madame. There's no way Aralyn would approve something like this."

"Mm, tell her I said hello. Now if you're done, I'd like to get some rest. I have quite a long day tomorrow. But don't worry, Princesa. It's just for a couple nights. I'll be out of your way in no time." The smug look on his face makes me want to rip him a new one, and just as I'm about to, he closes the door.

I yell out, "You know what, since you clearly want to be here so bad, why don't you just have the fucking house! I didn't ask for this, anyway! I didn't ask for any of this!" I storm back to the master room, quickly pack a night bag, and out the door I go.

This is the final straw for me. I've barely lived in this place for a full week and already I've experienced an invasion of privacy more than once, and a plethora of anxiety I really don't need. Gift or not, it isn't worth it.

I hardly know this man who, from the moment I met him, seems highly uninterested in getting respectfully acquainted in the least bit. He's an arrogant, obnoxious, incredibly disrespectful, pompous toolbag and if I ever see him again, I'll be sure to tell him just that! I'm so sick of people thinking they can walk all over me. One would think I had a sign on my chest that says, *"Please, use me as carpet!"* This complete disregard for my space and time is going to end at once.

I march to my car and toss my bag into the back seat. When I make it around to the driver's side, I come to a halt. There's an envelope stuck to the window. In frustration, I snatch it and tear it open. Inside is the same kind of black card as the one I received a few days ago. I look around me, hoping to catch a glimpse of its scribe, but the only person I see is the little old lady across the street tending to her flower beds.

Nervously, I open the card and am confronted with a worrisome reminder:

Stay away from him!

Great. As if things couldn't get any more complicated.

6

throw open the double doors of La Maison des Papillons, "The House of Butterflies", the kink den that's to be my new place of work. I'm on a mission to find the infamous madam and obtain her assistance, since the crazy man in my guest room won't see sense.

It's my first time here, and I'm dazzled by the sight of the large entrance lobby. I'm not sure why I had expected the aesthetic to be dark and moody elegance, but this place is far from it. It's light and airy, and smells extremely clean, like a doctor's office, but luxurious times ten. A magnificent chandelier commands attention in the center of the room. Its long strands of crystals cascade like a waterfall, and the light glints off the white walls and ornate gold trim. Black leather seats line the walls, and large black-and-white photographs are displayed in gold frames to match the trim. I soon realize that the photos are artistic shots of individuals taking part in various kink scenes. They remind me of the photos Aralyn has at the house, though far more intimate and erotic in nature.

"Jess?" Jovana walks out from around the corner. *"Salut!* What are you doing here? We were not expecting you till Monday."

"Hey! Yeah, I've, uh, been trying to get in touch with the Madame but she's not answering. I went down to the salon, hoping she might be there but since she wasn't, I thought maybe I could find her here. Anyway, what are *you* doing here?" I'm so used to seeing her around the salon, I didn't really think she'd be hanging around the den."

"Surprise! Madame Chérot hired me to be your assistant! I'm here to set up."

My mouth falls agape in shock. "No way! No way!" Did Madame Chérot actually consider what I'd like for once?

This is fantastic! I adore Jovana! Quite unexpectedly, she is becoming a good friend. Our connection began to grow beyond a stylist-client relationship not long after my final meeting with Aralyn. She kindly came to check on me, and I was in the middle of crying my eyes out over a romantic comedy that was supposed to make me laugh, but instead just made me depressed. As soon as I opened the door and she saw my puffy eyes, she hugged me and comforted me. I was touched by such an act of empathy.

I then invited her in for a drink and we ended up talking for hours. It was so interesting how much more relaxed she became around me compared to how she was before. Perhaps it was because her boss and I had no more contact. Or perhaps she genuinely desired a friend in me. I'm not sure. But I'm grateful for it. I discovered this whole personality that I would have never guessed she had based off previous interactions. Charming, funny, though shy at times, she is a woman with immense passion for her career, and in-depth thoughts about the worldliest topics. I even learned a lot about her Brazilian heritage.

"Jovana, I had no idea you were even interested in the position!"

"I wanted to surprise you! When I heard Madame was looking, I knew I wanted to apply. Now you have an assistant *and* a personal stylist." She winks and giggles. It's such an incredible relief to know I will be working closely with someone I actually know well! Learning the ropes of my new position while also trying to navigate managing someone completely new is now one less thing I have to worry about.

"That's the best news I've had all day!"

"Bien! I am happy! You said you were looking for Madame, oui?"

"Oh yes, do you know if she's in today?"

"Ah, what I hear is the Madame does not come in much. But maybe you can try to call from the phone in your office. She might see the number and answer."

"My … office?"

"You have not seen it? Oh, come, you must see! It is magnifique!"

I follow my boisterous assistant, and she gives me a quick tour around the facility. After a while we walk down a hall where a woman, completely covered from the neck down in tight red latex, with a matching corset around her torso, speaks in hushed tones with someone on the phone. Another woman at the far end of the hall is facing our direction, on her knees with her head bowed and her hands placed palms up on her thighs. I'm not entirely sure what the story is with these two, but I've learned enough on my own about BDSM lifestyles that I'm willing to bet the submissive on her knees is patiently waiting for her Mistress as commanded.

We pass her and reach a dead end where we stand in front of red double doors; two other black doors are on the left and right of us. Jovana points to the double doors. "If you go through here, it will take you down to the den. Madame will show you later." She struts over to the black door on the right, opening it. Once we enter, I'm again impressed by the grandiose elegance of the space. It's certainly fit for a boss, maybe even a queen, with a black and red aesthetic similar to that of the private back room at the Madame's salon. "Wow, this is… this is something."

"Madame De la Rue used to have more furniture here, but Madame Chérot wants you to have space for your own things." How thoughtful. I didn't think the woman had it in her to consider what I'd want. "My new office is the one you passed when you came in. I share it with Amélie, who assists the clients who come in." I can tell Jovana is extremely happy about her new position. I'm both surprised by it and not so surprised. She's been loyal to Madame Chérot and Aralyn for many years. And though she was mainly a hair and makeup artist, I imagine she probably did have dreams of being a part of the erotic, alluring team that was the Diamond Butterflies.

"Where does that other black door across from mine lead?"

"Madame Chérot's office."

"Ah, well, I really am so glad you are with me in this," I say, switching our conversation to French, knowing that it is easier for her speak and understand. Although her English has been getting much better. "I'm not sure I'd feel as comfortable going through all this if you weren't, especially after everything that's been happening."

"What's happened?" Her expression shifts to one of concern.

I sigh heavily. "Just a massive wake-up call that I seriously need to set boundaries with certain individuals."

"You know, if someone is bothering you, I believe the Madame can arrange a bodyguard for you." That's quite an interesting statement. I didn't realize a bodyguard could be so easily acquired. Although I'm sure the Madame would not arrange a bodyguard to protect me from herself, it is something I take mental note of. If these suspicious cards keep popping up with no explanation as to whom they're from or to what purpose, I might just ask for one. I have developed a very long list of reasons I no longer trust most people, and I'll be damned if I'm going to take some ominous messages about staying away from Alex as well intended.

"Anyway, the phone is there on the desk. Dial six. I will leave you."

"Wait, before you go, what do you know about Aralyn's brother, Luca?"

"Oh, well, I know he used to manage the Madame's den in Spain."

"Really?" So, it would seem working in the fetish industry is something else that runs in the family. I'm so curious to know how this all came to be, how the De la Rue twins ended up managing the kinky little secret of one of the most renowned hair professionals in the world. I hope Aralyn is more detailed in her journal about that introduction than she has been about her late teenage years.

"Mhmm, he was here at this den for a couple years before asking to be transferred to Spain. From what I heard, that wasn't too long after the Madame chose Aralyn to be her protégé. I don't really know why he eventually stepped down, but he still lives in Spain and he and the Madame are still closely connected."

"Interesting. I'm guessing you've met him?"

"He's very nice. At least he is to me. Though I've heard from others that he can come off as intimidating." Or a huge asshat, but I can see intimidating too. "Why do you ask?"

"I've had the unfortunate pleasure of meeting him recently. And despite the fact that we hardly know each other, he seems insistent on making me uncomfortable. It's like he's purposefully trying to irritate me, but I'm not sure why. Though, Madame Chérot did say he was upset that I moved into Aralyn's home."

"Well, I would not worry. He probably won't be here for much longer. He must go back to Spain at some point, right?"

"Yeah, I suppose you're right." I look forward to it.

She smiles. "If you need me, I'll be at the front."

I thank Jovana and walk over to the antique-looking telephone on the desk. *My desk.* It's a bizarre thing to wrap my head around. I try to remember that I've chosen this adventure. I've made the decision to follow the stream of Aralyn's life to wherever it may lead. I said to hell with it, and chose curiosity over logic. However, I can't deny that I'm worried. I'm dreadfully worried that in my pursuit of insight, I will lose myself to her world. Here I am, in possession of yet another thing left to me by her, and the weight this adds to my internal struggle is heavy.

The phone rings three times before the Madame answers. I explain to her my situation with Luca and my frustrations regarding his inconsiderate nature. She lets me get out everything I need to before speaking. "I'll make a call. He'll be gone by this evening. Is that all?"

That's it? Just like that? I'm skeptical of her response and suspicious. "Are you planning to call Aralyn about it?" I ask because it will be interesting to find out if the Madame is still in communication with her. I don't even know if Aralyn is still in touch with Alex, but, seeing as she views Madame Chérot as a mother figure, I'm willing to bet they remain in contact often.

"That need not concern you. Bonne soirée, mademoiselle." There's a click followed by a dial tone.

I set the phone down, perplexed by the sudden feeling of dismay that washes over me when I should be relieved. Problem solved, right? But as I glance around the room my mind wanders, lost in the tumultuous sea of over-analyzation, and I'm slowly being overcome by the waves of troubled thoughts. Suddenly, my eyes catch sight of a small, framed picture tipped over on one of the shelves. It's the distraction needed to help me surface, if only for a small time.

The picture is the only thing on the shelf, and it's covered in a thin layer of dust. I pick it up, turn it over, and stare at it; my pulse races, and my throat becomes dry. It's of Aralyn and… "Alex," I whisper. My fingertips sweep across his image. It looks like the two of them are in a garden and they are both all smiles, glowing with pure joy. It's surprising seeing Aralyn in this photo dressed so … comfortable. She's not fashionably dressed, not even wearing much makeup. Her hair is pinned up, she's wearing a plain red dress with spaghetti straps, and her face is full and vibrant. I can tell this was taken before she became ill.

She's looking at the camera, and Alex is looking at her. It's that look a man gives a woman when he's truly in love. That look of intense admiration, as though in that very moment he's taking in every single aspect of who she is and radiating love toward each molecule of her being.

What I hold in my hands is absolute confirmation that Aralyn was indeed Alexander's whole universe, and he was hers. It's hard for me to see this. I've wanted to believe I can be as good for him as she was but, as with so many other things in my life at present, I'm really not sure. The more time goes by, the more I learn. The more I sit alone with my thoughts, the more it seems as though all I may ever be in his eyes is the replacement, even if he does eventually fall for me. And that's unsettling, because who really wants to be that?

I wonder briefly why Aralyn would have left this behind, or why no one caught it while doing a cleanup and moving things out. Was it fate that I was to come across this? Did she leave it intentionally? No, both those possibilities are silly. Aren't they?

I set the photo back down the way I found it, grab my purse from the desk and head out. I don't have a destination in mind, I just need to get out of this building. I need some fresh air.

I need to find control over my emotions again.

Journal,

Pierre has vanished. His father too. One day they were here and the next they were replaced. I've yet to figure out who I have to thank for snitching but I know my father didn't just dismiss one of his most loyal employees for no reason. And Pierre would have never knowingly left without saying goodbye, not after how close we've become over these last six months.

I think the normal reaction would be for me to feel devastated but instead, I feel somewhat relieved. I've anticipated this since the beginning of our relationship. I've stressed, sometimes relentlessly, over when this day would arrive. Now that it has, I feel lighter. I think that's the saddest part.

I miss Mama. Sometimes I think she would have found a way to whisk me away from here if she really knew what I've been through.

I turn eighteen in a couple months. I haven't told anyone yet, but I got accepted into one of the most prestigious universities in Europe! My plan is to wait till just after my birthday to tell Papa the news. That way, if there are any rejections, I can simply pack my things and walk out of here. But I'd like to do things as peacefully as possible.

In this family, status trumps everything. If university stands in the way of duty, then university is frowned upon. I'd be risking spite by bringing this to Papa's attention. But I risk spite every day just being alive.

He'll either approve of it or he won't. But I must try. This is my chance to live even a fraction of the life I envision for myself! I can't remain a prisoner in this tragedy of a home any longer.

I plan to tell him that I will go for a business degree. He will be more likely to approve of that. But you and I know where my passions really lie.

No matter what, I will do whatever it takes to feel the kiss of joy again.

Journal,

Luca is here, for good. Normally, this would be something to celebrate, but it's not, because him being here confirms one thing, Mama is gone.

My sobbing surprised me last night because I had already mourned her long ago. Haven't seen her since Papa took me away. I had surrendered to the knowledge that there was a likely chance I'd never see her again. How odd that despite my acceptance of that, I still wept in silence within the walls of my room for many nights until grief became slightly easier to bear.

Yes, the tears that flowed from me came as quite a shock. However, I'm not sure if the tears came because I'm really grieving her or because I'm grieving hope. Her being alive meant there was a sliver of hope to cling to that we'd be reunited. A small hope that she'd take me away from here. Hope that there was light at the end of all these years of darkness. Now, hope has died with her, buried in earth that I was not even permitted to go see.

And Luca, my poor brother. All I've heard Papa say since he's arrived is how he will beat the little boy out of him if he doesn't get over it. I know in the quiet of his room he weeps as well. The time for sleep will be the only opportunity he'll have to process her loss.

I pray that wherever Mama is, it's somewhere far better than the life she had here. Please, God, if there is a God, let her be happy. She deserves to finally be happy, to finally be at peace.

I love you so much, Mama. I always will.

7

$\mathcal{E}$xcitement courses through me like a rushing river. Genevieve, has arrived in Paris! I received a message from her saying she landed about an hour and a half ago so she should be here soon.

It's strange to think that no one from my life back home has ever come to visit me before. And the last time I visited friends and family from the States was three Christmases ago. I've been such a world away from the place and people I grew up around that it's now bizarre to be experiencing a piece of it all again. But I need this, I really do.

I've been preparing for her arrival all day, finishing up the unpacking, and sprucing up the guest room just for her. I also had enough time to officially move into Aralyn's room. The decision to do so was triggered by yesterday's intrusion.

This morning, I wasn't even sure about coming back to the house, even knowing Madame Chérot kicked Luca out. I felt overwhelmed and entirely over all the drama. I know I signed up for an adventure, but having my privacy continuously invaded is absolutely not my idea of one. And then there are the ominous notes. Whoever wrote them obviously knows where I live, and are perhaps watching me.

It's like I haven't any space to exist in peace. Despite how unnerving I find that to be, I can't leave… not yet. I refuse to run off like I'm some intimidated little girl afraid to stand her ground. This is my second chance. I've claimed it as such. It's my opportunity to prove to myself that I don't need to hide from or behind anything. I know why I chose to move here. I know what my mission is, and I'll be damned if anyone is going to get in the way of me achieving it. So, I left the hotel, deciding to return and reclaim *my* domain and, to me, a large part of that was making Aralyn's room my own.

Something I found quite odd, while sorting out the house, was an alarm system that no longer appeared to be working. Upon further inspection, I noticed certain areas on various ceilings throughout the home with mounts that may have contained something electronic. Could Aralyn have had cameras rigged throughout the place? I'd understand outside, but a camera in almost every room of your home, even sometimes more than one per room, seems like overkill. Even the doors and windows still have additional locks that seem totally unnecessary. Why so much security?

The sound of the door knocker echoes through the house and I run to welcome my dear friend. But as I swing the door open, my excitement turns to great disappointment. Aralyn's a-hole of a brother is leaning against the banister, looking scorned and irritated, similar to the day we first met. Is this a resting bitch face he has going on or does the sight of me really tick him off that much? Frankly, I should be the one with the attitude here.

"Uh, hi? What are you doing here, *again*? You're not staying the night so don't even think I—"

"We need to talk." I can't say I disagree. Although I'm still pissed about his intrusion the other day, I really do need to ask him the plethora of questions I have about his and Aralyn's upbringing, but damn he has poor timing.

"I would actually love to talk but I'm expecting someone any minute, so maybe we can arrange a good sit down a little later. What does your schedule look like next week?"

He gives one hefty laugh under his breath and then stands upright. "No, not next week. Now."

"NO. Maybe you didn't hear me, but I just told you it's not a good time." Who does he think he is, giving me demands?

"And I told you we need to talk right now."

I roll my eyes so far back in my head they might have gotten stuck were there any truth to that old wives' tale. "Goodnight, Luca." I begin to shut the door, but he stops it with his hand. I throw it back open. "Okay, what the fuck is your problem? No, means no, asshole!"

His tone lowers and his serious expression has an added hint of disgust. "I know you're fucking that billionaire." I let out a laugh in pure shock at his brazen statement. He follows that with, "Why?"

"I'm sorry, exactly what the hell gives you the right to come here and interrogate me about my personal affairs that are none of your business? I don't know you!"

"What the hell made you decide it was a great idea to get involved with my sister's lover?" I want to tell him to fuck off, but something dawns on me in this moment. What if he has no idea about Aralyn's wish for Alex? No idea the connection between her and I? If that's the case, I can only imagine what he thinks of me. Some strange woman he'd never met gets handed his sister's home on a silver platter, and then he discovers that same woman was also involved with her boyfriend. Well, ex-boyfriend, but still. I must look like a total home wrecker.

"It's not what you might think. Aralyn knows about me and Alex. She wants us to be together."

"I know about what she wants for the two of you. What I don't know is why you are going along with it. You're an attractive woman; you're telling me there was no other man you could entertain?"

Entertain? What is he talking about? "Not that it's really any of your business, but I'm not 'entertaining' Alex; I want to build a relationship with him. Why are you making such a big deal of this?"

"You're making a mistake, just like her."

"Oh, really?" I scoff. "That's what you thought, that your sister made a mistake being with him?"

An exuberant screech rings out in the air. "Jess! Aggghhh! I'M HERE, BABES!" We both watch as Genevieve gleefully jogs over with her bags in tow.

Luca grumbles and turns back to me. "We'll finish this later. Do yourself a favor and distance yourself from Aralyn's life. You don't need her home and you definitely don't need *him*." With that he takes off down the steps, leaving me a confused mess in the doorway.

Gen admires him as he passes, then mouths, "Who is that?" while mimicking a fanning motion with her hand.

I meet her at the bottom of the steps and give her a giant hug as though she's a long-lost sister I thought I'd never see again. "*Ooo*, it's so good to see you!" she squeals.

"You have no idea how good it is to see you too!"

As soon as we release each other, she looks at me quizzically. "Was that Daddy Moneybags?" Her nickname for Alex makes me cackle.

"Definitely not. I'd give you a run down about him, but it's a long story and honestly, he's not worth the time to tell it right now." I help with her luggage.

"Long story, huh? Mm, I bet something else is long." My eyes bulge with shock. "What? Like you haven't thought about it."

"Hahaha, oh my god, seriously, Gen, you *just* got here! How are you already trouble?"

We set her bags down in the foyer. "Yes, well, I wouldn't be myself if I didn't bring a little trouble, babes. Ah, come here!" She brings me in for another tight embrace. I've missed my friend dearly. "You look amazing! Did you sprout double Ds since we've last seen each other?"

I fold my arms over my chest. "Gen!"

She undoes them. "Oh, come now, let's see you! Don't be ashamed of your assets, love! Give me a twirl!" I do a little spin causing my teal dress to swish fluidly around me. "Ugh, you slut! You're gorgeous! Way to grow into your womanly figure!

You've really been holding out on me, living the life in Paris, two men literally fighting over you like fiends, one of whom happens to be one of the world's wealthiest men. AND NOW I find out you have a body blessed by the gods? Sheesh, leave some luck for the rest of us!"

I find this funny, because Gen has always been a stunner to me—dimpled cheeks, pouty lips, pretty blue eyes and gorgeous, straight black hair that extends to her waist. She's had some struggles with insecurity about her looks ever since I can remember, but I've always told her she could be on the cover of Vogue if she tried. "Oh, please. What about you? I am one hundred percent sure you did not have an ass like that when I left Nebraska." She blushes and does a little twirl herself, showing off an impressive derriere hugged tightly by yoga pants.

"I told you I'm a gym junky now. Leg day is my favorite day." She winks.

As I give her a grand tour of the house, she gawks, highly impressed by the decor, and is deeply interested in trying to figure out the psychology of the home's predecessor. I wish I could tell her. I'm trying to figure it out myself. Aralyn truly is a marvel.

Gen and I chat a little more as I help her up to her room, where she is once again completely intrigued by everything she lays eyes upon. "This is my dream. You're literally living my dream!"

"Trust me, Gen, it's not all rainbows and sunshine." I place a hand on my hip and stretch a bit after parking her hefty bags next to the bed. "But I suppose it does feel like a dream at times. A really vivid, surreal dream."

"I bet you never thought this is where your decision to move to Paris would take you."

"Very true. If you told me this is where I'd be I would have called you delusional."

She flashes a loving smile. "You seriously look good, Jess. Really good. I know things haven't been the easiest for you the past few months, but to be honest, you seem brighter and more yourself than the last time I saw you."

"Yeah?"

"Mhmm." She takes a seat on the bed. "More like the you as a college graduate, ready to set off on your grand Parisian adventure, except you're grown and absolutely breathtaking. I want to say the last time I saw you was when you came home for the holidays three years ago, if I recall correctly. I remember you seemed… I don't know… changed. Not in a horrible way, just not yourself, nor were you the visit prior, even." I understand her perfectly. And a small sense of pride swells within me, listening to what she's saying. This wild, unreal dream is the very thing that woke me up to the reality of my folly. In the midst of all the unexpected and mysterious happenings, it was Alex who challenged me to fly, and Aralyn who pushed me from the perch.

"Yeah, you're right. I definitely wasn't." My phone vibrates in my pocket and when I look at it, I see Carmyn's name on the screen. My heart skips a beat. News from Alex, perhaps? "Hey, I'm gonna give you a bit to settle in while I take this call. I'll get some snacks out downstairs so we can catch up, and then maybe we can find somewhere for dinner after, if you're hungry?"

"Starving!"

I laugh and make my exit, pressing answer. "Carmyn? Hey. What's up, is everything alright?"

"Ms. Rivers, hello. Is this a good time?"

I walk into the kitchen and begin pulling out a small charcuterie board I arranged earlier. "Yeah, it's perfectly fine."

"Splendid. Well, I don't want to cause alarm, but I wanted to call you because I've been receiving some slightly concerning messages through Mr. Marc's mail."

My stomach drops. "Let me guess, black cards?"

"Yes, exactly. How did you know?"

"I've been receiving the same here. They've been warning me to stay away from him and, unfortunately, I'm not sure who's sending them."

"Interesting. These notes have been instructing Mr. Marc to stay away from *you*." What is going on? I just don't get it. Clearly someone is trying to keep us apart, but who would go to such lengths? And with note cards? Of all the ways one could get a message across, why choose that route? "Ms. Rivers, do you think it could be that man you had a quarrel with at the banquet?"

"Arthur. Yeah, I've considered that, but the handwriting is not his. He was my close friend for years. I'd know his writing anywhere."

I've even considered the possibility of it being Ritter, trying to get some sort of twisted payback for what happened with the article, and Alex basically threatening to expose him. But I don't see Ritter having the time to spend on mailing out or delivering these bizarre cards. And for someone who was so bold as to have blackmailed Alex, why would he choose now to be so secretive, particularly with an agenda to keep us apart? Ritter is the type of man who would have played every card in the book to bring us both down somehow. Hell, he tried to taint my reputation after the banquet to keep me from publishing the article on Alex. But this? This makes no sense.

"Hmm, well it sounds like we have quite the mystery on our hands. I haven't spoken with Mr. Marc about this yet; I wanted to chat with you first, see if we could find out what we're dealing with and put a stop to it before bringing it to his attention. But by the sounds of it, it may not be able to be helped. I will let him know in the morning. If I were you, I'd anticipate his call soon after."

I can already picture his protective mode being activated by this news. Who knows what he'll do. He's Alexander Marc; it could be as little as just hiring an investigative team to figure this out, or as grand as requesting I lock myself away in some high-tech security bunker till everything is solved. "I understand. Thank you."

I pour two glasses of Merlot, adding some extra in mine to help ease the whiplash from the ride I've been on the past thirty minutes. "My pleasure. Since he'll be informed, I'll try to stay out of it, but if anything particularly noteworthy comes up on this end, I'll be sure to reach out."

"I appreciate you. And Carmyn? This is off topic but, woman to woman, how did Alex seem when he got back the other day?"

"Lighter." I can hear the smile in her voice. The uttering of that one simple word brings me more ease than an extra sip of wine ever could. Alexander's happiness means so much to me. Knowing our reunion did in fact have a positive impact, that our exchange did in some sense bring him closure too, blankets my heart with a comforting sense of peace. "We'll chat soon, darling, yes?"

"Yes. Thanks again, Carmyn." We hang up just as Gen enters the kitchen.

"Hey—Oh, I hope I didn't just interrupt your conversation."

"Not at all. It was done." She instantly takes the charcuterie board and follows me over to the living room couch.

"So," she begins, "do you have time now to tell me about the sexy man at your door when I arrived?" She waggles her eyebrows.

"Ugh, Luca. Luca is…" I'm suddenly zapped with an epiphany. What if Luca is the person behind the mysterious notes? Based off his confrontation with me, it would seem he has issues with my "entertaining" Alex for reasons he hadn't gotten around to mentioning. But it's clear he doesn't like that we've been involved with each other, and THAT is motive.

"Jess? You alright?"

"Yeah, sorry, something just dawned on me."

Tomorrow, I'm to meet with Madame Chérot to have my introductory lesson at the Den. It will be the perfect time to ask her to put me in touch with Luca. The conversation I want to have with him is now beyond a simple pull for information on the twins' backstory. I need to understand why this man is trying to keep me away from Alexander.

Journal,

For the past month I have stared out the window each morning for hours, plotting my escape. My attempts to run away have failed so many times, but the next time, the next time has to be different. Papa is forcing me to marry this stranger, a complete asshole with riches and ego but little of anything else. I cannot do it. I cannot. I may not survive.

This attempt to flee has to be different.

I'm so tired of it all. The more time I spend staring and plotting, the more I consider actually following through, flying away from here, never to return. Becoming someone new, someone I've always wanted to be but was never allowed to. I could be free!

Couldn't I?

Journal,

I can't remember if I ever envisioned myself married. In fact, I'm almost certain I never have. What I do remember is an event that led to a decision against marriage for me.

One night, when I was little, I walked in on Papa asleep in bed with two strange women and a bottle of liquor in his hand. Mama had been away that week visiting our dying grandmother. I remember feeling angry as I approached the bed. I was only eight, but I knew what love wasn't. It couldn't possibly have been the endless misery he brought to Mama's life. She didn't deserve it. None of us deserved that kind of careless "love." The sad truth is that the only reason we knew of the word was because of her.

My poor mama. The day she came home from her trip they had a horrible argument, fighting through the early hours of the morning. I huddled under my sheets, covering my ears, but it wasn't enough to block out the horrible sound of her tumbling down our enormous staircase, or Papa slurring and screaming, "That's what you get, bitch!" There was silence after that.

Luca ran into my room shortly after and held me tight, rocking me as I cried and telling me everything would be okay. But I knew, we both knew, nothing would be okay as long as Papa was around. Most children are afraid of monsters in their closets. But we were afraid of the real monster who lurked every day, threatening, tormenting, brooding.

That was the night I decided I would never marry. Papa had showed me that a relationship born of love could turn into pain and fear. And now, I'm so afraid Journal. I'm afraid that the man he's forcing me to marry is just as cruel as him, or may one day be. There is no way I trust Papa to choose a man who can cherish me the way a girl deserves to be cherished.

Mama was in the hospital for a few days following that incident, I don't recall how many. But when she came home, the light in her eyes, which over time had been fading, was nearly gone. These days, when I look in the mirror, I see the same dull look that I saw on her that day. And now I understand that she went from living to simply existing, as I do now. He killed a part of her that night and whatever that part was, it was something that even after their separation, remained deceased. I often wonder if it's too late for me too.

I fear that if I marry this horrid stranger, it really will be.

8

My first official day at the Den. And as with any first day, my stomach is a bundle of nerves. The number of times I questioned my sanity on the ride here was too many to count. Who does this? Who takes on a job in a field they know very little about? I know Madame Chérot must have been doing the same on her way to give me the proposal months ago.

Speaking of the platinum blonde devil herself, she rounds the corner to meet me in the lobby. After a greeting and exchange of cheek kisses, she scans the length of me, examining the gray jacket, white button up blouse and gray slim-fitted slacks I'm wearing. Her eyebrow quirks and her lips purse. She hates it.

It's not like I was given a dress code, so I figured I should just wear something professional. "What's wrong?" I ask blandly.

With a deep sigh she holds out her hand and says, "Give me your jacket."

I reluctantly take it off and hand it over. "Bien. Now, unbutton the top three buttons of your blouse."

I have the urge to challenge her request but decide against it, choosing peace over getting scolded. After doing what she requests, she nods her head in approval. "C'est mieux."

Better? I don't know if I'd say that. "My tits are practically popping out."

"Exactement."

"That's not odd? I assumed I needed to dress a bit more, you know, professional for this job." To my recollection, I don't think I ever saw Aralyn with her girls on display like this. Well … maybe once.

"Mademoiselle, take a good look around this place." I do as she suggests and see a man walk by in a well-fitted business shirt, slacks with suspenders, and very impressive dress shoes. The receptionist in the front office is wearing a short electric-blue dress with the top cut very low. The dress hugs her frame and she's wearing the most gorgeous blue open-toe heels I've ever seen. A woman walking in the door is wearing a stylish cream trench coat with fishnets and red pumps. She takes off her designer sunglasses and greets the receptionist. The Madame herself wears a black bodycon dress which, I must admit, highlights her figure in an exquisite way. "The only odd thing in here was you. There's board room professional and then there's professionally elegant. Learn the difference." I fight the urge to give a smart response.

"Amélie, apporte-le, s'il te plaît," she calls out to the receptionist, asking her to bring something over.

"Oui, madame." Amélie steps out from behind the reception area carrying a medium-sized gold box. The Madame peers down at my white pumps and points. "Take those off." There's no way she can say these aren't "professionally elegant." They are actually very trendy. I keep my mouth shut, however, and do as she requests.

She reaches into the box and pulls out a pair of brand new shiny black heels with a three-dimensional diamond-encrusted butterfly on the back of each. Similar to Aralyn's, but identical to the ones I saw the Butterflies wear at the kink club Alex had taken me to. She holds them out to me. "These are your required uniform. All service-providing staff members must wear either these heels or an approved shoe with the symbol embossed somewhere on it. This is to help everyone, clients included, understand who belongs to our team and who does not." Ah, well, there's an answer to a question I've had for quite some time. I take them from her and begin to put them on.

"You will never be expected to provide services. Unlike Aralyn, who started off providing services before becoming protégé, you have very little experience, and I haven't the patience to train you in that. So, you, mademoiselle, will be receiving the crash course to protégé. Consider yourself extremely lucky. Other employees, like Amélie here, have been hoping for this position for a long while." Oh, well, this is awkward. I finish putting on the second shoe, stand, and give the surely scorned receptionist a stiff smile, then immediately avert my gaze, embarrassed to hold eye contact with her.

Madame shoos Amélie away with a flick of her wrist and continues with her speech. "Because you will be a madam of this facility, you are required to wear them, simply to remind those you manage of our standards and expectations. Leading by example, as they say. Turn." I do a little spin. "Bien. How do they feel?"

"Um, they fit. And they are actually comfier than I expected. Though I'm sure they'll be painful in about fifteen minutes." I laugh. She stares, horribly unamused. "But, uh, nothing a little breaking in can't fix."

"Oui. You'll get used to them. This way." She signals for me to follow her. I grab my belongings and hurry to catch up.

I take the opportunity to bring up what I've been dying to ask. "Madame, would it be at all possible for you to provide me with Luca's number?"

"I thought he left the house."

"He did, but there are some things I'd like to ask him about Aralyn. It's for the book." I purposefully avoid telling her that my primary inquiry is regarding the notes. I don't care to have her in all of my business.

She stops and faces me, raising a brow. "Book? I thought you were writing an article."

"I was, but then I decided to challenge myself." She rolls her eyes and resumes walking. "I won't write any sensitive information about you. I promised I wouldn't, and I intend to keep my word."

We reach the red double doors next to my office. Madame Chérot ignores my statement. "Honestly, I don't understand you. First you hunted me down to get him to leave you alone, and now you want my help in contacting him again. You Americans astound me. Always so indecisive and entitled. As if I don't have more important things to spend my time on."

"Hold on, let's get something straight. My needing to speak with him does not mean I want him in my personal space uninvited."

"Ugh, s'il vous plaît, stop with the whining, mademoiselle. You got what you wanted. Moving on. As for your request, you can get Luca's number on your own when you see him." She holds one of the doors open for me and I walk through. There's a staircase leading down to what appears to be another hallway. She goes ahead of me, and I follow.

"But I have no idea when that will be."

We reach the bottom of the steps and I discover three hallways branching off. Every wall and ceiling as far as I can see is completely black. From here I count at least fifteen rooms, each with a red door that has a light hanging over it. I'm assuming there are more rooms around corners at the end of the halls. This is definitely where all the kinky fuckery happens.

We start down the hall to our left and I can faintly hear moans, groans, yelps, and slapping sounds. There's a window into each room with curtains drawn on the inside. "Why windows?" I ask. I have a guess and I'm curious to know if I'm right.

"Some clients like to watch or be watched. They are one-way viewing so only those on the outside can see." Just what I thought. I'm once again reminded of the kink club I attended with Alex, except those viewing windows were not one way.

"And the doors? What's the significance of the red?"

"A symbol. The entryway to pleasure."

A tall man rounds the corner ahead of us and walks our way. He's wearing only dark jeans and black boots. A black cloth covers the bottom half of his face from the nose down, like a mask, and his torso glistens with a thin layer of oil, causing the red lights to bounce off his tan skin, highlighting his impressive eight-pack abs. He greets the Madame and she replies in kind.

As we pass, I can't help but steal an extra glance back and so does he. Although I can't see it, I can tell he's grinning under that cloth and suddenly I'm incredibly bashful, immediately turning forward again. In an instant my body temperature feels as though it's risen a degree or two. If men like him are a regular around here, then I might be managing heaven!

Honestly, Jess, get a grip! You're not even an official manager yet and you're already making mistake number one by swooning over the staff!

The Madame stops in front of a room at the end of the hall. "This room," she says before opening the door, "Is the Eden room. It is one of three rooms specifically designed for those who are newer to the lifestyle. It provides a more comfortable setting. We have rooms to accommodate almost all fetishes, kinks and levels of experience within our legal means to provide services for, and we pride ourselves in having established such a model." Good to know.

When we enter, I see what she is talking about. There's nothing too intimidating about this room at all. It's a pretty shade of cobalt blue, with a soothing fountain in one corner, a stained cherry-wood floor, plenty of plants, and soft, moody lighting. Music that can be described as sensual R&B is playing at an appropriate volume. This space oozes comfort and class while providing naughty delights for the eye to behold in various spots around the room. Even the furniture looks like it's ready to aid in pleasure and I wouldn't at all be surprised if it does exactly that.

There's a man at the foot of a sex swing that's centered in the space. His black hair is pulled back in a low bun. The tan and toned muscles of his bare, tattooed back ripple as he tinkers with whatever it is he's tinkering with. I draw closer and now recognize a tattoo that portrays a scene of an angel and demon at war with one another. Fuck.

Madame Chérot addresses him in French, and Luca turns to us. An amused smile pulls at his lips at the sight of my immediate annoyance.

With a mischievous smirk, Madame Chérot responds to my silent question. "Luca used to be one of my most sought-after Dominants. Sadly, he doesn't work for me anymore but, after some persuasion, he's graciously agreed to teach you about one of the dynamic services we provide here at the Den, Domination and Submission. I thought we'd start you off with something familiar, seeing as though you've … spent some time with a Dominant before. Correct?"

I swallow my momentary embarrassment. Of course, she knows about Alexander's … tastes. He and Aralyn did have a dynamic after all. And I'm guessing Aralyn wouldn't have kept that a secret from her den mother. But why Luca? Why must he be the one to teach me?

She regards my silence with a chuckle. I guess she has a sense of humor after all, and it's twisted. Oh, joy. "You'll be introduced to the rest of the staff later. For now, I will leave you to it. I'll call to check in on you tomorrow."

"Please, don't leave me here with him." I quietly plead.

"Don't forget to leave your signed paperwork with Amélie. Bonne nuit." She smirks and makes an exit.

"This isn't happening," I murmur to myself.

Luca speaks up. "Right, then. Ready to begin?" I laugh in disbelief, and he glares at me. "I don't see what's funny."

"Really? Wow. I was so sure you'd be laughing it up right along with the Madame, delighted by my irritation."

He tilts his head slightly. "Are you irritated?"

"Are you an idiot?"

"Hm. Being a smart ass must be a thing where you're from. Either that or it comes naturally to you."

"Yeah? Does being an annoying prick come naturally to you?"

"Perhaps. Though I'd say it's a touch better than being a vulgar, entitled little princess. Now, is there anything else or can I proceed with what I'm here to do?"

I drop my belongings over by the wall. "Whatever. Let's get this over with." Please. The sooner the better.

His jaw works as he glowers. "In this room, you'll refer to me as Master Rue." He can't be serious.

He efficiently undoes his belt and swiftly pulls it from the loops of his jeans. A knot forms in my throat, both from concern and, to my annoyance and confusion, arousal. "What are you doing?"

"I'm here because I've agreed to assist Madame Chérot by helping you understand the difference between a good Dominant and a bad one. Part of your role as a soon-to-be madam yourself is to ensure a safe environment is maintained at all times. You need to know how to tell when a client crosses the line, and the rare occasion when an employee may do so also. Do I make myself clear?" Is this man truly the best Dominant for the job? Hell, he accessed my home without my consent; that's got to count against him. Clearly red flag energy.

He holds the belt between his fists, bending it, then straightens it back out with a snap. I jump in shock. "I said, is that clear? I greatly dislike repeating myself. Don't make me do it again."

"Yes," I reply with an agitated tone.

"Yes … what?"

It takes everything in me not to roll my eyes. "Yes, Master Rue." I add an intentional dash of sass. "Crystal clear."

"Bien. On your knees." Despite the fact that he could have been chosen to teach me due to his experience, it's hard not to think I've somehow been set up by the Madame to endure this degradation. After everything I've had to go through with him in just a week alone, it's cruel.

The second my knees touch the cold floor, he sucks his teeth and blows with an air of frustration before stating in a controlled tone, "Up."

"But you just told me to—"

His voice grows more commanding, "Jess, *up*." Back onto my feet I go, confusion surely plastered all over my face.

He walks up to me, standing like a massive mountain in front of my petite frame. I can feel the body heat radiating off him. I smell the intoxicating, musky scent of his cologne and suddenly I'm terribly discombobulated. "Lesson number one, Princesa. Never submit to a man who does not first walk you through a discussion of safety, boundaries and, if it's a play scene, the use of a safe word."

"Right. Sorry." The heated kiss of a blush blooms on my cheeks. I should know better. Alex had that discussion with me when we first had fun in his playroom. I'd even read about this in the multitude of articles I'd come across on the dynamic and in the handbook Madame Chérot had given me to read through.

"Sorry, *Master*. Don't forget your role in here." It's clear he's getting frustrated with me but, I don't think it has anything to do with my missteps.

I can't help but ask, "Master, why did you agree to teach me if you dislike me so?"

My question takes him aback, and I can tell it's momentarily pulled him from the role. "I don't dislike you." He pauses a few seconds. "I just don't trust you."

"Why? Because your sister is signing over her home to me?" He huffs and walks back toward the swing. "You act like I somehow conned it out of her. Like I had some great agenda to take her place. I didn't go looking to have anything of hers!"

"What turns you on?"

I'm now the one thrown by this abrupt change of conversation. "Excuse me?"

He turns to me again. His face is more concealing this time and his stare bores into my soul. "What. Turns. You. On?"

Before a thought can pass through my mind my inner voice says, *You*, and I'm mentally kicking myself. Focus, Jess! I cross my arms defensively. "Well, for one, respect, which I question whether you have."

"Stop taking things personally. I'm here to teach you, not care about your feelings."

"Obviously."

He mutters something in Spanish which, if I had to guess, was a few choice words of distaste with a side of cursing. Despite the resemblance, it's still strange to think he's related to Aralyn. Aralyn's accent wasn't the purest French, but I never heard her speak a word of Spanish. Luca, on the other hand, clearly grew up in their birthplace. Though I will say, he has the same fiery spirit, more so, actually.

"Just answer the question."

"I gotta say, so far your style of teaching sucks."

"No one is forcing you to stay. If you want to go, go." The stare down he gives me is intense, daring me to walk out the door. He'd like that. He'd feel victorious. And I simply cannot allow that to be the case. The last several years of my life have been spent showing others that I'm not to be walked over. He desires my obedience? Fine. I'll give it to him … for now. And then I'll make him give me what I crave, his secrets. I'll let him think he's winning. Little does he know the true upper hand resides with me.

My silence is response enough for him. "Thought so. Now, I need you to understand something, Princesa. If this … teacher-student relationship is going to work. I require your complete cooperation."

I display my most convincing smile. "Yes, Master Rue."

"I'm told you like to take notes. I hope you've come prepared to do so today." He gestures for me to take a seat on the black leather couch behind me. I do so, still highly annoyed. I'm just ready to get this over with.

He pulls his bottom lip between his teeth and whistles. The door opens and in walks an absolutely stunning woman. She appears to be in her late twenties to early thirties and potentially a bit taller than me, though it's hard to tell from this position. Not to mention, she's wearing heels, the same ones I have on now. She's a Papillon Diamant for sure. A radiant Diamond Butterfly.

She acknowledges my presence only briefly as she passes. Her green eyes glint with allure. Long, wavy brunette hair that extends down to the middle of her back bounces as she gracefully walks to Luca. He smirks upon sight of her and his eyes sweep the length of her scantily clothed body. All she's wearing is a strappy, rouge lingerie set, with a garter belt that dangles over her bare thighs.

He greets her as she comes to a standstill in front of him. "Hello, my pet."

"Master." Even her voice is sultry and smooth like silk.

He places his hands on her shoulders and positions her to face me. "Jess, this is Emory. She will act as my sub this evening as part of a demonstration."

"Pleasure to meet you," I say.

Her teeth are a dazzling white. "Tout le plaisir est pour moi. It's nice to finally meet the woman I've heard so much about."

"All good things, I hope." She provides only a half smile in response.

"Let's begin," Luca interjects.

I pay close attention as he runs through the proper practices that make for a safe and healthy Dominant/submissive play session, as well as an explanation of how such a session must adhere to the rules and regulations required to be followed by law. Madame Chérot called them the commandments. They are to be adhered to religiously. One of them, no penetration, was one I remember Alex explaining to me some time ago. I know now that with an establishment such as this, there is a fine line between fetish indulgence and prostitution that, for legal and safety reasons, must never be crossed. He also talked to me about common unhealthy practices within the dynamic, emphasizing that any disregard, by clients or staff, of safe practices was not at all tolerated.

Then, the demonstration begins. Luca orders Emory on to her knees and gently rakes a hand over her head. She gazes up at him with such … devotion. A memory of being on my knees before Alex springs to mind and instantly causes a fluttering sensation in my nether regions. I wonder if that very look is what he saw on my face back then.

"Remember, Emory and I will have already discussed what she's here for. I've received a detailed list of her interests and her hard limits already, and I've gone over with her exactly what will be done during her session this evening. For this example, let's say she explained to me that in addition to her love of submission, she's somewhat of a masochist as well and has chosen me for my ability to be the sadist that can fulfill her desires. We'd have communicated about her pain tolerance, which we've concluded to be moderate. Bruises are fine, but drawing blood is a hard limit. These are all things that must be thoroughly addressed and acknowledged before any play session begins."

He crouches down to her level, grasps hold of her chin tightly and draws her close to his face, looking at her as though she were a delectable dessert to be consumed. "Are you ready to begin, my pet?"

"Yes, Master."

He slaps her and I flinch, stunned by the unexpected act. Then he grasps hold of her jaw again. "I think you could sound a little more enthusiastic, yes?"

Strands of hair cover her face, jolted out of place from the impact, and a rouge mark begins to blossom on her cheek as she smiles wickedly and repeats, "Yes, Master. I am ready."

A low growl of approval rises from his throat. "Good girl." Dear heavens, do I miss being called that.

It was a relief to discover that I was not going to be the participant in Luca's demonstration tonight. Obviously, I find him to be incredibly aggravating and off-putting. However, after some time passes and I watch him strap Emory in the sex swing and hold a vibrator to her clit, teasing her with it over and over, while speaking deliciously lustful words to her, I suddenly find myself wishing I was the participant after all.

Ugh, I'm extremely sexually frustrated. That brief couple of hours with Alex teased the hell out of me the other day and I've been desperately desiring him ever since, craving touch, craving ecstasy, craving release. It's maddening.

Emory writhes with pleasure, moaning against the ball gag that's keeping her from yelling out in the way I imagine she must want to. And Luca toys with her, pulling on the clamps he placed on her nipples, every so often stopping to smack her clit.

After multiple rounds of orgasm denial, she can't take it anymore and cries out in an explosive orgasm. And when she finally comes to, her eyes apologize to Luca. He says nothing; he simply removes the gag, undoes her restraints and moves her to what he refers to as a spanking bench, strapping her wrists to it once she's bent over the hump. He selects a whip from the vast array of choices on the wall. His selection is long and frayed, with thick black cord.

"You came without my permission."

"I am sorry, Master." She says out of breath. Her chest still slightly heaves after the intense climax. "I deserve to be punished, Mast- AH!" The whip that just snapped against her ass, instantaneously leaves its bright red mark as evidence. My eyes grow wide.

Luca paces slowly behind her. With every step the anticipation of his next move grows. It's clear there will be no warning of when the whip will kiss her delicate skin next. I catch sight of the bulge in his pants. He's very much turned on, and I find it hard to pull my focus away from the sight. I have to admit, though he's an immense pain in the ass, he's truly divine to look at.

With a swift sudden movement, the whip lands on target and Emory cries out again. "Merde!"

He grabs a fist full of her hair and lowers himself close to her ear. "You keep that up and I may have to gag you again. Shut up and take your punishment like the filthy little whore you are."

"Oui, Master." She chokes back tears.

He continues to whip her several more times. Her muffled yelps have me wanting to help her. But then I remind myself she actually enjoys this treatment. Many people across the world actually enjoy this treatment. It's baffling, and yet wildly fascinating. It tickles the part of me that's interested in understanding the psychology behind it all.

And now another thought comes to mind… I wonder if Alex is a bit of a sadist. Or perhaps Aralyn was more so a masochist. I remember seeing an array of different whips displayed in the toy closet of the playroom he had, as well as the ones I came across in her closet. Was pain a part of their pleasure? Would he want it to be part of ours? I don't know if I could ever be down for this kind of fetish.

"Jess!" Luca yells out.

"What? Why are you yelling?"

"I've called your name four times. Clearly you haven't been paying attention."

"I was listening! I was just … thinking about something for a moment is all."

"Oh? What was the last thing I said?" His face is the picture of annoyance.

"Uh, I believe you were telling Emory to take her punishment … like a whore."

He drops his head, shaking it and closing his eyes momentarily before looking up at me again. "I said that will be all for the night and that the rest of this week the Madame has arranged sit ins for you to learn about the other services provided here."

"Sit ins with you?"

"I don't believe so."

Thank god. "Great. Got it."

He huffs, then goes to work undoing Emory's restraints. I stand and take my leave before he has the chance to say anything else to me. This was actually a very informative and educational experience. My only complaint was that the hospitality was less than average. I give the overall lesson a solid seven out of ten. I think that's reasonable.

I make a stop in my office to finish signing the Madame's contract and non-disclosure forms and drop them off to Amélie on the way out. I step outside to discover that it's pouring rain. *Ugh.* I should have told Jean-Philippe to wait for me, but I thought it was so silly to utilize a chauffeur for a destination that was less than a mile away. Now I'm wishing I would have at least checked the weather before releasing him for the day.

I pick up my phone to text Gen to see if she can hop in my car and come get me, and notice that there are six missed call notifications from Alex. Shit! He now knows about the notes.

9

I call Alex back and he picks up on the first ring. "Jess, hey, where are you?" Thunder rumbles overhead and the rain comes down harder. I tell Alex to hold on a second, and try to go back inside but the door is locked and Amélie doesn't seem to be at the desk right now. Crap.

I cover my other ear with my hand to hear him better. "Hey! I'm uh, just getting out of a meeting of sorts. What's up?"

"Where are you, specifically? I just landed in Paris about an hour ago."

"What? Oh no, Alex, please don't tell me you came back here because of the notes."

"You're bloody right I did. Jess, I don't wish to sound harsh, but I should give you a proper lashing for not telling me about this sooner. I haven't given you reason to think you can't ring me if you're in trouble." A lashing? Well damn, maybe he really is into dishing pain. "Now, please, tell me where you are so I can come collect you. I already went by the house and your friend said you weren't there." Ugh, that was not at all the way I envisioned Genevieve meeting him, but there is nothing I can do about that now. I'm sure she will have a lot to say when I get home.

Now that I think about it, how does he know I'm staying at Aralyn's home? I never gave him that bit of information. I don't even think Carmyn knows. That's gonna have to be a question for later, though. There are apparently much bigger things to address, such as his sudden arrival and how he might react when he learns where I am. "I'm, um… I'm at La Maison des Papillons."

There's silence for a good seven seconds. When he finally does respond, it's void of emotion. "I know where it is. Don't go anywhere. I'll be there in a few minutes."

"Okay," I watch as Emory walks out of the building far more clothed than earlier. She strolls to the opposite end of the covered entry and lights a cigarette. "I'll see you soon," I say to Alex and then the call ends. Well, this will be interesting. I knew there was a chance he'd do something drastic when he found out, but I never suspected he'd interrupt his schedule to fly out here. Not that I'm entirely upset about it. Any opportunity to see him is one I'd gladly take.

Emory looks over at me and with a smile says, "I didn't bring an umbrella."

Placing my phone in my purse, I smile back. "Neither did I. The weatherman is a damn liar."

"Haha, yes. I'm certain it will pass soon, though."

"I'm guessing you're walking too. Do you live close by?"

"Not really. I was just an idiot and parked my car a few streets away, thinking I could use the fresh air and extra exercise."

"Your English is incredibly fluent."

"We get a lot of English-speaking clients from out of the country. Many of them travel simply for our services. I've studied English since I was a child, but several years of working as a Papillon has helped fine tune my fluency." Makes sense.

"I've been excited to learn all about the Papillon Diamants. If you don't mind me asking, do you Butterflies actually have fetishes yourselves? Or is satisfying the needs of others in this way just about paying the bills?"

A plume of smoke rolls out from between her ruby lips. "Both. You have to love what you do in order to do this job. Better yet, you have to understand what you do and respect it. For many clients, indulging in their kinky fantasies isn't just an occasional thing, it's a lifestyle. And it's a lifestyle for many of us too.

"I am what you'd call a switch. I can be a Domme or a submissive. In my personal sex life, what I choose to be depends on my mood most days. But when I'm working here, I'm a Domme, always. Unless I volunteer for the sake of education, as I did tonight." She winks.

The vision of her bare ass marked with red welts is still seared in my memory. But I find so much of what I'm learning extremely intriguing. "Do you only work with regulars? Do you get to choose when you work? What about location; do you work at some of the clubs around town, or just here?"

She smirks and flicks her cigarette into the rain. "My, my, the Madame was right, you are a curious creature full of many questions." I can only imagine what else the Madame must have told her about me. "Allow me to ask you one now."

"Sure."

"Why are you doing this? From what I hear you have a good career and reputation, little to no experience in the BDSM lifestyle, and I was recently told you have Madame De la Rue's extremely wealthy lover quite enamored with you. You don't need to be here. Yet here you are."

I'm feeling mighty put on the spot, and I'm unsure of what to say. "Madame Chérot gave me this opportunity because it was Aralyn's wish."

"It sounds to me like she had quite a few wishes, and every one of them seems to involve you. You're not the least bit interested in figuring out why that is?"

"Of course I am."

"You could have turned down Madame Chérot's offer. You still can. But so far, you've chosen to stay. You've chosen to take the place of a woman you barely know. Why?"

"Like you said, I'm curious. So much so that I've stepped into her shoes just to see where the journey leads me. Just to understand a woman I barely knew but desperately wanted to since the moment I first saw her. To dive deeper into the story she left behind for me to uncover." There it is. The answer I've struggled to bring to the surface for a while.

"Ah, well, you've chosen the shoes of a very complicated woman."

I chuckle softly. "Oh, don't I know it."

"Just be careful. In my experience, not much good comes from inserting yourself into the business of others. Though, I suppose as a journalist you're used to taking those kinds of risks."

"What can I say? I can't resist the lure of a fascinating story."

"Mm, yes, though not all stories have happy endings. Just watch yourself. If you go diving too deep, you may not be able to make your way back up again."

I take note of Emory's concern. It's good advice, however, I can't help but feel like she's telling me this as a warning. Like perhaps she knows something she's not at liberty to share. "Thank you for the words of wisdom."

"My pleasure. Tell me, does the Madame know you're only invested in this opportunity for the experience of it all?"

"I'm not sure."

"You should tell her. It's only right. She's looking for a protégé, not a temporary fill in. Madame De la Rue was next in line for her throne, so to speak. Madame Chérot was supposed to retire in a few years and pass along the entire business to her. If she still has plans to do so, she hasn't the time to waste on anyone who is not serious about taking her place."

This is new information. I didn't realize the Madame had already been considering retirement. Next in line for the throne? Even if I'm here for a year, could I even fathom being ready for that? Would I even want her title? "I wouldn't suppose you'd want to be her protégé?"

She laughs. "Never. Far too much work. I like to have enough free time for the pleasures of life."

"You don't think Aralyn had that? She seemed to have time to build a relationship with her 'extremely wealthy lover.'"

"And I'm certain he was the only pleasure she granted herself."

"Huh. Interesting. It sounds like you knew Aralyn—Madame De la Rue, pretty well."

"Well, enough. She was a very private woman. To be honest, I'm not even sure she kept many friends, if any. She'd come, do her work, and leave. Plenty of us tried to befriend her. And though she was kind, she seemed guarded." She peers out at the rain, which has settled to a light drizzle. "Finally."

"I'll take what you said into consideration. You're right. Though I am very invested in learning about everything that happens here, I don't wish to waste anyone's time."

She smiles at me as she pulls up the zipper on her jacket. "I like you. There's something about you that reminds me of someone. I'm not sure who just yet, but I'm sure I will figure it out. I'm going to make a run for it. Have a safe journey home. Bonne nuit."

I bid her farewell and watch her walk down the street. What a day this has been. I'm not entirely sure what to make of it all, but I've gained some solid insight on a few things, and that, to me, is positive progress. I'm beginning to see a bigger picture of Aralyn's life and it fills me with confidence. This book might just come together after all.

The front door opens again and out walks Luca. He barely looks at me as he breezes past. "Goodnight," he grumbles.

Earlier, I had been so quick to get away from him that I totally forgot I had wanted to speak with him. I still have questions. "Wait, hold on!" He stops and I watch his shoulders move up then drop as he exhales a deep sigh before turning to look at me. "I have a bone to pick with you."

"A what?"

"You don't like Alex. Why?"

"How is it that when I came to you wanting to have a conversation, you were ready to slam a door in my face. Now, when I'd love nothing more than to go rest, you want to talk?"

"Well, look on the bright side, it's not like I'm showing up to your house unannounced, or worse, breaking in."

He laughs incredulously. "Fine, let's do this. Alexander Marc is a pain in my ass. He has been since the day he found his way into my sister's life. He's a selfish cabrón who cares only for his own interests."

"Then we aren't talking about the same man. Alex is the least selfish person I know."

"Then you don't really know him." My eye begins to twitch. I'm so sick of this man's ridiculous assumptions and statements.

"You sent those notes to us, didn't you?"

"What are you talking about?"

"The notes! The stupid black cards warning Alex and I to stay away from each other."

"I haven't sent either of you anything. But whoever did has the right idea. There's no reason you should be hanging around with him."

"Why, because he's *sooo* selfish? Give me a break. Even if he was, why would you give a fuck?"

"He leaves a path of ruin everywhere he goes!" Luca bellows. But I can't understand what would cause him to loathe the man I cherish. A trail of ruin? From what I've gathered all,

Alex ever seems to do is try and hold things together and give assistance. That's why he's here in Paris now, to help and protect me. Granted, I'm sure it will be in whatever way he deems best, but he cares, deeply. How can a man like that leave devastation in his wake?

The anger that flashes in Luca's eyes is not there without reason. There's either something I'm not seeing clearly or something he is misinterpreting about Alex altogether. The disconnect is profound, and I'm currently unsure of the angle I need to approach this in order to connect the dots.

The sound of tires can be heard rolling to a stop on the wet pavement. I look behind me and see a black car pull up. Without being able to see through the tinted windows, I know Alex has arrived. My stomach begins to churn with worry.

The driver walks around to the back passenger door, but it opens before he can get to it. A brown Italian leather shoe steps out onto the sidewalk and Alexander emerges, his gaze fixed on Luca.

Luca glares at him and in a low tone, almost a growl, he says, "YOU."

This isn't good. This isn't good at all.

10

lex strides over to my side, his demeanor calm. He greets me with a hand placed gently at the small of my back. "Hi, Brown Eyes." I give him my sweetest smile, hoping to mask my apprehension. He then turns his attention to the man who looks like he's about to have a conniption. "Luca, good to see you. I didn't realize you and Jess had met."

Luca just stares him down. I respond instead, hoping to avoid what could certainly become a disaster. "We met just last week, actually."

"Yes." Luca finally speaks up. "And then we met here today so I could teach her what a real Dominant is like."

OH. MY. GOD. I swear whatever color was in my face has drained. "Luca, what the hell?"

"What? He should know what we've been up to, don't you think?" His emboldened smirk enrages me.

"That is beyond inappropriate!" I step forward to get in his face, but Alex throws out his arm in front of me, drawing me back beside him.

Luca laughs, but Alex maintains the same stoic expression. I remember now how good he is at remaining calm until he's triggered to the point that he's not. There's no telling what's really going through his head at this moment. He replies, "How interesting. Well, I'm sure that boosted the ego a bit. After all, the only time you ever seem to make an effort to assert real dominance is in a playroom with a woman you barely know."

I do my best to hold back my snicker. This is a side of Alex I haven't seen before. I should have known the man had a lethal way with words. I'm so proud and so here to soak up every delicious word he throws at Luca, whose grin quickly turns into a sour frown.

"Now, any more juvenile remarks or can we have a mature conversation for once?" Alex asks.

Luca continues to stare at him in detest. "You're not worth saying much else."

"Is that what it is? Or is it because you can't handle what you shell out?"

Luca's nostrils flare and he takes several paces forward, getting in Alex's face and saying something in Spanish that sounds like he just cussed him out. The two of them are eye to eye and Alex doesn't back down; he barely even flinches. Instead, he just smirks and responds with, "It's unfortunate you feel that way." Then, in a lowered tone that I strain to hear, he says, "I'll always have respect for you for the simple fact that you're Aralyn's brother. However, don't ever mistake my respect for being permissive of your ill-mannered behavior." The atmosphere is so tense it's suffocating.

Luca's eyes bore into his like a wolf prepared to attack. "Fuck your respect."

"I see. We should be going. Always a pleasure to see you again, Luca." I note the hint of sarcasm. He gently grasps my hand, entwining his fingers with mine, then leads me away to the car.

Luca calls out, "It's your fault she's dying, Alex! I pray that knowledge will always haunt you!" Chills run through me, stopping me cold. "I'll never forgive you for taking my sister from me!"

"This is ridiculous," I mutter as I whirl around, preparing once again to chew him out.

In a tone only I can hear, Alex says, "Leave it be, Jess. It's okay. Just get in the car." There's a long tense pause. Each of us is motionless, frozen in the thick intensity of the moment. But I eventually do as he says, just as the rain begins to fall again.

After Alex gets in, he orders the driver to proceed. "Are you alright?" he asks.

"Me? I'm not the one who was basically accused of being a murderer! Why would he say something like that to you? What happened between you two?"

He exhales and runs a hand over his face. "I believe he blames me for the decline of his relationship with Aralyn and the ill treatment he endured from their father as a result of her decision to be with me."

"He and Aralyn had a falling out? I assumed they were very close, especially being twins and all."

"They could have patched things up after she left me, but they had gone nearly two years without speaking to each other when we were together. He disliked that I continued to pursue a relationship with her, despite his multiple pleas for me to leave her be. And he absolutely detested me when he found out his pleas didn't work and we gradually became a couple. Trust me, there were a few times I tried convincing Aralyn that we should perhaps not continue the relationship, because I became worried about the potential repercussions, especially when I found out that her father was a tyrant. He was really the one who wanted me out of the picture; he just sent Luca to make it happen."

He drifts into thought. "I've seen the lengths her father went to make her miserable. I didn't want that for her, no matter how much I wanted to be with her, but she wouldn't hear it. So, despite the possible consequences, our relationship continued.

"Luca made a couple major mistakes; he chose to do his father's bidding over finding a solution that would keep Aralyn well and safe, and he did not fully take the time to know the woman she had become. At some point in her life Aralyn found her strength, and she refused to allow anyone, her family especially, to get in the way of what would make her happy and bring her peace. I respected her choices and loved her even more for the voice she had developed. However, it ultimately led to there being a rift between them and she refused contact with him, until recently, perhaps."

It's good to finally get some information about what's caused such foul energy between Alex and Luca. However, something still doesn't add up. "But Alex, why would any of that lead him to say it's your fault she's dying?"

"If I had to guess, I'd say he thinks he could have somehow helped her get better if I hadn't been what he believes to be the cause of their distance."

"It's madness to blame you for that."

"Yes, well, when it comes to her family, madness doesn't even begin to describe it. Aralyn was the exception to a very toxic rule." He turns in his seat to face me. "Listen, I can tell you are curious to learn more about her; perhaps that stems from your journalistic nature. While I understand, I urge you to be careful. Her father is deceased, but that doesn't mean his legacy is. There's no telling what you may come across if you go digging too deep."

There is so much I don't know about Aralyn and her family. It's clear, from what I've read of her journals so far, that her father was a monster. But Alex makes it sound like there was, and perhaps still is, something more sinister at play with them than meets the eye. I briefly wonder if Luca could still be tied to that man's "legacy." Could he still be connected with the same unsavory individuals that his father was? Could I see him potentially hurting me? Sure, he's an asshole, and I wouldn't put it past him to write cryptic notes to me and Alex to scare us, but he doesn't seem like the kind of guy who would actually do anything to harm either of us. Certainly, the Madame didn't think he was that type of man, if he was under her employment for years, especially not with the kind of standards she upholds. However, that look he gave Alex a few minutes ago does give room for speculation.

"I'll be careful," I assure him.

The rain falls even harder now, pounding against the car, and the traffic ahead is keeping us at a standstill. Despite the lengthy delay, I'm grateful for the additional alone time with Alex. "You know, any chance I get to see you makes me happy, but you didn't have to drop everything for this note situation."

He frowns. "To be honest, I'm not sure you're taking it seriously enough. It's not as though you're aware of who is doing this, Jess. Neither of us are. So, neither of us has any insight into who this individual is, their motive, or what they are capable of. These things aren't to be taken lightly." He does have a point. Perhaps I've been brushing it off because it's easier to be ignorant than to acknowledge the potential for real trouble.

"I feel kind of bad. You seem to always come to my aid somehow, and it's at your inconvenience. I don't wish to be an inconvenience for anyone, especially you."

"Ensuring your health and safety is never an inconvenience for me. I truly care about your well-being, Brown Eyes. Even when I wasn't there, I always made sure I knew whether you were safe and well."

"What do you mean?"

"Over the past several months, I hired someone to keep an eye on you. You were a sore subject for quite a while, so they were only to report to me if they suspected you to be in danger or if you were ill or injured."

My eyes grow wide and I giggle with shock. "Mr. Marc, are you telling me that all this time you had assigned me a personal stalker?"

A rich belly laugh rolls from his diaphragm. "That's an interesting way to view it. They didn't follow you all the time, only periodically. You must have been doing just fine, because I never received a report."

"Are they still keeping tabs on me?"

He grins. "Maybe."

"And if I don't consent to being followed?"

His grin turns into a frown. "Shit. I had been so caught up in the need to know you were alright that I hadn't even considered it as a potential breach of consent. I sincerely apologize."

I chuckle. "It's okay, Alex. I think it's endearing, actually. You didn't track me out of some weird desire to know my every move, you did it to make sure I was okay. I had assumed I had become an afterthought after what happened between us. But it's nice to know I wasn't. Despite everything, you still cared about me."

His brow creases and his eyes bore deep into mine. "More than you know." Then, he clears his throat and looks away as though he's keeping himself from connecting too deeply. "Well, um, speaking of having you looked after, I'm certain you can imagine my shock when I called them to inquire about your current address today and they gave me Aralyn's." I knew this conversation was coming. When he mentioned earlier that he spoke with Gen, I knew the only way that would have been possible was if he showed up at the house. Of course, with everything else going on, I didn't have time to think too much about it.

"Right. I suppose I should explain."

"By all means."

"Apparently, she's arranged it so the house is mine once she passes. I don't really know why and, like you, I was absolutely shocked when I found out. Though, after some time to process, I figured accepting it and moving in for a while would be a good way to try to understand her more." He's silent for a bit, thoughtful. "I'm sure it must seem so strange to you."

"Mm. Well, I suppose more than anything, I'm curious as to why you'd go to such lengths to understand her." There's no time to satisfy his curiosity as I notice we're turning down my block. Not enough time, either, to prepare myself for Alexander's reaction as we make our way to the house I'm sure he once frequented, the house bearing many memories that are surely sweet yet heartbreaking. I catch his frown as he glances out the window at it. "Alex, if being here is going to be too hard for you, I—"

"It will be fine," he replies with a stiff smile. His words may say one thing, but his energy says something different. Being here is going to be triggering for him. It already is, and possibly already was, since he had stopped by earlier to find me.

He clears his throat, "Look, um, I think it best you pack some belongings, anything you feel you'll need for a couple weeks at least. I'd like for you to return with me to London till all this note rubbish is no longer a threat. We'll take the jet this evening." He exits the car, reaching in and offering his hand to help me out.

I take it, then stand, stunned and confused, "Wait, what? Alex, you know I'd normally be so thrilled to go with you to England, but I have responsibilities here now; I can't just up and leave."

"I'm guessing your responsibilities have something to do with those." I follow his line of sight straight to my feet. I totally forgot that I'm still wearing the diamond butterfly heels. I'm actually shocked I've lasted in them for so long. They are way more comfortable than I anticipated.

"Um, yeah, about these, I uh… I can explain these too."

"Oh, I look forward to it." He starts walking toward the front steps. "You'll have plenty of time to tell me all about it on the flight."

"W-wait! My friend Genevieve is visiting; I can't just leave her."

Swinging open the front door, an exuberant Gen pops out. "There you are! I was hoping the storm didn't—" She notices Alex and can't restrain an impressed grin. "Why, hello. Back again, I see." Her gaze sweeps the length of him.

"Pleasure to meet you again. Genevieve, is it?"

"Pleased you remembered. Come in!" She moves aside to let us through.

Alex takes a step forward and then hesitates. Something is keeping him from crossing the threshold into familiar territory. I think quickly and move next to him, grasping his hand. "Gen, how would you like to go to London? Alex has invited us there while we figure out what's going on with the weird notes." I sense him looking over at me, having picked up on what I'm doing.

"London? Are you telling me this has just turned into a two-for-one trip? Sign me up, babes! Agh, I'm so excited! When?"

"Uh, tonight!"

"Flight leaves in two hours," Alex chimes in.

"I can be packed and ready to go in twenty minutes!" She practically runs up to her bedroom, leaving us standing on the stoop.

I reassuringly squeeze Alexander's hand and face him. His eyes are soft and filled with unspoken gratitude, for the save, I'm sure, but I think also for no longer putting up a fight about traveling back with him. "I hope it's okay I invited her along."

"Of course. I wouldn't ask you to leave her behind."

"Thank you. Also, you don't have to come in with me." I give a small, knowing smile. "I think I'll be safe enough to pack on my own."

The smile he flashes in return is sweet as he cups my chin, sweeping his thumb delicately across my skin. I can tell there's much he wishes to say right now. I can also tell he's keeping himself from saying anything at all. Anything but, "Alright then. I'll wait by the car."

The ache I feel as his hand drops away and he walks down the steps is excruciating. Being close to him in any capacity is hard enough. But when I yearn for him the way I do, emotionally, physically, sexually … that ache quickly becomes a burn. Now, I'll be around him a lot more in London. How will I put out the embers before they ignite with mind-boggling intensity?

As soon as I make it into my room, Gen rushes in, seating herself on the bed and grinning dramatically, as though she waited ages for this opportunity to chat. "Oh my god, Jess, he's more perfect than I thought, and absolutely gorgeous! I swore I was dreaming when he first came by. You have my blessing to marry him immediately."

I let out a laugh, "Honestly, Gen, you just met him." But she's right, he is perfect.

"I'm just saying, I will literally throat punch anyone who tries to object, before they can even move their lips to breathe a word."

"Hahaha, your dramatics never cease to shock me. Shouldn't you be packing?"

"Already done if you can believe it! Must be the excitement. I didn't bother to fold shit, I just threw everything into my bags."

I smirk and start on my own packing, but I notice Gen's excitement fades the longer she keeps her eyes trained on me. "Crap, I've been treating this like a spontaneous vacation, and the whole reason we are headed to London is to make sure you're safe! I didn't even consider how you might be feeling right now."

I shrug. "I feel fine. It's happening at an inconvenient time, but I understand it's for the best."

"What about you seeing Alex again? Did you even know he was coming?"

"Not a clue. In terms of how I feel about seeing him again, I'm not quite sure, Gen. I love seeing him. I love being near him. I love that I'll be spending more time with him, even if this wasn't how either of us envisioned that happening…"

"But?"

"But … I'm worried that the more I'm in his presence, the more my emotions will get involved. It's taken me a lot to be, well, okay after all that happened. Alex was hesitant to even speak to me and now, here we are in a position where he's once again present, and I'm just going along with things praying I'm not left heartbroken for the second time."

"I see." She goes quiet as I continue packing. Then, after a minute or two she says, "I've been wondering something. I remember in one of our conversations, before you found out about him and Aralyn, you mentioned you felt like he could be your soulmate. Do you still feel that way?"

"You must have thought me insane."

"No, but I mean, don't get me wrong, what you've told me about him and his lifestyle sounds absolutely amazing, but you knew each other for about a month before things went downhill. How do you know this isn't infatuation getting the best of you?"

I understand her questioning. I have asked myself the same many times over. One of the things I love most about this woman is that she's always kept it real with me. She doesn't sugar coat, and she speaks her mind, but in a way that's mindful of my feelings. I can't help but think if we'd been in touch more these last few years, our conversations could have kept me from so much trouble.

I sigh. "It's hard to explain. I guess, as cliché as it sounds, there's this magnetic energy I can't shake. For a while, I wondered if it's because he treated me better than any man has, but it's deeper than that, sacred and spiritual, in a sense. And you know me, I don't usually buy into all that, but I can't deny how I feel. No matter where I go or what I do, I only ever want to be where he is."

"Strong chemistry doesn't always equate to soulmate energy."

I take a seat next to her. "I'm telling you, Gen, it's not just chemistry. I can't quite put my finger on it yet, but all I know is that if I could imagine what it could be like to come across a soulmate, this would be it."

"Aww. Well, what do I know? I haven't ever really had that type of connection with anyone. But hey, you know what they say, when you know, you know, right? I actually think that's really beautiful. My inquiry might come off as though I'm being a Debbie Downer, but I hope you know I'm cheering you both on."

"Thank you, that means more than I can express. But, Gen, what if I really am delusional for thinking what's between us is something worth fighting for? Although he says he won't close the door on what we could be, I'm not entirely sure he feels the same way I do about him. I mean, I really thought he wanted me just as much, but I was pretty much tossed to the side that night. And there is a small part of me that wonders if the only reason he's choosing to continue contact is because he doesn't want the burden of my pain."

"He was hurting, Jess, and scared of his emotions, I'm sure. From the sound of it, a lot was unloaded on him that night. You said yourself, he and Aralyn were madly in love. I can't imagine it was easy for him to unpack what was happening, let alone to make the decision to let you go. To him, he was probably doing the best thing in that moment to protect his heart that already wasn't fully healed. I don't think that means he doesn't, or is unable to feel the same way you do for him."

"Yeah, you may be right."

"Chin up, babes! Whatever happens, you are going to be okay. When all is said and done, if he's not ready to choose you, keep choosing yourself, no matter what."

Her words of encouragement and validation bring me instant relief. "I love you."

"I love you most. Now, hurry up and finish packing. LONDON'S WAITING FOR UUUUSSS!"

Yes, London's waiting, and thirty minutes later, so is Alex, standing exactly where he said he'd be as we approach the car. I peer up at him, curiously observing his sweeping gaze. I swear, I may never get used to the way he looks at me. "Welp, I'm ready to be whisked away to safety." I catch longing in his expression. His eyes dart across my features as though he's taking note of every detail of my face. "What? What is it?"

"Nothing. I'm just … thoughtful." Oh, what I'd give to get a peek into this man's mind right now. A look behind the curtain where he keeps so much hidden. It's just like when we were first getting to know each other. I had to work my way up to gaining his trust and openness, and now I find myself having to do it again. But this time he also has to work his way to mine. I believe he knows that. He knows that even though I made my intentions to fight for us clear, it won't be as easy for me to believe his efforts to be genuine. It won't be as easy for me to spill out my soul to him.

It's as though there's glass between us. We clearly see each other, clearly yearn for each other, but if I try to reach out and touch him, or him me, there's a barrier in the way. How and when do we shatter such an obstruction? How do we give ourselves the freedom to be what we once were? Will I discover the answer in London, or will I simply be left questioning and immensely unsatisfied?

He gives me a reassuring smile. "Right, then. Let's whisk you to safety."

Journal,

I met the man Papa is forcing me to marry. Edward is his name. Some chauvinistic idiot from Berlin. I've never met someone so educated yet brainless. No real passions other than to take over his family business. He has all the degrees to pull it off, yet, when asked, seems to know very little about the position he'll one day take on. This tells me one of two things. Either he's lying, and is in fact not at all interested in his father's plans for him, or he is interested but has probably skated through everything in his life to even make it to this point.

The way I had to resist the urge to vomit every time he mentioned what a lucky man he will be to "possess" me, as if I'm some prized toy to be won at a festival. Not to mention, the way he talks to the house staff is disgusting. He actually spit out something he didn't like onto the floor, laughing as the server knelt to clean it up, and poking fun. And everyone else, including Papa, laughed right along with him.

I can't marry that man. I refuse. So, here I am at a train station in Venice. I'm catching the next train that comes, no matter where it goes, as long as it takes me far away from it all.

Every time I run away I'm caught by Luca and brought back home. My poor excuse for a father always sends him to do his dirty work, and he willingly does it each time. I feel sorry for my brother, I can tell he's trying to fill a void. And even though his search for me will be a major inconvenience to all of my plans, I'll continue to forgive him.

Maybe one day he'll see things as I do. Maybe one day he too will tire of our father's manipulation and abuse. Maybe one day, when he goes in search of me, it will be because he wishes to join me. Maybe one day.

11

Carmyn warmly greets us as we ascend the jet's stairs. She gives me one of those cryptic smiles as she glances between Alex and I, alluding to her content in seeing us together again. She and Gen sit across the aisle from us as we get settled.

It takes about twenty minutes before the plane is ready to take off. When we do, I stare out the window, watching Paris get smaller and farther away. Madame Chérot is going to be livid when she finds out I took a spontaneous trip out of the country without her approval. I wonder if she'll accept the excuse of a potentially life-threatening situation.

As soon as the plane levels out, Alex gestures toward my foot, "May I?" I nod and he grabs my leg, gently lifting it onto his lap. He slides off my heel and gives it a quick look over. The diamond butterfly glistens, all shiny and new. "So, I'm quite curious, Brown Eyes, how exactly did you end up becoming a Diamond Butterfly?"

I hadn't spent much time thinking about having to tell Alexander of my kinky new endeavor, and in a way I'm glad, because I would have obsessed over how he may or may not respond. "I don't know if I could really be called a Butterfly."

"It's my understanding that you aren't simply given these if you aren't."

"Right. I suppose that's true. About four months ago, the woman in charge of the den asked me to take Aralyn's place as her protégé." He raises a brow but says nothing. Per usual, it's difficult to get a good read on him. "Apparently it was Aralyn's request that I be given the position. I wasn't going to take it. In fact, I thought it absurd that she'd even go through with asking me, but after some time, I thought it would be a good opportunity to learn about Aralyn and the BDSM world."

"And … I'm assuming Luca was part of a learning opportunity within this new position?"

Begrudgingly, I reply, "Well, yeah, unfortunately. However, he certainly wasn't my choice for a teacher."

He nods in acknowledgment, and is quiet for another moment of time. His focuses on my foot, where he begins to apply pressure in circular movements.

"Why did you go through with the Madame's offer?" he calmly asks.

"Well, like I said, it seemed like a good opportunity to—"

"No, I mean why did you feel that taking on such a high position in an area you have very little experience in and knowledge about was the best way to achieve what you're hoping to achieve?"

"I-I don't know. I mean, I do, but I don't, if that makes sense."

He laughs. "Come now, Jess, you'll have to do better than that."

"I suppose, if I'm being entirely honest with myself, I have a thing for risk. Possibility excites me, and the idea of never knowing terrifies me. Not because I fear the unknown will lead me somewhere bad, but because not pursuing the unknown could mean I miss an opportunity I may come to regret not taking. So, if I see the potential, if I see the possibilities, and I like what I see, I have to go for it."

"And … is that reasoning what's keeping you tethered to your attraction for me? Do the possibilities excite you so much that you view me as a risk potentially worth taking?"

I calculate what I'm about to say carefully, because how he words it makes what I said sound horrible, somehow. "There's always a risk in the pursuit of intimacy and partnership; it doesn't matter with whom."

Uncertainty creeps past the layer of stoicism he displays. Alex is a man who takes time to think through the risks before deciding whether it's worth it. This is one of our differences. Many times I make quick decisions based on feeling. He needs to believe risk has a high probability of success, especially when he feels there's a lot to lose. Perhaps I should attempt to be more like him in that regard, to balance myself out.

"Alex, I know it may seem like I don't always make the best judgement calls, like I'm reckless. And yeah, perhaps I am. But I hope you know that I care about you very, very much. You're not just some tempting risk. You're so much more to me than that."

"That's comforting to know. Regarding your decision with the den … you know I adore your ambition and curiosity; I just don't want you to get in over your head. If you really feel this path that you've started down is best, I still support you."

"But you don't think it is the best one, huh?"

"Like you said, it's a risk. And if you want my honest view of things, I think you're choosing to take on quite a lot in the name of a woman you didn't know much about. Anyone else would think it's madness."

"Trust me, the insane nature of it all is not lost on me. I question my decisions daily."

"Just promise me, if any of it feels too overwhelming, you'll let go of whatever you deem necessary in order to maintain your well-being." I promise, and he hits a pressure point in my foot that sends tingles drifting up my leg and spine. I let out a small, delighted moan. Fuck, I needed that.

Gen can be heard quietly giggling at me across the aisle and I look over at her as she fans herself with her hand. With an amused grin, I shake my head and then allow myself to relax into my seat, relishing in Alexander's caring touch.

━━━━━━ ♥ ━━━━━━

We're driven to the front entrance of a fancy hotel. Alex said we'd be staying here instead of his place. Since we have no idea what's going on, he felt it better that he keeps me close enough that he can reach me quickly, but far enough that it's not drawing unwanted attention. For all we know they could be staking out his home too. Considering this unknown enemy is trying to separate us, I couldn't agree more.

As the bell boys offload our bags, he goes to the reception desk to check us in. Carmyn walks up to me and places a hand on the small of my back. "How are you feeling, love?"

"I'm okay. A little shocked that I'm in London under these circumstances, but I'm also happy to be here. Especially with Gen and the two of you."

"I tried to reason with him, but I'm sure you know by now that when Mr. Marc makes a decision about something it's rather difficult to dissuade him." Which makes the fact that he's willing to remain open to a potential relationship with me fairly impressive.

"I appreciate your help, as always."

She grabs hold of my elbow and guides me out of ear shot of the others. "I heard you had a run in with Ms. De la Rue's brother." I can see the concern in her eyes.

"Well, I don't know if I'd call it a run in, per se; I've actually encountered him a few times prior to today. I'm guessing Alex told you want happened?"

She shakes her head. "No, I heard it from a reliable source."

"What source?"

"Never mind that. You should know that word spreads like wildfire within connected networks. And the word is that man is bad news. He's not like Aralyn. I wouldn't go as far as to call him evil, or anything like that, but he certainly has his faults."

So, Carmyn clearly doesn't trust him either. It's validating to know I'm not the only one who suspects there is something seriously off about him. "Yeah. Alex mentioned Luca has some issues."

"'Issues' is a generous term. Her brother made every attempt to make his life utter hell when he was dating Ms. De la Rue." I'm about to ask her for details, but Alex has finished checking in and comes over to meet us with the keys. She whispers a final word of caution, "Just watch yourself around him, love. He may seem like the charmer, but he's really the cobra." He hasn't seemed charming to me whatsoever, but I value her advice and store it in the memory bank.

"Alright, well, we have you and Genevieve situated. Carmyn, would you mind showing Genevieve to the room? I'd like to take Jess for an evening stroll before heading home. We shouldn't be too long." Alex turns his head my direction. "If that's alright with you, that is." I nod with an enthusiastic "yes!" It's like an unexpected treat.

"I'd be happy to, sir. Good evening Ms. Rivers." I bid Carmyn good night in return, and she walks off with a giddy Gen following after her.

━━━━❤━━━━

*I*t's a warm summer's night, but there's a cool breeze that makes the temperature feel perfect. I'm enjoying the view of the city as we stroll the streets of London, not too far from the hotel. His security team is following us. They aren't close enough to be noticeable to anyone looking, but they aren't too far that they can't quickly jump into action if something goes down.

Neither I nor Alex have said much since leaving the hotel. In a way, it's as though he's been taking a moment of silence to think about what he wants to say. I've simply been waiting for him to be the first to say anything, unsure of where his head is at, especially after all he's discovered since picking me up.

He takes off his suit jacket, undoes his cuffs, and folds the sleeves of his shirt up to his elbows, showing off those beautiful veiny forearms I've so terribly missed. I catch myself rolling my bottom lip between my teeth while envisioning things I'd be embarrassed to tell him at this time. Thankfully, he doesn't notice.

Finally, he speaks. "*Ehm*, so, I uh, bet you're probably thinking we're walking without any destination in mind."

"Are we not?"

"No. I have somewhere I'd like to show you."

"Let me guess. You're not going to tell me what it is till we get there."

He flashes that charming smile. "You know me well. Speaking of which, I had the pleasure of reading a very fascinating article recently—yours." I'm both nervous and thrilled to hear this news. I had no way of knowing if he had read it. One would assume he would have, given that it was about him, but I had my doubts.

"I want you to know that I'm incredibly proud of you, Jess. What you wrote was … profound and very flattering, honestly. I knew you had it in you to write from a place of more depth and understanding, but I didn't expect the level of brilliance behind it. Though I really shouldn't be surprised. It was poetry, and I'm incredibly honored to have been a part of it."

I'm relieved and joyful. "I have you to thank for that, you know. You saw the greater potential I had, and even though you can be a smart ass at times," I snicker, "you were right to challenge me. I'm the one who's honored." Alex, despite us having barely known each other during the early period in which I was interviewing him, believed in me more than some of the closest individuals in my life. Something compelled him to take a chance on me, a couple different chances. I'm beyond grateful he did.

What he showed was a gentleness and attentiveness that I hadn't received from a single man before him. Not even Arthur, whose obsession I mistook for love. How could I ever want to break away from the way he makes me feel? "I hope the media hasn't swamped you since. I was a bit worried about that."

"It was intense for a spell, but you know how I handle the media. Once they realized there wasn't anything they could get from me, it all returned to normal." Funny how 'normal' for him involves still being bothered by nosy information fiends, which is made even funnier by the fact that I'm one of them. "So, what's your next big story?" he asks earnestly.

"Do you really want to know?" I'm not sure how to give him the news about my "next big story."

"Of course, why wouldn't I?"

"Well, because … it's about Aralyn." He stops abruptly and I come to a halt as well, gauging his facial expression to get some comprehension of what he's thinking or feeling, but it's hard to tell, per usual. I take his silence as an invitation for me to explain. "A few days after I met up with her, you know, to find out what had happened and why she did what she did, I received a package from her. It was four of her journals, along with a note implying that she'd like me to tell her story."

I pause, allowing him the opportunity to say something, but still he says nothing, lost in thought. "I had considered just writing an article but, there's so much about her that I believe deserves more than a couple page spread. I'm going to push myself a little further and write a biography."

To my astonishment, a small smile dawns on his face. "Good. It will be brilliant."

"You're not opposed?"

"It's not my story. Whether I oppose or not doesn't matter. What I love is that you are branching outside your realm of comfort, not simply limiting yourself to what you know. And I have no doubt that you will do the memories of her life justice." It's a relief to hear him say that, and in many ways affirming.

"I've only recently started reading her journals. I haven't gotten to any parts about you yet, but I want you to know I won't mention you by name. I value your privacy just as much as you do." We continue with our walk.

"Will you be giving me an alias?" He jokes. A nod to my Isabella Evens era, surely.

"Mm, most likely. Do you have a preference?"

"Surprise me."

"If you in insist. Maybe I'll call you Mr. Bright Eyes, then your alias can pair well with your pet name for me."

"Ah, so we could be Mr. and Mrs. Eyes, yes?"

I scrunch my nose, "Oh god, that was corny."

His laughter is deep and hearty. "Ugh, agreed. Though you bloody well started it."

"Hahaha, true, but I'm just saying, if you want me to surprise you, don't be disappointed if you end up with that sobriquet."

"I find it endearing, actually."

"Stop lying."

He grins. "I'm not lying. Call me whatever you like—Mr. Bright Eyes, Mr. Ten Toes, Mr… ah, I don't know, Mr. Smart Arse, it doesn't matter to me. I know it will be given with the best regard."

My laughter gradually subsides as I notice an acute longing stirring within me. There's an even greater sadness that follows soon after upon the realization that this day, this precious time with him, will come to an end. He slows to a stop. "Remember that destination I told you about?" I nod. "We're here. Look up."

I do as he requests, and my sight ascends a tall building at least twenty stories high. The glowing white sign toward the very top reads *Ether Inc.* My eyes grow wide as I gawk at it. "Ether? Oh Alex, your company! Is this the headquarters?"

"The one and only." He steps forward and beams with delight, placing his hands in his pockets while glancing up at his pride and joy. "I've wanted to show her to you for quite some time. Since back when we had discussed you moving out here with me. At that time, I just thought it would be a good thing for you to see. I thought perhaps you would have wanted to write about it at some point. But now, I just find myself more thrilled that I get to show you at all."

He looks over at me. "This may not seem like much, showing you a building, but this building is a large part of what makes me who I am. At the core of it, it represents my dedication and commitment. I don't give up easily. When I say I'll fight for something, I'll fight for it until there's no reason to fight any longer. I wanted to bring you here tonight to open up a little and prove that I meant what I said when agreeing not to shut you out. It will be hard for me, but I'm dedicated to the vision, committed to exploring the possibilities, even if it's gradually. I can tell you're concerned about where I stand, even after our discussion last week. Please know that where I stand in this is right next you."

And with that, the barrier between us is thinner, and things appear more promising. "Alex, I can't find the words to express how comforting that is to hear. It continues to amaze me how you're always so attentive to my energy and emotions. And it means so much that you wanted me to see Ether. You put your all into making this company as influential as it is today. Your father would be incredibly proud of you. Thank you for sharing this with me."

"Thank *you* for being patient, for being willing to take things bit by bit. I know it's not easy."

"You've got that right," I say playfully.

He begins to stare at me in a certain way that I'm finding hard to read. It's almost as though he's flustered, but also, perhaps, turned on? "What is it?" I ask.

He turns his face away, grinning, appearing like a child who was caught being mischievous. "There's a certain look you've been giving me since I picked you up earlier. I just remembered why it was so familiar. It reminds me of one you gave me the night I fuck—" He pauses and quickly clears his throat before continuing, "Um, the night we were first intimate."

I watch his cheeks turn a light shade of rouge. "Are you blushing, Mr. Marc?"

His grin widens and his fingers sweep across my cheek, his touch feather light. "No more than you are, Ms. Rivers."

Bashful, I avert my gaze downward as I notice a tingling heat rising in my body. He steps close, very close, and with a hook of his finger beneath my chin, tilts my head back up. His thumb traces the edge of my lower lip causing my body to ache for him in the most sinful way.

"Now, this look… It's always terribly difficult to resist you when you look at me like this," he says.

"Like what?"

"Like you'd give the world for just one kiss." He really does *see* me. He pauses, and I can see the uncertainty in his eyes. Then, his features soften, his shoulders drop as he exhales, and I catch the exact moment he gives into a decision. He lowers his face close to my own and, with such tenderness, asks, "How about you get the kiss and keep the world? Would that be alright?"

My breath hitches. "Would it?" I desire him immensely in every beautiful way imaginable, but I want him to feel comfortable. I want the actions he takes toward me to naturally and fully be what he desires as well.

His answer comes swiftly, when only a second passes and his mouth presses against mine, gentle yet claiming. Entranced, I reach up and place my hands on either side of his face, drawing him closer, making the kiss deeper. I've craved this for too long, and now I'm greedy for it, greedy for his touch, greedy for this gesture of adoration and affection that I know, if triggered, he could revoke at any moment.

In a single tantalizing kiss, I once again sample possibility. I can see all the potential of a life with him flash behind my closed eyelids, dreams I had forced myself to tuck away. I am utterly enamored, and my heart is undoubtedly at his mercy. Perhaps I am a fool for him, a silly little fool. But I'd willingly own that title a thousand times over just for any piece of heaven he blesses me with.

I've become oblivious to the amount of time that passes before we stop for air, our breathing heavy and in sync. With his arms wrapped around my waist, my body flush against his, it's the safest I've felt in a while. It's a feeling that comes with a deep sense of nostalgia. Here, like this with him, was once my safe, happy place. To revisit it brings a sense of peace that's hard to describe.

His forehead touches my own. "Summer rain," he murmurs.

"Hmm?" I slowly open my eyes in a slight daze.

"That's what kissing you is like. The blessing of summer rain after a hot day. Refreshing and invigorating."

I'm glowing, mesmerized by his ability to make sweet words ever the sweeter. I'm dizzy with bliss, but even in this state I can't help but wonder what this means for us. It's not an unreasonable thing to ponder. Although I may be a fool, I'm not so much of one that I think a passionate, long awaited make out session means everything is back to normal between us. But, despite such questioning, I allow myself to melt into him, his scent, his warmth, his energy. All delicious. All divine.

If only the earth could stop spinning for a minute. If only time could stand still. If only I could capture this heavenly moment in a glass bottle, to have and hold forever.

Journal,

Caught again. But I refuse to sit around and be sad about it. This time I'm putting all my energy into finding a way out for good.

Journal,

There was a dove that came to perch on my windowsill every night for the past two weeks. At first, 1 hated it. 1t felt as though it were taunting me with its ability to come and go as it wished. 1t was almost as though it were some cruel prank from fate. But a couple nights ago, it tapped its beak against the glass to get my attention. 1 went to the window and tapped back rather aggressively, intending to scare it off, but it didn't go anywhere. 1t just tilted its head and stared at me.

A few minutes passed of us staring at one another before 1 remembered the dove is a symbol for hope. 1 thought to myself, perhaps the dove isn't here to taunt me after all. Perhaps it's here to give me some of the hope 1've lost, to remind me not to give up on my dreams, even if they seem more distant every day. 1 said to the dove out loud, "1 understand." And only then did it fly away.

1 haven't seen it since.

12

As I sit in bed, within the confines of a lavish penthouse-style suite, I place a bookmark between the pages of Aralyn's journal and reflect on what I've read. It was silly of me to think I could read her journals in a day or two. Not only is the process a little slower because I'm translating the French they are written in, there's just so much about her experiences to unpack. These have to be approached in doses. I'm still on the first one. Her early years were so fraught with trauma and tragedy.

I reach into my bag to grab a pen to take notes. As I do, my hand comes across the strange notecard from several days ago that was attached to my car. I pull it out, analyzing it. The handwriting is exquisite. I wish it was recognizable.

I hate mysteries. Yet somehow, mystery is looking to be the theme of my year. I lean my head back against the bed frame and close my eyes in an effort to collect my scattered thoughts and emotions. I shouldn't let this note phase me. I have enough on my plate. However, it's impossible to ignore that intuitive sense alerting me to the fact that these are things I should in fact be phased by.

Perhaps Alex isn't being overly cautious; his decision to bring me all the way here might be quite reasonable. I don't want the things I can't see to sneak up on me like they did before. I didn't think anything could be worse than how things ended up back in February, but now I'm not too sure I think that anymore. There's something ominous looming in the energy that surrounds my life. It would be stupid to ignore it … even if ignorance truly is bliss.

It also hasn't helped that Alex and I haven't communicated much since the night we kissed. He checks in via text, mostly, calls every so often, but usually has an excuse to rush off the phone and he has the security team watching out for us twenty-four seven, likely reporting on our well-being. My expectations for what could happen between us moving forward weren't very high on purpose, but I'm starting to worry he's avoiding me because he's perhaps regretful.

I open my laptop to finish some work on an article I'm writing, in the hopes that it will distract me from my burdensome thoughts. Suddenly, Genevieve bursts into my room, startling the shit out of me. She throws herself right in front of me on the bed, causing papers to fly everywhere. "Hey, watch it!"

"Are you not incredibly bored?"

"Not really; I'm working."

"Right. Of course you are." She huffs. "Seriously though, we've been confined to this room for over a week now. There's a whole city out there we've yet to explore! Why are we wasting precious time staring down at it all from the sixteenth floor?" I understand her sentiments. This room is more and more like a luxury prison cell each day. And it's not to say we aren't allowed to go anywhere; it just has to be approved first.

Now, I'm not one who enjoys restriction or limitation from anyone, but I think I've allowed myself to hide in the "safety" of it this time. I'd be lying if I said I haven't become slightly paranoid about going out. Here, under guard, within the shelter of this hotel room with my best friend, and a mere phone call away from the man I treasure feels quite secure and comfortable. But have I gotten *too* comfortable?

"You know Alex wants us to remain here for our protection. They haven't found anything on this note writer yet. So, until we get the green light, we should stay put."

She rolls onto her stomach and smirks. "Do you always do what Daddy Big Bucks tells you?" I give her the side eye and she groans. "Come *ooonn*. I thought you're supposed to be a big shot journalist! Doesn't your job entail breaking the rules from time to time?"

"Trust me, I know it's far from fun to be cooped up in here. It really would be awesome to go explore London, but this is one risk I don't think we should take."

"How much trouble could we possibly get into, with two armed guards who will quite literally be following us everywhere?" She gives me her famous puppy dog pout, something she perfected when we were children. "Please?"

"Ha! Oh no, you're not getting me with that this time."

"Ugh, fine then. You leave me no choice." In the blink of an eye, she closes my laptop, grabs it off my lap and hops off the bed.

"What are you doing?"

"Jess, babes, I regret to inform you that you're a workaholic and a total Debbie Downer. Luckily for you, your bestie has the cure." I rush around the bed and reach out for my laptop, just missing. "*Aht aht*! You'll get this back at the end of the night once we've returned."

"Gen, honestly, you're being ridiculous." I make another attempt to retrieve my device but she outmaneuvers me, rolling across the mattress to the other side.

"OR I can keep it for the duration that we're stuck up here and we can just be bored to death together." With my hands on my hips, I stare her down incredulously. She waves the laptop in her hand. "Your choice."

"If Alex finds out we've disobeyed his orders and something happens to us—"

She laughs out loud. "Disobeyed? Dear god, Jess. You make your lover boy sound like a premium Mr. Grey." If only she knew. "Relax! *If* something were to happen, I'd never let anyone hurt you. I'd seriously take a bullet for you!"

"Yeah, that's not making me feel any better about going out."

She struts toward the adjoining door and enthusiastically replies, "Get dressed, bitch, we're going!"

"Going where, exactly?"

She pops her head back through the doorway. "A nightclub." Then she disappears into the next room.

I let my head fall back as I groan. I can't recall the last time I went to a club. It had to have been in college. I don't know what she's thinking. Of all the places we could "break the rules," a nightclub has got to be one of the worst. Too much opportunity for anything and everything to go wrong. Though, I can't deny that it would be nice to get out and let loose a little. There's been so much tension as of late. And though I'm not big on dancing and spending time amidst large groups of people, this would provide the perfect distraction from all the noise in my head.

I sit on the edge of the bed and collect myself, slowly but surely allowing myself to sink into submission to Gen's wishes, or rather, defiance of Alexander's.

❤

*T*he bodyguards we were assigned implored us several times to remain on the hotel premises, but feisty Gen was hearing none of it and basically told them they could either drive us to the nightclub or follow after us once we procured a black cab. They reluctantly agreed to take us, and very soon after we left the hotel I got a call from Alex. Apprehensively, I ignored the call and texted him one word: *sorry.*

I could have answered, but I wasn't yet in a position to explain our questionable choice. Which, I suppose, was a questionable choice as well. But alas, I powered off my phone, fully aware of the high probability that I'd catch flak for it later. I've yet to see Alex truly upset with me, but I could almost bet that tonight would be the night that changed.

The nightclub Gen chose is very much a rave type of scene. It reminds me of the nineties rave vibes—colorful flashing lights, whistles, dance music, and tons of people jumping up and down to the beats. The energy is high. Most people have come to release all inhibitions, but I feel completely out of my element. Do I even remember how to "let loose" like this?

Gen so conveniently happened to have a sultry, short white party dress with gold chains as straps that she lent me. It fit perfectly and garners attention as soon as we enter.

As we make our way through the crowd, Gen yells out to me over the music, "I've been talking to this guy on a local meetup app. He says he's got a table in the VIP section! We can head up that way."

"What? Did you know he would be here?"

"I invited him."

"Gen, we shouldn't be hanging out with anyone we don't know!" She rolls her eyes, takes my hand, and leads me through the sea of sweaty bodies toward the stairs. The guards try to catch up, slowed down by their inability to slip through the crowd as easily due to their body mass.

The table we go up to has four men seated, watching us as we approach like we're pieces of mouthwatering meat being served on a silver platter. I would have thought I was naked the way they are gawking. Gen introduces me to the guy she'd been chatting with, a bald man who I'd place somewhere around thirty, with a huge build I'd almost guarantee is credited to steroids. "Hey there! I'm Adrien." His greeting reveals an Irish accent.

"Jess. Nice to meet you."

One of the other men calls out, "Ay, Adrien, you didn't tell us they were so fit! You've been holding out on us, bruv!" Whoever that man is, his comment is enough to make my skin crawl. I absolutely detest being ogled like a high-ticket item at an auction. And surprise, surprise, I have the unfortunate privilege of sitting next to him. "Fancy a drink?" he asks me, while pouring a shot of tequila. I shake my head and avoid eye contact, not wanting to give him any reason to think I'm even remotely interested.

Despite my attempts to give him a hint, he doesn't take it, and instead makes a move to place an arm around me. That is, until he notices our security team walking up. "What's all this about then?" He nods toward them.

Gen shouts across the table, "My friend here has a very caring and protective admirer!" He immediately shifts in his seat and inches away from me. I can't help a small smile at his discomfort.

After several long minutes of observing dull chatter among the boys, I excuse myself to the restroom in hopes of taking a break from it. As expected, one of the guards, who I've come to know as Jonathan, follows. The club is packed, making it difficult to get around. I try to walk slow enough so he doesn't lose sight of me. However, just as I finally work through the large crowd and make it to the entryway for the restrooms, there's a sound of glass shattering behind me. I turn to see him, a few people between us, covered in what I assume is alcohol, and there's an embarrassed bottle girl apologizing profusely.

Suddenly, there's a firm grip on my arm and before I know it, I'm roughly tugged into the hallway. I swing my arms like a wild beast, throwing my fists at whoever has the gall to place their hands on me like this. "Get the fuck off me!"

"Hey! Calm down! It's me!" I stop fighting and focus on the man gripping me.

What the actual hell. "Luca? What are you doing here?"

"I'll explain outside. Come."

He starts to pull me toward the exit and I resist, trying to yank myself from his firm hold. Flashes from the night Arthur lashed out at me and grabbed me in a similar way play in my mind, immediately causing me anxiety. "I'm not going anywhere with you!"

He scoops me up over his shoulder, and those standing in the hall whistle and cheer while he takes quick strides to what I can only assume is a back exit. Fucking intoxicated idiots. This man is literally taking me against my will. Why is nobody doing anything to help me?

I punch his back, yelling at him to put me down, but it isn't till I feel the cool outdoor breeze whip up my dress, when he steps into a side alley, that he does. I slap him across the face. "Don't you EVER do that to me again!"

He takes the lick with surprising acceptance, laughing lightly. "Okay. I probably deserved that."

"What the hell do you think you're doing? I can't believe you flew all the way from France just to stalk me and, what, kidnap me?" He wipes the trickle of blood that springs to the surface on his cheek, not far from his scar. I almost feel bad for catching him with my nail. Almost.

"Trust me, if I wanted to kidnap you, I would have done it in Paris, rather than bring myself to the slums of Europe to do so. This city is awful."

I look at him in astonishment and turn on my heels. He hurriedly follows after me. "Come now, there's no need to get so upset, Princesa."

No need? My anger has far from subsided, and I now have a mighty urge to rip him a new one. I whirl around, and he runs into me, his chest colliding with my face. With all the force I can muster, I push him back. "Ugh! Since you don't seem to possess the intellect to figure it out, let me make something extremely clear. I've reached my tolerance level with you! Besides this obscene violation tonight, your behavior with Alexander at the den was grossly uncalled for. You are such a fucking prick. You have been nothing but insanely intrusive and rude since you first walked through my front door."

"Aralyn's front door."

"Oh, this is so not the time to debate me on this."

"Look, I get it, but can you put the anger away for a moment? Yes, I have been following you. I followed you over here from the hotel and then saw an opportunity to get you away from those guards, so I took it. But trust me, it's for a good reason."

"Guess your tracking skills are still sharp. Can't say I blame your sister for constantly trying to find ways to outrun you."

"If I were you, I'd be careful speaking on things you don't understand."

I cross my arms. "Or what?" He only responds with a smirk as he shakes his head, opting to hold his tongue—the first smart move he's made since I've known him. "What do you want, Luca?"

"I am traveling back to Spain in a couple days. I told you before, I really need to talk to you. So, I'm here to talk."

"It never crossed your mind that a call or text would be, oh, I don't know, more appropriate? I mean, honestly, what could be so important to discuss that you'd skip those two primary options just to stoop to the level of a raging lunatic?"

"Your life! You don't realize the hornets' nest you stirred when you agreed to take on all of my sister's responsibilities, her lifestyle, her job … and especially her partner. If you don't make some serious adjustments and decisions soon, you may not even live to regret the choices you've made."

A knot forms in my throat. "What do you mean, I may not live to regret them?" He gives me a look implying that I know exactly what he means. "You're scaring me."

"Bien! Good! You need to be scared! This is serious shit, Jess!"

"I don't understand; why would my life be in danger?"

"That's what we need to talk about. And it comes with a long explanation that is best discussed in person. It's why I made the decision to come to London rather than take a chance on you ignoring me, or simply not picking up. But we can't talk here. I don't want to keep you away for too long or those guard dogs of yours will find us out here."

"Luca!" The figure of a woman hurries down the alley toward us. "Elle doit y retourner! They are looking everywhere for her!" She steps into the dim alley light.

"Jovana? You brought Jovana here too?"

Luca responds with a sly grin, "Are you so shocked? Madame Chérot made her come with me to meet up with you. She is your assistant, after all. I hope you didn't think you'd get to take off from your responsibilities just because you've been taken out of the country to supposed safety." God, I just know he had to have irritated the hell out of Aralyn. I can imagine him being the annoying older brother, and he's not even older than her, just more of a smart ass.

"I really despise you. I hope you know that."

"Aw, I'm wounded, truly." His smirk widens to a large grin as he laughs, which irritates me further.

"I am sorry, Jess. She made me come." Jovana's concerned dark brown doe eyes pull at my heart.

"No need to be sorry. It's my fault for dipping so suddenly with such little communication the past couple weeks. Is she pissed?"

"Pissed?"

"Yeah, like really upset."

"Ah, oui, she is not happy." Great, I'm sure this will all make for a fabulous conversation with her when I return.

Luca interjects our exchange. "We need to get you back in there."

"Wait, when are you wanting us to have this talk, if not now?"

"You said yourself, I'm an excellent tracker. I'll find you." I don't recall using the term 'excellent' but whatever. It will be interesting to see him pull this off. After all that's happened tonight, lord knows when Alex will allow me to see the light of day again.

Jovana winces and reaches out to touch Luca's cheek. "Merde. What happened?"

He beams, looking straight at me. "Cat scratch." I stick my middle finger up at him and he winks.

Jovana glances around, oblivious. "What cat?"

Luca brushes by us. "Let's go."

As we head out of the alley, Jovana lets me know she will message me with an address of where she'll be staying. Then Luca informs me that they will be going back inside the club as well so they can grab a drink before going on their way. We make sure to enter through the front entrance to make it appear like all is normal in order to hopefully avoid unwanted attention. Then, once we are in, Jovana and Luca break off toward the bar, and I make my way to the stairs leading to the VIP lounge.

Seemingly out of nowhere, Gen hops in front of me. "OH. MY. GOD! Where have you been?"

"I, uh, just needed to grab some fresh air; it's so hot in here!" I fan my hand in front of my face, while feeling a bit guilty that I'm not telling her what's really going on. But it's entirely too much to explain to her right now. She'll get the real version later.

"For future reference, when I say I'll take a bullet for you, I do not mean that I'm willing to be murdered by Alex because you want to take a stroll without telling anyone! I'm pretty sure he's about to fire Johnathan right now!"

"What?"

"Yeah! He's upstairs flipping his shit. Come on!" She grabs my hand and leads me away. Alex is here? What am I saying? Of course he's here. I've completely ignored his attempts to contact me. What did I expect from a man who hopped on a jet just to come collect me in Paris because he's concerned about a couple ominous notes? Why, oh why, didn't I just choose to be bored to the death in the hotel room?

This whole night is some terribly surreal experience, a domino effect of utter chaos. And it would be me going through it, because I can never seem to stay away from situations that could blow up at any second. I should be used to it, but I expect I'll never truly get used to life's impeccable curve balls. Damn, does it have one hell of a pitch.

When we approach the table, I notice that the boys from earlier have cleared out and Alexander is on the phone, pacing back and forth, running a stressed hand across the back of his neck. A mixture of worry and anger covers his face like a dark mask. But when his eyes fall upon me, a bit of light comes back as relief hits.

He hangs up and grasps my shoulders. "Christ, Jess, are you alright?" I tell him I'm fine and his hands move to my face, cradling it as he glances at each side, then scans the length of my body. It's as though he needs to check for himself that I haven't been harmed in any way.

When he's satisfied with what he sees, he visibly relaxes, dropping his shoulders upon exhaling a sigh of relief. Then, he draws me into an embrace. I can feel his heart hammering against his chest, and it triggers the kind of sadness that settles in my throat, and in the tears that wait at the rims of my eyes, ready to surface if I let them. I did not wish to cause him so much concern, and to know all of it could have been avoided had I just kept my ass in the room makes the disappoint I have in myself ten times worse.

Only when his heart rate slows to a normal rhythm does he let me go. Then he leads me to the now empty table where we all take a seat while we wait for the security team to return. His thumb brushes my hand, tightly clasped in his, and he asks once more if I'm okay, noticing the somber mood I'm in. I rest my chin on his shoulder. "I'm so sorry I disappointed you. I knew better than to leave the hotel." He shifts sideways on the seat and delicately brings my hand to his lips, planting a kiss on each knuckle before rubbing them.

"Jess, it doesn't bother me that you wanted to come here and spend some time with your friend. I only wish you would have asked me along."

"Um, you do?"

"If I'm with you I can help protect you." Here I was, worried he was busy avoiding me, and he actually would have preferred to be in my presence. "If something were to happen to you…"

I giggle and joke, "You'd what, tear the world apart to avenge the injustice?"

I catch a hint of concern in his gaze, "I just might."

"Well, whenever I have the opportunity to meet her, remind me to thank your mother for raising such a chivalrous son. Speaking of protection, could you maybe not fire Jonathan? It's not his fault. I should have just stayed close to him."

"Hmm. I'll think about it."

"Alex!"

"Trust me, it's better that I think about it than give you the answer I want to give." He looks down at the dance floor and his bright smile returns. "How about a dance?"

"Ooo, uhhh, yeah, about that, dancing is one of the many things I'm horrible at."

"Well, have you ever tried dancing with a partner?" I shake my head no. "Would you care to try it with me? I think you'd quite enjoy it." With a surprising lack of hesitation, I give him a nervous nod. We rise from the table and I take notice of his outfit for the first time. It's not often I see him outside of business attire, but when I do, he always looks so damn good. He's wearing gray denim jeans, black boots, and a white shirt that hugs him perfectly.

Gen sips her drink and winks as Alex whisks me away. We head down to the dance floor and, as if he planned it, the song changes to one that's still upbeat, but with a slower tempo. Upon reaching the center of the floor, he brings us to a stop, turns to me, and bows. I laugh and curtsy like it isn't the oddest thing to do to such a track. But I remind myself that Alex is one of the most confident people I know. He couldn't give two shits about what anyone thinks. I adore him for it and aspire to follow his example.

He brings me close to him and says, "Do you still trust me?"

"More than you know." I follow his lead as he steps out and in, in sync with the rhythm of the music. He spins and twirls me a few times and then holds me flush against him, his front pressed to my back as his hips flow and rock. I allow myself to flow, too, falling into the depths of his motion, sinking deep into the bliss of his presence.

"You know, I used to be an awful dancer. Always so rigid," he says with his cheek pressed against my temple, raising his voice to be heard over the music. "It was my mum who first taught me to dance. When I was a young lad, she used to place my feet on hers and guide me around. Then, to challenge me, she placed me in Salsa lessons, of all things."

I laugh, facing him again. "Talk about throwing you in with the wolves!"

"I got paired with a lovely girl who was my first crush. And of course, I didn't want to be embarrassed in front of her, so I practiced till I became… well… not embarrassing."

I laugh harder. "Yep! A crush will make you realize your capabilities, that's for sure."

"You do that to me a lot."

"Do what?"

"Show me what I'm capable of." I blush as he spins me around again, making me beam so hard. I turn and hook my arms over his shoulders, gazing at him in awe, captivated by all of who he is. It seems to me as though it is only me and him in this whole building … until it's not, for, with the slightest shift of sight, my eyes connect with another's. Luca is standing at the bar, staring at us with disgust. I observe him down the rest of his drink in one gulp and walk off, disappearing amidst the sea of reveling souls.

The mere sight of him brings me back to reality and serves as a bitter reminder that no matter how much I want it to be otherwise, pleasure is fleeting. But the threat of pain … or worse? That is forever imminent.

13

lexander's finely built arms wrap around me as we lay in my bed watching "Gentleman Prefer Blondes," my movie of choice. I've adored Marilyn Monroe since I can remember. My mother is obsessed with her, and I recall times while I was growing up when we'd spend hours some nights binge-watching her films. So, this sweet dose of nostalgia, along with laying in the arms of a man who, just a few weeks ago I thought I may never see again, is the perfect comfort. And though dancing with Alex at the club tonight was an incredible treat, there's just something about this time with him that I find to be much more meaningful. No loud noises, no large crowds, no worrying about our safety, just me, him, and the enchanting Marilyn.

I get the sense that Alex really appreciates it too. When I suggested the movie earlier, he was excited, as it was something new for him. Apparently, he'd never seen any of Marilyn's films. He told me he didn't have the opportunity to watch a lot of television or movies growing up, especially during his high school years.

His young life consisted of school, extracurricular activities, and learning the ropes of a massive business empire. At first, it made me a little sad to hear that he missed out on some of the best parts of being a teenager—sleepovers with friends, movie nights, family game nights, and more. But he assured me that despite the lack of such things, he was quite happy in those years. He was just a content young man who grew up differently than most. His greatest aspiration was to become successful like his father, so he never minded his busy upbringing.

After some time, my mind begins to drift, and I become incredibly distracted by the texture of his abdomen beneath his shirt. It's been far too long since I've seen him exposed. Far too long since he's ordered me into some risqué position and fucked me till my knees gave out. I've held back certain advances because I'm unsure where he stands and what he's ready to do with me.

In the midst of mental analysis, another thought pops up, giving way to burning curiosity. "Alex, can I ask you something kind of personal?"

"You know you can ask me anything."

"Perhaps, but you don't always answer."

He laughs and pauses the movie. "Fair. Go ahead and ask. I'll answer, promise."

"The night Aralyn came to your house, and I was hiding in the other room, I recall seeing her kneel at your feet. She wasn't just your girlfriend, she was your submissive, correct?"

"She was. It was a dynamic that started almost as soon as she agreed to date me."

"And I'd be right to assume she wasn't your first submissive?"

"Mhmm."

"But she was the best?"

His hand, which is caressing my head, stops. "Jess, look at me." I look up at his fine face and see an affectionate expression, and a dash of concern. "What's going on in that beautiful mind of yours? Why are you asking me this?"

I sit upright, facing him nervously. I really wasn't sure if this was a good time to bring her up at all. But I can't avoid that nagging part of my consciousness which continues to remind me that Aralyn is still very much a huge factor in our connection. I have to know if I may always be second best to the woman he treasures so highly.

"I'm just a little worried that I may not be enough for you. Aralyn is this bold, fierce, stunning woman who I know loved you immensely, and surely would have devoted herself to you any way she could have. But me? I'm brand new to so much that your life consists of, especially BDSM. I like to think that I could be the woman who would bend to your every desire. But in truth, I'm still trying to figure out if that's me. And I'm concerned that even if it is, I may not be able to satisfy you in all the ways she did."

He responds with a kind smile. "Making the choice to build a connection with you isn't because I thought you could replace her, Jess. I chose to because I'm incredibly attracted to who *you* are. You are driven, enigmatic, loving and passionate, talented, and committed to your work. You have such an inquisitive nature which I find rather amusing at times, but it's fascinating to watch you in that element. I will tell you a thousand times over how insanely gorgeous you are, because it's true. And I can hardly resist the way you look at me. I think it's adorable." He gently guides me into a straddled position on his lap. "You're a little wild as well for the fact that you tend to do whatever you bloody well please. But believe it or not, I sometimes enjoy your moments of defiance, because it gives me pleasure to tame you."

"*Tame me?*" I scrunch my nose. "Makes me sound like some sort of rogue jungle cat."

"Or, just what we in the BDSM world would call a brat."

I playfully roll my eyes and a firm hand falls upon my ass with a loud *smack*. "*Sss, agh!*" I cry out and he smirks.

"And THAT just provided the perfect opportunity to demonstrate how I deal with bratty defiance."

"Right, sorry," I murmur, having forgotten his dislike of me rolling my eyes, playful or not.

"My love, I would never expect you to be like Aralyn. I only expect you to be you. And as far as submission is concerned, I'm quite alright with training and guiding you on such a journey. It's actually something I look forward to. Together, we can figure out what kind of sub you are, or if you even resonate with the title at all."

"And if I don't resonate with it?"

"Then you don't resonate with it, and we'll figure out a solution that can satisfy us both." His response brings a smile to my lips. How was I so blessed to cross his path? It's something I wonder about frequently. I've never been so bold to envision that a man like him existed, certainly not one I'd form any measure of relationship with. Yet here I am in his arms, enraptured by the very essence of who he is.

"Anything else I can help clear up?"

"I am curious, was there only a Dominant and submissive dynamic between the two of you, or did you dabble in other things as well?" Part of me doesn't want to know anything about what the two of them were into. A greater part of me, however, wishes to know everything, yearns to understand the depths of their relationship with one another. Surely theirs is a love story as complex as it is profoundly beautiful. If I'm going to write Aralyn's biography, I'm going to need all the information I can get.

"Hmm. Well, I'd say that Domination and submission was the core of our dynamic, and anything additional was like an accessory to it. For example, Aralyn was very much an exhibitionist. She thoroughly enjoyed being on display, shown off, so to speak, whether she was wearing a gorgeous dress, lingerie, or nothing at all."

Wow. Something that made her and I complete opposites. Not too long ago, I was the girl who'd hide behind boring and even baggy clothing, forsaking makeup, having a nonexistent social life, just to keep the attention off me. It seems that Aralyn, however, craved it. I'm certain she collected quite a lot of admirers, being the all-around attractive woman that she is.

"That never made you jealous?"

"Quite the opposite. I was delighted by it. I loved the admiration she received. There was something about others lusting over her, but never being able to have her, that made me incredibly hard." A blushing heat rises to my cheeks. "I had no cause to be jealous. She was mine and I trusted her wholly. I knew that, regardless of the attention, regardless of the number of individuals who ached for her, I was always who she wanted in the end. No number of gazes, compliments, and uttered wishes could match how I made her feel mentally, physically, emotionally, and even spiritually, and she never gave me reason to believe otherwise."

I'm beginning to realize more and more that Alexander is the type of man who doesn't let his masculinity and desire for dominance snuff out his partner's freedom to be who they are. He, in fact, nurtures those parts of her and compliments them with his own energy. He may have a kink for control, but he also makes room for free will in a way that brings balance to a relationship. I admire him so much for that.

A vision of Aralyn's closet of toys and naughty trinkets springs to mind, and the collection of whips that stunned me. "What about pain? Was she into things like being whipped?"

"It wasn't a hard limit, but it wasn't a kink of hers either. She much preferred to be the one serving pain, and commanding something like a whip was oftentimes part of her job."

"Oh, that's right. I remember hearing that she provided services before becoming a madam."

"Being a madam suited her better, I think. She had a knack for it, and a certain appreciation for it as well. As I'm sure you've likely read by now, if she's mentioned it, she had a difficult upbringing and was stripped of any real independence. The den represented freedom, the key to release her from those shackles." It makes even more sense now, why she was so immensely devoted to her position, even down to wearing the company colors constantly. La Maison des Papillons was her sanctuary, her pride and joy.

"She had such a miserable start to life. It's so sad."

He gives my hand a gentle squeeze. "It is. I'm grateful life didn't always remain that way for her. She had some truly wonderful moments too."

"Like her time spent with you."

His eyes shine as he smiles. "Yes. Like that." I push back some strands of hair that fell loosely over his brow and he grasps my hand, pressing my palm against his cheek. "I mean what I said. Please, don't compare yourself to her. You are you, and I adore you just as you are."

"Just gotta work on the obedience, right?"

"Haha, I'm not worried. As we spend more time together, your obedience will improve magnificently." He leans in and kisses me softly. Then, with swift action, he flips me over onto the bed, and soft kisses turn into a full-blown make out session. Between the amazing sensation of the silk sheets beneath me, and him pressed down on top of me, my senses are delightfully overpowered.

I grasp the back of his neck, drawing him as close to me as possible. I am eager for this man, and all concern about where we stand with each other, sexually, is out the window. The greedy part of me gives not a single damn. My legs wrap around his hips just as his hand wraps around my throat and he draws himself back ever so slightly. His brilliant gray eyes bore into my own and he grins. "I quite enjoy how desperate you are for me." I respond by raising my pelvis, pressing it against his to feel the depths of his lust for me, too, and it's hard, rock hard. A throaty growl rumbles from within him, "Mmm. I bet it's been tearing you apart to have waited so long."

I nod my head, wiggling my hips, begging for merciful release this night. "Beautiful," he replies before lowering his mouth to my ear. "Though, I think you have it in you to wait just a bit longer. Can you do that for me, love?" He plants kisses under my ear lobe and down my neck as I whimper with both pleasure and utter frustration.

If it were any other man, I'd have said fuck waiting, pulled out my vibrator and never have spoken to him again. But it's not just any man, it's Alexander. My Alexander. I'll wait as long as it takes to have him again, even if I do so begrudgingly.

"You take too much pleasure in teasing me," I say with a heavy sigh.

He chuckles, "You have no idea."

"Well, in that case, Mr. Marc, I'm kicking you out of my room."

His brows shoot up in surprise and the dimples in his cheeks become craters as his grin widens. "You're serious."

"*Shoo*! *Shoo*! Out!" I push him till he rolls out of the bed, laughing.

"I take it we won't be finishing the movie, then."

I sit up on my knees and place my hands on my hips. "You deprive me of you, I deprive you of Marilyn."

His fit of laughter continues as he grabs his jacket off the chair. "That's fair." Then he steps to the bed, looking at me adoringly in that way that touches my very soul. "Will you also deprive me of a farewell kiss?"

I can't keep the smile from my lips. "I don't think I could ever deprive you of that."

His lips are soft and sweet, bearing the promise of his return to me and that's all I could truly ask for at the end of the day. "See you tomorrow night, Brown Eyes."

As soon as he exits the room, I feel his absence profoundly. I curl up under the covers, embracing the pillow that still bears his body heat and his heavenly scent, then turn the movie back on. The movie is watching me, however. I'm somewhere else, far away in thought and longing and wonder. My mind becomes hyper-fixated on my worries and dreams, and they swirl together like paint on a canvas, exquisitely chaotic. It's the very manifestation of my life at present, and here I lay, immersed in its process. What more is there to do?

❤

I found it incredibly difficult to sleep last night after being placed in a chokehold of sexual frustration. My mind could not stop fantasizing about all the delightful things I'd let Alex do to me. And though I entirely respect that he still wishes to take things slow, every time he's around me he's the ultimate tease. My desire for him increases with the delayed gratification from each recent encounter.

If I'm being real with myself, I've lost the taste for masturbation, simply because I know doing so will not provide me the satisfaction I crave. I *need* his touch. I need to hear him ordering me into whatever position he wants. I need to be thrust into that space in time where the only thing I could even remotely focus on is the gripping wave of pleasure that takes over my body when I climax.

As the masseuse digs his fingers into my back, it takes everything in me to keep my mind from sending me right back to the very thoughts responsible for my current state of agitation. I am, however, grateful for this time of relaxation and tension relief. Gen and I spent the entire morning hanging out in the hotel's impeccable spa facilities. She wants to do some sightseeing later, and we've been granted approval to do so, under the supervision of the bodyguards, of course.

I was relieved to see Jonathan this morning and apologized to him so much that I'm sure he's sick of me. Hell, I even bought him an entire bag of pastries from the hotel café. Come to find out, he has a gluten allergy, which made me apologize even more. I just hope nothing else occurs that will put his position in jeopardy once again.

Unfortunately, there's no telling what could happen, knowing Luca is lurking somewhere seeking the opportunity for a conversation with me. He wants me to meet with him, yet has given no information as to where or when. And based on his mood last I saw him, I've no clue what he could be cooking up to try speaking to me without Alexander's knowledge.

We finish with our massage and the staff steps out to allow us privacy to change. Gen rolls onto her back, stretching out like a cat who's awoken from a glorious slumber. "I think she hit knots from ten years ago! That was amazing."

"Yeah, it was! Really needed. I feel like a new woman."

"Oh, I'm sure a certain dashing young billionaire had something to do with that new woman energy. You looked so happy last night. Actually, each time I've seen you two together you have this glow about you that's so refreshing to witness. Everything you've been telling me about him and how he makes you feel makes complete sense in person." I kick my feet and bite my lip while trying to contain the joy ready to burst out of me at hearing what she's saying.

"I know you've had some concerns about whether he does or ever will feel the same about you as you do him. But trust me, babes, if there's one thing I'm good at, it's reading people. The way his eyes shine when he looks at you, and the way he softens when you're close to him, there's no way he isn't completely enamored by you. So, no more worrying, okay?"

I can't help but grin from ear to ear. "Okay."

She hops off her bed and onto mine, throwing her arms around me. "Oooo, I just love you so much!"

I giggle as she holds me tightly to her chest, "Oh my god, Gen, I love you too, but must you literally have your bare tits in my face?"

She pats my head. "Shhh, just think of them as nice pillows, and enjoy these next few seconds with me, won't you?" I settle into the awkward yet endearing moment a while longer, till there's a knock at the door; one of the guards calls out, checking to make sure we're alright.

We gather our clothes and quickly change, ready to see what else the day has in store for us. I'm hoping we can keep to the theme of fun and relaxation, especially tonight, when I meet up with Alex for his friend Tommy's special event. I still need to find a dress that will help me accomplish my goal. Tonight, I'm on a mission, and my inner goddess is absolutely delighted by my intentions. Let's see what happens when the teaser becomes the teased.

14

The driver stops at the entrance of the venue and I take the opportunity to collect myself before he opens the door to let me out. Usually, big events that draw attention are something I'd absolutely avoid. But when I exit and smooth out the fabric of my electric-blue cocktail dress over my hips, I feel calm, collected, and incredibly alluring.

This dress hugs me perfectly. Jovana is truly a style genius. She went out with Gen and I earlier and helped pick it out. I'm excited to see Alexander's reaction when he sees me, though I'm equally nervous. The last big event I was at was the charity banquet, and knowing how that ended is still a trigger spot for my fear. Already this night feels like my do over, my chance to have the ending I didn't get, or at least some alternate version of it.

I make my way up the steps with a few others who have arrived at the same time. A couple of them I recognize as being in the entertainment industry. And as I enter the venue, I recognize a few more faces, including the face of the man I'm most excited to see.

Alex spots me at the same time, excuses himself from the conversation he was having, and meets me, kissing me on the cheek. "Hey! I'm so sorry, darling. I had every intention of meeting you at the car, but I got sidetracked by a few individuals."

"That's okay! Don't worry about it. I—" I pause, caught off guard by his astonished expression.

He gives me a twirl. "My god, woman, you look absolutely breathtaking." I glow, enraptured by his compliment.

"Hey, hey, hey, look who it is!" Tommy struts over alongside Carmyn. He's wearing a cream suit that is magnificent against his dark brown complexion. Carmyn matches him with a long cream-colored evening dress that she wears like a dream.

"Hi, Tommy!" With outstretched arms he scoops me up into a huge hug, spinning me around joyfully. I haven't seen him since Monte Carlo. "Oh, it's so good to see you. Congratulations on the nomination!"

"Ah, thank you, love. Congratulations to you too! Not many women can get this lad to stop sulking and right his wrongs." He gives Alex a light punch on the arm. "I told him he was an absolute pillock for leaving you."

"Honestly, Thomas. Must you bring that up?" Alex chuckles.

Tommy laughs out loud. "Oh, settle down mate, I can't embarrass you any more than you already embarrassed yourself with that blunder." There aren't many people I know who could get Alex so flustered, so I'm enjoying this rare event.

A man kindly and loudly asks everyone to take their seats, and those of us standing make our way through the large banquet hall, which is decorated with flowers and elegant raindrop chandeliers of various sizes. Portraits of those who are nominated for awards tonight are displayed along the walls. The dedication to detail by event planners always amazes me. They clearly take pride in ensuring everyone's experience is magical.

Not long after everyone is seated, a delicious appetizer is placed before us. Thank heavens! I've barely eaten all day in preparation for tonight's delicacies. The reimagined crab cakes inside of a beautiful shell, gleaming with mother-of-pearl, are both a delight to the eye as well as the palate.

As the evening goes on, the presenter announces awards, along with introducing entertainers during short intermissions. The night has been shaping out wonderfully. In the company of people I enjoy, with Alexander's hand on my lap or rubbing my back, there's a sense of ease that allows me to be worry-free.

Finally, Tommy's name is mentioned as a nominee for outstanding chef. Every one of us at the table holds our breath in anticipation of the results. And in unison, we release a cheerful gasp and stand in boisterous applause when he wins. His acceptance speech is touching, mentioning everyone he has to thank, including Carmyn for her unwavering support, and Alex for being a motivating factor in his well-earned success.

After a while, I'm not sure if it's the oysters or the champagne, I begin to develop a … craving, for something other than food and conversation. That craving intensifies when Alex's hand leaves my lap as he changes seats to have a conversation with a gentleman across the table. I never did get the man's name, but I couldn't give a shit right now. My focus is elsewhere.

Normally, it's either my mind or my heart that makes decisions, but tonight, it's my body. I'm consumed with an overwhelming urge to satiate my desires. I had a mission in mind before coming here, and my mission has never been clearer than it is right now.

My foot takes on a mind of its own under the table and slowly glides up Alexander's leg at the same time that a flirtatious smirk lifts my mouth. I watch him become momentarily caught off guard. His eyes flicker over to me, intrigued, but not yet where I want him. He clears his throat, loosens his tie ever so slightly, and regains his composure, continuing his conversation. I like this. Love it, actually.

The knowledge that little ol' me can make THE Alexander Marc squirm, turns me on like a flame that's been kissed with lighter fluid. I want him to want me. No, more than want me, *yearn* for me. To give me his full undivided attention. Maybe I shouldn't push for that so much. Maybe this really is a pace too quick for him. But my body has given the middle finger to dwelling on pace. There's no denying the energy he's given off the whole time he's been beside me tonight. I know that beneath that calm, cool demeanor he has, he's dying to have me. And if he won't give himself permission, I'll grant it to him instead.

The sexual energy I'm pushing in his direction screams of my desire for him to quench this thirst I have. I decide to test the limits and turn things up a notch. I grab the juiciest syrup-covered strawberry from my plate of cheesecake and take a bite, purposefully allowing the sticky juice to fall upon my bosom. I feign surprise as it dribbles down my chin and into my cleavage.

Using the napkin on my lap, I go to work, slowly and delicately cleaning the mess. The man Alex is talking to takes notice first, unable to keep from watching me. I give him a small smile and he averts his gaze, embarrassed. Alexander witnesses it, of course, and looks back in my direction. I keep my eyes trained on him the entire time he's looking at me with a mixture of annoyance and arousal.

He'll soon discover that he's no match for my newfound confidence and seductive tactics. No match for the woman he awakened within me months ago. He has not a clue that I've mentally prepared myself for this. I'm going to win this unspoken challenge. I'm going to make him cave. Who's the tease now?

I watch him murmur something to the man and then he rises from his seat. He takes off his jacket and roles up his sleeves while making his way back around the table to me. "Come, Jess. Why don't we take a few minutes and get some air?" Bingo!

He places his jacket on his chair then leans down, a breath away from me, and grabs my plate of dessert. "You seem to enjoy this," he says as his eyes glisten in a delicious way. "Let's take it."

I grasp his outstretched hand and he leads me out of the bustling room and around a corner into a small nook behind a curtain, just out of view of the attendants who are busy going in and out of the entertainment hall as necessary. Almost immediately, he pins me against the wall and overtakes my mouth with his own. He tastes of whiskey and chocolate, wholly divine.

After many thrilling seconds of passion, he stops, his mouth hovering a few inches from mine. "Please," I plead in a quiet, nearly breathless tone, "Don't stop."

"Mmm. Do you know how lovely it is to hear you beg? You've made the choice to dangle yourself in front of me, tormenting me. But it's not so fun when it's the other way around, is it love?" Fuck. I definitely did not think that all the way through. What better punishment for my naughty behavior than for him to return the favor? As if I haven't experienced his denial enough. If I'm going to have any chance of getting things to go the way I want them to, I need to recover from this, quick.

"Like you would've had it any other way. Admit it." my hand moves from his chest and wanders south till it wraps around his firm package, gloriously erect, to my delight. A small, shivering gasp escapes his lips and I ache from the sound. His eyes darken with pure unbridled lust as I slide my palm across the bulge of his cock. "You live for the torment." I extend myself on my toes enough to kiss the soft spot on his neck where the rhythm of his heart thrums at an accelerated speed from the adrenaline of this moment.

With a sudden movement, his hand grips my hair and yanks my head back, forcing me to look up at him. "I think you've teased me enough for one night." He steps forward pressing me against the wall once more. Then he speaks in a low tone. "I won't go easy on you for this."

"Good," I breathe.

With a smile he takes a berry from the dessert plate he'd set down next to us and proceeds to run a trail of syrup down my neck and across my collar bone before setting it back on the plate.

His tongue begins to follow the sticky path he created, and my body quivers with delight.

As he continues, he hooks my dress with his finger, right at my cleavage, and slowly pulls the fabric down till my tits burst out, ready to be admired and enjoyed. Then he stops to witness how flustered I am, and there's a flash of extra heat in his gaze when he glances down at my bosom. He grins. "It appears you missed a spot earlier."

With his index finger, he collects the neglected drop of liquid sugar between my tits and then drags the same finger across my bottom lip before gently dipping it into my mouth. The flavorful syrup dances across my taste buds, and in an instant, his mouth connects with mine once again, kissing me deeply. In the best of ways, the taste of berries and desire is a potent combination.

"You're so divine," he groans while worshipping my tongue. And then, the same lips that praised me, fall upon my breast where he licks the remaining syrup while rolling one of my nipples between his thumb and index finger. My fingers grip his hair and I let out a small cry as the slight tinge of pain from the pull of my tender flesh mixes with the pleasure of his kisses, setting fire to my spirit.

When my body can't take much more of the teasing, he takes a firm hold of the back of my neck and guides me over to a service cart, bending me over it. With my eyes now adjusted to the low light, I see the space we are in is used as a small storage for dining items. And here I am, with my dress now hiked over my hips, and my panties torn from my body with one swift movement of Alexander's hand. He spreads my legs, exposing my needy cunt. The anticipation of his cock filling me makes the hair on my arms raise up. I am feral for this man, more than I believe he will ever know.

I hear him undo his belt and then his pants. "I do hope you remember our safeword, Jess." I tell him that I do. "Say it."

"Red." Fuck, I want him inside me so bad!

"Good girl. I'm impressed. In the event that your mouth is covered and you need the safeword, you are to firmly tap my arm three times. Understood?"

"Yes, Sir."

I can hear the smile in his voice. "Very good." He leans over me, his manhood pressed firmly against my slick entrance. He cups a hand over my mouth and, in a low honeyed voice right at my ear, says, "I just want you to know one thing, my little tease. I have no mercy to give you tonight. I will fuck you till your legs give out, and then I may find delight in fucking you again." There's no time to register what he's said. He thrusts into me so hard it knocks the breath from my lungs. I quiver in ecstasy as he does this again, and then again, ravaging me.

His hand mutes my pleasure filled cries. The loudest noises are the voices of the dinner guests in the other room and the sound of him pounding me, groaning softly. All I feel is the delicious, rhythmic pressure against my cervix and the nerves in my body firing off from my head to my toes.

"You're sopping wet. You must have been a desperate little slut for me all night long. That's exactly what you are for me, aren't you?" He moves his hand from my mouth to my neck, giving it a delicate squeeze. "I want to hear you say it."

"I-I'm your slut."

"Louder."

Louder? What if someone hears us? I raise my voice only slightly higher. "I'm your slut."

He stops, his cock still buried within me, and he lowers his mouth to my ear once again. "Are you shy, my sweet girl? Worried we might get caught? Hear me when I say I don't want you thinking about anyone else right now. Focus on me. I'm the only one here. I'm the only one who will truly hear you." He sucks in a shuddering breath as he slides deeper inside me. "The only one who will understand your body's irresistible urge to moan." Only us. Imagine it's only us. That shouldn't be difficult. The world oftentimes fades away when I'm with him.

I close my eyes as he continues to fuck me. This time, however, his pace is exquisitely gentle and slow. He's playing to the tune of my energy, so attentive to the fact that this is the momentum I need in order to focus and do what he asks of me. "Now… louder, Jess. What are you?"

He's against me and inside me and all around me. His body heat is comforting and his scent intoxicating. He's cocooned me and, in this, I feel safe. In this, I really only sense him. I only give a damn about him. "I'm your slut, Sir!" I cry out.

He rewards me by planting soft, sweet kisses upon my cheek and temple. He's proud of me, so proud. It contributes to a profound sensation of pride within myself. Then, his lips fall to the tender spot between my neck and collarbone. After placing two more kisses there, he nips the area lightly with his teeth and it sends a wave of pleasure flowing through my system. My back arches and I sense my body slowly building the toe-curling orgasm I've dreamt of for months!

His voice spills into my ear, "Oh, no you don't. I'm not finished with you yet."

He pulls out and turns me around, lifting me onto the cart, then hooks my legs over his arms. His girthy cock, slick with my wetness, jumps with excitement at the sight of me like this, his for the taking, however he pleases.

Both hands support the back of my neck as he tunnels into me again and this position provides a totally new sensation that's mind numbing. He starts slow at first, taking his time with me and enjoying witnessing how my body responds to him. Then he picks up speed once more. My hands grip tight onto the edge of the cart and the dishes below clatter against each other as he plows me hard and deep, hitting all the right spots with such lustful vigor. I bite my lip, whimpering and trying hard not to scream out the way I so desperately want to. God, this is everything I've needed.

Light suddenly fills the nook as a female wait staff member draws back the curtain. I feel myself start to panic as she witnesses me getting railed. Alex briefly looks over his shoulder but he doesn't stop, he just smirks and looks down at me, my face now flushed from both satisfaction and mortification, and chooses instead to go faster. This is sensation overload. The waitress closes the curtain quickly. "Looks like someone just found out what a slut you are for me, darling." He glows with knowing. "How does that make you feel?"

"Like I'm yours," I breathlessly reply. This position makes me feel wildly sinful in the best way. Here, held in this space, legs spread and raised, body used, I really do feel … his … and I love it. "I'm your slut."

After a scorching kiss he says, "Don't you ever forget it. Mine."

My pussy clenches, bearing down on his cock, and with a low moan, he continues what he started. Soon, in the heat of it all, my head drops back as my previously interrupted creeping orgasm reaches a point of no return. It shatters me and I yell out while Alexander's pace slows, fucking me through it. He groans and his muscles tense as he cums soon after.

I'm overwhelmed. Even as my heart rate gradually starts to settle, I'm still completely overcome with sensation and a heavy state of euphoric bliss. Loud clapping and cheering can be heard echoing in the air around us. I'm tickled by the sudden thought that the audience is applauding our grand finale.

Several moments pass in which we catch our breath and Alex continues to kiss me, almost as a form of gratitude. Then, he buttons himself up and wickedly grins as he pushes aside some strands of misplaced hair from my face. "We were actually caught." I softly state the obvious, still bewildered.

"Mhmm, that we were. And you know something? I think you liked it." I feign disbelief of the validity of such a statement, and he chuckles.

"You think she'll say anything?"

"Most likely. I imagine this will make for great gossip to satisfy her mates with. Though I doubt it will reach much further than that."

I collect myself. "You know, I've known since meeting you that you're a man who cares little what people think about you, but I think I've still underestimated the level to which you truly don't give a shit."

"You pick and choose what you allow to bother you in life, Brown Eyes." He pulls me against him, wrapping his arms around me. "After all, no one is getting punished." I playfully roll my eyes at his remark, and his firm hand lands on my ass with a *smack*, "Though, that *could* change."

With a giggle, I take that hand in mine. "Come on, let's not make Tommy feel like we've only come here on his special night for the chance to act like a couple of horny teenagers at prom."

We stop at the restrooms to freshen up and then, arm in arm, we return to the table, where almost everyone is thankfully too wrapped up in conversation to pay us much mind. But as soon as I take my seat, Carmyn leans over to whisper, "I have a bit of concerning news."

I laugh, thinking she's joking, but her face shows she's very serious. My joyous mood rapidly dissipates. "Oh god, what is it?"

"While you two were away, one of the waiters delivered this to me." She slides something discreetly into my lap and I quickly take a peek down at the black note card I now hold. My stomach instantly flips.

In a hushed, irritated tone I say, "They seriously sent Alex *another* note? And here of all places?"

"Darling, this one isn't for him. It's addressed to *you*."

Dread befalls me. They know I'm in London. Not just London, they know I'm at this event. I feel even more clueless as to what the hell is going on. But one thing is for certain, this has become way more dire than any of us thought, and not knowing how it could all end is terrifying.

15

$\mathcal{U}$nsettled. It's the best word to describe my current headspace. I'm still unsure what to make of the note that found me last night. I couldn't bring myself to tell Alex about it just yet. What we experienced together was so incredible. I was afraid to sour the high energy with such news. Carmyn kept quiet about it also. I believe she was of the same mind about the matter.

Today is a new day, and though I'm concerned about the threat looming closer than I had ever imagined it would, I've little time to dwell on it. I've been entirely too occupied with the work related to my new position. I had chosen a nice restaurant that wasn't overcrowded in which to meet with Jovana. She was adamant that we go over some documents the Madame made her bring along. So, here we sit at the bar. Jovana patiently explains the numbers on the pages, and I make an effort not to lose my mind trying to understand it.

"Jovana, none of this makes any sense to me. I thought being Madame Chérot's protégé entailed being knowledgeable about whips and chains, overseeing safety, ensuring order, not doing math."

"The Madame is very strict about documentation of the finances and inventory." She smiles faintly. "You will get used to it. I heard Madame De la Rue hated it too." I groan and let my face fall into my hands.

My phone chimes and I see that Alex has messaged me.

Just checking in. How are you?

My fingers speed across the screen.

> *Trying not to suffocate under the weight of seemingly poor life decisions. Save me!*

"I can save you." I turn my head, and my gaze falls upon Luca, standing directly behind me. Jovana's eyes dart between the two of us, surely feeling the awkward tension polluting the air.

Annoyed, I set my phone down and tend to my drink. He places a hand upon Jovana's back and asks her in French, "Jo, would you mind giving us some time to speak privately?"

She glances at me for approval and I give her a nod. "It's okay, let's just call it a day. I'll check in with you in the morning." Hesitantly, she heads out and Luca takes her seat.

Before I know it, both guards are by my side. "It's alright you guys, he's … a friend." They don't immediately back off, especially Jonathan, but they eventually head back to the table nearby, where they were seated.

"Fancy." Luca sarcastically remarks. "And how interesting to hear we're friends."

"I hope you know how gross it felt to say that."

He places a hand over his chest. "You wound me, Princesa. Especially after I've come all this way to protect you."

"As you can clearly see, I have plenty of protection."

He snickers. "It always amazes me how naive you can be."

"Just get to whatever it is you want to discuss, Luca."

"Sure. Have you ever researched my sister?"

"Yes, months ago."

"No, I mean *really* researched her. I'm willing to bet you did a quick internet search hoping to find something on her but came up with nothing. Only, you missed everything. You missed the key information attached to her last name. You missed our father."

My mind takes me back to the night I first typed Aralyn's name in the search engine. It was the same day I learned from Jovana what her last name was, the very day I told Aralyn I was done scheming with her to gather information on Alex. I had found nothing on her, not a picture, not a single mention of her name anywhere. But there was indeed a man's name that came up several times. I can't recall what it was.

Could that have actually been her father? If so, then Luca is right. I overlooked it because I did not think the names that came up were of any importance. I was so focused on Aralyn, I didn't consider what lingered in the shade of her family tree.

"His name is Maxime De la Rue. Our father is what you might consider an oil tycoon. He is very wealthy, very intelligent, and very intimidating."

"I'm sorry, *is*? As in *currently*? I thought he was deceased." I could have sworn that's what Alex had told me.

"I'm not sure where you got that information, but no, he's not dead. He was and still is a prominent figure within European high society, and a man who gets what he wants by any means necessary." I have an idea, from what I've read so far of Aralyn's life, exactly what he's getting at. "Let me ask you something. Before agreeing to be so involved in her life, how much did you actually know about my sister?"

"Not much, honestly. She kept a lot to herself up until we last spoke. And even then, it was hardly anything."

"Allow me to educate you then." He waves the bartender over, who tries to flirt with him, but he doesn't give her the time of day, and instead requests a vodka on the rocks. "Aralyn and I were born in Spain, to a French father and a Spanish mother. When we were ten, my parents had a very troubling divorce. In the midst of it, our father wanted to move back to France, but Mama did not want to disrupt our lives further to go there, and certainly not for his satisfaction.

"Unfortunately, he's not the kind of man you say no to; he is relentless. He made it even more of a mission to make her life as miserable as he could, sabotaging her any way he could think of. It was not long before he went after her for full custody of us. Not because he really cared to be in our lives, but because he wanted to win. So, in an attempt to get him to leave her be, she presented the option of splitting us up between them, with the arrangement that Aralyn and I would be allowed to spend every major holiday together." The bartender gives Luca his drink and he twirls the glass in his hand before downing it like a shot. "I'll give you a guess as to whom he chose to raise."

The difference in the twins' accents is a dead giveaway. "I sense you're pretty bitter about that."

"A boy needs his father, especially as he gets older. I felt abandoned and I hated him for it. We both did, Aralyn for other reasons. He's a selfish and cold-hearted man. I questioned why he even accepted our mother's offer, especially assuming that it would have brought him greater pleasure to take us both from her. To this day I still don't know why he made the decisions he made, but for many years I had thought it was because of me. I thought maybe his agreeing to it and not choosing me was a cruel punishment, his way of letting me know that he considered me to be weak and not worth the effort of raising. He was, after all, very vocal about his dissatisfaction with me back then."

His eyes flicker and I can see the hint of pain lying within their piercing depths. "That very thought should have been enough for me to never care to be in his presence again. How he treated Mama, me, and my sister even more so. But … the unfortunate truth is that I didn't want to hate him. Despite everything, all I ever wanted was his approval and his love." He laughs lightly. "Love. I doubt he was ever capable of it."

I find the story of their upbringing so heartbreaking, and for the first time since meeting him, my heart softens for Luca. "I have always felt I cannot complain too much. My sister was chosen but she unfortunately had it far worse than I did. She grew up lonely, emotionally neglected, and treated like a pawn in his messy game. She was never happy." Luca orders another drink before continuing on. "When we were seventeen, our mother died. Car accident."

I was aware she had passed, but Aralyn did not mention how in her journals. "I'm so sorry."

"Me too. She was a wonderful woman. The kindest. Always did the best she could with the life she had. Aralyn is just like her—feisty, determined, but with the soul of an angel. So, after Mama's passing, Papa took me in. Only then did I discover the extent of how horribly he treated my sister. It wasn't long before I realized I was no exception."

"Is that how you got the scar?"

"Yes, actually. Got it two weeks after I had moved in. I stood up for myself, just like Mama had instilled in me to do. Got a fist to the face for it. His ring cut me."

"The more you talk about him, the more my blood boils for you."

"Unfortunately, mine didn't boil enough. Despite his treatment, I was determined to find his good side and be on it. As I mentioned, though there was much I resented him for, I wanted to make him proud. So, when he told us on our eighteenth birthday that he arranged a marriage between Aralyn and the son of a friend of his, another very prominent societal figure, I regretfully stood by and watched her world fall apart. Worse, I assisted in making sure she stayed in line and did everything she was told as we waited for the date they would be married. She ran away seven times in a year, and each time I was sent to find her and bring her back, back to the life she detested."

I remember reading something in her journal that spoke of this mysterious man she was supposed to marry but didn't want to. "She must have been so terrified to be married off."

"It wasn't marriage that frightened her, but the desire for death. She knew that if she married him, her miserable life would have been all the more so, and she knew she would not survive it."

Dread and sadness take form as a knot in my throat. "In her journal, she mentioned considering 'ending it all.' Is that what you mean?"

"The very last time I went to bring her back home, the seventh time, she begged me not to. And when I refused, she begged me to take her life, or she'd do it herself. That broke me. I saw the terror in her eyes … and the truth. She was serious. That was it for me. I couldn't be a part of contributing to that kind of pain. So, I returned home and said I was unable to find her. No matter how much I felt I needed that man's approval, I needed Aralyn far more."

It's devastating to hear she loathed her life so much that she would have chosen death just to end her misery. Now I truly understand the depths of her anguish. I can tell that Luca is giving me the watered-down version of events, most likely to save time, because whatever happened in that household was far more disturbing than he's letting on. A young girl doesn't favor death over returning home because of strict rules and an arranged marriage. What she did manage to write of her torment I'm sure was only a fraction of the bigger picture. "Where did she end up staying?"

"Madame Chérot took her in."

"Was this before or after you started working for her?"

"After. I had actually been going to the den several months prior for some Dom training. I'd been aware of my naturally dominant nature for some time, and further research led me to the den. The Madame was pleased with how well I picked up on it and offered me a job providing services as a Dom.

"Aralyn had found my coming and going at odd hours of the morning and night suspicious, and I suspect she was envious of it. So, she followed me one evening. Madame Chérot caught her sneaking in, but I can honestly say I have no clue how it came to be that the Madame formed such a connection with her, nor what led her to eventually offer Aralyn the position of protégé."

"Were you okay with her participation at the den?"

"Not at all. In fact, I was furious at first. But Aralyn, of course, called me a hypocrite and threatened to tell our father about my involvement at the den if I said or did anything to stop her. So I held my tongue. I'll admit, after a while it was good to see she found somewhere that felt like home to her. It was the first time since we were small children that I saw her happy. I couldn't strip that away."

"And what about when Alex entered the picture? Wasn't she happy then too?"

His expression hardens. "That's an entirely different story."

Obviously, I hit a sore spot, but it doesn't dissolve the urge to dig deeper. "I have time to hear it."

"I'm sure you do. You seem to have a lot of time for anything to do with him." His voice is laced with spite. To me, it doesn't make sense for someone to be so bothered by Alex. Unless they were like Arthur, with no real reason other than pure jealousy.

Though Alex has his guesses, I still do not understand what Luca's reason could possibly be for having such an issue with him.

"Are you jealous of him?"

"Ha! Not at all. That fucker has nothing worth me being jealous over."

"Then what is it? Why do you dislike him?" He goes quiet, his jaw moving in that way it usually does when he's irritated and trying to reign in his emotions.

"I mentioned to you that my father is a very powerful man. He knows people, dangerous people. After a few years, when he grew too suspicious of me 'not being able to find Aralyn,' he used his connections to help find her, instead, and there wasn't anything I could do about it but try to warn her as best I could. I warned both of them.

"She was eventually tracked down. However, at that point she had already been given the position of madam at the den, and she had also found it within her to stand her ground. She wasn't returning home, and made that very clear to Papa. But his pride and relentless nature would not allow him to accept her decision. He had made a deal to marry her off and fully intended to see it through. He tried multiple tactics to get her to comply, including an attempt to have her forcefully taken from her home, which was a different home than the one you're in now. The tactics failed, and to help keep her safe, Madame Chérot hid her away for nearly a year. She was once again out of his reach.

"That's also where Alexander came in. A large part of that year in hiding was spent with him. And when my father caught word of his involvement, I was sent to make sure that relationship ended immediately. I tried everything I could to get Alexander to see that he was risking my sister's safety for the sake of his supposed attraction. But he would not see sense, and she was too blinded by his charm to pull herself away."

"But she loved him, Luca."

"I do believe she loved him, but he didn't love her."

"How could you say that?"

"I just know it to be true," he replies with irritation.

"*How?*"

His anger breaks. "If he loved her, he would have never allowed her to get hurt!" The other voices in the restaurant are silenced as heads whip in our direction. Luca has a death grip on his glass. The ice clinks inside as his hand tremors with rage. "He should have let her go. He should have said something, anything, to get her to leave him, and then stayed away so she could move on with her life. But he's too weak of a man to do what's right. He has no idea what true love is—" His voice cracks, and he looks off into the distance.

I wish he would tell me what happened to her. Whatever it was, it doesn't sound like it has anything to do with Aralyn's illness, like Alex suspected. Hurt? How did Aralyn get hurt, and who was responsible?

The guards are once again at my side, ready to tell Luca to fuck off, but I urge them to let us be, insisting that everything is alright. As soon as they walk away, I place my hand over his to help keep it steady. "Hey, it's okay." I'm not sure where he's gone, but he's not here. Some dark memory has dragged him into a place far from my reach. "Luca. Luca, hey, come back to me." The ice in his glass begins to quiet. He squeezes his eyes shut, and when he opens them, those blue-green orbs of his stare straight at me, calculating my features, reminding him of where he is.

He looks at my hand covering his and I quickly pull it away. Needless embarrassment builds. "A-are you alright?"

He turns his head from me, clearly feeling some embarrassment himself. "Fine."

"Look, I don't know what all happened to Aralyn. And you don't have to tell me right now if you're not comfortable. I can tell that, whatever it was, was traumatic for you also. But what I will say is Alex would never in his life intentionally hurt anyone, especially her. I truly believe he loved Aralyn with all his heart… I'm certain he still does."

"You barely know him," he sneers.

"I think I know him more than you'd like to believe I do."

Frustrated, he rises from his seat and throws some English pounds on the bar top. "I'm traveling back to Spain in the morning. I just came here to inform you what you are up against. Maxime De la Rue is very much alive and continues his search for my sister. He has no idea that she is ill, and she has asked that I never tell him. All he knows is that she is no longer in Paris. I will, of course, honor her request and say nothing to him about her whereabouts and what is happening with her. But his lack of knowledge puts you at risk every minute you walk further in her shoes.

"He knows about you, Jess. And he's not sure how you know her, but he is suspicious of your intentions, especially after finding out you are a journalist. A well-known journalist, who just so happens to have covered a rare story on a man he deeply resents. He will stop at nothing to protect his secrets. Even if you may not be a threat, you appear as one to him. The more he suspects you as such, the more your life is in danger." This is suddenly so overwhelming. When I chose to explore this path, I never predicted anything this deep, that I could be caught up in a madman's life-shattering power trip.

"Alexander has his money and status to protect him. And no matter what you may wish to believe, no matter how many security guards he employs to keep you safe, he won't be able to protect you, not always." As I process this information, he places a firm hand on my shoulder, drawing my focus back to him. "Please, Princesa, save yourself a lot of potential pain and end all of this. Leave her home … and leave him too. Do what my sister could not."

He walks off and my heart races. Fear strikes me like a lightning bolt to the chest. Who would have thought that claiming a first-class ticket into Aralyn's world would mean I was putting my safety in jeopardy? Not only am I now aware of the perilous predicament I'm in, but it also dawns on me that the length of time in which I have to resolve these issues is unpredictable. I am dealing with an enemy I've never met. At any moment, in any manner, he can make the drastic decision to change my life.

Journal,

When I was a girl, one of my favorite things was watching my breath float through the winter air and then be absorbed by it. I suppose that's why I picked up smoking. The way the smoke dances and rolls then dissipates reminds me of those sweet, delicate moments. It's something happy to cling to, especially during stressful times.

If Mama were here, she'd probably shame me for such a nasty habit. Luca certainly does. He doesn't get it. Then again, he doesn't get a lot of things. Truth be told, sometimes I just smoke in front of him out of spite. If he didn't keep coming after me, I wouldn't be here. So, who cares if I make him uncomfortable.

Besides, he's not innocent either. I've seen him sneaking out at night or various times during the day. Nobody chases after him, probably because he always comes back. I wonder. I wonder where he escapes to.

Journal,

Well, I found out where Luca goes. You'll never believe it! I hardly do myself. A fetish den. That's at least what I was told it was by the facilities owner. She's a bold and beautiful woman, seemingly in her fifties, named Madame Chérot. She caught me while I was following my brother. I followed him in and all the way down to this corridor of different rooms. Everything was so black and red, so elegant and so—sexual. I've never seen or heard such things like what I saw and heard last night. I'm not sure I yet have the right words to describe it all.

Sex isn't something that's talked about in my household, although I'm very aware of what it is. I've caught Papa a couple times "entertaining" women. And a girl like me has plenty of time to read, so I often find myself lost in romance novels.

I'm almost hesitant to say this here. But if not here, where, right? I've had sex with a few guys. Three to be exact. Pierre was my first. We did it in the garden in the greenhouse. That was awkward, and quite painful, I might add. Once was all we attempted, and he was gone before we talked about doing it again.

The second time was with this older guy, I think he was twenty-eight. It was almost two years ago, a week after my eighteenth birthday. It was also during my first successful attempt at running away, and I lasted a whole two weeks before being caught. 1 met him on the bus and he offered me a place to stay for a few nights. One thing led to another. 1 actually enjoyed myself that time.

The third guy was the brother of this girl in our neighborhood who 1 detested. Papa is close friends with her parents, so they are always coming around and I'm usually forced to entertain her. But one particular day she made a comment that 1 should consider myself lucky to have an arranged marriage because 1 would never catch the attention of any sensible man. That 1 was too depressing to keep a man satisfied. So, 1 seduced her older brother and fucked him out of spite. 1 made sure she knew it.

Witnessing what 1 did at that den, however, had me feeling incredibly shy. It was as though 1 knew nothing at all. Have 1 been wrong about sex this entire time, or is it that 1 happened to stumble upon a completely different aspect of the sexual experience?

Anyway, when the madam discovered me lurking and asked what 1 was doing there, 1 of course asked her what my brother was doing there. You can imagine my shock when she said he was WORKING, providing risqué services! My own brother!

Oh journal, 1 don't know what to make of any of this. The world 1 entered last night was so far removed from the one we know, so vastly opposite, wild and unusual. Though, perhaps, that is why he has chosen to escape there. Perhaps, within those walls, lies his own personal paradise, a place where his freedom resides, a place where pleasure is bountiful.

After answering my questions, Madam Chérot gave me her number and said that if I had any more concerns about Luca being there, I could call her and ask, rather than sneak in. "Or, you can call me if you're looking for work too," she said next.

Work? At a fetish den? Me? I questioned why she would even plant that possibility in my mind, but maybe she knows. Maybe she knows the life Luca and I come from. Maybe she knows that, like Luca, she can offer me a similar form of escape from such a life. Or maybe it's something else entirely.

16

The hot water in the shower runs down my back, easing the tension in my muscles. My mind replays every interaction I've had with Aralyn like a movie reel, and I consciously observe each frame carefully. Was there something I missed, some sort of clue that could have warned me she was so closely affiliated with a man who might as well be at the helm of a Mafia? Was there ever any hint that her safety was at risk? Perhaps she no longer cared to hide in the shadow of fear, and chose instead to strut boldly around Paris, living her life on her terms, all the while taunting her wicked father. Even more so, I wonder why she failed to tell me that he could be a serious problem.

I had hoped that some of my worry would flow away with the suds that swirl down the drain. But though the hot water provides some relief, it doesn't quite have the desired effect I'd anticipated. I can't help but wonder if I had known at the time Madame Chérot asked me to take on the role of protégé that my life would become so complex, if I would have still made the same decision. My inner self is screaming *not a chance!* I signed up for an adventure, but not at the potential cost of my life. So far, the plan I had going into this—to always be two steps ahead—is failing miserably. I'm now lost in the ensuing chaos, and this may not even be the peak of it.

When I exit the shower and head over to the sink area, I notice the corner of the note I received last night, sticking out of my open handbag on the counter. I set down the towel I was drying my hair with and grab it, slowly turning it over, once again searching for any clue I could have overlooked that would indicate its origins. But to my great disappointment, I can't find a thing.

The door to the bathroom swings open and I shriek, dropping the note in the sink and hugging my arms tightly across the damp towel wrapped around me. Alexander stands in the doorway, laughing. "Are you alright? It appears I gave you quite a startle."

I instantly relax. "Yeah, sorry, I wasn't expecting anyone to come in." My nerves are definitely on edge.

"I did knock a few times. Didn't hear an answer." I can understand now why he rushed in the way he did. He was likely remembering how he found me in shambles the last time I didn't answer to his knocking.

I tuck my wet hair behind my ear and grin timidly. "Wow, I must have really been in my head."

A worried look springs to his face. "Mm. Wouldn't be the first time."

"True. I'm okay though, really."

He walks over, eyeing me with subtle suspicion. "Why is it that nearly every time you tell me you're alright, I find it dreadfully hard to believe?"

"I just don't want to worry you." I know better than to conceal anything from this man. The way he listens to his intuition is unlike anyone I know. Or perhaps it's that he's extremely attentive, closely studying the way I move, the pitch of my voice, my expression, my mannerisms. And maybe it's a combination of both. In either case, I always find it endearing, even when I wish he wouldn't catch on. I often wonder how on earth Aralyn managed to hide her terminal illness from him before she left.

"Just so you're aware, your attempts to keep me from worrying will only cause me to worry more." His hand cradles my cheek, and his thumb strokes my skin in a soothing motion. His soft smile transforms into a mild frown. "Though we are still working though some things with one another, I do hope you'll become comfortable enough to tell me anything."

I clasp my hand over his, pressing my cheek deeper into his warm palm. "Oh, Alex, after everything that has happened, I know you aren't someone I need to hide anything from. I know you'll listen and hear me out before harsh judgement and criticism. In truth, I am more comfortable with you than I am with most people. It's just … I think it's going to take me a little while to adjust to having someone I can tell anything and everything to. Hell, I love Gen to death, but there are certain things I haven't even been able to bring myself to tell her yet. I'm not used to being very open … especially with men.

"The thing is, aside from my childhood years, I had never quite felt understood, or like my voice ever truly mattered. It may be why I clung to journalism. Creatively structuring words on a page was like a playground for me where I could practically say whatever I wanted on whatever topic I was covering without harsh judgement. There was power in that. There still is. And then, after what happened with Arthur…" I trail off momentarily. "Arthur was the first man in my adult life who I allowed myself to be open with in any large capacity. And, well, when that chaos erupted at the charity banquet, I-I…"

"It's okay, love. I get it." His sweet smile returns.

"There *is* however something that I should be up front with you about. I saw Luca earlier today."

His brow quirks and his eyes search mine for an explanation. "He flew out here?"

"Yeah, I couldn't quite believe it myself. I was furious with him at first, especially since he also had that bizarre outburst at the den. But he came to warn me about his and Aralyn's father, Maxime."

"Why on earth would he come all the way to London to warn you about his deceased father?"

"According to him, Maxime isn't dead; he's very much alive, and a threat." Alexander's Adams apple juts out as he swallows. He looks away, his face muddled with confusion. "Alex, who told you he had passed?"

"Aralyn. I'm not sure why she would have lied to me about that."

"I might. Let me ask you this, how long after she told you about his passing did she leave you?"

He takes a bit of time to think, and I catch the exact moment realization dawns on him. "About a month. She must have thought that if I believed he was gone, I wouldn't go in search of him seeking answers to her disappearance."

"I think that's exactly it. I mean, what reason would you have had to question it back then? I called Luca a little while ago to clarify some things, and he told me she had asked him to tell their father she had left you, to satisfy his desire to have you separate, and I'm sure to also keep him from bothering you. She must have wanted to make sure that when she left, you didn't risk your reputation or even your life in search of her." He runs his hand along his face as he slowly paces across the bathroom floor.

I continue, telling him everything Luca had warned me about—getting too involved with Aralyn's affairs, and the vendetta Maxime still has against him that, if tested, he could act on at any time. I mentioned that he also isn't aware that his daughter is in Spain, dying. "I wouldn't be surprised if he's had you followed, and hasn't done anything yet because there's been no sightings of his daughter. He would have been moved to trust that you have indeed separated, especially if he had heard you were asking all of Paris and parts beyond about her." I hop up to sit on the counter. "I have a feeling he may be the one sending the notes. He knows about me. He knows what I do and that I'm too close to Aralyn's business for his comfort."

"If he's truly alive and he's aware of you, then I one hundred percent believe he's having you followed." My fear intensifies. "However, though I can see how one might suspect his involvement, Maxime isn't the type of man who would send obscure notes to get a message across." Makes sense, but shit, that would mean there's more than one threat looming out there.

"I see now why you didn't want to talk to me about Aralyn's family when I asked before. I know you said it was because you didn't want me getting roped into all this, but it looks like it was already too late for that."

"Let's hope that's not true. There's still a chance he might leave you alone. In any case, I'll have my investigation team look into it. Speaking of notes." He picks up the black card I had dropped in the sink. I don't know what to say as I watch him open and read the message.

How cute. You thought you could hide from me. I am everywhere and nowhere. Keep testing my patience and watch what that wins you. STAY AWAY.

This triggers something in Alex. His tone becomes low and menacing. "When did you receive this one?"

"Last night, while we were at the event. I didn't want to put a damper on such a lovely evening, so I thought it best not to bring it to your attention at the time."

He scowls. "Jess—"

"I know, I know. I should have told you right away. But can you blame me? There have been too many times when we have the opportunity to enjoy each other's company that something comes along to ruin the moment. I *loved* everything about our time together yesterday. I just wanted to keep the peace. Please, give me some grace on this?"

The crease in his brow cuts deeper and I can see the wheels turning in his head. He exhales a long, drawn-out breath and his lips pull into a smile. "I loved everything about it too." Then he tucks the card in the back pocket of his pants. "Right, then. I'll have this one dusted for prints as well. In the meantime, I'm going to need you to do something, Jess. Something you're not going to like." I already don't like it.

After another heavy sigh, he comes forward, placing himself between my legs. He's silent for a while, most likely contemplating how he's going to say what it is he has to say. "Christ, I hope I don't regret this," he mumbles. "Until all these unpredictable threats can be snuffed out, I need you to return to Paris. And no matter what, Jess … don't contact me."

My breath hitches, "Why would you ask me to do this?"

He shakes his head. "Not asking, darling, demanding. I thought having you here, close to me, was the safest arrangement for you. However, Luca is right, Maxime is a madman. It's his way or the hard way, and he hates me even more than Luca does. Assuming he doesn't already know, if he finds out we are connected romantically, I'm afraid he'll use you to make me pay for dating Aralyn against his wishes. I wouldn't dare put it past him to do it. I know very well what he's capable of." His fingers softly glide along my jaw. "I'd be a bloody fool to risk it."

Within my stomach swirls a complex clusterfuck of emotion. I don't get why all this has to happen. It seems insanely unfair. "Please, Brown Eyes, tell me you'll keep your distance, no matter what."

My response comes out in a tone barely above a whisper. "I just got you back. I JUST got you back, Alex."

He drops his head forward, touching his forehead to mine. I close my eyes, doing my best to keep myself from spilling the tears my utter frustration is brewing. "I know, love. As soon as we're in the clear, I'll come back for you." I hate this for us. "Hey, look at me." My wet lashes flutter up as I meet his penetrating gaze. "I *promise* I'll come back for you." He seals his promise with a kiss.

The first kiss is delicate and soft. The second is just the same. The third starts off that way, but as his tongue pushes insistently between my lips, overtaking my mouth, it quickly becomes scorching. My hands instinctively grip the back of his neck, pulling him deeper, and he responds with a low groan. He draws me to the edge of the counter, pressing me so close to him I can feel his bulging erection between my thighs. I murmur, "Fuck me. Please, fuck me." His teeth gently nip at my bottom lip and I moan, overcome with carnal desire for him.

I make a move to undo his belt, but he grabs my wrists and pins them down by my sides on the counter. My makeup and hair products tumble everywhere with a clatter. He smirks against my mouth. "Always such a greedy girl."

He tucks his finger into the fold of my towel and with one small tug, it falls open, exposing me to the steamy air and his smoldering gaze. The way I want this man inside of me is shamefully desperate, but I'm too far gone to care.

With his index and middle finger, he slowly charts a path up my inner thigh, getting closer and closer, warmer and warmer, until he's hot. I inhale a shuddering gasp as he slides his fingers over my soaking wet folds. My back arches, my head falls back and my toes curl as he inserts them inside me and rolls his thumb over my throbbing clit.

"Look at me, baby." I gradually bring my head back up and do as he commands, in a slight daze and quivering with every tinge of sweet pleasure pulsating from my cunt. "I want to see those gorgeous eyes while I'm enjoying you."

He keeps unbreaking eye contact while he fingers me. Then, he removes his fingers from within me and sucks the middle one clean as though he's just dipped it into a pot of honey. "I can never get enough of your taste." My pussy clenches. "Open that pretty mouth." I do as instructed and he inserts his index finger, ordering me to suck it clean. A salty sweetness coats my tongue, and with enthusiasm I watch him expertly undo his belt with his free hand. He swiftly unzips his pants, setting his cock free. It's a breathtaking sight. I watch it twitch with delight as he continues to observe my lips working around his finger.

He strokes himself. "Is this what you want?" Fuck what I want, it's what I need!

"Mhmm."

"Good. I'll give it to you." He could melt ice with the heated look in his eyes. "But, ladies first." I'm mesmerized as he lowers himself to his knees and gracefully unbuttons his shirt. He shakes it from his shoulders, and it falls to the floor, revealing his beautifully sculpted torso. Then he grins and spreads my legs up and apart.

His sight is trained on my face as his lips connect with my aching mound. When his tongue parts my sea, I cry out, thrust into a divine plane of existence. Before Alex, never in my life had receiving oral given me a borderline out of body experience! I've missed this sensation so damn much. I could easily become addicted to it. His tongue twists, roles, flicks, penetrates, all consuming. My body shutters, overcome with joy for such a blessing.

After several minutes in heaven, he rises to his feet and leans in, kissing me again and placing my arms around his neck. There's something about tasting myself on his tongue that thrills me. For a moment, I feel powerful, as though *I'm* the one to have claimed *him*.

I hear his pants drop to the floor, and he slides his arms beneath my thighs, picking me up off the counter. The head of his shaft probes my entrance and as soon as he gets it positioned perfectly, I find myself steadily lowered onto it. The sensation of my pussy being gradually stretched and filled by his girth is unlike any other. But when he suddenly thrusts into me, it drives me insane!

My tits bounce as he holds me steady and pounds me harder and faster. Every stroke sends me deeper into myself, as though I'm on an exploration and he's the guide and catalyst for profound ecstasy. The experience is all too thrilling and, quite rapidly, a soul-splintering orgasm is building toward its highest point. He can sense it, and he pulls out, denying me my release. I rest my head upon his shoulder as I quiver and try to catch my breath. Damn him for torturing me so much!

He plants kisses across my shoulder as he walks us into the bedroom, then lowers me onto the bed. While he hovers over me, his slick cock presses against my lower abdomen and his hand grasps my neck, applying the perfect amount of pressure, signaling to me that he's claimed ownership of my very being in this moment. "You haven't said it yet. I need you to say it, Jess."

My chest heaves, and my head is still spinning with adrenaline. "Say what?"

"Tell me you'll do as I said. Promise me you won't try to contact me till I come for you." I can see the seriousness in his eyes as much as I can see his longing. The fact that this is still of such importance to him in the midst of intercourse speaks volumes.

I'd give a lot to not have to do what he requests. It's as though someone has dangled my greatest desire in front of me and then the moment I reach for it, it's stripped away. My fingers trace over his fine face, his brow, his nose, his cheeks, his lips, locking in the memory of how striking he is, body, mind and soul.

"I won't try to reach you till you come for me. I promise."

I notice the muscles in his shoulders relax and he kisses me again. I revel in this moment with him, floating within a pool of passion. Slowly, he slides into me and it sends us adrift in a cosmic ocean of seemingly perpetual bliss. It's a wave we ride for some time before he flips me onto my stomach and lifts my hips. My back dips into a low arch as he tunnels into me again. My walls expand and I gasp as, suddenly, his thumb circles my asshole. "I'd very much like to enjoy this part of you, just a little. Is that okay?"

I nod my head, stunned by my lack of hesitation, and he slips his thumb in gently, gradually stretching it. It's a surprising sensation. Anal play is not something I'm experienced with at all. It's strange at first, but as he continues to move it in and out as though giving a sensual massage, going deeper and deeper with it each time, I begin to find the sensation very enjoyable. "Such a tight little hole begging to be filled," he says.

I quiver when his other hand lands a firm smack upon my ass and his hips quicken. He collects a fist full of my hair and pulls. My head jolts back as my body is being jolted forward and I feel completely under his control. I love it.

It's hard to believe that I'm still needy in the midst of all this, but I am. I need this feeling of being owned, being his, always. It has become one of my favorite feelings in the world. More. I crave more of it. I can practically hear his smile when I push my hips back. "Like how that feels, I see." He slides his thumb in as far as it can go and gently circles it around, stretching me wider and my eyes roll back. "One day I'm going to claim this too." He spanks me again then removes the finger, and I whimper.

He leans forward till the weight of him brings us both flat onto the bed. His hips continue to rock as he softly nips my earlobe while gripping my neck and hair. God, there's nowhere I'd rather be!

He continues to ride me hard until my body can't take it anymore and it convulses beneath him as he talks me through it. "That's my good girl. Take it. Fuck, you're so beautiful." I feel his body tense and his pace slows while he cums. I moan and squirm, burying my face in the sheets I grip as a second wave of climax overtakes me by surprise. "Mmm, shhh, it's alright my sweet girl. I've got you. Let it all out."

He moves dampened strands of hair out of my face as I come down from my exhilarating high. Then he rolls over, bringing me with him, and positions me into a comforting embrace. We lay breathless in each other's arms. I'm settled in this serene space of gratitude. Grateful to be here with him. Grateful to have been gloriously fucked for the second day in a row after many months of yearning but no real solace. Grateful for the opportunity to be a part of his life again, regardless of nothing being made official and the question of "will it ever" still lingering in the air.

I'm quite impressed with how involved Alex has been despite the concerns and fears he expressed to me a couple weeks ago. And it's so immensely frustrating that after everything, we will be thrust apart once more. I do believe we'll make it through okay … but what will we have to go through in order to find the peace we both deserve? It's a question that I'm sure will keep me up at night in the near future.

His fingers stroke my back as he, too, lays silent in thought. I wonder what's going through his mind right now. Is he happy? Worried? Regretful? Fearful? I kiss his chest and that pulls him from wherever he is. He looks at me and smiles, sweeping his knuckles along my cheek. "I know I say it a lot, but I'll never tire of the way those sweet, big brown eyes gaze at me." I grin and nuzzle my head against his shoulder.

Suddenly, we hear the entry door close followed by the sound of footsteps. Anxiety grips me. Gen appears in the doorway and her mouth falls agape at the sight of us laid out, completely nude. "OH MY GOD!" Her eyes light up and her lips pull into a giant grin.

I scurry beneath the sheets, grabbing the cover to throw over me as much as I can, which isn't much; these sheets were tucked in with incredible skill. Alex stays as still as he was moments ago, laughing. I'm surprised he finds the situation amusing.

She places a hand in front of her eyes and pivots toward her room, "Oh, please, don't stop on my account!" she calls back as she saunters away. "I'm gonna go mind my business. You two have fun!" Flushed with embarrassment, I finally manage to pull the cover over my head.

In a low tone, Alex says, "Something tells me this isn't the first time she's walked in on something like this."

I peek my head out. "Something tells me you don't mind that she's seen us like this."

"I don't. Now she'll know you've been properly fucked, and won't keep pestering you about it, like I'm sure she has." Well, he's not wrong. Gen has mentioned numerous times over the course of a week that we "need to quit tiptoeing around each other and just give into what we both obviously want."

"How did you guess?"

He chuckles, "She's been pestering me about it too."

My eyes widen, "She has?" How mortifying. But that's so Gen. I groan and slip back beneath the cover.

Gently, he pulls it down and looks at me adoringly. "She's a gem for wanting to make sure you're happy." He pauses momentarily before asking, "Are you happy?"

I can't keep the smile from my face. "Very."

"Good. That's my top priority, besides your safety, of course. But that's something we're still in the process of ensuring."

With a sigh, I surrender to the reality of our position. I'm not thrilled about any part of this plan he's developed to keep me safe, but it's necessary. I only hope it will all be over soon. "Right. Any guesses on who will be my temporary knight in shining armor? Jonathan, perhaps? He's grown on me."

"Well…" He clears his throat, appearing uneasy. "I do have someone in mind for the job. However, I'm going to need you to trust me with this decision. I mean really trust me."

"Now I'm getting nervous."

"Believe me, Brown Eyes … I'm nervous too."

17

"WHAT IS *HE* DOING HERE?" Arm in arm with Alex, I'm in disbelief as we approach the jet and see Luca De la Rue by the stairs. His face is the very picture of annoyance.

"Thanks for coming," Alex greets him. He says nothing in return, however, only sweeps him with his eyes, glowering with loathing, the same way he did the last time the three of us were all face-to-face. "Shall we?" Alex gestures up the stairs.

I lean close to Alex and whisper, "*Please* explain to me what is going on."

"I know this seems quite jarring, but it will all make sense soon. Trust me. Please."

"Fine, but what about Gen and Jovana? Where are they?" They were behind us in the car, but it doesn't appear that theirs has pulled in yet.

He gives my hand a gentle squeeze. "I'll have their driver bring them shortly and then all of you will be on your way. Everything is going to be alright." He leads me into the jet, though it doesn't appear to be the same one that brought us to London.

We take a seat across from Luca, who glances back and forth between the two of us before gruffly speaking, "Alright. What do you want, Marc? Why am I here?"

There's a squeeze of my hand again, but this time, Alex holds it tight. "I'll get straight to the point. I need you to take Jess back to Paris and look after her. Make sure she's safe."

I shift in my seat. "WHAT? This has to be a joke, right?"

"I'm quite serious." My face contorts with confusion. What does he mean he's serious?

Luca snickers. "You've made me miss my flight home just so you can ask me to babysit your new toy?"

"I'm sorry, what did you just call me?"

He looks me straight in my eyes. "A toy. That's all you are to him, you have to know that, right? He can't love you, Jess! This idiot has no comprehension of the word. He'll only delude himself into believing he does."

"Enough!" Alex's voice booms. "Don't push my tolerance for you any further off the edge it's teetering on. What I *want*, Luca, is for you to take care of the woman you so graciously took the time to fly out here for. Did you not?" There's a moment of intense awkward silence that follows in answer to his question. "It's my understanding that you felt the need to warn her about the potential ill intentions of your father. So, if you can do all that, then I'd say you sure as hell can put in the effort to protect her from him."

No. No way. Absolutely not! I'm not entirely sure what's going on here, whether Alex seriously believes Luca should be charged with ensuring my security, or if this is some weird way of playing into a pissing match, but I don't like it one bit.

"Yeah, I came out here to warn her because it was the right thing to do. I'm not heartless. You know as well as anyone what he is capable of. She's innocent, at the end of the day. But that doesn't mean I'm on board to do your job."

"Why not? You were certainly adamant that you could have done my job when it was your sisters well-bei—"

Luca launches out of his seat and slams his hands down on the table in front of us with such force the jet sways from the tremor. Alex didn't even flinch. Luca leans in close to his face. "You didn't deserve her! Me cago en tu puta madre!" Then he spits on the floor next to him. I'm concerned that anything Alex might say in response will only provoke him to do something he'll regret.

I look around for the security team, but we are the only ones on here. They must have been ordered to leave us be. "Let's just go, please, Alex. He's not going to do it. There's no point in continuing this. It's not worth it."

They continue staring each other down. Alex replies, "He'll do it. He'll do it because he has a point to prove—that he's more capable of protecting the people I care about than I am. I also suspect there's a part of him that does … admire you. To what extent, I'm not yet sure, but I'm not convinced he would have traveled all this way if he didn't." I witness the few seconds of softness in Luca's expression at that statement, as he's caught off guard by a truth he most likely preferred to keep hidden. Then, he quickly resumes scowling.

Alex carries on. "I don't have many favorable things to say about this man, Jess, but if there's one thing he is, it's fiercely protective." He breaks their eye contact to look at me. "And I need you fiercely protected."

It's in this one look that I can practically hear him plead, *"Please, trust me. It's for the best."* For some wild reason, it melts away my fear. My mind flashes back to every moment where he has shown that he places my well-being as top priority. The times he didn't want me to go outside without a coat in winter, or to be unshielded from the pouring rain. How he cared so greatly about my mental health, making decisions to ensure I'd be okay, or the time he bandaged my wound after I fell, with such sweet consideration. Or more recently, when he flew to Paris just to bring me here to keep me safe and within close reach. And most notable of all, when he defended me from Arthur.

He needs me fiercely protected, so he's choosing to provoke a response from Luca that would cause him to do just that. I nod, and he once again focuses his attention on the man before us who, though still clearly heated, has taken his seat again. And Alex says, "All I want is for you to do for Jess what you would have done to protect Aralyn from Maxime. And I'm not asking you to do it for me. In your own words, do it because it's the right thing to do."

Luca rolls his eyes and leans back in his seat, folding his arms and shaking his head. I make a quick decision to follow Alexander's example, and add something that will hopefully be that extra *oomph* to trigger him and steer him toward the desired outcome. "Personally, I think you're going to be absolute shit at this. But by all means," I cross my arms over my chest as well, feigning an attitude. "Prove me wrong."

He grins and rolls his bottom lip between his teeth. "Alright, fine. I'll watch the princess." Challenge accepted. "But just so you know," his mischievous gaze darts back to Alex, "the only way my keeping close tabs on her is going to work, is if my father believes we're dating." I'm hoping that was some idiotic attempt at a joke.

I catch the twitch of Alexander's eye, and so does Luca, whose grin grows even wider. "Don't worry, though. I'll be sure to take *very* good care of her."

The tension in the air is so thick it's suffocating. I'm not even breathing, but, despite it, I interject. "Abso-fucking-lutely NOT! I refuse to accept that's the only way."

"Afraid so." His eyes are bright with amusement. He's really enjoying pissing me off. But what's new? "Do you want my help or not? This is how it has to be if I'm going to be a part of this. I'm willing to help protect you from my father, but not at the risk of looking like I might be working against him. He already suspects you're close with Alexander. Besides the very in-depth article you wrote, there's also the photo of the two of you at some event."

Shit, the charity banquet. I completely forgot about that key piece of physical evidence linking the two of us together. It's not like it was a photo that one could interpret as us being intimate, but I am the one and only woman ever to be publicly photographed on Alexander's arm. That certainly can't look good to Maxime.

"Do what you need to do," Alex says sternly. "Just keep her safe, or it's me you'll have to worry about." I see I don't get a say in any of this. But I admit it's fear that's keeping my mouth shut. The truth of the matter is I have no real clue what I'm dealing with, and I don't trust many people. But I trust Alex. So, if I have to put up with Luca, I'll grit my teeth and bear it for the time being.

"Ha! Do what I need to do, huh? If only you had applied that same energy with Aralyn."

Alex sucks in a long breath. He is the epitome of a gentleman. I just know it's paining him to give Luca this much leniency after being so disrespected. "I expect you'll never understand the lengths I would have gone, the lengths I'd still go, to keep Aralyn out of harm's way. I've accepted that there may never be a way of changing your mind about what my intentions with her were. And I've graciously allowed you to be offensive with your accusations and derogatory remarks."

He leans in, pressing himself against the table to get as close as he can while remaining seated. His voice becomes dark and menacing. "But I need you to hear me well when I tell you that if your stubbornness and ignorance causes anything to happen to Jess, you *will* find out what it's like on the other end of my patience. And I promise you, that's an end you don't want to arrive at. I don't give a shit that you're Aralyn's brother; I will make you pay. Dearly." I can't tell if I find his statement more frightening or attractive, possibly both, but in any case, I'm highly impressed.

"Weird way to say thank you for an unearned favor."

"You'll get your thank you from me when the job is done, no sooner."

Luca's jaw works, showing his repressed anger at the threat. But then his eyes flicker over to me, as if needing the visual reminder of why he needs to check his pride and keep his cool. I can tell he knows how serious this is and that, despite differences, he's willing to hold his tongue in order to push forward and do whatever is necessary. He responds with a brusque nod.

"Good." Alex clears his throat and sits back. "Will you require payment?"

Luca glowers at him, appearing disgusted by his question. "I don't need your fucking money."

Alex ignores his attitude. "Very well, then. This jet belongs to a good mate of mine. I figured it would be best to use it in case mine is being closely monitored. I've also made arrangements for Jess to stay at a hotel in town until we can work things out."

"No," Luca interrupts. "Keep her at the house. Normally I'd suggest she stay far away from it, but he already knows she's staying there. Any sudden diversions will just cause more suspicion."

He has a point. Maxime has likely had his people keeping tabs on me ever since I set foot in Aralyn's home. I've no clue if they are aware I've come to London, but at some point they are going to grow suspicious of my whereabouts. Though, something does make me curious. "Do you know when it was that your father started to take notice of me?"

"A couple days before you left to come here. At least, that's when he sent out the message to all of us in his close network, asking if anyone knew who you were. Attached was the photo of you and Alex at that event. He let us know one of the men he hired to find Aralyn had confirmed you moved into her house. Which, to him, was also peculiar, considering Aralyn had left the home vacant for over a year."

"He didn't mention anything about that man seeing Alex?"

"No. Only that he suspects you may be closely connected to him, and he feels you might know something about where Aralyn currently resides. So, he dispatched a couple men to collect more information on you."

"You mean spy on me."

"Sure."

Alex addresses him again. "If you think keeping her at the house is the best option, so be it. But how are you going to convince Maxime that she isn't a threat? I doubt saying you're … together … would be enough to steer him away from her."

"Don't you worry about that. I know how to spin this. Just make sure you don't interfere, and everything will be fine."

Worry plasters Alexander's face and I sense him second guessing everything. "It's alright, Alex. I'll be okay. This is going to work." It's still shocking to me that he would make this decision to have Luca safeguard me, but he is one of the most brilliant men I know. There's a method to this madness, and I am at least able to see the general logic of this choice.

"Alright, then. You all should be on your way. Jess, will you walk out with me for a moment?" I've never been so happy to get off a plane.

As I start down the aisle, I look over my shoulder in time to catch Alex leaning down to whisper something to Luca. Then, he straightens his tie and continues forward, following me out.

When we reach the bottom of the stairs he asks, "How are you feeling about everything?"

"Well, I'm quite taken aback by all this, but I'm fine."

"I'm sorry, love. I knew if I told you ahead of time, you'd fight me on it." He's got that right. "I hope you can understand why I've done this. Luca is far from my favorite person, but I'm fairly confident he will keep you safe. It's important that I put my pride aside regarding your security."

"I adore you. You know that, right?"

Sunlight bounces off his dazzling smile and he takes hold of me. "I do, and I will carry your adoration close while we're apart." I nuzzle my cheek against his chest. "Oh, speaking of being apart, I took the liberty of letting Vivienne know that your absence is entirely my fault."

I gaze up at him, puzzled. "Uhhh, who's Vivienne?"

"The Madame. Vivienne Chérot." Oh, right. I remember now. I had learned her full name during my research, back when I wrote an article on her over a year ago. It's odd hearing her referred to as such. "I sometimes call her Vivie, depending on her mood. You have to time your greetings just right with that one. Anyway, she was irritated with me, of course, for whisking you away without notice, but she seemed to accept my responsibility for it. I hope she will not be too hard on you when you return."

"Um, wow! I figured you two knew each other via association with Aralyn, but I didn't know you *knew* her, like on a first-name basis."

He laughs lightly. "You'd be surprised just how well acquainted we are. Before Aralyn and I met, Vivienne was my Mistress."

I'm struck with shock. "Wait, wait, wait, stop. Did you just say she was your MISTRESS? As in, you were like her—her submissive?"

With a chuckle he confirms, "I was indeed."

"YOU were a submissive?" I'm having such a rough time wrapping my head around this.

Two cars drive up, and Gen and Jovana step out. "It appears we'll have to continue this discussion later," he says. "Time to go, love. I'll be checking for when you land. Oh, and try not to worry yourself too much about Luca. I may have given him the responsibility of keeping you safe, but you do have backup. I contracted a team to keep an eye on you from an acceptable distance. Remain vigilant, regardless."

I'm still stuck on him having been a submissive. In a million years I wouldn't have guessed Alexander Marc, one of the world's youngest and most prominent billionaires, and the epitome of a take-charge man, was anyone's sub. And he wasn't so to just anyone, but to the very woman who employed and mentored his ex. There's got to be something about this in Aralyn's journal that I've either missed or haven't gotten around to yet.

"You remain vigilant as well," I counter. "After all, you made a promise that you'll come back for me. Stay safe." It still hasn't registered that this will be my last moment with him for a while. I'm sure it will all hit me in a rush very soon.

I clasp my arms over his shoulders as he gives me one last kiss goodbye. My stilettos come off the ground as he lifts me up, and I giggle, grasping him tight. I wish for ten-thousand more moments like this in the future.

"Ugh, you two are nauseatingly adorable," Gen comments as she and Jovana approach. "I'd just like to say, Alex, that I am single and a definite catch, you know, just in case you have a cousin or a friend who could use some companionship."

"Haha, I can see why Jess considers you a good friend. Humor can be very beneficial for the soul. Do me a favor, if you please, and don't let her get into trouble."

"You're asking the wrong person to keep me out of trouble," I chime in, and Gen blows me a kiss, followed up with a display of her middle finger.

Alex chuckles, "I trust you'll be in good hands." Then he kisses the top of my head. "Bye for now, Brown Eyes."

After we are loaded onto the plane, I watch him closely out the window while the flight crew does the final preparations before taxi. He finishes talking with his security team and then looks up, smiling at me, with his hands in his pockets. His poker face is impenetrable. On the other hand, I'm not sure how good a job I'm doing keeping the dismay off my face.

The plane begins to move, and now the realization kicks in. Gripping fear and sorrow build in my chest. I wave to Alex, and he blows a kiss before waving back. Our eyes remain locked on one another as he grows more and more distant, until he's out of sight and I'm left to deal with the grueling reality of our separation once more.

Journal,

I called and asked Madame Chérot if I could speak with her a bit more about the den and what occurs there. Her response was an invitation to lunch. I told Papa I was going shopping today and was able to give his men the slip by making an escape out the back door of one of the stores while they thought I was trying on clothing.

When we met, the Madame explained to me the ins and outs of the business she runs and how, if I were to work for her, I'd first need to be trained. She said she can see me preferring a position as a dominatrix. When she explained what that is, I laughed, unsure what could have possibly made her think I'd enjoy, let alone be good at having dominance over anyone.

"It's quite simple," she said. "Call it intuition, but I get the sense you desire control in your vanilla life. You crave it. As a dominatrix you can have it. Within reason of course, there are always hard limits. But for once, you're in charge." She told me not to turn my nose at it until I give it a chance.

I admit, the more I consider it, the more it sounds appealing. Everything she said sounded appealing. What I appreciated most is that she is clearly a woman in control, and not just control over others, but control of herself. Her confidence and energy, her sense of self-worth and self-love, is refreshing to be around. She's awe-inspiring.

I desire that kind of existence, more than I do control. To be the type of woman who commands a room by aura alone is the true mission.

18

The flight was incredibly awkward, to say the least. Every one of us felt the tension that Luca's presence caused. Nobody spoke a single word. Jovana, who was seated across from him, looked like she had no clue what was happening. Nor did she attempt to ask. She stared at him quite a bit, bewildered, and he just slept the entire time.

Gen was seated across from me, and I think she could tell I was in a strange headspace. She allowed me my space and I was grateful for it. Speaking to anyone was the last thing I felt like doing. All I wanted was peace.

Now we are in a car headed home, or so I thought. Because, as we roll to a stop, I realize we aren't at the house, but at the den. "Um, Jean-Philippe, why are we here?"

Luca speaks up. "I asked him to bring us here. Madame Chérot's orders."

"So, now she also dictates where my driver takes me. Great." I huff and exit, not caring to wait for my door to be opened. Gen and Jovana follow after me.

Madame Chérot stands at the entrance of the building, looking like a no-nonsense mother who's ready to scold her children for not being home by curfew. "Rapidement!" She calls out, telling me to hurry. "We've a lot to catch up on and little time to waste, mademoiselle." I exchange a questioning glance with Gen. "You move at the pace of a slug." Can't say I've missed her sharp remarks.

"Is that *her*? Seems a bit tense. She could use a good tune up, if you know what I mean." I snicker at Gen's quiet commentary.

Madame Chérot's brow arches high as she notices Luca coming around the car. "Are you going to explain to me now why you are here and not in Spain?" Luca responds to her in French, letting her know he would catch her up to speed later. She rolls her eyes and walks in ahead of us. I find it curious. Why would she care so much whether Luca had returned to Spain or not?

As we step inside, Gen's face lights up. "Holy shit! This place is so fancy! Not at all what I was expecting from a fetish den." My exact thoughts when I first came here.

"Who is this?" the Madame asks sternly.

"Oh, um, this is my friend Genevieve. She's visiting from the States."

"Pleasure, madame." Gen extends her hand.

The Madame doesn't take it. She simply frowns and addresses me, "In your office, mademoiselle. Now." I just can't win with this woman. She asks the receptionist, Amélie, to hand Gen a non-disclosure document. Gen was right, she really is entirely too tense.

I begrudgingly follow her, and as soon as we step into my office she shuts the door behind us and begins her rant. "You don't seem to take this position very seriously. Leaving without notice—"

"But I thought Alex told you that I—"

"—no communication with me while away, and now, bringing uninvited guests into this establishment!"

"I wouldn't have brought Gen if I knew I'd be coming straight here! *You* didn't communicate with *me*, so here she is. The only thing I will take blame for is not reaching out to you while in London. It was irresponsible of me, and for that I'm sorry. Okay?"

She's silent for a time, considering my words. "Do you need my help? Are you in trouble, Jess?"

Her questioning surprises me. "What makes you think—"

"I am not a naive child. I can pick up when something is not right. Alexander whisking you away, Luca shockingly still here, by your side, instead of fulfilling his obligations back home, and the stress clearly evident in your body language." Damn, she's good. "I care about the well-being of every single one of my staff, including you. *Especially* you. As my protégé, you will become anchor to this ship, and this ship requires a strong one. If you need help, please know I offer it."

This is the first time I'm understanding myself to be a part of the team. Prior to this I felt like a lost lamb, trying to find her place in the flock. But the Madame telling me how important my safety is to her, to everyone, opens my eyes to the fact that I'm very much a real and necessary part of this den, even if I am brand new. I think it's time I allow myself to either fully fall in line with the role, or step out now while there's still time. It's clear I can no longer teeter in the middle. Commit or bow out.

It would seem like the logical answer would be to bow out. However, I can't. I can't pull myself away from this. That would mean going backward. It would mean stepping away from understanding Aralyn De la Rue more profoundly. No matter the threats that lurk in the shadows, my passion for my craft won't let me give up this opportunity. I've committed first and foremost to exploring the depths of who she is in order to create a riveting biography. And when it comes to the art of storytelling, no matter the story, once my heart is in it, it's in it. There is no going back.

"I appreciate the offer, madame. I think I'm alright for the time being. But if the need for assistance does arise, I'll be sure to let you know."

"Très bien. Let's move on." She goes to a rack of black and red clothing that had been placed in the middle of the office.

"I'm sure there will be something suitable here," she says to herself.

"What are you looking for?" She ignores me and starts rummaging through the outfits. "Fine. I'll try a different question. How well do you know Alex?"

"I assume you're speaking of Aralyn's ex-fiancé, oui?"

"Wait, ex-fiancé? They were engaged?"

"Oui. For about a year before she left him." I'm thrown by this additional twist. I haven't gone far enough in the journals to learn of their engagement. But how come Aralyn did not tell me about that? As a matter of fact, why didn't Alex?

"And you in no way thought it might be worth mentioning to me that you were his Mistress?"

She looks over her shoulder, scanning the length of me while puckering her cheeks, as though she's either passing judgment or is irritated by my questioning. Though with her, I wouldn't be at all surprised if it's both. "It was not my place to bring it up." The corner of her mouth quirks. "But I see he's had that conversation with you."

"Not entirely. We weren't able to talk about it much. I was hoping you might help me understand why such a dominant man would become a submissive."

"Ah! This is the one!" She grabs a tight, red, knee-length latex dress off the rack and walks to me, then holds it up to my frame. "Well, you certainly have the right curves to fill this out properly." Her eyes meet mine, noticing I'm still hell bent on answers, and she sighs. "Just ask him."

"I will… but I want to hear from you. After all, you are supposed to be my mentor. This could be an excellent chance to educate me."

She sucks her teeth but finally gives an explanation. "He came to me with the intentions of better understanding the role of a submissive by placing himself in their shoes. He told me he'd only ever known control and dominance. He was concerned because, at the time, he had particular expectations of his subs, and questioned if his desires and demands could accidentally compromise their well-being." This intrigues me even more. I wonder what desires he could have had that he worried might interfere with a submissive's well-being, be it mental, emotional or physical.

"Here. Try this on." I take the dress and strip down as she continues. "I personally found it commendable. I wish more

Dominants would have the maturity and mindfulness to put themselves in a submissive's role. Too many uneducated boys with large egos to stroke and a wish to be served simply slap themselves with the label without really understanding the nature of true dominance. Alexander sought to be the best Dom he could by making the choice to kneel at my feet.

"He was a tough one to break, though. To this day I'm not sure he ever really did, and after he and Aralyn met and grew closer to each other he became less inclined to stay mine." Her gaze drifts out the window. "My sweet girl, with all her fierceness and strength, found the one man who could get her to willingly bow her head in servitude." She turns back to face me and I stand before her in a dress that was a great struggle to get into, and even more of a struggle to zip. It's like I'm being constricted by layers of saran wrap.

She turns me around and glides the zipper the rest of the way. "The two of them were perfect for each other. Aralyn probably thought I often disapproved of her choices. I'll admit, I was seldom vocal about my approval, but I trusted her judgment a great deal. She's bold, brilliant, a risk taker. She reminds me a lot of myself when I was in my twenties."

After she fastens the clasp, I turn to her and ask, "Is that why you chose her to be your protégé? Because she reminded you so much of yourself?"

For the first time since I've known her, Madame Chérot smiles a true, genuine smile. "Oui."

"I remember her telling me that she saw you like a mother. She really admires you."

I watch her eyes grow watery. Then, she averts her gaze, exhales and snaps back to her stoic demeanor. "This dress will do. Keep it on for a couple hours to get used to it, and then wear it tomorrow night. There's somewhere I'd like to take you."

"Am I to assume you're not going to tell me where?"

"You've assumed correctly as I've yet to decide the exact location. Just be prepared to participate in some—risqué activities."

"How does one prepare themselves for unknown sexually adventurous events, exactly?"

"You try not to be so unnecessarily nervous and have a willingness to learn new things." Right. Just peachy.

She checks her watch. "I need to go. I'll have Jovana reschedule a few things to get us back on top of your training. I am giving you a one-time pass, Jess. Don't run off on me again."

"Yes, madame. Apologies." For a second, I was so tempted to call her Vivie, but I've been daring enough lately. Better to save that one for another day.

She wraps up her conversation by giving me a rundown of what I will need to do this coming week. My brain is entirely too jumbled to retain her long list of orders, so hopefully she will have given the same list to Jovana.

What a draining day. I could seriously use a good, lengthy nap right about now. It's the first time in a while that I am ecstatic to go home.

*a*s soon as Gen and I make it to the house, I bolt upstairs and throw myself onto the bed. I exhale as much as this tight ass dress will allow, and stare at the ceiling, happy for a modicum of solitude. But of course … nothing sweet ever lasts, does it? A knock sounds on the bedroom door. I groan and squeeze my eyes shut, hoping that if I pretend I never heard it, then it never happened.

"Jess, open up," Luca's voice calls out from the other side.

I grab the nearest pillow and use it to cover my face while I scream. Even if this only serves as temporary relief, it feels good to release the mounting tension in my body.

I have to roll onto my stomach in order to get up in this suffocating fabric. Walking in it has been a whole other challenge. I'm sure I look like I'm mimicking a penguin.

When I open the door, Luca's gaze rakes over me and he whistles. "You know, I've pictured you in something like this, but I didn't imagine I'd ever be so blessed to see you in it."

I want to tell him to go screw himself, but I don't think I have the energy at this point. Leaning my head against the doorpost I reply, "I see you've somehow finagled your way back in here. What do you want, Luca?"

He mockingly pouts. "You appear disappointed to see me." Understatement of the century.

I notice the duffle bag he's carrying. "I hope you don't think you're staying."

"Oh, it's not just what I think. It's what I intend to do."

Gen stands in the guest room doorway. "Sorry, sweets, he climbed up to my bedroom window."

"Of course he did." I stare him down. "We don't have any room for you."

Genevieve interjects, grinning flirtatiously, "Well, if you *have* to stay, my bed has room for two." God, she's so not helpful right now.

He winks at her. I don't recall ever meeting a man so blatantly irritating. "Luca, this wasn't part of the deal."

"This wasn't *not* part of the deal either. If we are going to pull this fake relationship off, we are following my rules. And my rules involve me being present, right here in this very home, with you." Heaven help me. "And the lovely Genevieve, of course." She blushes like she was just paid the highest compliment one could receive.

It would be well within reason to throw a fit, but I did agree to allow Luca to do what was necessary to keep me off his father's apparent hit list. "Fine. Whatever. Just try not to be in my way. And for all that is good and holy, please inform me when you want to use my shower."

He chuckles. "I will be the perfect guest." Entirely doubtful. "As much as I'd be happy to share a bed with your friend, I'll be respectful and take the couch until she returns home. I'll need linens."

"I'll get you some."

"Great. Now for the next order of business. Have you eaten?"

"Um, no?"

"Well, that won't do. We need to find you some proper nourishment."

"Since when did my nourishment or lack thereof become a focus?"

"Since I was adamantly charged with your care. Besides, we're dating now, remember?"

"PRETEND dating. Emphasis on 'pretend.'"

"In either case, I wouldn't be a good partner if I didn't make sure you are satisfied. And that includes the satisfaction of your stomach, Princesa." I open my mouth to argue, but he beats me to the next words. "There's a restaurant not too far from here. You may want to get changed into something a little more comfortable. Though, if you were to wear what you have on now you certainly wouldn't get an argument from me." His heated gaze sweeps over me once more.

"You're insufferable."

He laughs and heads downstairs, calling out, "I love you too, amor."

Gen just stares at me from across the hall, grinning like a Cheshire cat and mouthing to me about how hot he is. I give her my most unenthusiastic look. That man may be hot, but he is going to be hell on earth for the next several weeks. I can only pray this whole threat ordeal is resolved much, much sooner.

❤

I read Aralyn's second journal as I sit in the living room waiting for Gen to finish getting ready while Luca is in the kitchen, doing heaven knows what. I've still yet to reach the part where Aralyn has come across Alex. Then again, I'm only midway through it and she's just now mentioning meeting Madame Chérot.

I think about the interactions I had with her, remembering how fierce and confident I thought her to be, yet always noticing a hint of sadness in her eyes, peeking through the enigmatic barricade she'd built around herself. I knew she had suffered a great deal. To find out just how much has been both interesting and gut-wrenching.

Gen descends the stairs and pauses just shy of the living room. "What's this?" She picks up something off the floor by the front door, then looks at me with concern.

"Please, don't tell me that's what I think it is."

"Another note," she replies nervously.

"Give it here," Luca commands while exiting the kitchen. She hands it over to him and he opens the envelope, pulling out the black card. He reads it in silence. "Are these the notes you were referring to, Princesa?"

I nod. "What does it say?" I have an intense desire to know, despite also not wanting to.

"I'm going to make a phone call." He proceeds out the front door. "I'll be right back."

After he leaves, Gen takes a seat beside me. "Things are getting stranger by the minute. I'm honestly afraid to leave you here when I go back home in a couple days."

"If things get any wilder, I might just hop on that plane with you. I can't keep doing this; I can't just sit around wondering if notes are going to become actions, and when. I can't be expected to do nothing while Alex, Luca, or whoever tries get to the bottom of it. It doesn't feel right."

"I get it, babes. So, what do you think you need to do?"

I'm inwardly groaning at the plan I'm about to let her in on. "Right now, there's only one person I haven't spoken to yet who I suspect might be responsible for this. I kind of dread it, but I think it's time I reached out to an old friend. I need to find Arthur."

19

I have put a lot of thought into what I'm about to do, but I've still been a nervous wreck all morning. The unpredictability of my upcoming meeting with Arthur today has me wanting to renege and say forget it. For months I have been quite content not having any communication with him, but I must have answers. I have to know if he has been sending the notes, and if so, it needs to stop.

I initially ruled him out as the culprit. After all, it wasn't his handwriting. But he is smart; I'm sure he could easily change it up or get someone else to write them for him. In any case, it would be foolish to leave any stones unturned.

Last night I purchased a burner phone and used it to text him, not wanting to give him access to my new number. He was naturally surprised I had reached out. And though I anticipated him being upset about it, he was instead excited. I'm still unsure whether to be relieved by that or unnerved. After all, this is a man who got far too comfortable with the idea that we would be something more than just friends, so much so that he made some toxic decisions. What if he sees this meetup as an attempt to rekindle a connection?

I suppose it doesn't matter. My intentions will soon be clear enough. If he comes into our conversation with grand expectations, he'll unfortunately have to be disappointed.

I head out the door with Luca and Jovana. We're on our way to whatever naughty event Madame Chérot is having me attend. Luca is going for obvious reasons, but Jovana wanted to go for the experience. I was shocked to learn that, despite having worked closely with Aralyn and the Madame as a stylist and makeup artist for years, she was rarely involved with any part of the fetish scene.

I tug Luca's shirt as he's about to get into the car and pull him off to the side. "I need to talk to you about something."

"Clearly."

"I need to make a stop before we get to where we're going, and I need you to be as calm as possible when we do."

"Why don't I like the sound of this?"

"It's not a super big deal, just a quick meeting with someone I know. But I don't want you getting all overprotective, as I've been told you can get."

He crosses his arms. "I'm not overprotective."

"Sure, whatever, look can you just, please, be chill?"

He stares at me for several seconds, pondering. "Fine."

"Thank you. Okay, let's go."

He throws an arm out as I proceed forward, stopping me in my tracks. "If things go sideways…"

"Relax. Everything will be perfectly fine." Man alive, do I hope so.

I'm not sure I'm convincing enough. His arm is still extended across me. I look up at him. "What is it?"

His eyes search mine, perhaps looking for some reason to refuse. When he seems to find none, he lets me go. I stay put a while longer, unsure if he intends to answer me, but after a few moments more he gets into the car.

After informing Jean-Philippe where I'd like him to take us first, we are on our way. As soon as we arrive at the entrance of the park where Art suggested we meet, the nervous tension moves from my chest to the base of my throat. The realization that I'm really about to do this quickly pushes stress throughout my body, making my heart race.

Jovana speaks up when she sees where we are. "This is not the right place."

"I'm just making a quick stop. I'll be right back."

"I should go with you." She begins to undo her seatbelt.

"No, that's okay, it's not business related. Besides, I already have Luca. I won't be more than ten minutes." She glances at Luca nervously, then back at me. I smile in hopes of reassuring her, but I can tell she is still bothered. I didn't realize my security had been such a concern for her. It's sweet how much she cares.

Luca and I exit the vehicle and enter the park. I pause momentarily. My eyes search around and then I spot the man I've come to see, seated on a bench across a pond from us—Arthur Reed, my once close friend and the man who betrayed my trust like no other.

Taking notice of our approach, he rises from his seat. "Jess. Hey." He looks different than I've ever seen him. He's let his wavy brown hair, which used to always be slicked back, grow down to his shoulders, and he's grown a beard. It's not bad, it's just … shocking. He had told me many times before that I'd never catch him dead with a beard.

"Hey, Art. Thanks for meeting me." He smiles in response, though it doesn't reach his dark blue eyes, which dart to Luca. His smile drops and his brow crinkles with confusion.

"Oh, uh, this is Luca."

"Ah, new boyfriend, huh?" He chuckles and it fades as he catches my unamused expression. "Too soon. Got it. Sorry." Fuck. I'm already regretting this.

I don't even have to peek over my shoulder at Luca, I can feel the judgement and distaste radiating off him like body heat. He takes a long, drawn-out breath and I quickly say something before this becomes any more awkward and tense than it already is. "I just have a couple questions for you and then I'll be on my way." This doesn't please Art, and it's evident in the frustration that momentarily appears on his face.

To distract us from this lapse, he points at the café cart about twenty feet away. "How about an espresso? Double shot, right?"

"It's okay, I don't—"

"See? Still remember. I'll be right back." He hurries off to the cart and I stand baffled, trying to wrap my head around what the hell is going on with him.

"Alright," Luca grumbles, "who is this guy?"

"His name is Arthur. It's a long story, but to summarize it, we used to be close friends until we had a pretty big falling out. I asked him to meet with me so I can hopefully get to the bottom of something I've been curious about."

"Is something about him troubling you?" It's a genuine question and I'm unsure how to answer, or if I should. If I tell him that I suspect Art to be the note sender, he might do a whole lot more than just stand guard.

He regards my silence. "Fine, don't tell me. But be honest with yourself, can you trust him? Especially at a time like this?"

"I hardly trust anyone, including you."

If my words stung, he did a good job of not showing it. "I hope you know what you're doing." Truthfully, so do I.

It doesn't take Art long to come back with two drinks and he immediately notices the defensive energy Luca is giving off. "Everything alright?" he cautiously asks, handing me the small cup of double espresso.

I take it and then Luca grabs Art's own espresso from out of his hand and remarks, "Todo estará bien una vez que te hayas ido," before taking a sip. I haven't a clue what he said and neither does Art, which I'm certain he was betting on. Though Arthur appears highly irritated by him, he opts to say nothing and Luca walks off to brood in the shade of a nearby tree.

Arthur and I find a bench and as soon as we take a seat, he's quick to speak. "You're still so beautiful." Did he anticipate that I would have been less so? His underwhelming attempt at flattery bores me, and I'm certain my expression shows it. "So, uh, I know you said you have some questions for me, but before you ask them, I want you to know how sorry I am, Jess. I regret my actions immensely. It really hurt me to see the pain in your eyes that night."

I'm not convinced his words are genuine. Perhaps it's the lack of authenticity in his tone. The apology sounded robotic, scripted, even. "Yeah? What were they? Your actions that you immensely regret."

"I was far too rough with you. I should have never handled you the way I did." My mind is thrust back to the memory of him gripping my arm with bitter rage when I denied his request to talk things over, then insulting me when he realized that Alex might have been more than just the man I was interviewing.

"Is that all?"

He's searching my now frustrated gaze for the answer, and that's frustrating me more. "I won't apologize for what I said to him," he murmurs. "He shouldn't have butted in."

"What about what you said to me? Or do you still believe I'm a whore who sold myself to Alexander Marc for a fancy life? Maybe you still believe I needed you to swoop in and save me by making decisions on my behalf?"

"I said those things out of anger. I didn't actually mean any of it. Come on, you know me."

"Do I? I thought I did. But you showed me a completely different side to you Art, a terrifying side."

"I'm sorry, I really am. I was just… I was just afraid of losing you. Try to understand, I spent years developing this beautiful, strong connection with you, envisioning what my life could be like with you as … well … as my partner. And then all of a sudden, those dreams and desires were falling apart at the seams. You were slipping through my fingers, Jess. I had you, and then you were just … slipping through."

"Art, you never had me! I was never yours. We were really good friends. And sure, yes, there was something between us deeper than friendship that I, too, had wanted to explore, but you know how difficult it was for me to actually make moves in that direction. We talked about it, remember? Several times we talked about how I wasn't sure I was ready to take that step with you. In the end I decided that it would be best not to."

"Because you wanted him more." There's a bitterness in his tone that I can't miss.

"No, because I didn't want the restrictions that a relationship with you would have come with." I witness pain and surprise flash across his features. My words hit him like a train he didn't see coming. "You held on to your dream of us so tightly that you suffocated our future, Art." It's a truth I'm certain is hard for him to swallow but there it is.

He gazes out at the water, unsure of what to say. I look upon him with such sorrow. Memories of the best times we had together now flood my mind, and my heart aches because it misses my friend. My heart misses what we had when trust existed, and emotions weren't so muddled and tainted by the shadows that consumed us in the end.

"Despite it all, I do forgive you." I do. I had forgiven him not long after what happened. It didn't erase the hurt, but it did bring me a small measure of peace, which was sorely needed amidst all the chaos of the time.

"So, where do we go from here?"

I knew this question was coming. What I didn't yet know was what my response would be. There is a part of me that wants my friend back, but I know things will never be the same as they once were.

Was there ever really a genuine friendship to begin with? He said himself his focus was developing a deeper connection with me in the hopes it would be something more. Seems like the friendship I miss was simply a façade. There's also the fact that I no longer trust Art. Any trust I had in his care, consideration, and even my safety around him has gone. It would take time for him to earn it back, and I'm not ready to give him the opportunity.

"I wish I could say we go back to being friends, but I don't think it's a good time right now."

"I suppose it would be too much to ask when a good time might be?"

"It would."

He drops his head in defeat, nodding. "I get it."

"I might be more open to it someday, but I think my life needs to be more settled first."

"No, I get it, I do." He looks at me with a weary smile. "Don't worry, Jess. I hear you loud and clear." There's a lingering silence between us before he speaks again. "I guess it's your turn, huh? What did you want to ask me?"

Right, my questions. "First, how have you been? I've worried about you."

"Oh? That's a shock. Didn't think you cared."

"Please, don't."

"Don't what? Tell you how I feel? Tell you how fucked it is that you can say you were worried about me after half a year of no contact?"

"Don't twist this to make it something it's not."

"You mean the truth?"

"You hurt *me*, Art, in more ways than one. I didn't feel safe around you anymore; *that's* why it's been so long with no contact." If it weren't for my need for answers, it would have been longer.

"So, why don't you just stop beating around the bush and tell me what's changed your mind all of a sudden, hm? What do you want?"

Great. Let's get this over with. I dig in my purse and pull out the black notecard from last night, handing it to him. "Have you seen anything like this before?"

He opens it and reads the note in silence.

Welcome back. Hope you finally ended it.

Remember, I'm always watching.

"What is this?"

"Someone has been sending me these unsettling, and sometimes threatening notes." I observe him closely as he closes it and looks out at the water, tapping the card against his palm. "Most of the time the notes tell me to stay away from Alex."

"And you think I have something to do with this."

"Do you?"

He looks at me with disbelief. "God, I'll always be the villain in your eyes, won't I?"

"I'm just asking, Arthur."

"And the fact that you're asking says all I need to know." He stands and chucks the card onto my lap. "Good luck with your mystery. Sounds like you'll need it." He turns to leave and almost runs into Luca, who was quick to get over here. He stares him down as Art cautiously scoots around him and proceeds to storm off.

"You good?"

I shove the card in my bag. "Yeah. Thanks. That didn't quite end the way I had hoped. We should go; I'm sure Jovana's wondering what happened to us." I head for the park exit and he quickly follows behind.

"Just a moment, we need to have a little talk about something."

"Can it wait?"

"Princesa, stop." I halt and he moves in front of me.

"What?"

"I'm curious. What is it about you that has everyone wrapped around your finger, hmm? Alexander, my sister, Madame Chérot, Jovana, and now apparently this poor idiot. All of them are willing to do anything for you. All of them are making sacrifices for you. Why is that?"

"Why would you assume Arthur has made sacrifices for me?"

"He may be upset, but anyone can see he's very attracted to you. That right there is a man who would go great lengths for you, if he hasn't already." Oh, he doesn't know the half of it.

"Okay, you should be able to answer your own question, because with that logic, it's fair to say I have you wrapped around my finger as well."

He chuckles. "Not at all."

"No? Alright then, let's talk about it. You didn't have to agree to be my personal bodyguard. No one was forcing you, yet here you are, *sacrificing* your time and risking your reputation with your father to protect me." I step toward him. "If I didn't know better, I'd think you actually care about me more than you let on."

He quietly laughs, grins, and then bites his lower lip for a moment before responding. "I'm afraid my two reasons for taking this job are rather selfish, Princesa. Your Alexander said I have something to prove, and I'll admit, he's not wrong. I'll get great pleasure from proving to both of you that I can keep you from harm better than he could."

"Not shocking in the slightest. Okay, get on with it. What's the second reason?"

He smirks. "You'll figure it out soon enough." Then he closes the gap between us, gazing at me with heated intensity. In a low tone he says, "In the meantime, allow me to make one thing very clear. I'm not here because you have me wrapped around your precious finger. If anything, you'll be wrapped around mine."

That last sentence does something to me, causing a delicious ache I'm astonished by. Speechless, I watch his gaze slowly move from my eyes to my lips and back up again, until I can no longer help but bashfully look away.

"We'll be late. We should go," I mutter.

"Mm. We can't have that. Come then, Princesa. Let's get you to the ball."

Journal,

I've been training for three weeks now, though it has been incredibly difficult. The difficulty comes with sneaking away. The first week was hell to pull off. I had to miss nearly a weeks' worth of sessions because I got caught one night and my punishment was being confined to the house with extra security.

I then decided to have Luca help. He objected at first, pissed that I'm doing this, and refused to help me, even though he comes and goes as he wishes. I threatened to out him to Papa. That got him to give in.

It's been easier since then. Papa trusts that I'll return home if Luca is with me. But it's still difficult to make every session because of timing.

Madame Chérot sat me down for a private conversation the other day asking what was going on. I surprised myself, telling her everything as though she were a therapist. It's as if everything I had pent up for years just flooded out as soon as she asked. But she listened. She listened for a long time. And finally, when I had nothing left to say, she handed me a set of keys and said, "Welcome home."

Oh journal, she gave me the keys to her guest house! She's inviting me to stay with her until I can get on my own feet. I visited today. It's a beautiful home outside the city in a neighborhood that's secured so I'll be safe from Papa's men in the event they somehow find me. And she is hiring a chauffeur who will take me anywhere I need to go, especially the den.

Could this be it? Could this be the key to a better life?

Journal,

I've been at the new place for two weeks now. Every moment has been indescribably blissful. Every moment has been peaceful. I can breathe as though I've never truly experienced what it's like to take a breath. I've been learning so much in a short span of time.

My old life still lingers like a dark cloud, but at least it's no longer directly overhead. Luca has been tasked to once again bring me home. Knowing that I have been at the den consistently, he decided to question the Madame and he found out where I was. He told me he'd give Papa my location if I don't come with him willingly, and I told him he might as well end my life. I won't go back. Not this time.

There are only two options: this new life or no life at all.

20

As I observe my surroundings, Madame Chérot explains to me that we are at one of the three major kink clubs here in Paris. Unlike the one Alex had taken me to earlier this year, this particular club is within the main city and caters to those of many walks of life, not just the wealthy. I'm actually surprised that the Madame, with all her grand and proper ways, would consider servicing clientele whose pockets weren't lined. But I'm happy to know she appreciates inclusivity, regardless of status.

The atmosphere of the club feels more relaxed than the others as well, but it has no shortage of risqué indulgences. The whole place is an exotic buffet for the eyes. Everything, and I do mean everything, is black-lit. Neon colors on the walls, and paint on bare bodies glows bright. Even my red latex dress, that I changed into when I arrived, has a luminance about it.

In the main lounge, a DJ is playing sensual music, and a few individuals make out and grope each other against a wall or in a corner. However, most sit and socialize. Jovana rests in an arm chair, like me, closely observing everything taking place. Luca is at the bar engaging in conversation with a couple ladies who have been watching him like a hawk since we walked in.

"This way. I need to show you where the Papillons work from." I follow the Madame to the other side of the spacious lounge where she leads me into a back hallway. It too is lit only with black lights.

At the end of the hall is a glowing red door, and when we walk in, we are met with the sight of multiple Diamond Butterflies, all getting dressed and talking among each other. The chatter immediately dies down as they realize we've entered. But Madame Chérot doesn't seem to notice. Or she doesn't care. She moves through the dressing room with the complete confidence of a boss, and I follow in step feeling increasingly uncomfortable at the attention I'm receiving. But the thought that these people will be in my charge soon makes me roll my shoulders back and correct my posture. *Fake it till you make it, Jess. Don't give them a reason to think you're weak.* This is all so far removed from my comfort zone it's not even funny.

In through another door we go, and this time there's only one person before us, Emory. She sports a sleeveless black latex bodysuit, with a corset of the same color around her midriff. Her hair is in a tight, high ponytail showing off her impeccable facial structure and, of course, she has on the signature heels. Her green eyes immediately lock with mine and I suddenly find relief at the sight of her. She's a familiar face, a likeable person, and I don't have to go through the painstaking process of explaining who I am and what the hell I'm doing here.

"Jess, Emory is in charge of staff operations at this particular club; consider her like the assistant manager at this location. She will eventually report to you regarding what takes place here, including staff needs and client complaints and requests, as well as provide you with the profit list at the end of each night. Tonight, she is tasked with giving you a tour of this club and answering any questions you may have in regard to operations and protocol. Est-ce que tu comprends?"

"Oui. I understand."

"Bien. I am leaving now; I have other business to attend to. Emory, take good care of our girl."

"Oui, madame." Once she leaves, Emory addresses me. "I am guessing you haven't told her yet."

"Told her what?"

"That you don't wish to be protégé long term." Oh yeah, that.

"I don't know… maybe I'll change my mind."

"You're actually considering running a fetish den empire?"

It sounds silly, incredibly silly. But now that I am in this, I'm not ready to say I'd for sure turn down such an opportunity. What if this does grow on me? Granted, I have my doubts, and it's certainly nothing I've ever envisioned doing. However, what if that's the beauty of it? From journalist to fetish den CEO. It's unheard of and thrilling and … possible. "I'm not ready to overlook the possible."

Emory sighs and grabs a full-length mirror, dragging it across the floor and placing it in front of me. "What do you see?"

"Um, myself?"

"Look closer. Actually, *see* yourself. Look at the outfit you wear, the heels on your feet. Who are you?" My mind instantly responds with Aralyn's name and I close my eyes for a moment, doing my best to strike it from thought, to force my own into its place. "Jess," she says gently, "do you even know?"

My lids raise and I'm once again confronted with my image. *Do I* even know? Once upon a time not too long ago, I found myself pondering a similar question regarding my identity, torn between my made up alias, Isabella Evans, and the woman I was at the time. After my life started rapidly shifting, there was a point I thought I had figured it out. I thought I had finally found balance within myself when I realized that Isabella Evans was, in many ways, the part of me that wanted to be released from the cell I placed her in. When I opened that cell, I thought I was free.

But now, here I stand, addressing the question of my identity once more. In a dress that's not my dress. In butterfly stilettos I truly haven't earned, in pursuit of a title I'm unsure if I really want, completely enamored with a man whose heart is still held by the very woman whose life I've stepped into.

So, who in fact am I? A fraud? A fake? A phony? That's sure as hell what it seems like to me, and I think Emory may see it that way too.

"I'm a woman who's still discovering herself and what she's capable of." And that, in essence, is true.

Emory smiles faintly, but I can tell by her face that she believes my answer to be a cop-out. And maybe it is. Maybe I'm kidding myself and making excuses for my life gradually shifting into that of another's. But what I'm also not ready for, is to acknowledge that I've gone too far. Not yet. Not when I'm so close to getting the story that would ultimately propel my career further and fulfill Aralyn's dying wish. And not when I'm growing closer with Alex again.

"Okay," she replies, simply accepting my answer, seeing little need to question me further.

"You don't appear satisfied with my response."

She shrugs a shoulder. "As you have said, you're still discovering who you are." She places the mirror back. "If you are being honest with yourself, then who am I to question that?"

"You're not the first person to be concerned about me. I can imagine how this all looks to everyone. But I have my reasons for taking this path. And though I may not know the outcome, I do believe I'm doing the best I can to get to where I'm trying to be."

"You have guts, I'll give you that. Not many people are bold enough to make the type of choices you make, or take the risks you take. I commend you for it. Just don't lose yourself in the process." I nod, taking her warning to heart, because I completely get how easy it could be for me to do just that. I'm already walking a very fine line. The smallest gust of wind could blow me off it. "Come. Let's give you that tour."

She escorts me through the employee area and toward the door to the main club. "As madam, you will be expected to pay regular visits to the clubs we service, including this one. You will likely visit some of the other dens and clubs we are contracted with internationally as well. Madame De la Rue favored a club in Toronto called Nectar. I'm sure you'll go at some point." I wouldn't have guessed that her favorite spot would be international. It always seemed like her heart was tied to Paris.

I thought we were headed back out to the lounge, but instead, we go straight to a series of back rooms that I didn't notice coming in initially. "What are these for?"

"It's where we conduct our business. Similar to the den, every room is a private space for each client to receive their desired pleasures. Tonight, you will shadow me as I conduct a session for a special client of mine. He already knows you'll be observing and has consented to your presence."

"Please don't tell me it's Luca."

Amused, she says, "No. Luca is not a man who cares to be controlled, and tonight"—she grabs a crop from a variety of whips displayed in the hallway—"the control is all mine."

She walks to one of the back-room doors and throws it open. A middle-aged man, with a beer belly, a chest full of hair, and a long black beard, is standing, startled, in the middle of the room in nothing but his underwear. It's a sight I was very unprepared for, and I had made every attempt to come prepared.

"Samson! Why are you just standing there? On the ground!" Emory's voice is loud and commanding, also a shock.

The man falls to his hands and knees, bowing before us. "So sorry, Mistress Em."

"Oh, you will be. I'll make sure of it." She gestures at me to step in the room and close the door behind us. When I do, I notice a woman seated in the corner. Surprise number three within sixty seconds. This has to be a new record.

The woman looks to be around the same age as the man. She sits, stoic, with her hands folded over the purse in her lap. She gives me a faint smile and I return it, still trying to wrap my head around what's going on.

Emory takes slow paces toward her client. "Today, we have a guest." She squats down by his side and lightly taps his back with the whip, motioning him to sit up. "I know how much you love to be watched, so I'm sure you'll enjoy this."

"Yes, Mistress Em. Very much." His accent sounds American.

"Good. Why don't you go give our guest a gracious welcome. Kiss her shoes."

Woah, what? "Oh, that's not necessa—" Emory's eyes shoot daggers at me, and I shut up, clearing my throat.

Samson quickly crawls to where I stand and kisses the toes of my stilettos multiple times. Emory snaps the whip against a wall and it makes me jump. "That's enough! Don't overindulge. Remember your place."

"Ye-yes, Mistress." He scurries back and she crouches to his level once again, lifting his chin up with the tip of the crop.

"Good boy. Being greedy is not suitable for any slave of mine." Her demeanor is so controlled, and dripping in sex appeal, from her body language, to her voice, to what adorns her body. It's hard to wrap my mind around this being the same woman who, submitted to Luca. But I'm enjoying this. It's like another sneak peek into Aralyn's life—dominatrix by day and then, behind closed doors, submissive to Alexander only.

Two sides of a coin. Two extremes that are so opposite, yet Emory and Aralyn are have shown an impressive ability to dance between them with such fluidity. Could I ever see myself being so fluid? In some ways I feel as though I already am. I almost have to be dominant in my role as a journalist and, because of my adult life experiences, control is something I naturally acquired a desire for.

Then, I met Alex and he tapped into the part of me that desired softness, security, and letting go of the control I'd take on any other time outside of his presence. That's not to say I'd ever want to brandish a whip or take on the kink driven, sexual role of a dominant, but I can see and even appreciate how someone could be both.

Emory orders the man face down on the floor and then she lifts her foot, pressing the stiletto of her black heel into his back. "Ah! Oh, thank you Mistress!"

"Did I tell you to speak?" He says nothing in return, just the way Em wants it. For the next thirty minutes I observe her in this different element. I watch with interest as she provides her client with the pain and pleasure he craves. His pleasure, in fact, simply happens to be pain, pain and submission, nothing too sexual in nature.

I'm intrigued by the woman in the corner who must be his wife, gauging by the ring on her finger, and has not looked away once. I can't tell if she's into watching or if she's here because he wants her to watch. Perhaps Emory's services provide them both with something they long for that they don't really get within their own home, let alone outside of it.

When their session draws to a close, Emory begins to provide the man with what appears to be aftercare. She allows him to lay his head on her lap while she strokes his hair and coos sweet words, commending him for how well he did and telling him how much she cares for him.

All in all, this experience was less … overtly sexual than when I witnessed her get toy fucked and slapped around by Luca, though, it was harsher in the type and amount of pain inflicted. I continue to have trouble understanding the idea of anyone finding gratification in such actions being done to them.

As Samson stands to get dressed, Emory struts over to the corner of the room where the woman sits. She leans down, and plants a long and passionate kiss upon her lips. The surprises just don't end.

The woman gazes up at her afterward with awe and appreciation. Then, with not a word exchanged, Emory grabs my hand and leads me out of the room, closing the door swiftly behind us. She leans against it and smiles. "Well? What did you think?"

My eyes grow wide and my face flushes from suddenly feeling put on the spot, "I um, I think—I thought … it was, uh … different."

She giggles at my response. "You're still so fresh. It's adorable. We've got a lot of work to do with you. Isn't your lover a Dom?"

"Alex? Yeah. But to be honest we haven't explored BDSM together too deeply."

"Mmm, yet. You should speak with him about perhaps diving into it a little more. If you're ready to, of course. He might help you understand this way of life better."

"I'll be sure to do that." If I ever get the chance to be with him long enough. I hope there won't always be something that comes along to separate us again. "Though, Alex told me he's more of a sensual Dom. As far as I know, he doesn't much care for inflicting a lot of pain."

"That may be true. And that's absolutely fine, but even a Gentle Dom might be able to provide you with insight into the heavier stuff. Alexander had to experience some things in order to realize what he liked and the type of dominant he wanted to be. It's likely he understands firsthand a lot of what you've been shown recently." I wonder if she's aware of his short-lived dynamic with Madame Chérot. "And just so you know, pain and humiliation aren't the primary services we provide. It's merely an accessory to something bigger. What we sell is a variety of kinky experiences. We appeal to various fetishes. We make naughty dreams come true."

"Have you ever been a car salesperson? You'd be good."

"HAHA! I'd probably look incredible in a well fitted suit too."

"You'd absolutely pull it off. So, what's their story in there? Are those two a couple? Does she actually get off on what she saw?"

"Oui. They are married. They fly out to Paris every month just for this. He enjoys pain, but what he really loves is humiliation and degradation. He finds pleasure in his wife watching another woman treat him like filth. She, on the other hand, simply finds pleasure in the fantasy, the idea that I'm humiliating him for *her* as a token of my devotion and affection. They will both return to their hotel now and fuck each other senseless. I suppose you could view this as very dramatic foreplay." I find this all so bizarre and mind blowing. "Anyway, come, I have to finish giving you the tour." She hooks her arm in mine and off we go.

She takes me to every single room in the club, explaining the uses of each, the expectations of me, and the expectations I should have for the Butterflies and club management. She gives me a thorough rundown of how to handle any client complaints or disputes, and instructs me on the various methods I can utilize to ensure the Papillon Diament's impeccable reputation remains intact. By the time we finish, I am bogged down with information.

"Questions?"

"Uh, no. I think I really just need to digest everything first. You sure you don't want this job? Haha. You seem to have all the ins and outs down."

"You're going to do great, Jess. It will take some getting used to, but remember, we are a family here. If you ever need help, use us." She kisses each of my cheeks and bids me farewell before walking off.

I sigh, incredibly overwhelmed, then I take the opportunity to go outside and get some air. Pulling out my phone from my pocketbook, I scroll through the call log. My thumb hovers over Alexander's contact.

"Promise me," his voice echoes through my conscience. It's a reminder that I can't do what I crave to do right now, which is to talk to him. Perhaps he'd calm me and reassure me that despite my insane choice to pursue Aralyn's job, everything will work out, that between this and the messy situations I'm in, I'm going to be alright. All I'd have to do is click his name and I'd have a direct line to that possibility.

It's not fair. He put me in such a vulnerable position when he asked me for that promise. I would have said anything at that time just to savor such a delicious moment. So … it doesn't actually count … right?

Fuck. I can't bring myself to disappoint him. I'd ultimately disappoint myself. Heaven knows I've done that enough times this year.

I lean against the wall, watching as the Parisian night life ramps up. Tourists and locals alike stroll up and down the streets, going about their lives, making the most of the warm evening weather. A couple men whistle at me as they go by, and it makes me want to revert back to old habits, and run for the hills while wrapping myself up in an oversized coat. But I'm not that woman, who's terrified of a man's gaze and what it could mean, any longer. I remind myself of it, choosing instead to ignore them.

I return to people-watching, and my eyes catch a figure dressed in all black standing in the shade of a tree across the street, their face obscured by the shadow of the hat they wear. Perhaps I'm paranoid, but although I can't be certain, it seems as though their stare is aimed straight at me. I squint in an attempt to get a better view of who they are.

"See anything fascinating?"

I yelp, startled by Luca's sudden appearance. "You're awful jumpy, Princesa." He laughs.

"Why must you always creep up on me?"

"It's never intentional. However, I might start doing it just to hear your little squeak."

"Squeak? What are you talking about? I don't squeak."

He laughs heartily. "Oh, you do, like a little toy you give playful pups. Don't be ashamed. It's cute."

I roll my eyes and glance back across the street. But the figure, whoever they were, is gone. I let out a frustrated sigh. "I'm ready to go. Where's Jovana?"

"I sent her home."

"What? Why? She wanted to stay and immerse herself in the environment. She didn't have to leave early."

"Relax. I'm confident she saw all she wanted to see. Jean-Philippe dropped her off. So, since it's just the two of us now, how about a date?"

"I'd rather eat glass."

"Trust me, it's not without reason. That man you were staring at has been following us since we left the house."

"Wait… you know who that was?"

"His name is Emil. He works for my father. If I had to guess, he's likely been sent to keep an eye on you, which means at some point he'll make an attempt to speak with you."

My stomach is a tight ball of nerves. "Why would he want to talk to me?"

"To figure out your intentions, of course. And to find out what you know about my sister's whereabouts." He takes my hand in his, interlocking his fingers with my own. "So, we are going on a date. That way, when I inevitably have to explain what we are doing together, it won't seem so suspicious."

With each passing day, the threat on my security grows more severe. Now, there's actual proof that I am being watched by Maxime. Luca was right. I hold on tight to his hand, not for appearances, but because I'm terrified, and his hand has become a life raft to cling to, providing some measure of comfort.

He squeezes gently, as though in an effort to reassure me that I'll be alright. "How about we have our companion follow us to the Italian restaurant down the road? I don't know about you, but I could devour an entire pan of lasagna right now. I'm starving."

"Ha! Perhaps, since we're dating and all, it would be more gentlemanly of you to offer me a slice first."

"Mm, perhaps not. We're not *that* serious yet. But nice try … babe."

Babe? I drop his hand, turning from him. "Never mind, I can't do this. I'll take my chances."

He suddenly grabs my wrist and pulls me tight against him, then wraps his arms around my waist and grins. "You seem to forget you're not the one in charge here. Until otherwise specified, you're my responsibility, Princesa. The rules we play by are mine. The things we do are my call. And to anyone wondering, you belong to *me*. Object all you want, but it won't erase those very real facts." Being this close to him cloaks me in his scent and warmth, and his tone, so matter-of-fact, so dominant, tickles that part of me that would gladly fall to my knees if commanded. I'm missing Alex something fierce. It's the only explanation for my naughty thoughts that makes sense to me.

I place my hands on his chest and push him just enough that we break apart. Then, I gently touch his cheek and display my most convincing smile. "Whatever you say, my love." On my tippy-toes, I plant a soft kiss right near the edge of his mouth. His low cut, well-groomed beard tickles my nose.

His brow cocks upward as the shock on his face grows evident, and he stands, frozen, completely taken aback by my actions. I give a cunning smirk, take hold of his hand again, and lead the way to the restaurant.

If he wants to play … let's play.

21

The restaurant we go to is a quaint little spot with an outdoor seating area that is decorated like a tea garden. We get seated in a corner, which is perfect for keeping an eye on our surroundings. Lights entwined with draping vines twinkle above us, and a rose-shaped candle is held in a delicate crystal bowl in the center of the table, adding to the ambiance. This place is a bit more romantic than I would have gone for, but to my enemies, it will look realistic enough for the story we are creating.

Luca glances over the menu eagerly as I continue to glance around, twiddling my thumbs, while wondering if I'll catch a glimpse of the man who's been tracking me. "Your anxiety is giving me anxiety, Princesa," Luca says, noticing what I'm doing.

"Yeah, well, we've every reason to be anxious."

He sets the menu down and pours a glass of water from the bottle placed on our table. "Here, drink this and calm down. Don't focus on anything but what's going on right here at this table. You don't want Emil catching on to the fact that we're on to him."

"You're right; it's hard not to worry, though. I keep wondering if Maxime is going to find some opening to get access to me."

"Not with me here. Now, please, drink up and focus on what you want to eat." I don't even have an appetite for food. What I'm hungry for is some information.

"I never asked you this before, but what is your current relationship with your father? You mention all these things about how cruel of a man he is, what he's capable of and what you know of his intentions. But where do you stand with him?"

He sighs and leans back in his seat, preparing to get into the details. "Our relationship is naturally a complicated one. Think of it this way, I see him more as a boss than a father."

"A boss? So, you work for him."

"Working for him would imply I'm getting paid. I do receive many privileges for being his son, but no, I do what he asks of me or suffer the consequences."

"So … you haven't tired of him yet."

"What?"

"In her journal, your sister said she hoped you'd grow tired of your father's treatment and find freedom, like she did."

He looks away, pondering. There's a sadness that shadows his face for a moment. "If I find freedom now, Aralyn loses hers."

"What do you mean?"

"Have you ever been curious why my sister, despite her illness, hasn't been found yet? It's because I've made sure she won't be. I could run from my father, and everything and everyone he's connected with tonight if I wanted, and never look back. But then, there will be nothing keeping him from her."

Realization strikes me and I quietly state, "You must know where she is, then. In my last conversation with her, she told me she was moving to Spain and that the only remaining family she had was there. And just yesterday, Madame Chérot mentioned you had obligations back in Spain. Aralyn is your obligation, isn't she?"

"Yes, to all of it."

I knew they had contact with each other, but I never suspected Luca was largely involved with keeping Aralyn hidden. Considering his numerous attempts in the past to get her to return to Maxime and do things such as leaving Alex, I figured she would have also hidden her whereabouts from him.

"I want the end of her life to be peaceful. Her best chance of that is for me to remain "obedient" to him. My job, so to speak, is to play the role of the perfect son, collect information, particularly anything that could put her security at risk, and do everything in my power to keep him from finding her. It's a self-appointed task, but I couldn't live with myself if my dying sister lived out the rest of her days in agony under his roof."

I'm overwhelmed with emotion at this. Of all the questions I could ask, though, the most important one to me is, "How is she doing?"

He gives a weary smile. "Her mind and spirit are doing great. Her body is very weak."

The waitress comes to take our orders and after she walks away, I ask, "Who's watching her if you're here?"

"She has her own security team. I don't spend much time with her because I don't want to draw attention to her location, but I do check in as often as I'm able."

"Does she know you've been tasked to protect me?"

"No. She has no idea that our father is having you followed, either. I intend to keep it that way. She isn't in a good state of health. I'm concerned that any additional stress could cause her issues."

I nod. "That's understandable."

He looks at me questioningly. "It's a mystery to me how you ever became entangled with her life."

My mind drifts back to my first memories of her at the cozy café she had frequented for weeks before initiating a conversation with me, to my great surprise. I was enchanted by her very essence. Captivated, not only by her beauty, but her unique style, her enigmatic nature, and the manner in which she consistently carried herself. The answer to the conundrum he ponders is that she herself was the mystery, one I couldn't ignore the opportunity to solve.

"Anyway," he continues, "as I said, you don't have to worry. You're going to be just fine." Everyone keeps saying that to me. Hell, I even say it to myself, just to quell the rising stress that's triggered each passing day. I wish I could say it helps to hear it, but it doesn't, because how do they know? How does anyone really know that it will be "fine" or "okay"?

"Sure. Yeah."

"I'm going to the restroom before the meal comes. Will you be alright till I return, or would you feel more comfortable coming along?"

I laugh. "I don't think I need that much protecting. I'll be fine. You go on."

My phone chimes just as he leaves, and I check the notification. It's from Genevieve.

Hey, sooooo, are you on your way back?

Why do I get the feeling she's asking because something's wrong?

Out with Luca. Stopped to get dinner. What's up?

Okay, so, crazy thing happened. I accidentally knocked the coffee table and one of the journals fell off. Out slid this…

The next text is a picture. I squint my eyes in an attempt to process what I'm seeing. Oh my god. An *ultrasound* picture?

She sends a follow up question:

Did Aralyn ever say anything about being pregnant?

Not at all.

I click on it and zoom in closely on the not yet fully developed fetus and the name listed in the upper corner. It's Aralyn's name. So, it really is hers. Questions flood my mind as I text Gen back.

What does the journal look like?

I anxiously await her response, feeling increasingly unsettled.

It's black with some gold swirly designs on the front.

Her third journal. I haven't read it yet, but I know with near certainty that it covers the time when she was with Alex. Which means … there's a big chance the baby belongs to him. Though, what if it doesn't?

My hand begins to shake, and I set the phone down, taking slow, methodical breaths. I don't understand. Why has no one told me about this? A child is such a huge thing not to mention. Neither Alex nor Aralyn ever thought it would be a good idea to bring this up? Does Luca know? If I ask him, I run the risk of mentioning something he may not have been privy to.

Does the Madame know? She was like a mother to Aralyn. She must have known.

I call the waitress over and ask her to cancel my order. Then, I pull out a receipt from my bag and write a quick note on it to Luca, telling him where I'm going and that I'll meet him back at the house soon. I have to get out of here. I have to get to the bottom of this.

------ ♥ ------

*L*ucky for me, I knew exactly where Madame Chérot was going to be tonight, at one of her studios giving a master class to up-and-coming stylists. I took a service car straight there. There was no way I could sit through dinner and then go home without some answers. It would eat me up too much.

I storm into the hair and makeup room filled with models and novice stylists. My eyes scour the room till my sight lands on the woman I've come to see. I make a beeline for her as she helps a student with a model.

When she spots me coming toward her, she places her hands on her hips and exclaims, "I said I'd meet you tomorrow, not tonight. You'd better have a good reason for being here, mademoiselle."

"Did you know?"

"Know what?"

"That Aralyn was pregnant!" With a snap of her fingers, she signals to one of her assistants to take over, and pulls me aside out of earshot.

"Have you no respect? You could not choose a more private occasion to bring up these things?"

"All these secrets are giving me whiplash! I have to know how this has completely slipped any conversation I've had with literally anyone associated with her. Please."

She glares at me, but after a moment of frustration she finally gives in. "Oui, I knew she was pregnant. And you must never tell Alex. He must never know."

"Why not? Was he not the father?"

"He was, but he must still never know."

"I'm sorry, are you seriously telling me that Alex has no clue Aralyn had his child? I'm pretty sure this is information he has a right to know about."

"Don't be a fool," she snaps at me. "If you really knew what happened, you'd never say such a thing. Her pregnancy was a miracle. Aralyn was told she'd never have children. During the first year she started working at the den, she had been tested and treated for ovarian cancer. Having it at such a young age was rare, but she did manage to catch it early enough and beat it. The treatment was harsh on her system however, and the doctors believed her to be infertile because of it."

Ovarian cancer? In the last journal entry I read, she spoke about having to go to regular doctor appointments, but she hadn't yet mentioned why. This could have been the pre-existing health condition she told me about that kept her from making the heart transplant list.

"I won't ever forget when she came to me with the news of the positive test. She was so happy. I'd never seen her with that much joy in her eyes." She sighs. "But things went from joyous to devastating, because two weeks later she had a miscarriage."

My chest seizes with sorrow. My god, she just couldn't catch a break. I feel like such an idiot for my assumptions. "Oh, Aralyn."

"She was waiting for Alexander's birthday to tell him about the pregnancy. The miscarriage happened three days before. She wanted to spare him the emotional distress, so she made the choice not to mention anything of it to him at all."

It's astonishing how she placed her partner above herself in such drastic ways. She truly wanted to protect Alex from the heartache of loss and the long road of grief again. It seems to be something she repeated throughout their relationship. I am, however, torn in my perspective.

I get it, I do, and I can't imagine what it's like to take on the weight of everything she went through. But I can't help but wonder what the outcome would have been if she allowed Alex the opportunity to support her through the aftermath of the tragedy. The same regarding the battle with her heart. Just maybe, it would have made a difference somehow, or at very least eased the weight of her trauma.

I've been picking up on an interesting pattern between the two of them. They both keep so much hidden to protect those they love. Whereas Alex has kept secrets from others in order to protect her, she has kept secrets from him in order to protect him. And though they both have the best of intentions, they've carried such great burdens because of it.

"You're right. That truly is devastating."

"Oui. Well, now that you know, can I please return to my class?"

I nod, still bogged down in the quicksand of thought. She notices and addresses me once more. "Jess, we are all living in one world while operating within our own personal little worlds. There will always be an untold story to discover, unimaginable truths to stumble upon, shocking secrets brought to light. My advice to you is to get used to it, ma chérie. You've entered her world looking for her in the fragments she's left behind. You're finding her. Don't be upset about it; don't send yourself into depression by mourning her losses either. Instead, acknowledge her footprints in the sand, pay tribute to their existence, and then, like you must eventually do with all things, let them go."

As I watch her walk away, I take a deep breath in hopes that it may reset my emotions. I was taking things so personally, as though some great wrong had been done me by not being told of Aralyn's pregnancy. Meanwhile, the whole thing is so far removed from me.

In a handful of minutes, I've been slammed with new information I never saw coming. And the Madame is absolutely right, I went looking for it. I was the one who made the decision to explore Aralyn's world. For the second time tonight, I'm having to remind myself not to get lost in it. The question remains, when all is said and done, when I have uncovered all the pieces of her precious life, will I be able to find my way back to *mine*?

I exit the salon, preparing to hail a service car home. Luca will undoubtedly be pissed. I'm sure I won't hear the end of it. However, I don't really care. To be honest, the more I think about what he told me tonight regarding the connection he still has with his father, the more I wonder if I truly am safe with him.

Even though he claims to only maintain a relationship with Maxime to keep Aralyn out of reach, what's to stop him from giving me over if he were asked to? I'm not his sister. He might be willing to make the sacrifice of facing his father's wrath for her, but if it came down to it, would he really do everything in his power to do the same for me, a woman he barely knows?

"JESS!" I groan and turn in the direction of the voice bellowing from down the block. A very irritated Luca makes quick strides toward me. "Have you completely lost all sense?"

"Must you insist on lecturing me like a child?"

"Must you insist on behaving like one? A lecture is too merciful! You deserve a thrashing for the shit you pulled!"

I wave him off. "Whatever. What is it with you Dominants always wanting to spank someone as punishment?"

He folds his arms across his chest as he reaches me. "I was right, you really have lost it. What the hell were you thinking? Were we or were we not just trying to deceive someone who's intent on watching your every move? And how about the part where you left behind the man tasked to guard you from him? Tell me you have amnesia because that's the only explanation that will pardon you from such an insane decision as the one you've made."

"I get it, okay? I made a stupid choice. Happy? Can we go now?"

"Christ, you're so stubborn! Do you not understand that your life is in danger, or is that a concept beyond your comprehension?"

"WHY are you yelling?"

"BECAUSE I'M ANGRY! Angry that you'd risk yourself like this! Angry that you'd jeopardize everything for the sake of doing whatever you want to do!"

"Oh, right, I forgot. If something happens to me, you'll never be able to prove to Alex that you're the oh-so-superior protector." His brow creases as he struggles to find a proper response.

I *almost* feel bad for being so difficult. He's right, after all, it was not a smart move to go off on my own, considering the current circumstances. But my emotions have been yanked in so many directions tonight that I think any filter I had holding them back has become nonexistent.

For a moment, I consider apologizing. But why should I? I didn't say anything that was a lie. Luca isn't in this for me, he's in it for him. The only thing he's trying to protect is his pride.

Jean-Philippe drives up and Luca opens the back door. "Get in."

I fold my arms. I'm growing quite sick of him ordering me around. "I'll get in when I'm ready."

He steps forward till he's standing only inches in front of me. "Get in the car, Jess, or so help me God, I'll—"

"What, *spank* me?"

He swiftly grabs my arm and shoves me in the vehicle. "Let go of me!" I kick my leg out and my heel strikes him in the thigh.

"*Ssss*, mierda!" he yells out. Next thing I know he's on top of me in the seat, my body pinned by his, and his hand grasps my jaw, forcing me to look at him. In a deep tone he cautions, "Try that again and see what happens."

"What would Alex think of you handling me like this?"

"Has anything I've ever done or said given you cause to think I care?"

I glower at him. "I wonder if you'd still say that if he were here."

I continue to stare him down and observe his hard expression gradually soften. "I am not the enemy, Jess. Despite what I said on that jet, I wouldn't be here if I truly didn't wish to keep you from harm."

"What's the second reason?"

"What?"

"The second reason you agreed to look after me. What is it? What do you really want out of all this?"

His thumb softly runs along my chin as he studies my face, then his frown transforms into a mischievous smile. "You really want to know?" I glare at him, annoyed by the question. "Alright then, if it will make you feel more … at ease." He lowers his head to my ear and in a low, velvety tone says, "What I *want* is you on your knees before me. I want to own you, claim you, devour you. I want you trembling beneath me as you cry out my name." I gasp quietly and my belly flutters. The way he speaks, the way his words float through my ear like music that reverberates throughout my body, has a hold on me I can't quite shake. No, no, no, this is *not* how this is supposed to go.

The only thing I can do is feign disinterest. "There's no way on earth I'd fall for you."

He shakes his head. "Mm. I suppose this is the selfish part I spoke of, because it's not your heart I want, Princesa. Your body, on the other hand…" His eyes darken in a lustful way as they sweep to my chest and back up again. "There's so many beautiful things I could do with that."

I need to gain control of this situation and fast. "So, basically, you just want to use me as some worthless fuck toy and walk away."

"Who said anything about worthless? And who said anything about walking away? You can keep me if you'd like." He grins wickedly. "I'd gladly have you as many times and in as many ways as you wish." I'm not sure what pisses me off more, what he said or the fact that it turned me on, and that's incredibly bothersome.

"I don't know why you pretend to give a damn about my safety."

"Oh, I do care. But I can't pretend that my intentions are completely pure. I intend to keep you safe just as much as I intend to have you, to fuck you slow and deep till you lose all sense of your body and you can't see anything but the stars that aligned you with me." The warmth of his breath tickles my skin as he softly nuzzles my neck. My back slightly arches as I give into the tantalizing sensation.

The next thing I know, he swiftly lifts himself off me and gets out, leaning down to say a few last words through the door. "I'll sit in the front, give you time to think things over." At a loss for words and thought, I gaze at him with confusion. He smirks knowingly, and then closes me in.

To hell with him bringing me to my knees, if I'm not careful, he might just bring me to my ruin.

Journal,

I'm so thrilled with this new life! It's been almost a year since I left my father. Almost a year free from his tyranny. I think I might make a special occasion of it. Do something to commemorate such a huge event, one that has truly shifted the course of my life.

I may soon have something else to celebrate as well! Madame Chérot has been incredibly pleased with my progress at the den. I've been the most requested Dominatrix for seven months straight now, and I've heard whispers of a promotion. As to what kind, I'm not sure, but it's such an exciting prospect!

I'm so proud of myself. I went from not knowing a thing about the fetish lifestyle to becoming masterful within it. Since my first lesson, I've been so hungry to learn everything there is, and the more I learn, the more I fall head over heels with it. THIS is where I'm meant to be. THIS is home. After so much trial and struggle, it really did find me.

Journal,

Protégé! Oh my God! Madame Chérot has asked me to be her Protégé!

Oh, I never imagined anything so magnificent. ME! I'm going to be trained to eventually run the company! I've cried more happy tears than I knew I could today.

This is my era for greatness! Countless times I've wondered what greatness tasted like. No more wondering. No more sampling. It's mine to possess fully.

Journal,

I saw them in the window. The perfect pair of stiletto shoes. A glossy black with rich red soles and plain heels that begged to be elevated with a personal touch. I received my bonus today. Guess who got them customized?

These are the type of shoes that make a statement. Now, with the addition of a butterfly on the back of each heel, they will also be unmistakably me. The butterfly is so symbolic of my own personal metamorphosis. With slow agony, I crawled through the dirt while others looked down upon me, watching me with either interest or disgust. Then, I found my sanctuary, a place I felt comfortable enough within to cocoon myself from the world and those who sought to make me miserable. Now, finally, I'm emerging with beautiful, vibrant wings that will take me places I once could only ever dream of.

With this fresh new wave of energy, I am reclaiming who I am. I am fashioning my identity piece by elegant piece. I am becoming the woman I always dreamed of becoming and so much more. Brilliant, beautiful, free.

22

I help Gen with her bags as we enter the airport. She's headed home today. The realization that I'll no longer have her around has made me depressed all morning. I've cherished her presence immensely, especially with everything going on.

It's been years since we've spent quality time together like this, yet it's as though no time has passed at all, which for me is fantastic. Not having had many friends in Paris to begin with, what had happened between me and Arthur was discouraging, causing the concept of friendship to feel warped. I'm unable to express how truly grateful I am for the reminder that true friendship really does exist.

"So, you were out with a certain someone quite late last night," she quips as we stand in line to get her bags checked.

My mind flashes back to the intense and steamy moment we shared in the car. I immediately try to shake it away. "We had to go on a date, you know, for appearance's sake."

"Mhmm. Sure." Her brow arches.

"Don't look at me like that."

"You don't think there's any chance of you developing feelings for that heartthrob of a man?"

I scrunch my nose. "Absolutely not. I know where my heart is."

"True, but you're technically a single woman." She grins. "There's nothing wrong with having options, babes, and he certainly wouldn't be the worst option to have."

"No, he in fact *would* be the worst option. He's Aralyn's brother, first of all. I'm not hooking up with the brother of the woman who's dying wish was for me to be a part of her ex-fiancé's life. Also, he's a menace, a menace who still maintains questionable contact with his psychotic father whom, if I must remind you, is having me stalked. Third, he's an arrogant asshole who thinks he can get his way all the time. My intentions are to gravely disappoint him when I inevitably prove he can't. So, there's no way in hell he's an option."

The man standing in front of us turns around, eyeing me with annoyance. "Occupe-toi de tes oignons!" I remark, telling him to mind his own damn business. He rolls his eyes but faces forward, as he should.

"Hahaha! Damn, I like feisty Jess. Didn't realize Luca was such a touchy subject."

"I'd rather he not be a subject at all."

She continues to laugh. "Fine. We won't discuss him anymore. But seriously, until Alex gives you the commitment you deserve, don't keep yourself from having fun and exploring. Like I've told you, I'm all for him, he's incredible, but I'm team Jess at the end of the day. Speaking of exploring, have you figured out what you're going to do about the whole Aralyn having been pregnant thing?"

"Nothing, I guess. Since the Madame wants me to keep it from Alex, per Aralyn's wish, I'm just going to stick with her request."

"But what about your book? This is an important part of her life. I'm sure she suspected you'd write about that when she gave you the journals. If you do include it, and Alex decides to read the book…"

Then he'll find out the truth. I've thought about that myself. Will it open up old wounds? Surely it would shock him, and who knows if her illness and the pregnancy are the only secrets she kept from him. How do I honor her wish while also protecting his heart? Though, the desire to protect his heart is what's led to so much shock and chaos to begin with. Perhaps it's better that he finally knows every truth she stowed away.

"Honestly, Gen, it's probably one of those 'cross the bridge when you get to it' type things. I might drive myself nuts if I think too much about it right now."

"Completely understandable. I know whenever it's time, you'll figure it out."

"Yeah… *Ugh*, are you sure you have to return to Nebraska?"

"Unfortunately. *But*, listen, if I can figure out a way to move out here, I will in a heartbeat. It would be amazing to explore more of what Paris and the rest of Europe has to offer. To be close to you again would be the cherry on top." I'll do everything in my power to help her make that happen. I need my friend.

Once we get her bags situated and make it to the security checkpoint, I throw my arms around her, and we hug for a long time. "I'm going to miss you like crazy," I tell her.

"Not as much as I'm going to miss you. Keep living your best life, okay? Luca better do his job right, or I'll catch the first flight out to kick his ass."

We release each other and I laugh. "That's if Alex doesn't kick his ass first. Have a safe journey home. Call me when you land?"

"You can count on it." She moves into the line ahead and waves one last time before disappearing into the sea of travelers.

I'm suddenly struck with an overwhelming sense of loneliness. I'm now apart from everyone I care deeply for. It's just me, myself … and Luca.

As I sit in the living room, trying to finish an article I need to have in to the publisher in two days, I find it hard to maintain focus. I glance at Luca who is seated in one of the armchairs, scrolling through his phone, and I begin to sense an all-too-familiar itch. An itch for answers. Although I told Genevieve that the whole ordeal with hiding Aralyn's pregnancy from Alex was something to deal with when it seemed most necessary, it's leaving me gravely unsettled.

"Luca."

"Hmm?" He chuckles, finding something he's watching amusing.

"Can you put me in contact with Aralyn?"

His eyes snap up. "What?"

"You know where she is, and you two have frequent contact. It shouldn't be hard for you to get me in touch with her, right?"

He shakes his head. "No way. Not doing it."

"Why not?"

"First of all, I'm not supposed to be here with you. Remember? She has no idea what's going on."

"Yeah, but—"

"Second, by not having contact with her, you clear yourself of both knowing her whereabouts and having had recent communication with her, in the event you do end up questioned by my father."

"But if I can just talk to her, I'd be able to find out what of her journals she wants me bring to light and what she wants to remain hidden."

"She didn't give you those instructions when she gave them to you?"

"All she said was that she wanted me to tell her story and to keep certain locations and identities a secret."

"Well then, sounds to me like she made it clear what she wanted."

Why is he being so difficult? Sure, I get that not having contact with her makes it easier for me to pass any interrogation by Maxime. However, it would also make it easier for me to know what of her life I should expose to Alex. I can't stand the thought of keeping anything else hidden from him; at the same time, if I somehow go against her wishes, regardless of her eventual passing, I risk the emotional turmoil it could cause him. There's also the fact that I'd likely sour my relationship with the Madame, which is already in a questionable state. In addition, I'm not even sure Luca is aware of Aralyn's pregnancy, either, and if he isn't, who's to say him finding out won't create a whole new set of issues?

I won't be able to please everyone, that much is clear, but it would be nice to choose the least damaging option. If I can just speak with her, perhaps Aralyn can help me in that regard. Folding my arms, I huff in agitation. "I understand your argument, but trust me, I wouldn't be asking this of you if I didn't feel it would be important."

"There's a lot I'd do to help you, Jess, but I am sorry. I can't help you with that."

"Fine, I'll just get Madame Chérot to help me." I haven't a clue whether she can, but it's worth a try at this point.

I pick up my phone from the coffee table, preparing to give her a call when, as quick as lighting, he springs from the chair and grabs it from my hand. "Luca, what the hell are you doing?"

"Why are you so insistent on disobeying me? I told you to leave it alone." I rise to my feet and rush him, lunging for my phone. He holds it higher, just as my hand reaches it, and then looks down at me as his mouth curls with mirth. His arm is wrapped around my torso, keeping me in place against him. "Are you done?"

Just as I'm about to raise hell, the doorbell rings. Our attention is swiftly drawn from our spat. "Are you expecting anyone?" he asks.

"No. Not at all."

The bell rings again, followed by a powerful knock. "Stay here," he says, handing my phone back as he goes to answer, taking a few moments to listen at the door before opening it.

My heart beats ferociously at the thought of who might be on the stoop. However, I don't hear an exchange of words. Instead, Luca steps out. Then, after what seems like entirely too long, I go to the doorway and watch him on the sidewalk, looking anxiously up and down the street.

I call out to him, "Did you see anyone?" He glances back at me, his face marked with worry, then comes back inside. "What is it? What's wrong?"

He looks out one last time before closing the door, then holds out his clenched fist, revealing what's within it. I look at the object, confused. "A business card?"

"My *father's* business card. It was lying on the top step." I take it and give it a proper look. It's white with gold lettering and an unfamiliar emblem depicted on the front. Maxime's name is clear as day.

My stomach jumps to my throat. "He was just here?"

He shakes his head. "It's more likely someone dropped it off for him, perhaps Emil. The bad news is, this is a clear message to you that he wants to talk."

"So, he doesn't believe the whole façade of us being together, then."

"Of that I am unsure. We haven't been seen together long enough for him to draw a firm conclusion. However, what I am sure of is I'm going to have to talk to him myself, first. I'll need to leave you for a few days. I think it's best we arrange for you to stay with the Madame until I get back."

"You can't just give him a call?"

"If it were only that simple. No… There are some things I must discuss with him in person if he's to be convinced you are innocent in every way that counts." I've been mentally preparing myself for something like this all week. I knew it was only a matter of time before Maxime would attempt to speak with me. I guess I had hoped it wouldn't come this soon, and I can tell Luca had hoped so as well. Now he's on a mission to buy us time. How much time will likely be unclear, even after they have a talk, but the longer I can keep away from both his interest and wrath, the better. Suddenly, the idea of fully investing in the role of Luca's girlfriend is like a dream opportunity.

He takes the card and tucks it in his jacket pocket. "This is why it's so important for you to keep a low profile. This is why you shouldn't contact my sister. The closer he gets to you, the closer he might get to her too. So, for now, please, if you've any care for her security and yours, don't do anything reckless by going to look for her."

"Alright, fine." I drop my head in defeat. Lately, it seems like no matter what I do I'm met with trial after trial. In this case, I'm met with a dead end. Damn it, Aralyn. You're so close, yet so incredibly far.

I exhale a long sigh as dread swirls like a tornado on a rampage within me. With no other direction to go, it's now up to me to dictate the outcome of events regarding the unveiling of her life story and the potential unleashing of her secrets. What I choose to write will determine the future.

What an unnerving power to wield.

23

It's been a little over one month since leaving Alex in London. Surprisingly, it's also been over a month of peace. Since Luca spoke with his father, there hasn't been a single ominous note, and neither has there been any sighting of the man who was sent to follow me. It's been so peaceful, in fact, that I've started to become comfortable, allowing myself to relax in the stillness. However, I can't ignore the intuitive part of me that is paranoid about the potential dangers that could still very well be lurking.

Just as planned, I stayed with Madame Chérot while Luca was away. The visit to her estate wasn't as uncomfortable as I thought it would be, particularly because she wasn't around. She had gone overseas to Canada to do an event. So, I enjoyed the week of freedom and quiet. No Madame, no Luca, just me and the house staff, who were instructed to make my stay as pleasant as possible, which they absolutely did.

I could see why Aralyn felt comfortable staying there while she found her wings. There was something about the place, perfectly tucked away, and gated, in the outskirts of Paris. It felt secure, and I was able to focus and get a lot of work done.

When Luca returned, I too returned home. I had tried multiple times to inquire about the conversation he had with his father, but he urged me not to worry about it, and insisted that, for now, Maxime believed him enough that he'd leave me be. It didn't instill a lot of confidence, but I ultimately left it alone, especially as the days and weeks began to roll by without incident.

We continued playing the roles we agreed to take on in public. Shockingly, despite him being ever present, he hasn't been as much of a pest as he started off. Generally, he keeps his distance while also looking out for me as often as necessary. The one constant, however, is the way he looks at me. Although he gives me my space and doesn't say much most days, unless he deems it important, his eyes … they have a language of their own and they speak, LOUDLY. I try to pretend I don't understand. Try to act like I can't tell he's taunting me with his energy, patiently waiting for the day I decide to give in to him.

I don't know what I prefer more, having him say what's on his mind all the time, or his silence layered with heated gazes. I'd be lying if I said it wasn't starting to get to me, tugging at my burning curiosity for all things sexual these days. Of course, it absolutely doesn't help that my body has been yearning for touch and affection. Being around sexual energy at the den several days a week has me severely horny, so he's only making it worse.

Can I be strong? Is my willpower developed enough? Can I be successful in holding out for the man I crave touch and affection from most? Would it be a bad thing if I don't? What am

I saying, of course it would be! I shouldn't be entertaining the idea of Luca at all.

Despite the way my body aches for passion and wild, mind-numbing sex, my heart aches tremendously for Alex. There hasn't been a peep from him. Though I know he's a man of his word, and he meant it when he said no contact, I can't help but wonder if he misses me just as much as I miss him. Does he think about me multiple times a day, every day? Does he crave my touch the way I crave his? Often times when I find myself tumbling down that rabbit hole of thought, I do all I can to re-center my focus on other things, as it does no good to keep on. I wish I'd hear something though, *anything* at this point.

Life at the den has indeed been interesting. After more shadowing and mentorship from the Madame, and occasionally Emory, I've begun going solo, growing stronger in my new position of management, though I still struggle with it. There are so many things about the various lifestyles and elements of the kink world that shock me and are a bit difficult to wrap my head around. I am, however, enjoying the learning process, even if it can become overwhelming when I also have journalism demanding my attention.

It's bizarre. There are times when I'll be conducting an interview for an article, and I'll catch myself wondering if my subject happens to dabble in BDSM. I begin to wonder if I might come across them sometime at the den. It's distracting, though as soon as I catch myself in that web of thought, I do my best to shake it away. Yet, my mind always wanders back eventually.

Today is a work day at the den, and thankfully it's nearing an end. I have one more fetish room to do inventory in and then

I'm free at last. I enter the Ruby Room and halt in my tracks, as I'm faced with the scene of one of the Mistresses giving a client a firm lashing across his ass. The frayed whip cuts into his skin causing dark bruises and abrasions, some of which bleed a little. My stomach churns at the sight.

The Mistress whips her head toward me, confused, and seemingly irritated. "Pardon!" I mouth and swiftly back out, shutting the door and leaning my head against it, doing my best to control my breath in the midst of my queasiness and mortification.

"Are you okay, Madame Rivers?" I quickly stand erect and see a concerned Emory staring at me.

"Yeah, totally." My embarrassed laugh only makes it more evident that I'm lying through my teeth. "Um, actually no. If you couldn't tell yet, I'm not the best at this job."

She gives an amused smirk. "What happened?"

"I must have gotten the timetable mixed up, or maybe the rooms? I don't know. I thought this room was unoccupied. I came to do an inventory check but there's a session."

She gestures for me to hand my tablet to her and then takes a look at the availability chart. "Hmm, no you got it right. Let me guess, Mistress Mel is in there?" I nod. "Thought so. The Ruby Room is her favorite to work out of. She has a bit of a rebellious streak and doesn't always do well with authority. Most of the staff will follow the rules religiously, as they should; they certainly get paid well enough. But there are one or two who, from time to time, like to break them. My guess is she's testing the waters with the new girl to see how much she can get away with." She hands the tablet back. "Don't let anyone here walk over you or take you for weak. You are the boss. You'll need to talk to her."

"Thank you."

"Of course." She begins to leave but pauses. "Hey, you're done here soon, right?"

"Yeah, now I will be. I'll probably just come in early to do the inventory for this room tomorrow. Why do you ask?"

"A few of us are going to the bar for drinks. Would you like to join? There is a good one not far from here and their food is also très délicieux."

I laugh. "Are bosses allowed to have outings with staff around here?"

"I don't see why not."

"Did Aralyn?"

Her smile is warm. "Who cares? You are not Aralyn." Something about the statement brings me a surprising amount of comfort. This struggle to separate my own life from the auburn-haired beauty's has still been difficult, especially as I delve deeper into her role. Even the thigh-length, black, leather and lace dress I'm wearing is reflective of her style. Any validation I receive that I am in fact not her, is music to my ears.

"Well, when you put it like that, I'd love to go."

"Bien! I'll be outside when you're finished. Oh, and you'll want to have a talk with Mistress Mel before we go. She shouldn't be too much longer. Don't allow her to leave here thinking she got away with, well … disobedience." She winks and proceeds toward the exit.

I sigh, still haunted by what I saw a few minutes ago, and try to rebuke the image from my mind. I'm not sure I'll ever get used to the things I'll be exposed to with this job. However, I suppose the unpredictability of it is what makes this a true adventure.

❤

$\mathcal{M}$istress Mel storms out of my office, loudly expressing to herself her feelings regarding my "audacity" to flaunt my "uneducated authority" around the den. Yeah, she's going to be a handful. Perfect. I close my eyes and pinch the bridge of my nose, sensing a slight headache coming on. I suspect it's partially due to her yelling, but more likely due to the stress that my first full day as madam has placed on me.

There's a knock at the opened door, and I lift my head to the sight of Luca leaning against the doorpost, with both hands in the pockets of his denim jeans. His hair is down today and flowing over his shoulders. The De la Rues have truly been blessed with beauty.

"Long day?"

I groan. "The longest."

"The way Mel is throwing a fit down the hall, I can imagine so." He struts in. "I saw Emory outside. We are going for drinks?"

"Hope that's okay. I don't know about you, but I could really use one."

"Of course. It will probably be the most thrilling place I've followed you to so far."

I chuckle and shake my head. "No one is ever forcing you to go with me, you know."

"Ah, but then I wouldn't be a man of my word, would I?" He comes to a stop in front of me, a little too close for comfort. His very scent makes me squirm in delicious ways, and it annoys me to no end that that's the case.

Per usual, I must be doing a horrible job keeping the lust hidden from my body language. He's caught on to how he's affecting me and laughs lightly. "Anytime, Princesa. You don't have to keep torturing yourself. All you have to do is tell me you want it."

"Yeah? Well, I don't, so."

"Look me in the eyes and say that if you mean it."

My lashes flutter as I look up at him. I open my mouth to speak, but his gaze catches me off guard. He's once again staring at me like I'm a precious jewel he's pleased to possess.

"I don't know why you insist on continuing this," I say.

"Well, despite your stubbornness and consistent attitude toward me, I find you to be an attractive woman. I could have some fun with you." He grins. "I like fun."

"*Ugh*. Get over it."

He leans in, placing both hands on my desk on either side of me. His eyes, those piercing bluish-green eyes, bore into my own, locking in. "Is that what you're trying to tell yourself right now, to get over it?" I squeeze my thighs together, doing my best to control my body's explicit urges. He notices this little movement and chortles. "Now who's the delusional one?"

I inhale sharply as his face inches dangerously close to mine and his breath brushes softly against my lips. "I'm with Alex, Luca." This will be my one and only gentle reminder to him.

"Are you?" He cocks his head to one side and his mouth pulls into a playful smile. "Because a little bird told me your beloved Alexander is so heartbroken over my sister that he can't possibly commit to you right now. Doesn't sound like you're with him to me."

What little bird? And what am I doing still sitting here, letting him talk to me like this? I should have left five minutes ago. I should slap him for even having the gall to invade my space as he is now. There are so many other things I could be doing besides sitting here taking this, this … taunting.

I push him aside as I stand, my knees knocking with adrenaline. "You don't know Jack shit about me, or my relationship with him."

"Oh, but you see, I do." He steps up to me again, hovering so near that I can feel the lustful energy pouring from him, enveloping me. "I know that he's simply been entertaining you while you waste time waiting for him to offer you his love. You're a smart woman. You and I both know how Alexander Marc can be. He'd rather suffer in silence than give in to his desire to have you, especially while Aralyn still breathes."

"You're wrong."

"Am I? Sure, I may not know all the intimate little details of your connection. But I've known that man far longer than you. If you think that by sticking by his side he'll choose you in the end, I urge you to seriously reconsider how much hope you put into that outcome." In this moment, I'm not sure what's worse, that he's telling me this, or that I think there could be truth to what he's saying.

"Come now, Princesa. It's about time you were honest with yourself. I've studied the way your body reacts whenever I am near. You keep yourself closed off, and for what, a man who has deprived you of what you want? What you need?" He takes another step closer and gently cups my cheek, running his thumb across my flushed skin. "I can at very least satisfy your body's needs if you let me."

"Once again, you're delusional."

"And you're in denial." He leans in, nearly touching his forehead to mine. "Tell me then. Tell me you don't want me, and I will walk away." As I fumble my words, my breathing quickens. He gradually lowers his mouth toward mine, carefully gauging my reaction as he moves in. I stand frozen, so uncertain, because what my body cries for and what my mind screams at me to do are two separate things. I shouldn't yearn for this, certainly not with him. It would be ridiculous. It would be going too far. Aralyn asked me to cherish Alexander's heart, not mess around with her brother. But … I'm not stopping him. Why am I not stopping him?

With no request to halt his actions, his lips fall upon mine. His tender kiss is like being wrapped in a fleece blanket in winter, soft, warm, and gentle. It soothes the nervous chill that had raced through my body and brought rise to the goosebumps on my flesh.

Against my better judgement, I kiss him back, soaking in the sensation. He places both hands on the small of my back, drawing me against him, and slowly walks forward, causing me to step back till I'm once again trapped between him and my desk. His bulging erection is pressed firmly against my abdomen, and his tongue sweeps across mine as he deepens the kiss. Then, he gently nips and tugs my lower lip with his teeth. I moan, completely exhilarated by this moment. Fuck, he's so damn good at this.

To my surprised disappointment, he stops, pulling back ever so slightly to gaze into my eyes. "There it is, that's the response I've been looking for," he coos.

My brain has another go at logic. "We shouldn't be doing this."

He silences me with his index and middle fingers pressed delicately against my lips. "*Shhhh*. Let's not ruin a good time with needless worry." Those same fingers gradually travel south, sliding across my skin. "Tell me when to stop." Down, down, down they go, over my collar bone, over the peak of my right nipple that's straining against the lacy fabric of my dress. Down over my abdomen, where my nerves fire rapidly, causing the muscles deep in my belly to constrict in a delicious way. All the while his eye contact is unbroken, as he watches me closely to not miss a single reaction, and waits for me to give up the need to control my responses, challenging me to say the word he hopes I will not utter.

My mind insists that I tell him to fuck off like I've managed to do every time before. But I'm full of hesitation at present, especially as his fingers reach the bottom hem of my dress and slowly start to reroute up my inner thigh. I should be pushing him away, but I can't. I can't move. And I can't tell him to stop because I … I don't think I want him to.

His fingers finally reach their target, and to his delight, he discovers I'm not wearing panties. Of course, this would happen on the one day I opted to be without them. He instantly feels the slick pool of my arousal, and grins with enthusiasm. Then, with a deep groan, his other hand grasps the back of my neck and he slides his knee between my legs, pushing them open.

"God, I love how wet you are for me. You can lie to yourself as much as you want, Princesa, but I know the truth." His thumb circles my clit and I shudder against him. "Alexander can have your mind and your heart, but your body is mine." I want to argue his bold and ignorant statement, but as his fingers slowly plunge into my slit, I can do nothing but gasp with pleasure. Taking advantage of that, his mouth encloses around mine, his tongue dancing while his fingers enact a soul-snatching dance of their own that is almost too much to take.

Any chance I had of talking myself out of this is gone. Logic no longer stands a chance. It's all lust. Pure, unbridled lust, and I'm lost in it.

The motion of his hand accelerates, and with expert skill, he's hitting my G-spot while the edge of his palm grinds against my clit. My legs tremble. My knees can barely hold me up. "It's okay to let go, mi amor. You don't have to fight it." He's right, I am fighting it. I'm fighting hard. Perhaps logic still has a chance after all.

As much as my body desires release, it's quite difficult to allow myself permission to give in to it. If I give in, he knows for certain he has won. If I give in, I will be proving to myself that I do in fact crave this man, something I've been desperately trying to convince myself isn't the case. But fuck, this feels so damn good, and he looks, smells and tastes so damn good.

He works his fingers so methodically and masterfully that I become fully aware I'm losing the battle. What control I've tried to maintain is slipping from my grasp to his. "Luca, please," I whimper and moan, but it's too late for reasoning. I close my eyes as they roll back into my head, and I buck against his hand as a large tremor radiates through me and I cry out in ecstasy.

After a few electrifying moments, my knees give way, and I crumple to the floor, heaving, as my pussy continues to clench and pulsate. Luca crouches down to my level, his hand glistening with evidence of his good work. He cracks a devilish smile and slowly licks his fingers clean while observing me trying to catch my breath. "You taste better than I dreamed you would. Maybe next time, I'll let you taste me too."

"There won't be a next time." My voice quavers.

He laughs and rises to his feet. "Oh, how I enjoy proving you wrong." He reaches a hand down to help me up. "One day, you will see what I already know."

"And what's that?" I ask, ignoring his offered help and lean against my desk for stability as I stand.

"That no matter what happens, I'm the man you won't be able to stop thinking about in the end. The man you'll want to return to, over and over again." He gestures toward my office door that is still wide open. "Let's not keep our friends waiting, and go get that drink. Besides, I feel like celebrating."

I am flushed with a mixture of satisfaction and guilt at war with one another in my spirit. What have I done? What am I doing? What will I do?

Journal,

I had a bizarre interaction today, one I can't quite shake from my thoughts. The Madame came by the den to work with a trainee client, which is rare. Only a select handful of individuals have the honor of calling her their Mistress. Prior to her session starting, she had told me she'd been expecting a call, and requested that if the call were to come while she was giving her lesson, that I contact her immediately.

The call did come through and, per her request, I brought the phone to her while she was in the middle of a play session with the trainee. She gave orders to the submissive man to finish cleaning up the coffee she had purposefully spilled on the cream carpet, and I waited as she walked to the corner of the room to take the call. Despite her demands, however, the sub didn't move. He just stood there, staring at me with eyes that were strikingly gray behind the black leather eye mask he wore.

I criticized him. "What are you looking at? Did you not hear your Mistress? Get back on the floor and scrub!" He slowly dropped to his knees, but his eyes, those soul-piercing eyes, never left mine. I started to panic! How was I to respond? His session wasn't with me. I didn't know all his needs. I'd barely even witnessed how the Madame was with him.

All I could think was, would I be crossing a boundary if I give commands? And if I didn't, would I look foolish? Would I look exactly how I felt in that moment, inexperienced?

I tried to place my attention elsewhere, but I could feel his gaze locked on to me and it was hard to ignore. In a firm, yet lowered voice, as to not disturb the Madame's call, I said, "You worthless idiot! Have you been given permission to look at me?"

"No, Mistress." My breath hitched, caught off guard by his response, said with such calm defiance.

I bent down to meet his eyes, still heavily trained on mine, and in a much lower and more disciplinary tone I replied, "I am not your Mistress. Don't ever refer to me as that again." Then he just smiled at me! I couldn't believe it. It was like a complete mockery!

"As you wish," he responded.

Being as close as I was to him, I could clearly see the subtle joyful expression on his face. He knew exactly what he was doing. That man wasn't like Madame's other pets. He knew I had no real authority over him, and he loved it.

Oh, journal, I felt so embarrassed! I quickly stood upright and did not hesitate a moment longer when Madame walked over and handed me back the phone. I made a hasty exit. As I did, I could overhear her scolding him for not doing as she had asked, letting him know he'd be promptly punished. I glanced back as I was walking out the door and, for the first time, his focus was not on me. He proceeded to bow to her and apologize.

No client has ever challenged me the way he did, nor looked at me the way he did, and I'm still trying to understand what that look even meant. Whatever it meant, I've been unable to shake the memory all day. Perhaps I am overanalyzing things. Maybe he's simply a strange man with no manners and a developing fetish for pushing my buttons, but why would I be so turned on by that?

Anyway, that's my rambling for the day. Hopefully it's all back to normal tomorrow, whatever normal actually is, haha. Learning the ins and outs of the business is no easy task, but I've been enjoying every bit of it! No day is ever the same. It's an exciting, thrilling little life.

24

I wouldn't say I'm completely inebriated, as I stumble through the front door, giggling like a loon. I'd say I'm one drink shy of drunk, though some might argue I'm already there. The wild thing is, I'm not laughing at anything other than myself. What happened with Luca tonight is still frustrating me. I'm being hard on myself, perhaps unreasonably so, but my heart is feeling terribly guilty.

I sit on the stairs in the foyer and lean against the staircase, still a giggling mess. Luca closes the door and looks at me questioningly. "Care to fill me on what's so amusing?"

I blow some strands of hair out of my face and smirk. "Oh, nothing. Just laughing at silly ol' me and my silly little decisions that get me caught up in silly predicaments."

He squats down in front of me. "Mm. Care to elaborate?"

I drag my finger up in the air and point at him. "You and I can never happen again."

"Where was this energy twenty minutes ago when you practically pleaded with me to kiss you before we left the bar?"

"I'm under the influence of alcohol, which makes me severely sex crazed. You can't hold that against me." I grip the rail and pull myself to a stand and he rises too. "NEVER again, Luca. All I really want is Alex."

"He will never truly be yours, you know." Here we go again.

My eyes narrow as I glare at him coldly. "Right. I'm sure you wish that was the case. I personally really wish you'd shut up about your distaste for him. It's obsessive and weird."

"I'm just trying to help you see clearly."

"News flash, I don't need your help. I'm not some damsel in distress that needs to be rescued from the clutches of Alexander Marc."

"I think you might be. Only, you don't see it."

I scoff. "God, you are so atrociously hellbent on talking shit about him, and for what? Because Aralyn was hurt by your father during the time she was in a relationship with him? You, of all people, know that man is a raging lunatic! But you'd much rather believe that Alexander being with your sister is what hurt her the most, and not the man who was supposed to love her all her life."

Silence lingers like a thick plume of suffocating smoke between us. He exhales a long, drawn-out breath before replying, "You read her journals, yeah? So, I'm sure you know she was pregnant and miscarried."

So, he *is* aware of her pregnancy after all. I fold my arms across my chest to keep my hands from shaking with frustration. "I haven't reached that part of her journals yet, but yes, I know."

"Are you also aware of how she lost the baby?"

"No."

"Then you don't understand. I warned that man that every minute he stayed with Aralyn he was putting her in danger. He told me not to worry, that he'd protect her; he told me he'd never let anything happen to her. HE PROMISED ME! And then our father had information retrieved from her doctor shortly after her appointment and found out about her pregnancy.

"Not only would a baby ruin the plans he had for her, he couldn't stand the thought of having a blood tie to Alexander. So, he hired a few men to go to her home and attack her. Told them to be certain they left her face clear of any injuries." My stomach turns, nauseous at the notion that a man could be so cruel to his own child. Oh Aralyn … you deserved so much better.

"If it wasn't for me rushing in when I did and spooking them, they likely would have taken her to Maxime. I was the one who had to witness my poor sister lying on the floor, in the dark, hemorrhaging and barely conscious. I was the one who took her to the hospital. Marc never even showed his face!" Luca's fists ball up at his sides. "I wanted to kill him. And the ONLY thing preventing me from doing so was her. I didn't want her to wake up from such horror to news of her lover's demise, and at my hand. Her love protected him so much more than he'll ever know."

"Oh my god." Realization strikes me like an electric shock. "Luca, Alex didn't know! Madame Chérot told me he had no idea she was pregnant. I doubt he ever even knew about what Maxime had done to her that night!"

"It doesn't matter. She paid for his arrogance. If he would have left her alone, none of it would have happened." I see it now. There truly isn't anything I can do or say to convince him that

Alex is innocent. He already condemned him, completely vilified him for ignoring his pleas to leave his sister be. And the most twisted thing about it is that Alex truly does not know why he's so hated, and may never know. For the knowledge of any bit of what's just been revealed to me will surely shatter him.

At the sight of my dismayed face, Luca softens. "I'm sorry for upsetting you, Jess, but I don't believe he can be the man you want him to be, no matter what he may say to make you feel otherwise. For him, it's not about love. It's merely about possession."

He reaches for my hand and I snatch it away. "I can't believe you," I say with disgust.

"Please, try to understand. He—"

"You're so horribly wrong. You know, maybe if you weren't so blinded by rage you'd be able to see that the fault doesn't lie with him. It lies with you!" His face contorts with confusion. "You feel guilty because *you* didn't protect Aralyn. So, you'd rather force the narrative that Alex is to blame for what happened."

"What? No, I—"

"You were too much of a coward to stand up to your own father! Why not take some accountability and admit you begged Alex to leave her to spare you from the shame of not being man enough to protect her yourself." His mouth falls agape, but nothing other than air comes out. "And, you know, maybe that's what irritated you the most about him, knowing that he had bigger balls than you ever did." He knows there isn't anything he can say in defense that wouldn't be a lie. He knows it.

"Loving someone isn't a crime, Luca. If so, then the only thing he seems guilty of is loving her deeply. I'm not sure the same can be said for you."

There's another long period of intense silence as both of us stand, staring at one another incredulously, consumed by our emotions. He's trying to wrap his head around what just happened, and I … I am exhausted. My whole being has been pulled every which way tonight, and this eruption has drained what little I had left keeping me together.

I can tell I bruised this man's ego, big time. I can tell my words were like a gut punch he didn't see coming. What I can't tell is whether even an ounce of what I've said has gotten through to him. Was all this energy I've used up trying to get him to see the error in his thoughts and projections worth it, or wasted?

After a few more moments, he throws his hands up, appearing hurt and deflated. "Do what you want. After all, protecting your heart isn't part of my job description." He breezes past me up the stairs and I sigh in defeat.

Wasted.

<hr>

*T*here have been so many times in the past couple months that I have questioned my choices. And far too many times I seemingly choose paths that thrust me deeper into chaos. I reflect on this as I uncomfortably sit on the patio of a local restaurant for breakfast with Luca. Not that it was at all my choice to have him here with me. I've been checking my phone several times an hour since early this morning, wondering if I somehow missed a call or text that would let me know this arrangement between us can finally end.

For the most part, he hasn't said a word to me, which I prefer. There's no use in exchanging words. The man is foolish, arrogant, and maddening. He'll never take accountability for his own faults; clearly, it's far too difficult for him to set aside pride and admit that he's projecting on Alex something he cannot face within himself.

There is a part of me wondering if I had perhaps been too harsh on him last night. He was, after all, quite vulnerable in opening up to me about a situation that was traumatizing to experience. But the way he's acting today, unconcerned, as though the argument we had never occurred, has convinced me I may not have been harsh enough.

I stare at him for a while as I sip my tea, trying to work out exactly what fuels his utter audacity. Several minutes go by before he finally notices. "What's wrong? Don't tell me you're still upset over yesterday."

"Don't tell me you still hate a man just to deflect from your own guilt."

"Not this again," he huffs, bringing his cappuccino to his lips.

I take his desire to change the subject as an opportunity to ask something I've been curious about for weeks. "Tell me, what did Alex whisper to you when we were getting off the jet?"

A sly smile glides up the side of his face. "He told me I'd better keep my hands to myself."

"And you find that amusing?"

He shrugs. "I find it interesting. He likely foresaw the possibility you might … *enjoy* my company."

"I don't." My cheeks grow hot, and I look away, irritated. I don't understand what's wrong with me. I don't know how I could have ever let Luca get that close. No matter how many times I've tried to chalk it up to being incredibly horny, and even tipsy at one point, I can't help but wonder if those are sufficient excuses. Those things have never kept me from dodging a man's advances before.

So, why didn't I push him away? Why did I allow myself to go there? Was I that desperate for affection? Do I lack so much self-control? Or is it something else entirely, something I may in fact be choosing to turn a blind eye to?

Sure, he is an attractive man, very attractive. I've known that since day one. But physical attraction has never been the sole stamp of approval that would give my legs cause to spread. And it couldn't possibly be his character that made my knees weak. So, where is the crack that allowed him to seep through, that allowed him to penetrate my defenses?

"Don't worry, Princesa. It will be our secret."

I glare at him. "I don't appreciate how much joy you're getting out of this."

"And that is your issue, right there. You never allow yourself to just enjoy having what you want out of life, even if it's as simple as my touch satisfying your deep need for pleasure. I always knew I'd win you over."

If I could imagine how I look in this moment, I'd picture one of those cartoon characters with steam billowing out of their ears right before they're about to throw a fit. "This is all a game to you, isn't it? This was never about an interest in me, it was just some challenge to get in my pants, all so you could feel like more of a man for fondling the woman your enemy is infatuated with. No wonder you're still lonely and bitter. Who wants to be with someone who finds satisfaction in making pawns out of women? Guess that's one thing you got from good ol' dad, huh?"

Luca stares at me, wide eyed, bewildered, and horribly speechless. I quickly rise from my seat and throw my cloth napkin on the table. "I'm out of here."

"Jess, don't. Jess!"

I rush out of the restaurant and make my way down the street. I have no idea where I'm headed, but as long as it's away from him, I don't give a shit. He can't keep getting away with treating people like toys he can fuck around with whenever he wants, with no repercussions. Screw him! Screw his poor excuse for a father! And screw Paris, I am so sick of this place!

I come upon a fountain a few blocks away and sit on the edge of it, burying my face in my hands. Besides the tragedy that was last night, the gravity of everything else weighs on me like a boulder upon my back. This is not the life I pictured for myself, a life of constant chasing and being chased. A life of secrets and schemes and deception. All I want is to continue growing in my field as a journalist, and to be by Alexander's side without having to fear for my life. Is it truly too much to hope for? Am I an absolute idiot for once again thinking there could be a happy ending waiting for me at the end of all this?

The thought of packing up my most important belongings and hightailing it back to America in the dead of night to regroup and start again sounds more tempting every day. And logically, I'd be safe there; I could remain until this all blows over. I'd put great distance between myself and my unknown stalker *and* I'd be out of Maxime's sight. That has to be a far better alternative than putting myself through all of this. Aralyn would understand me turning down the house and her position as madam. I'm certain she would. This can't be what she envisioned for me, either.

I wipe my tears with the beautiful red handkerchief she had given me the very last time we spoke, retrieved from within my pocketbook. Then, I turn it over in my hands and run my thumb along the gold butterfly stitched in the fabric. I wonder how many of her own tears she wiped away with this before passing it to me.

The wind whips through the small courtyard, bringing with it a slight chill, along with all the other signs that fall is upon us. I wrap my arms around myself and then spot a crumbled ball of paper tumbling toward me in the breeze. I catch it with my heel and pick it up. Once I get it unraveled, I inhale sharply as I fall into shock, in disbelief of what I'm looking at. It's a missing person flyer, and to my astonishment, the missing woman pictured is Aralyn De la Rue. There's a one-million-dollar reward on any information that leads to her return.

The wind whips harder, and amidst the rustling of leaves, the rustling of paper can also be heard in the distance. I glance up and gaze at the wall of a neighboring building, covered with these flyers that are flapping in the breeze. The lump of fear in my throat is hard to swallow.

These flyers can only mean one thing: Maxime is tired of waiting for results. He's taking any means necessary to find his daughter, even going as far as to involve the public, which is the last thing any of us thought he would do. He's a dangerous man on a desperate mission, which is a potent combination.

The question is, what does his any-means-necessary approach mean for me?

Journal,

Luca came by the other day and begged me to return home. Tried to use the fact that I've been receiving treatment for my cancer as a reason, implying I'd have better access to the resources I need to heal quicker. But no reason is good enough.

My brother is blind to reality and possibly terrified of truth. The truth is, though my body may be ill, I don't feel as ill as I did when I lived under our father's roof. There is a toxicity there that makes cancer seem like a simple bout of the flu. Imagine that.

What's incredible is, when I went to my doctor appointment today, I received the most amazing news. I'm in remission! I cried such joyful tears. I can't express how proud I am of my body and how proud I am of my mental fortitude. With a mind that tortured my spirit so many times in the past with the desire to give up, I made it through.

My father would rather me be weak. He'd rather I be so weak that I need him.

Instead, I'm so much stronger than he'll ever know.

25

a nightmare, that's all this is. I tell myself this as I'm being ripped away from Alexander by a tidal wave in the sea.

He's trying his hardest to get to me as I cry out for him, but it's no use, we drift farther apart from each other. In an instant, I'm pulled underneath the water by some unseen force, internally begging for breath. My body begins to convulse, and the shaking becomes more and more violent until my eyes fly open. I'm met with Luca's panic-stricken face and his hands gripping my shoulders. "Jess, get up. Get up now!"

"Wha-what's going on?" I rub sleep from my eyes, trying to get my bearings.

He hurries to my closet grabbing a suitcase and placing it open next to me. "I put some clothes for you on the bathroom counter. Hurry and change, then come grab whatever is important to you and let's go."

I'm so incredibly confused by what he's saying. The room is still blanketed with the darkness of night. "What's happening?"

"No time, Princesa. Hurry!"

I groggily roll out of the bed and make my way to the bathroom to change into the short white summer dress he laid out for me with a navy sweater. When I finish, I return to the bedroom to see him busy throwing any clothes he can find into a suitcase. I hurry as best I can to collect my toiletries and my satchel, with all my work documents and Aralyn's journals. It's still not hitting me that I'm about to be whisked away somewhere. Hell, it's still not hitting me that I'm awake. Somehow, this feels like it's just an extension of my nightmare.

"Quickly, Jess! Quickly!"

I look at the time on my nightstand. It's four in the morning. I groan, "Please, for the love of all things good, tell me what I'm doing all this for." The doorbell rings and I turn, startled by the sound at such an unfavorable hour of morning. Luca doesn't even appear to flinch as he continues to grab clothes. "Who is tha—"

"Jess, pack!" The urgency in Luca's expression earlier is very much evident in his tone, and *now* it's hitting me that this is not a dream, but a very real threat is looming. I pick up my pace and finish grabbing whatever I can that is of importance to me.

In less than a minute, Luca zips up the bag and grabs his tote. Then, we both book it down the stairs. "Whatever happens," he says quietly as we make our way to the front door, "let me do the talking."

He opens the door and there stands a tall, slender man dressed in all black. He looks young, maybe in his late thirties, bald, and cold eyes with a look in them that would intimidate the hell out of anyone.

"Buen dia, Emil. Surprised to see you here," Luca says, feigning calm surprise.

The man speaks up, his voice low and raspy. "I could say the same for you."

Despite his Spanish greeting, Luca continues the conversation with him in French. "I'm visiting my—Oh, I suppose you may not know yet." He grabs my hand and pulls me out the door to his side. "Allow me to introduce you to Jess, my girlfriend."

I display my most convincing smile, praying he doesn't notice the terror I feel. Emil stares me down, highly suspicious of what he's hearing, and then looks back at Luca. "I'm certain you're aware of the interest she's stirred."

"I am, and I've already spoken to my father about it."

The strange man glances down at our bags. "Going somewhere?"

"We are, actually. I booked a trip for the week, and we happen to be running late. Good to see you." We start past him, down the stairs, but then Luca stops and glances back at him. "By the way … why exactly are you here?"

Emil looks at me again, his expression emotionless, but the way his jaw works tells me he's irritated. "You know why I'm here."

Luca looks at me before replying, "Ah, right. Seems unnecessary to involve you, though. If my father needs to speak with her, he can tell me that himself. I'm sorry you had to waste your morning this way. See you around, yeah?"

We start toward my car again when Emil calls out, "*Where* exactly are you headed, Luca?"

Luca's grip on my hand tightens and he pivots to address the man once more. "Respectfully, it's none of your business, Emil."

"I have my orders."

"And your orders are to what? Interrogate me?" He drops my hand and walks up to him. "I highly doubt it. Suppose I let him know of your unwarranted interrogation of me. You're also making my partner uncomfortable, which I have a problem with. Perhaps I will make him aware of that as well. I've known you for many years, and I happen to like you. Please don't give me reason not to."

The man remains as composed as ever; he even smiles slightly. "My apologies. Have a good trip." He said it a little too nonchalantly for my comfort.

Luca says nothing else; he simply comes back to me, reclaiming my hand in his and leads me away. "Give me your keys," he quietly commands. I slip them to him as discreetly as possible and we load into the car.

As we drive away, I catch Emil still standing at the bottom of the stoop, following us with his gaze. My stomach churns wickedly. "He showed up so early." I said it more to myself, but Luca heard.

"Most people are still asleep. The streets are quiet. It's the perfect time for a visit that could go wrong."

"He came to hurt me?"

"He came to suggest that you go with him."

"And if I refused?"

He's silent for a bit before answering. "Then he would have forced you to go." *Forced me to go*. The weight of those words sit on my spirit in a manner I've never experienced. Things could have gone so horribly wrong.

"Take me to the airport."

He looks over at me like I've lost my mind. "I can't do that."

"Take me, damn it! I need to get out of this god-forsaken city!"

"Don't worry, we're leaving, but it won't be by air."

No way my plans are going to be foiled yet again. "Turn this car around and take me to the fucking airport! Now!"

"For Christ's sake, woman! Would you for once trust me to do the job I'm risking my livelihood to do?"

I stare at him, stupefied. Am I being unreasonable here? It's possible. Luca hasn't given me reason to not trust him with my protection; even Alexander trusted him, despite their rift. Perhaps I do need to chill out and let him worry about getting me to safety, and see where this goes.

"You're right. I'm sorry. I was acting like a brat."

He smirks. "Wouldn't be the first time." I roll my eyes in annoyance.

I notice that Luca keeps looking up at the rear-view mirror, and it moves me to look at my side view mirror. There's a black car with tinted windows behind us. "Are we being followed?"

"Looks that way. Though I don't recognize the vehicle. We don't drive those."

After a minute, it dawns on me that this could be the individuals Alex told me he had employed to keep an eye on me. I can't be sure. However, the possibility brings me some comfort. I consider telling him this but decide to keep it to myself a bit longer. After all, who knows how he might take the knowledge of Alex procuring backup because he doesn't fully trust him to not fuck up. I want this man's focus to strictly be on getting us to safety.

"I have an idea. Hold on to something." In an instant, Luca's foot bears down on the gas pedal, and we fly down the street at an accelerated speed for several blocks while I hold on for dear life. Maintaining excellent control of the vehicle, he quickly turns a corner, peeling into a parking garage and racing up the ramp to the top floor. He then drifts straight into a parking spot.

"I'll get the bags. Run to the lift, quick!" I bolt out of the car and sprint to the elevator. Before I know it, he is behind me with our luggage and I hear the sound of a revving engine growing closer.

We both enter and just as the doors begin to close, I catch a peek at the car that was following us making it up to our floor. We breathe heavily as adrenaline courses through our veins. The minute the elevator arrives at the ground level and the doors open, Luca shouts, "Get to the exit! Vamos!" I book it outside and he orders me up the street to an area with service cars. I hail the first one I see, and we hop in the back seat, bags and all. In French, Luca explains to the driver, who's looking at us quizzically, that we are late for our train and need to get to the station right away. The man matches our urgency and is on his way before I can reach for my seatbelt.

As we catch our breath, I lean my head back against the seat and laugh, sweeping my hand through my sweat dampened hair. "I can't believe this is my life."

"You're surprisingly lighthearted about this," Luca says, unamused.

"Trust me, my laughter is to keep from crying."

"Everything's going to be fine."

"Yeah … sure. Anyway, how did you know Emil was going to show up?"

"About thirty minutes before I woke you, one of my father's men, who I'm good friends with, called to tip me off. Said Emil had been sent to come collect you. Despite the conversation I had with my father, I guess he still feels there's something you know about Aralyn's whereabouts that you're not telling him or me."

"Wait, had he said that to you previously, that he suspected I had that type of information?"

He sighs as though preparing to explain himself. "Yeah. When I went to talk with him, he mentioned his suspicions."

"Why didn't you tell me?"

"Would it have made a difference? If anything, it would have made you more nervous."

"Damn right it would have, but at least I could have better prepared myself for his potential actions as a result. Instead, I was settling into the idea that he'd leave me be!" My gaze drifts out the window, my mind riddled with worry. "Maybe I should just talk with him and get it over with. I don't know anything about where she is, nor am I able to get in contact with her. If he speaks to me, maybe he'll realize this and leave me alone for good."

"It's not that simple."

"How could it not be?"

"If he can't use you for information, he'll hold you as a hostage for the purposes of negotiating."

"EXCUSE ME? Hostage? Negotiating with who?"

"With me. I used to always be the one to find my sister and bring her back. Over the years, however, I know he's found it strange that the thing I did so well became such a great challenge.

He hasn't told me to my face that he suspects me of lying to him and hiding Aralyn, but I'm certain he'd keep it to himself. Keep his suspicions hidden from me until he can find the perfect pressure point that pushes me to do all I can to bring him what he wants. I told him we're dating, so, if I truly know the type of man he is, the pressure he'll apply is you."

I don't understand; it's like we are running around in giant circles. Telling Maxime that we're dating was supposed to be the best choice to keep me safe and not complicate matters more. How have we now reached the point where we are on the run from him? Even to face him in an effort to prove I don't have what he wants would still be risking so much. "That man is on a major power trip. The fact that he came into money and, of all things, chose to use it to torment his family and build his own personal Mafia is insanity."

"It's unfortunately much deeper than that."

The driver drops us at the train station and as we step out, I glance around, slightly paranoid that someone may still be following us. I spot no one other than a lady crossing the street with her own bags in tow. The sun hasn't yet appeared, leaving only streetlights to illuminate the eerily quiet street.

As we make our way up to the platform to wait for a train, it dawns on me that I haven't a clue where we are headed. "So, you gonna tell me where we're going?"

"Florence." Florence? Odd choice.

"Why there?"

"You'll see." Once again, he's keeping information from me, which is sending me into a tizzy. Since the moment Alex assigned Luca as my bodyguard, I've questioned his decisions and ability to ensure my security. I keep telling myself that if Alex trusted him, it must be okay for me to trust him too, but I'm beginning to see that reasoning may not hold for me much longer.

I'll keep my mouth shut on the matter for now, and see how this plays out. When we get to Florence, if something still seems off, I will separate from him and do what I need to do to protect myself, with no hesitation. For now, I change the subject. "Madame Chérot is going to be so pissed. Again."

"She'll understand."

"This is the second time I've bailed on her and the den. I'm not too sure that's going to be acceptable in her book."

"I've already told her there was a possibility I might need to get you out of here. You remember when I said I needed to make a call, when that note arrived at the house a while back? It was her I called. I let her know my concerns, and she understood. Your well-being is more important to her right now than your management of the den. She doesn't want to lose another protégé." I sense a sadness that overcomes him with that last part.

It takes fifteen minutes for the train to arrive. Thankfully, all was peaceful while we waited, with no sign of anyone having found us. As soon as I settle into my seat, I feel my eyelids grow heavy. I don't necessarily fault the lack of sleep last night, or the restlessness of it, rather the exhaustion from everything occurring in my waking reality.

Before my mind allows my body to drift into a space of relaxation, I go to grab my phone out of my bag, hoping to see if perhaps Alex has broken his no-contact rule out of concern. If the individuals following us really were the team he hired, they had to have told him what's going on by now. However, as I search in my bag, I realize my phone is gone.

"It's not in there," Luca says. "I threw our phones out at the station when I went to get our tickets."

"I'm sorry, you WHAT?"

"Can't have anyone tracking us. Don't worry, you'll get a new one."

I can feel the panic rising like a flash flood, without warning. That phone is my lifeline to everything—my job, my parents, my friends … Alex. "WHY THE HELL DID YOU HAVE TO THROW IT OUT?"

He sits up, frantically looking around. "Quiet down! You're drawing attention. I just told you why."

I whisper-shout, "You could have told me to leave it at the house or in the car! You didn't have to toss it like trash!"

"Oh, I'm sorry that I was entirely too busy worrying about *saving your ass* to remember to have you leave your phone at the house! Besides, it would have been too much of a risk. They could find it and access it."

"As opposed to what? Finding them in the trash bin at the station?"

"I destroyed them and snapped the sim cards. If they do find them, there will be nothing they can get but pieces."

I huff and tears brim in my eyes. "I hate everything about this."

"Yes, well, I'm not too fond of it either."

I throw myself back in the seat and cross my arms, furious and dismayed. On top of everything, I am beyond afraid. I wipe the tear that falls down my cheek and shudder at the notion that

I'm on my way to a completely different country, and no one, not Genevieve, not Alex, nor Madame Chérot knows what has happened or where I'll be.

"Jess, it's going to be alright."

"God, I wish you would stop saying that. Nothing about this is okay. Nothing about this will be alright until the threats are removed, and life goes back to normal. You can't promise me that will happen. You are as clueless about the future as I am, so please, just don't." My lower lip quivers as I sigh in distress, then I hold it between my teeth to keep it steady.

After a minute or two, I'm composed enough to say, "I'm sorry. I know you're doing everything you can to help. I really do appreciate you being here for me the way you are. You didn't have to, but you are. I'm just—I'm terrified, Luca."

He wraps his arm around me, drawing me into his side, holding me tight as my head falls upon his shoulder. "I know," he replies quietly.

No more words are exchanged between us as we chug along. The cityscape begins to turn to a seemingly endless sea of trees as I settle more and more into his warmth. His sandalwood scent covers me like a cloak, and the motion of the train rocks me gently to much-needed sleep.

26

$\mathcal{I}$ feel a tap on my shoulder, and my eyes flutter open. Immediately, I squint, blinded by the bright sun streaming through the train's large windows. "Madame? Madame, nous sommes arrivés à Florence," the train attendant says, letting me know we've arrived at our destination.

"Oh! Merci, Monsieur." As I get my bearings, I notice Luca is no longer beside me. In fact, he's nowhere to be seen. On his seat is a piece of paper with writing on it.

Before walking away, the attendant informs me that the train will be departing in a minute, which throws me into hustle mode. I hurriedly grab my belongings, taking quick note that not only is Luca missing, but so is the tote bag he brought with him. I snatch up the paper that was on his seat and hurry off the train, dreadfully discombobulated. Then, as soon as I set foot onto the platform, I read what was written.

Princesa,

Please forgive me, but I had to get off at the stop before. I cannot continue with you to Florence. You'll understand soon, I promise. I have asked the attendant to make sure you make it off at the correct stop. I've also arranged for someone to meet you at the station. They will be holding a sign with your name and will take you to where you will be staying. I'll be back soon. I beg of you, don't do anything stupid. Please, stay put till I return.

- Luca

You've got to be kidding me. In a fit of frustration, I crumple up the paper and chuck it into the first trash bin I see, then bound down the steps leading toward the station exit. When I arrive at the passenger pickup area, I immediately spot a dapper man standing next to a very expensive-looking vehicle. He's holding a sign with my last name, just as Luca said.

"Ms. Rivers?" the tall man in a well-fitted suit asks as I approach.

"Yes, that's me."

"Wonderful." He takes my suitcase, placing it in the trunk of the sleek, black car. This is one of those cars they chauffeur presidents and royalty in, surely. I certainly wouldn't have anticipated little ol' me being picked up in anything like this. The man opens the door, and I assume he opens it for me, but my assumptions are quickly proven incorrect when out steps a woman I wasn't expecting to see.

"Carmyn?"

She smiles softly. "Hello, Ms. Rivers."

I reach out and embrace her tightly. "Oh my god! Oh my god, what are you doing here?" Joy and relief flood my being. For weeks I've wanted nothing more than to be by Alexander's side again. Her presence leads me to believe that wish is about to come true.

Suddenly, her subtle smile becomes a sorrowful frown. "I see you weren't informed. I've come to fetch you. I need to take you to Mr. Marc rather urgently."

My excitement evaporates. "What is it? Carmyn, what's wrong?"

"We got the news yesterday evening. Aralyn has passed."

"What? No. No, that can't be. I was just with Luca—" Luca… Was this why he left me on the train? Does he know? Has he known this entire time?

"I was under the impression Mr. De la Rue had sent you here so he could go make necessary arrangements. At least that's what he told me the plan was when he rang."

Oh god, he *did* know. This whole time, he was aware Aralyn had passed, and he still dealt with this morning's threats, and made getting me to safety a priority. All the while he must have been breaking inside. I was such a bitch to him.

"He called me around ten last night to give us the news, and eventually mentioned that his father had sent someone to come for you, and that he needed to get you out of Paris. Then he asked if he could bring you to us, and I told him to bring you here to

Florence, as we've been here since early this week, staying at Mr. Marc's holiday home."

So, not only did Luca not tell me about Aralyn's passing, but he also wasn't being entirely truthful about the timeline in which he received word that Emil would show up. He'd known he was on the way for hours, not minutes. Something's not right. Why wouldn't he be forthcoming with me about what was going on?

Carmyn continues. "Mr. Marc doesn't know about your arrival. I haven't had the heart to discuss it with him. He's an absolute mess over this."

Oh, Alex. He probably prepared himself for that call for months, but nothing could have truly prepared him for the immense grief of losing someone he loved so dearly, even having experienced it before. Because, despite knowing that this time would come, I'm certain he was not ready for her to go.

I haven't a clue if there's anything I can do that will ease his pain, but I'll put my all into trying. "Carmyn, take me to him."

❤

*W*e pull into the driveway of a massive villa that looks like the setting of an Italian romance film, with stone walls, creeping vines, terracotta roofs, and large arched windows, surrounded by a lush vineyard. I'd spend a good twenty minutes at the entry, gawking in awe, if I wasn't on a mission.

As soon as we enter the home, I ask Carmyn to lead me to Alex. When we reach a set of double doors at the end of a long hallway that belongs to what Carmyn explains is the library, she places her hand on the handle, but hesitates to open it. "What is it? What's wrong?"

She faces me and addresses me in a hushed tone. "He's in bad shape, Jess. I don't think he's moved from that bloody chair for a second. Before I left to get you, I tried asking him if there was anything at all I could assist him with, but I'm not sure he heard me. It was as though he was caught in this unending trance. Tommy was here too. He says it's just shock, and to let him be, but I'm worried. I'm really worried. I've never seen him like this before." Her eyes well with tears.

I touch her arm. "I understand. We're going to help him through this, Carmyn."

With a nod she says, "I know, I just—" She places her hands over her chest. "It's so sad. That poor woman." I envelop Carmyn in a hug, rubbing her back in an effort to soothe her.

Then, after a moment of comfort and silence, we let go of each other. "I know there may not be much you can do," she says, "but maybe having you here might bring him some relief."

I smile faintly. "I'll do my best."

She opens the door and, when I enter, I'm confronted with a scene straight from some chaotic dream. Books, lamps, furniture, and other objects are torn, broken, and scattered all across the room. Alex is kneeling in front of the fireplace, in a navy T-shirt and black denim jeans, staring into the fire. His face is pale, and his eyes dark and haunted. His hair is disheveled as though he just rolled out of bed, though he appears far from rested. My breath hitches at the sight. The man I've always known to be so composed sits in a complete shambles.

What do I say to him? It's hard to believe there's anything to be said that would really help. I know that nothing but time and compassion will truly make the pain he's experiencing dissipate.

I approach him slowly, taking the time to consider how I should greet him. He finally takes notice of my presence when a couple shards of glass crunch beneath my heels. As his eyes fall upon me, he sets down his tumbler of whiskey and, surprised, softly says my name. "Jess…" I pick up my pace toward him and his expression switches to one of concern. "Jess, wait, there's glass everywhere, you could get cut." He slurs a bit, clearly inebriated. Look at him, despite everything he's going through, he's worrying about me getting hurt. How could anyone ever claim to know this man and call him selfish? No way, Luca.

"It's okay. I'll be alright." I brush away some debris on the ground when I reach him, and then kneel by his side. He quickly moves to wipe the trails of tears that stain his face, and turns his head away.

I gently place a hand upon his cheek, guiding his face back toward me and then run my thumb over a dampened area of skin. His gray eyes reflect the storm raging inside him and the tumultuous flood of sadness that burdens his spirit. "You don't have to hide the pain, Alex. Not from me." The misery projected from his aura is heartbreaking. Softly, I say, "I'm so very sorry."

Wrapping my arms around his shoulders, I draw him against me, allowing his head to fall upon my chest. I can smell the alcohol seeping through his pores, and it hurts to know he's been here for hours, alone, trying to drown his sorrows in liquor after the grief-fueled rage subsided. For a man who is normally meticulous in keeping himself and everything around him so in order, I can only imagine how out of control he must feel. How much I'm certain he wishes he was allowed the opportunity to try and prevent this outcome.

I rest my chin atop his head and hold him tight while gently stroking his hair. Within moments, his body begins to convulse under the weight of emotion. I say nothing; I just let him grieve.

Now, two of the people he cared for most in this life have departed far too soon. After hardly allowing himself to work through the passing of his father, and then taking on the weight of an empire—keeping secrets to protect it all … he needs this. He needs this emotional release so badly, although it's crushing to witness.

He sobs uncontrollably, barely able to get the words out. "I-I can't…"

"Shh, I know. I know." I kiss his head and silent tears flow from my eyes. I'm being strong for him, but I know my own time to mourn is coming.

For all that's been gained over these last seven months, there has been an equal amount of loss. Aralyn's death now trumps it all. In many ways I feel as though I've grown so much closer to her via the words she left behind on paper, a trail of memories that won't be erased nor increased, and they have deeply resonated in me, no matter how sad or joyful. Because of this, Aralyn has become a kindred spirit. And I'm heartbroken at the loss of my newfound friend, no matter how bizarre a short connection we had.

After a while, the fire begins to die down and the room grows quieter. Alexander has become still. I look down to see that he's fallen asleep on my lap and then I notice that he's clutching something in his hand. I slowly remove it, doing my best not to disturb him. It's a silver ring, and there's an inscription on the inside that reads:

Yours always, till the end of time.

It's a man's ring. Aralyn must have given it to him.

His body jolts and he stirs, groaning as though he's waking from a bad dream. "Okay, hey, let's get you to bed." I call out to Carmyn, who comes to assist me in getting him up. His lids are heavy and his speech slurs as he grumbles something we don't quite catch. Carmyn's foot accidentally hits a whiskey bottle that was lying on the floor against the couch. It shatters as it collides with a wall across the room. Alex lifts his head and snickers. Then he slumps again, his weight heavy on our shoulders.

"Come on, babe, we can do this," I encourage him.

We struggle to help him up the stairs, and Carmyn suggests maybe just bringing him a blanket and letting him sleep it off on one of the couches on the first floor. But I'm determined to get him to where he'll be most comfortable.

After what feels like a solid ten minutes, we finally make it to his room and drop him into the bed. As I slip off his shoes Carmyn says, "I've already canceled his flight and his appointments for the next few days. He might be miffed about it, but I reckon he'll just have to get over it."

I shake my head at the idea of Alex getting agitated about not working, when he should be resting and healing. "Don't worry, I'll put in a good word for your intentions. Thanks for your help."

"Of course. I'll pop by later in the morning. I stay in the guest house, so if you need anything at all, give me a ring, yeah?"

"You've got it."

She takes one last worried look at Alex, now fast asleep, and leaves. I get back to work making sure he's tucked in and comfortable, then I take his ring from my pocket and place it on the bedside table before getting up to leave myself. Suddenly, I feel a hand grasp mine. Alex squeezes it a little tighter.

"Please," he says as softly as a summer breeze. "Stay. I'd rather not be alone."

I reach down and gently caress his cheek. "Of course I'll stay." I climb on the bed and curl up on the other side of him, laying my head on his shoulder. We remain like this until we both drift off into the realm of dreams.

━━━ ♥ ━━━

*T*he clock on the bedside table shows that several hours have passed. Day became night and night has indeed become day, though you wouldn't know it due to the storm-darkened skies outside. To my surprise, Alex is awake. He lays quiet, staring stoically at the oversized windows that touch the floor and ceiling, as raindrops pound against them. I barely hear his breath. If it wasn't for the rise and fall of his chest, I would have thought he was not breathing at all. I can tell his mind and body are still exhausted, and I wish there was something I could do to take the pain away.

"Good morning," I say quietly, but he doesn't respond, seemingly stuck in a trance like Carmyn spoke of. My mind hurriedly attempts to figure out a solution that could lift his spirits, if only a little. Perhaps what he needs is intimacy—not the sexual kind, certainly not now—the kind of intimacy that allows him to feel safe, loved, and at ease.

My fingers gently run a trail up his arm and back down in a soothing motion. Then I whisper, "I'll be back."

In the bathroom, I'm pleased to see that there's a large soaking tub gleaming in the low light. Just what I was hoping to find. I turn on the faucet and start a hot bath with all the essentials: salts, herbs and candles, all of which were sitting in the small linen closet, perfectly in order and ready for use. There's a Bluetooth speaker on the wall and I connect my phone, turning on music I feel he'd be able to decompress to, a playlist of cello instrumentals.

Before long, I spot Alex in the doorway, witnessing me prepare his den of rejuvenation. He smiles softly. "What is this, Brown Eyes?"

I approach him, and then, without much thought, I kneel, looking up at him with eyes full of adoration and love. "It's for you … Sir." Dear god, I don't know what possessed me to do it. This is incredibly bold. I don't officially hold the title of his submissive, and he's certainly not expecting me to kneel at his feet; it just happened on impulse. Strangely enough, it *felt* like the right thing to do. It was as intuitive as running the bath, which I'm now realizing was in many ways an act of devotion that I naturally wanted to show. To show him that I care greatly about his well-being, and offer this bit of service to express it. "It will help you feel a little better."

His smile grows slightly, but I can see the weariness of life in his eyes. I see the uncertainty of how to react to my unexpected gesture. I quickly rise to my feet, not wanting to make him feel uncomfortable. "I'm sorry, I wasn't trying to take—" *I wasn't trying to take her place.* That's what I was going to say. But I stopped, scared that I may have just thrust him back into the state of unyielding grief I'm trying to relieve.

An amused smirk pulls at the corner of his mouth. "Always sorry."

"Haha, ugh, right, I'm sorry." I fling my hands over my mouth, embarrassed.

He laughs. "Come here." Pulling me into his arms, he gives me the most tender look and murmurs, "Thank you. This was incredibly thoughtful." He tilts my chin up. "And you look breathtaking on your knees." There's an enticing glint in his eyes, and his words send a rush of sensation shooting south, where desire stirs without mercy. I feel guilty for wanting him the way I do right now. It seems wildly selfish. I mean, the man just found out the light of his world is gone.

"Well, I'll leave you to get undressed," I say, undoing myself from the security of his embrace, and begin to make my way around him.

He lightly grabs hold of my wrist, bringing me to a stop. "You don't have to leave."

"I just thought you might want to—"

"In all my years I've never had anyone make such an effort to bring me comfort in a time of great suffering as you just have.

I wouldn't dare want you to leave, Jess." I'm stunned by his statement.

He walks to the bathtub and steps in, still clothed in his jeans and dark shirt. He settles into the warmth of the water and sighs pleasantly. I try to stifle a disbelieving laugh. He must still be a bit buzzed to do such a silly thing. His gaze meets mine in the low light of the candles and he holds out his hand. "Join me."

"Oh, Alex, you didn't even—"

"Please," he requests in a delicate tone.

I smile. What the hell, why not? He wants me to join him, and I gladly will.

In my white dress, I slip into the water, and he draws me against him, holding me tight. We remain like this, allowing the scents, sounds and sensations to wrap around us like a healing blanket. Not a word is spoken, but words aren't necessary.

In this moment of stillness, I dwell on the devotion and passion I have for this man. It burns like a raging fire within every corner of my being. I truly yearn for him in every way. But at the peak of my yearning is the desire to see him happy, the desire to make him feel safe, just as he's made me. I wonder if this is how Aralyn felt. If this very feeling is what led her to make the decisions she did, what led her to guide me to him.

Uncertainty still lingers in the air for the two of us. I think I have struggled with the need for control in this regard as well, with my need to know an outcome. But when does one ever truly know how their life will play out with their partner? In my case, my potential partner. Would it not be best to simply surrender to the present moment, the moment that exists, the moment that is certain?

If all I have is now, then I aim to cherish every bit of it.

27

It's a beautiful afternoon, now that the rain has cleared and the dark clouds have scattered. I was pleased to discover a grand, lush garden in the backyard, perfect for my stroll. Though it's the start of fall, I'm surprised to see so many flowers in bloom as if in their springtime glory. Whoever's in charge of the upkeep has done impeccable work.

The sun glows through the tall trees, and birds chirp, while honeybees are hard at work collecting pollen, some of which blows like pixie dust in the breeze. It's as if God himself crafted this place.

Alex went back to bed after the bath and is still asleep. I didn't want to wake him, although evening isn't far off. I know he needs rest. Carmyn confirmed with me that she's rescheduled all business affairs for the next few days. Both of us are in agreement that business is the last thing he needs to worry about right now. Could he be upset? Maybe. But I have a feeling it won't bother him for long.

As I round a corner heading toward the pond, with its lovely fountains arcing high, creating rainbows in their mist, I realize I've seen this setting before. But where?

After a moment, the memory hits me. This is the garden in that photo I found of Aralyn and Alex! The image is still fresh in my mind, and I can clearly picture the love that was captured just a breath away from where I stand now. Her cheerful face is imprinted on my mind, and I'm ashamed that I am unsettled by it. Unsettled because I worry her memory will forever haunt me here. That it will forever be a constant reminder that she was truly the Earth to his orbit. She kept him grounded. She kept him balanced. Then she handed the responsibility to me, along with her metaphorical diamond butterfly stilettos, which might be too big to fill.

I shake my head to clear away the thoughts, and exhale my feelings of overwhelm. Continuing forward, I walk past a row of rose bushes as I approach the pond, and spot a woman who appears to be in her fifties, on her knees picking roses. My presence startles her, and she yelps, holding a hand over her chest, and then bursts into a fit of laughter. "Oh, I'm so sorry my love, you gave me a scare!"

I join her in the nervous laughter. "I apologize! I had no idea anyone else was out here. I was just taking a little walk."

"That's quite alright. It's a pleasure to see a new face around here enjoying the garden." She rises to her feet. "And such a lovely face too."

I blush at the kind compliment. She's lovely as well, with a streak of silver standing out amidst her long, sleek dark brown hair, and her bright gray eyes gleam with kindness. The corners of them crinkle as she smiles sweetly. "Where are my manners? I'm Sofia." She has an interesting accent. I can't quite pin down where she's from; although it sounds British, it doesn't sound entirely so.

"Pleasure to meet you. I'm Jess."

Her face brightens and her smile stretches wide. "Jess Rivers?"

"Um, yes. How did you—"

"Oh!" She excitedly approaches me, pulling me in for a hug, then kisses my cheeks. "Oh, my son has told me so much about you." Her … son? I'm stunned, but the shock and curiosity are momentarily replaced by embarrassment. The rouge in my cheeks is surely visible as it dawns on me that I'm standing in front of Alexander's mother, and in a short, skimpy, red satin robe, of all things. After the hug, I instantly wrap my arms around myself a bit tighter. "No one told me you were here. I would have prepared a meal!"

My laugh is light and awkward. "Oh please, that's okay. There's truly no need. I'm just here to…" I trail off, unsure exactly what reason to give for my presence.

"Aralyn." Her eyes are sad. It's wild the way they change shade depending on mood, just the way Alexander's do. "Yes, that is very unfortunate. She was such a wonderful girl." She looks down at the white roses in her hands. "I picked these in her honor, the last ones of the season. White roses were her favorite." It's surprising for me to hear as I absolutely would have guessed red.

It's apparent to me that she knew Aralyn very well, perhaps even saw her as a daughter. A three-year relationship is long enough to establish that type of connection with the parent of your partner.

It's surreal to be standing in front of Sofia Marc. I remember being so hopeful I would meet her prior to our split. Of course, then I wasn't sure if I would. Now, here I am, before the woman he guards with his life, and rightfully so. The media would eat her alive for sure if they knew her role in the family secret.

"How is my son doing?" she asks. "Have you seen him today? I haven't checked on him yet. Carmyn told me he hasn't had much rest, so I thought it best to leave him be."

"Yes, a short while ago. He was really distraught last night, but he managed to settle enough to get some rest. He's still sleeping, last I checked."

"*Tsk*, my poor boy." She glances toward the house. "I really wish Aralyn would have let him be there for her."

My ears perk. "Do you know why she wouldn't?"

She sighs heavily. "I believe there were a few reasons. Chief among them being that she wanted Alexander to move on with his life. She didn't want him spending time worrying about her and watching her health decline. Apparently, they had a spat about it. Alexander told her he didn't care about her appearance, he just wanted her to tell him where she was going to be so he could be by her side, but Aralyn begged him to let it go. I visited him in London shortly after that last encounter with her, and he was so heartbroken. It was like he felt the weight of the world on top of him. Ever since his father..." She looks at me with uncertainty.

I give her a reassuring look, "I know about what happened. He's told me everything."

She nods and continues. "Since his father's murder, he's kept his emotions locked up tight. But after everything that occurred, having to part ways with her … and with you, I think his heart could no longer take the pain of loss. For the first time since he was a boy, I saw him break down."

"I think a lot about what that might have been like for him. It was difficult working through my own emotions surrounding what happened, so I know it had to be harder for him."

She sets the roses down in a basket and takes my hands in hers. "He really cares about you, you know. I can tell by the way he speaks about you."

The knowledge that he speaks of me fondly to his mother brings a smile to my face. "I really care about him too."

"And I thank you for that. From what I've heard, you make him feel seen and safe enough to be who he is. Not many people do that, and he doesn't make it easy. You have to be a special kind of soul to get past the thick walls he's built around himself. Whatever happened between you two in Paris, at some point, he realized this about you. The best advice I can give in regard to him is to be patient. It will take him some time to mend, but he's an excellent choice for a partner, and I'm not just saying that because he's my son, either." We share another good laugh.

It warms my heart to know that Sofia not only appreciates me, but accepts me, and all of this because of what Alex told her. A few months ago, I questioned where he and I stood with one another, whether he was simply attempting to see where things go with us to avoid hurting me, or if he actually wanted us to work out. She's given me some comfort in my hope that, although he's healing, he is committed to our journey, no matter where it leads.

"Come. I'll start preparing dinner. No guest should be without a proper home-cooked meal." I almost tell her she needn't go through the trouble, but not only might that be rude, my stomach would absolutely object.

"Can't wait!"

———— ♥ ————

While Sofia is in the kitchen, I quickly run up the stairs to go change. As I do, I come across Alex heading down. "Hey! You're awake!" He still has bed hair, and it's adorable.

He smirks. "Don't you look delectable." God, if only he knew I was looking "delectable" in front of his mother.

He continues down till he's a single step above me, eyeing me in that heated way that gives me heart palpitations. "You feeling alright?" I ask. "I hear there's a fantastic dinner being fixed. Maybe it would be good for you to—"

He grasps my neck right below my jaw and gently pushes me against the rail while keeping me steady with his other hand clasped on my waist, and his mouth encloses my own. A rush of sensation has me dizzy with delight and ecstasy, with an equal helping of confusion as his tongue, coated with the taste of mint, overpowers mine. I press my hands against his body, initially trying to push him away so I can question him about his sudden and surprising action during this time. But, when I feel the rippling of his abs beneath the fibers of his shirt, I grip the fabric and pull him toward me, bringing his body so close to mine, not even air can pass between us.

I take in every bit of this heaven, and yet I can't ignore the terrifying feeling that I shouldn't be enjoying this at all. *The man is grieving Jess, he's not in his right mind; he's trying to fill a void.*

Fuck!

I manage to move my head to the side, unlocking my lips from his, and he instead trails hot kisses down my neck. "Alex. Alex, wait. Alex, we have to stop!"

He halts and steps back, looking at me with a stunned and questioning gaze. We both huff, out of breath from the adrenaline of the moment. A heavy blanket of guilt then covers his face, along with another look. Could it be fear?

"Alex…" I whisper. "It's okay."

"Th-that was terribly inappropriate of me. I'm so sorry."

"What? No, no! You know I normally wouldn't mind at all. But Alex, you *just* lost her. I'm… This isn't really what you need."

"What do I need, Jess?" I'm not sure at first if his question is genuine, but it quickly becomes clear that he's truly asking for my guidance.

"I-I think… I think you need time. You need time to process what's happened. You need time to accept it as true, because right now… right now I think you want to do anything but believe she's gone."

He takes another step back and leans on the opposite side of the stairway, running a hand through the tousled curls atop his head while collecting his thoughts. Then he speaks, "I'm not used to this. I'm not used to letting my grief surface. I've buried cumbersome emotions for so long." He shakes his head. "I was a master at stowing them away. Skilled in avoiding them. I suppose now, my body is tired of hiding my pain, but I'm tired of feeling it too. I loathe it all."

I close the distance between us once more and wrap my arms around his torso, placing my chin on his chest as I gaze up at him. "I know. But once you finally give those pent-up emotions the proper attention, and then let them all go bit by bit, you'll begin to feel better. It won't be instant, but you will."

Considering what he must be battling internally, I think about how the closest I've come to experiencing this level of loss was when my gran passed when I was twelve. It was unexpected, and it shook me to my core. She meant the world to me and, besides Gen, I felt she was one of the only people in the world who truly understood me at the time.

Her departure was my first introduction to the cruel reality of loss and the consuming process of grief that followed. No day was like the next, and the highs and lows randomly alternated, seemingly more unpredictable than before. I recall my many outbursts over the course of a year. Though my parents knew what was happening, it took me a while to recognize that what I was doing was unknowingly expressing my sorrow and pain, something I then had to address more deeply within myself. I still miss Gran, terribly much.

"Thank you for that, Brown Eyes."

"Anytime."

He smiles coyly, then kisses the top of my head and murmurs, "I smell my mum's bread. Did you just come from meeting her?"

"I'm embarrassed to say I did. I certainly never dreamed of meeting your mother in a robe that, if the wind blows just right, she can see all the goods! Ugh. I was just headed up to change."

He grins playfully. "Well, I'm embarrassed to say she's happened upon women in the past less dressed than you."

"Yikes, that *is* embarrassing! You win."

"Hahaha. I'll see you in a bit, then."

We go our separate ways, and when I get to his room, I go to work to find something appropriate for dinner with one's parent. For whatever reason, I can't seem to find the belt that went with my dress yesterday. I check Alexander's hamper, thinking perhaps it was scooped up and placed there accidentally.

As I'm combing through the clothes, something falls out of one of his pants pockets. It's a folded up black card... A black card just like the ones I stopped receiving well over a month ago. I drop the clothes I'm holding and pick it up, smoothing the crumpled edges. Then, I slowly unfold and open it to read the note in white handwriting:

You think I don't know about your little game of hide-her-so-I-don't-seek? This is your final warning. If you know what's good for you, end it with her. End it now!

If you know what's good for you? This is far worse than any of the ones I've received, far more threatening. And for what? My anxiety surfaces rapidly as I ponder what this note means. It's baffling. While I was thinking we might be in the clear with this mysterious writer, Alex has continued to be threatened by them.

I was expecting fear to be the primary emotion causing my body to shudder, but it's rage. It's one thing for me to receive them, it's another to be holding one addressed to Alex. It feels even more offensive for some reason, like how dare they involve him in this twisted game!

Something has to be done. *Someone* has to pay … and it damn sure won't be him.

Journal,

Alexander. That's the name of the man who wouldn't stop staring at me at the den a few weeks ago. I came across him again today in the lobby and he stopped me, asking, rather politely, for my name. I of course asked him why he wanted to know. "Because I want to know you," he said.

I asked him what made him think he's earned the right to know me. He simply replied that he knows he's earned nothing, though he'd like the opportunity to prove that he's more than deserving of my time. It was shocking that Madame's sub could so boldly proclaim interest in pursuing me. However, I must admit there is something admirable about him. And I dare say he may not be submissive at all.

There's an aura about him that's different from other submissives. His eyes shine with a desire for dominance and a desire to obtain whatever he wants in this life. He gives off the energy of a man who is not only dominant but maintains exquisite self-control. His gentle yet assertive pushes are powerful. No aggression. He doesn't need aggression. No begging, pleading, demanding. He's skilled in a level of subtle persuasion I've yet to encounter. Alexander appears to be a man who's sure of himself without being cocky, and as such, had me feeling as though I'd be the one missing out if I turn him down.

Still, turning him down was exactly what I did.

Journal,

This man is unrelenting. Amélie must have given him my schedule. He always seems to be around these days, constantly placing himself in a position to come across me. And the worst thing is he says nothing to me, only looks at me, smiles, and goes about his way. But it's his presence that's driving me crazy.

He's consistently asking for my time without asking at all. Simply by keeping himself in sight, he serves as a gentle reminder of his offer. I'm to understand that as long as I continue to see him, his offer still stands. It's severely agitating, yet so damn clever. It puts him in the position of control. All he has to do is not show up, and suddenly I'll be sent reeling, questioning if he's moved on. Questioning my decision. Because he knows that the reason I turned him down has nothing to do with me being uninterested. Somehow, he just knows. He's playing the long game. Fuck.

Journal,

I gave in. I actually agreed to a date with the man. It's alright. I just need to go and get the curiosity out of my system. I'll see that he's exactly like any other man, and then I'll end whatever this is and forget I ever gave him the time of day.

28

The weight of exhaustion overcomes me as I sink into the chaise in the living room. Like most of the home, this room is also grand. All the tall windows are open, and the white curtains flutter as a soft breeze rolls through. The light of the setting sun streams in, causing the dust floating through the air to appear like glitter. I'm entranced, taken by the peaceful setting calming the chaos that has troubled my soul. I find myself once again wishing I could freeze time. Oh, how I'd encapsulate this moment.

Alex enters and gives me a tender smile before proceeding to one of the windows, gazing out thoughtfully, with his hands in his pockets. I admire the way the sun favors him too, as it kisses his skin, creating a heavenly glow and causing his gray eyes to shine like silver. I can't imagine a scene in which he'd ever not be mesmerizing to me.

"My mum is rather fond of you. It would seem that, despite the earlier introduction in your scandalous nightwear, you've made quite a positive impression." He grins.

"Haha, well that's great to know. I'm fond of your mother as well. And her food is some of the best I've had. I'd say it rivals Tommy's."

His laugh is rich. "Don't let him hear you say that, but yes, I happen to agree."

Dinner with Alexander's mother went better than I had anticipated. I didn't have many expectations going into it, and I was dreadfully nervous. I've never had the privilege of meeting the parents of any of the men I've dated or had an interest in, so this experience was not only unexpected, but new. I've always considered myself to be the type of woman a man would be proud to introduce to his mother, but I have the added pressure of forming a relationship with Sofia after she had already formed such a great one with Aralyn.

It's silly, really. Here I am worrying about how she might view me in comparison to her once future daughter-in-law, when I am very aware the only person busy making comparisons is me. It's hard to detach myself from the need to do so. Aralyn is—was—such a larger-than-life individual, bold, elegant, alluring and compelling, with an unmatched strength she'd had to develop. She was beautiful in every way that counted, and her impact on those who loved her was noticeably profound.

With every bit of responsibility I have inherited, I've become more concerned about my ability to match her energy and brilliance. Emory constantly reminds me to simply be myself, but that's difficult to do when you're placed in positions and situations that belong to someone else. Now, Aralyn's departure puts the spotlight entirely on me. What will I do with the things she left behind for me to take on? It's the unspoken question I'm certain is on everyone's mind. They'll be watching to see how I move forward from this.

I shift focus from my self-reflection, and my thoughts surrounding dinner with Sofia, and turn it back to Alexander, who I've noticed has become quiet. He continues to stare out the window, lost in his own little world. From where I sit, halfway across the room, I can see the sorrow in his distant gaze. I'm torn between checking on him and allowing him his moment to ponder in grief.

My heart, however, wants to kiss the wounds and make things better, even if to try may not be as much of a soothing balm as I hope. Eventually, I can't resist getting up and walking to his side. I link my arm in his and lay my head against his shoulder. We both stand in silence, taking in the view of the vineyard, which appears like a photo you'd find in a travel magazine, truly picturesque.

After a minute or two, he points out the window, "Do you see that tree?" I notice a large tree protruding from the vast rows of grape vines, seemingly out of place, its branches wide and its leaves moving in the breeze. I nod. "When I was a lad, it was much smaller, and I climbed it often. My father had wanted to cut it down to make room for more vines, but I begged him not to. I told him it was my magic tree." He chuckles. "Whenever we'd visit for holiday, I'd spend almost every evening sitting in it, watching the sun disappear over the horizon. And then I'd spend a bit of time after, counting stars as they appeared."

"That sounds so peaceful."

"It was." He pauses, then sighs before continuing. "Those were simpler, sweeter times, filled with wonder and innocence.

The boy who sat in that tree never fathomed how the passage of time would affect him, never considered what life would take amid its great generosity. That boy's biggest worry was missing the sunset. He never realized that, in the future, he'd have traded witnessing thousands of sunsets to share one minute more with those great loves he'd inevitably lose. He never considered that even if he counted an infinite number of stars, it wouldn't keep his joyful heart from breaking."

Tears glisten at the edges of his eyes. "It's true what they say. Time really is a thief, and I'm admittedly terrified of it, of what it could take from me next. It's become a constant worry, and I don't think I have it in me to go through this again."

Dear heavens, guide me on how best to respond. "I understand." I go quiet for several seconds, waiting for the right words to come to me. "Though I will say, in my experience, fear can often be the true thief, creating darkness in the cracks of the heart where light could fill, robbing us of joy that could sprout from whatever beautiful things and people time does place there. But the good news about that is we can choose to not let fear win.

"In regard to time—well—I can't speak on what time might take, but I can speak on what it gives. All these milliseconds that swiftly become hours, days, years, none of them are promised, but what we are granted is ours and can't be revoked." I reach up and grasp his face with both hands. "You're hurting, aching, devastated over your father, over her, and you've every reason to be. But their love, Alex, has not left you and never will. Their love resides in all the memories of *time* well spent with them." I take his hands in mine, running my thumbs along his knuckles.

"It's true, the path of the unknown *is* terrifying, but just know you don't have to walk it alone. I'm right here."

He wipes the trail left behind by the tear that has descended down my cheek. "I don't believe there are enough words to express how precious you are to me," he says. And then, with a gentle tug, he pulls me into his embrace.

I soak in his warmth as the sun fades, giving way to dusk. Time may not be the real thief, but it stops for no one, not for Aralyn, not for him, and not for me. We're all just cosmic dust, floating along in this breeze called life and, every once in a while, we find something to hold onto. I'm holding on, Alex. With everything in me, I'm holding on—for as long as time permits.

For the last week I've been staying in one of the guest rooms. As much as I'd enjoy lying next to Alex every night, I've made it a priority to give him space, which has been good for me as well. It's provided me with the opportunity to indulge in my night-owl nature and get some work done since, unfortunately, work doesn't stop simply because I'm away. Articles still need to be completed and there are managerial duties at the den that require my remote attention. I'd be lying to myself, however, if I said focusing on work is easy. "Restless" would be the best word to describe my current state.

As I'm in the midst of finishing up the review of some documents, there's a knock at the bedroom door. Carmyn enters, though appearing hesitant to do so. "Good evening, Ms. Rivers. I wanted to check on you before turning in for the evening."

"That's very kind of you. I'm doing alright." I gesture at all the papers and books around me, "Keeping busy, haha."

"I see. Not too busy, I hope. I hear you have a long day of traveling coming up soon."

I gaze at her curiously. "I wasn't aware I was going anywhere."

"My apologies, I thought Mr. Marc had already spoken to you. I've just come from seeing him, and he mentioned Mr. De la Rue is coming in a few days to take you somewhere safe."

Luca is on his way back? I experience both relief and frustration at the news. "I don't quite understand. Does Alex not know about what had happened prior to my arrival here?"

"Oh, trust, he asked me all about how you got here and more a couple days ago." Then why on earth would he think returning me to Luca is a good idea? Sure, Luca did do everything possible to get me out of the city safely. He's a great bodyguard, I'll give him that, but he's also the son of the man who's after me, the very man who sent Emil to my home to kidnap me. Unless Alex and Luca have come up with some sort of extraordinary plan, I don't see how this is for my benefit.

"What about Aralyn's funeral?" I ask. "I'm assuming if Luca is on his way back, he's completed whatever arrangements he needed to make regarding her passing. Did Alex mention to you any plans to attend her funeral?"

She draws her shoulders back, and with a sorrowful expression says, "There won't be one, love."

"No funeral? For *Aralyn*? Why the hell not?"

"From what I understand, Mr. De la Rue wants to keep the location of her remains private. He doesn't want to take any chances on his father discovering it."

Breath rushes from my lungs. I am both stunned and utterly dismayed. It was already shitty that Alex was not permitted to be with her during her last days, but to also be kept from his closure after her death? It's tragic. And I get it, I completely get Luca's desire to protect his sister's resting place, but it seems so cruel and unfair to Alex. Could there not have been a way for him to give his final farewell? I can't help but wonder if the reasoning that is keeping him from her is really an excuse Luca gave to enact some sort of payback.

"It's all such a fucked-up situation. Alex deserves better."

"I couldn't agree more, but there's unfortunately nothing to be done about it at the moment, and Mr. Marc appears to have made peace with it."

"I see. Well, since we're on the topic of things hidden, I want to ask you something." From between the pages of Aralyn's journal, I retrieve the crinkled black note card that had fallen out of Alexander's pants pocket. "I found this the day after I got here. Would you happen to know how recent it is?"

The expression on her face as she stares at it tells me she's about to be the bearer of some less-than-fortunate news. "I'm afraid fairly recent. There was a decent amount of time in which we didn't receive anything. Mr. Marc was nearly convinced the worst of the situation might be over. That was, until he received this note last week. The investigators he hired to figure out who is behind this are still stumped. There have been a few leads, and some footage of someone covered head to toe in black, but regardless, there's no definitive proof of who this individual is, nor their motive."

If the best team of professionals money can buy can't even figure this out, how will I? "Every time I think I'm close to solving who this is, I wind up right back where I started. It's madness. And to now threaten Alex? For what?"

She gestures toward the bed. "May I?" I nod and she takes a seat beside me. "If you want my opinion, the person responsible is either very close to you, or procuring information from someone who is. They seem to know far too much about your movements and whereabouts." It's a terrifying notion because it expands the suspect list to literally everyone I'm comfortable with.

"I feel like a laboratory mouse in a maze, hopelessly chasing the scent of a piece of cheese, and constantly hitting dead ends. I haven't a clue what to do, Carmyn. Cut everyone off? Isolate myself?"

"You may have to be more selective about who you share certain information with, and perhaps even limit what you do with others in your inner circle. Sometimes those closest to us are the most lethal."

"Yeah…" I'm already cautious about engaging with strangers, but I suppose I haven't exactly placed the same energy into my engagements with the few individuals I do associate with often.

"May I just say, the way you've maintained your composure throughout all these dramatic events is quite impressive, Ms. Rivers."

"Ha, if you only knew how chaotic it is in my mind."

"You're a brave woman. And I'm not saying that because of the dangers you're facing. You've got incredible grit and determination. It takes bravery to follow your own path while honoring another's in such a profound way, while also risking your livelihood. On top of everything you're also maneuvering through with Mr. Marc, I'm sure it's left you pondering what the future holds. It's not an easy path you're on. Someone should acknowledge the excellent job you're doing traversing it."

I grasp her hand, giving it a firm squeeze of gratitude. "I didn't realize how much I needed to hear that. Thank you, Carmyn. You always have a way of speaking such impactful words at the moments they are needed most."

"I'm pleased to have been of service." She smiles warmly, then rises to her feet. "I had best be off. I have a long day tomorrow. Our CEO's absence means a lot of potential chaos I need to ensure remains properly tamed and managed. But, before I go, here." She retrieves a box from her purse and hands it to me. It's a new phone.

"Oh, this is such a relief! Thank you."

"You have Mr. Marc to thank." She winks. "I assume you have everything backed up?"

"I should, yes."

"Marvelous. Have a beautiful evening, darling."

I bid her farewell and return to staring at the card still in my hand. I haven't brought it up to Alexander yet because I don't want to add any additional stress on him. It's clear, however, that the time is soon approaching when we will need to discuss this in relation to next steps, especially if there's talk of Luca coming back for me. Especially that.

This morning I awoke with a number of questions on my mind, specifically regarding Luca's upcoming return for me. I intend to address Alex this morning and ask why this decision hadn't been discussed with me before it was finalized. Although I understand that he may find it necessary, I believe another solution can be found. I want the chance to bring up the possibility of returning to America, just till things are resolved. It's not my favorite idea, especially considering how far I'd be from him, but it really might be the wisest choice.

I follow the smell of fried eggs to the kitchen, and see Alexander and his mother at the island, preparing breakfast. They don't see me at first, and it provides the opportunity to observe them in their element together. She cooks omelets on the stove while he's mixing something in a bowl, and they laugh and speak to each other in Italian. It's my first time hearing him speak another language outside of the occasional French. Not surprisingly, it adds greatly to his high level of attractiveness.

"Good morning, you two."

Alex beams. "Ah, good morning, love. Did you sleep well?"

"Very well, actually. The bed feels like I'd imagine a fluffy cloud to be. I'd have slept longer if my stomach didn't beg me to get up and eat. Speaking of which, it smells amazing in here."

Sofia smiles. "Thank you. Breakfast will be ready soon. Would you mind taking over for me, dear? I have to run up and make a quick call before we eat."

"Of course," I reply nervously. She explains to me what I need to do and then takes her leave. I'm happy to help, though the last thing I want to do is fuck up this woman's meal.

Alex snickers. "I must say, I've never seen anyone gaze at eggs in such a terrified way."

"It's that noticeable, huh?"

"Tremendously so. Here, let's trade. I just added the last few ingredients into my dough. How about you mix, and I'll take over the omelets?"

I breathe out a huge sigh of relief. "Yes, please, you're a darling."

Thoroughly amused, he trades places with me. I start to stir, and the aroma that wafts from the bowl has my mouth watering. "I didn't realize you could bake," I say.

"I'm half Italian, Brown Eyes; in my family it would be considered a sin for me not to know my way around a kitchen. I'm nowhere near as skilled as my mum when it comes to preparing a meal, but baking, I excel at. You can thank the tremendous sweet tooth I had growing up."

"Just growing up? Has your sweet tooth diminished over the years?"

He strolls back over and takes a pinch of the dough and samples it while eyeing me. "Diminished? No. I'd say it's become more refined, and has extended beyond my palate. I now yearn for sweetness outside of desserts." He winks.

He returns to the stove and I ask, "What is this dough going to be?"

"Chocolate hazelnut biscotti. I figured they'd be excellent with some tea or moka pot coffee later."

This man is so damn impressive that I continue to question how he's real. "How did you find the time to learn to bake, with everything else you had to do and learn growing up?"

"It was something I did in the middle of the night. I had bad insomnia, likely due to anxiety surrounding my responsibilities during the day. Baking would clear my mind, allow me to focus on something other than my stressors. It was therapeutic, and the bonus was having a delicious treat to indulge in before finally settling in to sleep. I don't do it as often anymore, but every once in a while, when I have the occasional guest or I find rest hard to obtain, I come right back to it."

"Ah, so it's a soothing hobby, like playing your cello."

"Exactly that." I'm glad to hear it. I can't help but worry about him, wondering how he works through the painful aspects of his life when his life, and those in it, demand so much of him. I learn more and more that he's been learning to adapt, adjust, and process for years, ever since childhood. It's painful to know, however, that he's had to do most of it in solitude. It has to be incredibly lonely.

I also wonder how much he had let Aralyn into his moments of anxiety and grief. As much as they cared for one another, they seemed to both suffer in silence, justifying it as protection in the name of love. I wonder if she ever knew, or witnessed him sneaking to the kitchen to bake when he was overwhelmed, or if she joined him. I'd ask but I'm afraid to bring her up, nervous that it will be too difficult a conversation for him to have at present.

He places the last omelet on a plate and then faces me. "Hey, so this is a bit off topic, but I wanted to have a chat about some upcoming arrangements I've made for you." It's a relief to hear, considering my intentions to bring it up.

"Right. Luca is coming back to get me?"

He looks at me questioningly, and I respond with, "Carmyn brought it up yesterday, not realizing you hadn't told me yet."

"Ah. Yes, he's on his way. Actually, he—"

Sofia enters with a concerned expression she's failing to hide. "Son, it looks like our guest has arrived."

I look at Alex. "Guest?"

A male voice calls out from the doorway. "Well, I certainly hope I am. I'd hate to intrude." Luca enters the kitchen with a broad grin as he gazes directly at me. "Hello, Princesa."

29

Luca leans against the kitchen island and grins, enjoying my shock. His hair falls perfectly over his shoulders, covered by his black leather jacket, and his blueish-green eyes peer into mine as he eagerly awaits my response to his presence. I find myself both thrilled to see him and highly irritated. My heart races and my left eye twitches.

"Hey, glad you made it in alright," Alex says. "Are you hungry? I figured we'd start off with a good meal before we get into more serious business." I glance at Alex, quite confused. Is Luca not the enemy, to some degree? Was the encounter on the private jet not headache enough? Why would he think sitting down for breakfast before a major discussion, that I'm assuming is about me, is a good idea?

"Sounds great. I'm starving," Luca replies before making his way to the dining table. This is far too weird. He's acting too … jovial. This man hasn't made one wild remark yet, and now he's happily joining us? Very off-brand for him.

Alex rubs the small of my back. "You alright?"

I keep my voice to just above a whisper. "When were you going to tell me we were having breakfast with Luca?"

"You must not have checked your texts from last night."

I pull my phone from the back pocket of my jeans, and check my inbox. Sure enough, there's a message from him informing me of exactly what we are discussing now. "Oops. I must have cleared the notifications when I stopped my alarm this morning. Sorry."

He smirks. "No need to apologize. Let's just try to get through this little meetup without incident."

The tension in my body is magnified by all of this. As I approach the table, Luca slides out the chair next to him with a smile. I roll my eyes and continue toward the seat across the table. He chuckles and says, "Distance certainly makes the heart grow fonder, doesn't it?"

"Don't start with me," I respond in a hushed tone. "You've a lot of explaining to do."

"I'd be happy to answer any of your questions, mi amor. But perhaps we should save that for later."

Alex and Sofia approach with the food and some drinks. Everything looks incredible, but the appetite I had minutes ago has diminished. My body is too full of nervous energy. As much as I'd like to believe we can have a dignified meal, I don't trust Luca to be on his best behavior, and I'm also not thrilled about the prospect of returning to Paris with him.

To my surprise, despite my concerns, we enjoy the meal peacefully. Sofia, being the bright ray of sunshine that she is, brought a lot of engaging conversation to the table that distracts from the thick fog of anxiety in the air. She asked Luca a lot about

Spain, and spoke of her time there. She even mentioned a past lover she'd had during her brief study-abroad venture back when she attended university. It was, of course, before meeting Alexander's father. And it was hilarious to witness how embarrassed Alex was at hearing this part of her past that he was unaware of, and how descriptive she was of her attraction for him and his … assets.

"My god, Mum, please spare us the details."

"Ha! My boy, I am a woman like any other. And guess what? I've still got it."

He drops his head into his hands, mortified. I'm in a fit of giggles as I reach across the table to give her a high five. Alex throws an arm in front of me to hold me back, while laughing in shock, "Christ! Don't encourage this."

"Your mom is a legend." I wink at her.

"Thank you, dear."

"This isn't happening. You're supposed to be on *my* side."

"Oh, Alex," I grasp his hand, "I *am* on your side … ninety-nine percent of the time. This just so happens to be a one percent occasion." All three of us laugh, but Luca only smiles, and it's gone as quickly as it shows. He seems distant, as though he's here but his mind is elsewhere. It's a look I've seen him wear before, the few times I witnessed painful memories of his past gripping him.

It's only now that I question how hard it must be for him to sit at a family table, where stories of good times are shared. I wonder if he's ever had this. Perhaps he did, once upon a time, until something abruptly changed in his father, and what was once so good became broken. Although I don't personally know the man, it's hard to imagine a time when Maxime could have been all about family. Though maybe, just maybe, the twins did sample moments like this before he became the monster responsible for destroying their chances at having what Alex and Sofia have today. I'm sure his sister being gone makes this more painful. She and their mother were the last true family he had, and now he's alone.

Alex takes notice of his current state as well, and the laughter dies down. "*Ehem*, breakfast was amazing, Mum. I think now would be as good a time as any to have our discussion. What do you say, Luca?" Luca gives a quick nod of approval.

"Right then, excuse me. I'll let you lot have your chat," Sofia says, clearing the table before taking her leave.

I speak up before the men begin. "Before we start, Luca, I'd like to give my condolences. I know there isn't anything I can say to help ease the pain of your sister's passing, but I want you to know you have my sincere love and sympathy." A large part of me also wants to inquire why he had lied and hid so much from me the day he brought me here, especially regarding Aralyn's passing. However, it doesn't seem to be the most appropriate time.

His jaw works, and he turns his head away, gazing out the window. "Yeah. Thanks."

"You have mine as well," Alex adds, sadly. "I'm certain I'm one of the last people you want to hear from regarding her, but it wouldn't feel right to not—"

"Yeah, okay. I got it." His tone is clipped, but not necessarily cold.

Alex nods and says nothing more. It's bizarre to see Luca like this. The man I know would have told Alex to shut up and fuck off. Instead, though visibly irritated, he's far more reserved than usual. It could be that perhaps his grief has caused him to lose his taste for a fight. Or perhaps, he accepts that Alex is the one person who comes close to understanding his pain, and because of this, he's choosing to keep the peace as best he can manage.

"Was it beautiful?" Alex asks, his voice trembling slightly. "Her funeral?"

Luca shifts uncomfortably. "Of course. Only the best for her." There's a momentary pause in conversation as we all struggle with what to say next. "Anyway," Luca continues, "I've made arrangements for Jess to stay with me in Spain for however long is necessary."

Alex asks the very question on my mind. "Why Spain?"

"I've inherited my sister's home there. It's where she had been hiding. My father never knew about it. I didn't even know about it until after we reconnected last year. It worked for her, so I'm sure it will work for Jess too."

"Hm." Alex looks at me. "What do you think? It sounds like a plausible solution, but I want to make sure you're comfortable with it. Spain will be new territory for you, and I know there's the matter of work and the fact you won't know anyone there."

Luca interjects, "She'll still have her responsibilities at the den. I'm sure Madame Chérot wouldn't mind you continuing at the location I once managed there."

"I think you're putting too much faith in that assumption."

He shrugs. "We'll work it out, don't worry."

"And journalism? I've already fallen behind; I had to cancel two interviews I had scheduled this week. I might be a favorite among the publication firms for now, but if I keep this up, I can kiss my shining reputation goodbye."

"Can't you conduct virtual interviews instead?"

"I mean, sure, but in person is more … personable. People find it easier to open up when they can be in your presence and feel you out."

He runs a hand through his hair, then leans into the table. "Look, I understand, but you might have to make some sacrifices here. Making sure you're clear of any danger needs to be top priority."

I hear what he's saying, but I can't ignore this gut feeling that something about this plan isn't quite right. "I'd like to propose another idea." I swivel in my seat, facing Alex. It's him I ultimately want to convince. "I think I should return home to the States. If I'm going to make sacrifices, I believe the best thing is to do it somewhere that would not only be difficult for Maxime to reach me, but that's familiar. Somewhere I will have a good support system—Gen, my parents, they'd be able to keep tabs on me."

Alex takes in what I've told him. Luca, on the other hand, appears unsatisfied with my plan. "I think Spain is the better option."

"Why? Do you really believe the best option for me is to be cooped up in yet another one of your sister's houses, surrounded by all of her belongings? As if losing her isn't enough, as if taking her place isn't enough, I'd be miserable within those walls, and you know it's true. Not to mention, I'd have no one in Spain."

His gaze softens. "You'd have me."

I'm careful not to respond in a way that would imply having him is not enough, even though it's true. "Luca, I respect you so much for everything you've done and continue to do to protect me, but I'm so tired of the cat-and-mouse game, always having the danger too close for comfort." With pleading eyes, I entreat Alex. "I want to go home."

Although I can tell he's worried for me, Alexander's mouth curls into an understanding smile and his knuckles sweep lightly down my cheek. "Okay. I'll make the preparations."

"I'll go with her, then." Luca's statement has both of us gazing at him questioningly. "If I'm not with you, things will look too suspicious."

Alex shakes his head in disapproval. "If you're with her, Maxime will know where she is. It will defeat the whole purpose of sending her to the States."

"We've already created the narrative that we're together."

Alex grows agitated. "Create the narrative that you split up, then."

"That won't work!" The rise of his voice makes the room tense once again. He realizes he's lost control of his emotions and quickly finds some composure. "I need to be wherever she is. My father doesn't have to know. He can wonder where I went, just like he would wonder where she had gone."

"And how exactly would that fare for you?" Alex asks, bringing up a very valid point.

"It doesn't matter. Now that Aralyn has passed, he no longer has control over what I do." His eyes connect with mine. "I'm finally free, just like she always wanted. And with that freedom,

I *choose* to do all I can to keep him from destroying your life too." Is it true? Is he finally free? Since being sent to live with his father, Aralyn was his Achilles' heel, the one person Maxime could use to make him dance like his own personal puppet. But now, if there's nothing he can do to Aralyn, perhaps there really is no longer anything he can do to Luca … except hurt me.

Beyond the story of a relationship between us, it's clear we do have a connection. Granted, it's a complex one, unlabeled. I don't feel confident calling him a friend, and he'd likely prefer to be my occasional fling, which in my mind is completely off the table. Somehow, we are something else entirely. Though what, I'm unsure.

Perhaps his desire to go with me extends past a wish to guard me from the ruthlessness of his kin. Perhaps there is something deeper he won't bring to light. It makes me nervous, because I don't wish to find out what could develop should we linger around each other more, sexual or otherwise.

"Yeah, I'm not much a fan of that idea," Alex responds.

"What's the issue? I've proven I can handle the responsibility."

"It's not about what you've been able to accomplish regarding her security. I find it strange that you're so adamantly pursuing a responsibility you bitched about previously."

"What can I say? The princess has grown on me," he says, winking at me.

"I simply don't find it necessary. I'll arrange for a team to stand by in case something should appear amiss at any point."

Luca glowers at him. "You're making a mistake, Marc."

"I do appreciate all you've done, truly. I had my concerns, but it's clear Jess has been well looked after, and for that, I'm incredibly grateful to you. You were the best man for the job while she was in Paris, however, I've got it sorted from here."

Luca's face appears as that of a man who has lost a wager, riddled with disappointment, though I can tell he's trying to mask it. "At least let me escort her back to Paris. She can get whatever belongings of hers are important, and perhaps even work things out with Madame Chérot and her other employers."

"That's not a bad idea," I say with a sigh of relief, happy that we're finally getting to a mutually agreed upon resolution. "Especially the part about getting things with work sorted out. Then, I can take a flight to New York and from there purchase an entirely separate ticket home, so the farthest I'd likely be tracked is that first flight."

Alex is quiet as he contemplates whether this is an acceptable plan. Luca glances between us, waiting patiently for a response, which is again surprising. "I don't know about this, Brown Eyes. I'd feel better if you left straight from here. If Maxime finds out you're headed to America at all, especially for longer than the length of a short visit, he'd easily suspect you returned home to Nebraska."

He makes a good point, once again. It's insane, the hoops I must jump through to avoid this man. If only Aralyn had also provided a guide on hiding from her father when giving me her journals.

Before I can speak, Alex continues. "It's too risky. As far as we know, he's unaware that you're here with me. I say we use that to our advantage, and get you out of Europe before he catches on to anything that's taken place. I understand how important your career is to you, darling, but Luca is right in that you may have to make some sacrifices."

Sacrifice. What a terrifying word, especially when it pertains to what I worked so hard to achieve. The need to do so isn't written in stone, but it could be, and to have that looming over me, for heavens knows how long, is draining to consider.

"Well, I see my assistance is no longer needed." Luca's chair screeches across the tile floor as he stands. "I'll see myself out." He takes quick strides toward the dining room exit, and I'm thrust into panic.

"Wait! That's it? You're just going to leave? No goodbye? Nothing?"

"You're in good hands. Bye," he says brusquely as he continues his exit, no hesitation, no looking back.

I've fallen into a state of disbelief. "LUCA!"

He whirls around and I instantly take notice of his watery eyes, expressive with frustration. He throws his arms out and he replies with, "What else does La Princesa require?" There's a secret hope in his look. Hope that I won't let him leave without a purpose, a purpose involving me.

I'm utterly dumbfounded by this emotional reaction, and irritated. He hasn't got the right to it. We are nothing. We share nothing. We can be nothing other than partners in a mutual mission to trick a madman into never getting what he wants. That is it. That is all. We stand united in the nothingness we are together. Doesn't he see that?

As he studies my reaction, he begins to see it too. "Alright, then." His expression hardens and he leaves the room.

I search through my own emotions, yearning to make sense of them, but they are so scrambled, my head is spinning. Alexander's hand on the small of my back guides my attention to him. "Well, he seems genuinely upset. Are you alright?"

"I need to go talk to him. I can't let him leave like that."

There's no telling if Alex understands why I want to do it, but he doesn't ask questions. With a stiff nod he says, "Go on, then. Ring if you need me."

"I won't be long." I make a mad dash through and out of the house. Luca closes the driver's side door just as I reach his car. I yell at him through the window, "Luca, wait, let's talk!" He turns on the engine. "Luca, come on!" The SUV starts to reverse, and I pound my fist against the window. "Will you stop being a bitch, and open the fucking door!" That should get his attention.

The vehicle jolts as it comes to an abrupt stop, and the window lowers. "*Who's* being a bitch?"

"You! Are you being for real right now? What is going on with you today? First you show up acting completely unlike yourself, and then you want to throw a tantrum and storm out because you can't have things the way you want them?"

"You wouldn't understand."

"Then help me understand."

"Maybe it's better this way," he grumbles, refusing to make eye contact with me, choosing instead to stare out the front window.

"What? What do you mean?"

No response. A few minutes pass in which not a word is spoken between us, and only the low hum of the engine can be heard. I study the emotion that wells in his eyes again, and the strange way his Adam's apple moves as he swallows. Then, he lets out a long jittery breath. "Can you just do one thing for me?"

I fold my arms across my chest as a measure of comfort, while worry fills me. "What do you need?"

"You. And Alexander too. I'll stay here in Florence for however long is necessary, just please meet with me before you leave for America. There's a box of Aralyn's belongings she asked me to give him. I would have brought them today, but I was still debating if I should."

"What's changed your mind?"

"You have." He finally looks at me. "I don't want to talk much about it. Please, text me when the arrangements for your flight have been made. We can meet up somewhere before you are taken to the airport. I'll give Alexander the box … and I'll give you a proper goodbye." He gives me a faint smile but his expression remains somber.

"Okay. I will." My heart hurts for him. Here sits a man riddled with pain, fighting a loosing battle with the torments of his past and present. I'm ashamed to only now realize that his "tantrum" was likely warranted after all, and this is yet another situation that isn't about me, not entirely. I'm merely witness to an undoing.

Without much thought, I open his door, rise to my tip-toes and reach in, wrapping him in a heartfelt embrace. "Goodbyes must be extra hard right now. I'm so sorry, Luca."

He's very still for a moment, perhaps taken aback by my act. But then, he gradually wraps his arms around me too, and holds me tight. "I am sorry also," he murmurs.

Once we release each other, I grasp his face in my hands, preparing to say something in the hopes of providing comfort. However, he instantly averts his gaze and grasps my wrists, gently pulling them away. "Don't. I'll be fine."

Not wishing to upset him, I take a few steps back, allowing him the opportunity to close his door. "I'll be texting you soon," I call out. "Have a safe drive." He says nothing in return, opting to give a quick wave before putting the car in reverse.

As he backs out the driveway, I am haunted by a looming dread. However, I can't pinpoint why. I understand that grief affects everyone differently, and Luca was bound to handle the loss of his sister in a different manner than Alex, and certainly me. But is it really grief that is responsible for this sense of doom I feel?

After his vehicle is out of sight, and before I make my way inside, my phone chimes. An email notification pops up for the confirmation of an airline ticket. I click it and see that the flight listed is for tomorrow night. Alex wasted no time at all.

Somebody hold me steady. Everything's moving too fast.

Journal,

What am I doing?

All I agreed to give him was one date. ONE. I was confident there wouldn't be another, in fact, I was determined to make sure there wouldn't be another. I did everything to be the most lackluster date he ever had. My goal was to get him to want to leave me be, that way he'd quit taunting me with his presence. But, I made the mistake of thinking I was in control that night.

Every bit of control I thought I had slipped away when I rolled my eyes at something he said and he calmly reached around the table and dragged the chair I was in till I was planted right next to him. Eyes from all across the restaurant watched as he drew me close and whispered in my ear that if I rolled my eyes again, he'd bend me over the table and give my beautiful ass the thrashing it deserves without shame. I should have been appalled but I wasn't, I was impressed. Impressed that after all the hell I put him through on that date, he was still there, and by the fact that he didn't give me a demand or an attitude the entire night. He was a pure gentleman, until this one naughty trigger brought out the Dom I've suspected was there.

I looked at him in shock and he held my gaze, promising me that, be it heaven or hell I was after, he would give me the time of my life. He inched in, gauging my body language, waiting to see if I'd pull away or welcome him. He kissed me and OH, he was hot, oh, so hot, and I was melting. I was melting fast. And while we were outside waiting for the car, I wanted to jump in his skin and melt some more. Fuck! Ugh! This is so wrong!

Men are not on my list of priorities. I couldn't care less if I spend the rest of my life single. All I really want is to live a self-indulgent life, with no shortage of mind-blowing sex to satisfy my body's desires. But a relationship is what he will eventually want, and a relationship is not in my life plan. But, god, he has me curious.

What if it could be?

No. No, I refuse to entertain such a thought. I know what I want. I won't let him fuck up the dreams I have for myself. But maybe, just for ONE night, it wouldn't be so bad if I let him fuck ME.

Date number two tomorrow. Pray I come to my senses.

30

I hesitate before knocking on Alexander's bedroom door. But just as I make the decision to follow through, it swings open. He stands shirtless, and my eyes travel from his handsome face, to his Adonis belt, that beautifully crafted ridge of muscle along his waist, leading to a V that disappears beneath the towel wrapped around him. I swallow hard, caught off guard by the breathtaking sight. Could the heavens have created a more finely sculpted man?

"Are you alright?" he asks.

"Um, y-yeah, I… Wait, how did you know I was at the door?"

"I didn't actually know it was you. I noticed a shadow underneath."

"Oh. Makes sense. Well, I came to talk to you about something, but we can totally just chat in the morning."

For the first time ever, I catch him rolling his eyes. Then he smirks as he takes hold of my arm and pulls me into the room, shutting the door behind us. I laugh, "Did I actually witness you do the one thing you consistently reprimand me for?"

He walks past me with an amused glimmer in his eyes. "Whatever you think you saw, you didn't."

"Uh huh. I won't forget this."

He takes a seat at the edge of his bed. "Mmm, forget, don't forget, it matters little. It won't keep my palm from your ass if I catch you doing it."

I step forward and chuckle, folding my arms across my chest. "Seems kind of hypocritical, but I'll do my best to be obedient."

He grins. "Perfect. That's all I ask."

"I received the confirmation for a flight tomorrow night. So soon?"

"I feel the sooner we can get you out of Europe, the better."

"Right…" There's no hiding my disappointment. "I hate that I'm leaving you. I hate that you'll be so far. You're being threatened too, remember? Maybe I should stay and we can face the dangers together."

"Come to me." I do as he calmly commands and he draws me into a straddled position on his lap. His hand sweeps through my hair. "My darling, you weren't supposed to be here in the first place. I was supposed to come back for *you*, not the other way around. But, I am tremendously grateful that I've had you with me through all of this. Though separating pains me every time, this is, again, necessary."

I bow my head, but with a gentle tuck of his finger beneath my chin, he lifts it back up again. "Brown Eyes, my circle is small, and I've lost too many from it whom I care deeply for. I'd love nothing more than to physically be with you through this, but I can't lose you too. I won't."

I lean forward and kiss him with a tenderness as sweet as his words. "You won't."

"Mm, good." He kisses me again and then, as the kisses begin to reach a point of easily spilling into the hot and heavy zone, he stops.

"Is something wrong?"

"There is another matter we should discuss."

My eyebrow quirks with curiosity. "What other matter?"

"Luca."

I'm not sure about this, but I have a guess. "If it's about me running out to check on him, I did it because he didn't seem like himself today. I was concerned."

He shakes his head. "No, it's not that. His behavior, though bizarre, was understandable. I'm glad you went after him. I certainly wouldn't have been the one for that job."

"Yeah, I can't imagine that would have gone over well. So, then, what do we need to talk about?"

He gently moves me off his lap and casually strolls over to the bar cart. I admire the way the muscles in his back and arms move and flex as he prepares a small glass of whiskey. "I observed the way he looked at you today," he responds before taking a sip. "Luca might be a fucking bastard, but he's always had good taste." He sets the glass down and faces me, crossing his arms over his chest. "He fancies you. A lot."

Shit. I don't know where this is headed, but I want to find a reverse lever fast. I laugh half-heartedly "Bastard, huh? I think this is the first I've heard you speak so ill of him to me."

"It's a well-earned title. He has placed himself in the position, several times, to be one of my least favorite people. And, now that I know he fancies you, he's ranked even higher on that list."

I smirk. "You seem little jealous."

"You seem a little guilty." My smirk fades. Meanwhile, his face glows with amusement. "I learn new things about you all the time, Brown Eyes. But the one thing I've known since day one is that you're horrible at keeping your feelings hidden. Your body language could use some improvement in the control department." He's not wrong. I'm embarrassed to think of what exactly he picked up on today, though I shouldn't really feel guilt. After all, Alex and I aren't together, and nothing has been confirmed as exclusive. But my heart feels shame, because it's my heart that feels committed to him. "I sense something happened between the two of you," he adds.

I am quiet, uncertain of how to respond yet. I mean, what is there to say? I do have an attraction to Luca, and though it's mostly physical, I haven't entirely worked out how deep or how intense the attraction is. I can't lie, I can't deny it, but I certainly can't confess to Alex that the man who's ranked one of the highest on his list of least favorite people had me orgasming against my office desk recently. No, I'm not about to set myself up like that. Best to say nothing at all.

"I see my suspicions are correct," he says. "Your silence is rather telling." His expression projects slight displeasure.

"I'm not innocent, that's for sure. I—"

He holds his hand up, signaling me to stop. "I don't need to hear details."

"Right. Okay… I'm really sorry I've upset you."

"Well, I'm disappointed. But upset? No. I don't believe I've earned that right." He steps toward me. "I've kept you at a distance for a long time, both physically and emotionally. And obviously, under the circumstances, I've been unable to be as attentive to your needs as I'd like. Not to mention I've given you nothing in terms of a commitment, so I'd be a bloody idiot to expect yours." He cocks his head. "Still … I simply cannot let this go unaddressed, my love."

My brow crinkles. "What do you mean?"

"I mean, on your knees."

"Alex, I—"

"Do it." His voice is tender but there's strength behind it. I rise from the bed and my knees fold beneath me. I look up at him with concern, followed by anticipation, as excitement also settles on my spirit. Most of the time this position has led me to some thrilling experiences.

He takes a few more steps, coming to a stop directly in front of me, and runs a hand through my hair and down my cheek. Like a kitten, I press myself deeper into the warmth of his palm, soaking in every beautiful sensation his touch brings. I gaze up at him, still shirtless and damp, with freshly washed hair falling over his brow as he looks at me with such affection. I've missed this more than I can express.

"I adore you," he says. "But unfortunately, I think you're starting to forget it. I believe it's time I remind you that the only person you should ache for is me." He crouches down, continuing to cup my cheek. "The only touch you should crave is mine. Understood?"

"Yes, Sir." The way he looks, the way he sounds, the way he takes control is like the world's most delectable cocktail. The perfect blend of sweetness, with a strong kick that will promise you an unforgettable time. He hasn't done much yet, and already I'm sold on whatever he's selling. If it's punishment, so be it, as long as he's the one to serve it. My body may have folded the other day, but my mind, and especially my heart, stand firm in the knowledge that I belong here by Alex's side. I've never wanted to leave it.

He kisses my forehead the way he always does, so lovingly. Then, taking one of my hands, he plants a kiss in the center of my palm, then on each of my fingers. He stares at me the whole time, eyes shimmering with heated devotion. "Now, with this hand, I want you to touch yourself." I rapidly blink with surprise, and he smiles, loving the fact that his request is startling. "Go ahead."

Like the obedient sub I aim to be, I part my legs, using the hand he blessed to lift the skirt of my dress and draw my panties aside. Then, I guide my fingers over and between my folds, tender to the touch because I want him so damn bad. My eyes lower, and I take notice of his erect cock straining against his towel. I moan softly, incredibly aroused by the sight.

"Eyes up here. I want you to look at me while you're touching yourself." This is a different level of exposure, possibly more vulnerable and intimate than any other kind. Not only is he watching me pleasure myself for him, and not only is he studying my every reaction to this act, but he's staring into my soul. There's something about eye contact in moments like this that open you up in a way nothing else can. He sees me alright, and it's the hottest thing on earth, scorching.

"Tell me how you feel."

"Needy."

He grins. "Good. Now, spank it."

I almost ask what he means, but I know exactly what he means. After a few seconds of hesitancy, my hand draws back a little and with a slap, I wince. My clit is extremely sensitive to any bit of pain or pleasure right now.

"Harder." Fuck, seriously? I roll my bottom lip between my teeth, slightly nervous for what's to come, but I do as I'm told. My hand makes contact once more and I yelp at the sting. "Mmm, that hurt a little, didn't it?" I nod. "Good. Now, tell me, did he kiss you?"

I look down to the floor in shame, a clear admission of my guilt. "Mm. You really have been a bad girl, haven't you? Alright then." He stands, and before I can even process what he's doing, the towel drops to his feet, revealing his glorious staff at full attention. My brow arches as I take him in, highly impressed, as though it's my first time laying eyes on his divine package. It's so … perfect. Not too veiny, but what veins are there stand out like reverse riverbeds in earth, majestic.

"Would you like to take a guess as to what you'll be doing tonight?"

"Um—giving you a blow job?"

His chuckle is low and layered with hidden knowing. "How cute. But no. No, you see, good girls get to give blow jobs. Bad girls… well…" He reaches down and runs his fingers through my hair, then grabs a fist full, yanking my head back. "Bad girls get their throats fucked." My eyes grow wide.

"Y-you mean like last time?" I'm transported to the memory of the time I spent at Alexanders Paris estate, when he also had me on my knees, servicing him, in his playroom. I remember a couple instances where he had me choking on his cock till my eyes grew watery.

"Baby, am I to assume that was the closest you ever came to a proper throat fuck?" Is he trying to say it gets more intense than that?

"Well, yes. I've given oral before, but nothing rough."

"You're adorable. *That* was merely a sample. I'm going to give you the full experience tonight. Open up." He must see the concern in my eyes as I take another look at his rock-hard member swaying inches from my face, questioning how much of him I can take. "Don't worry. I know you can handle it." I wish I had that kind of confidence in myself.

My lips part as I open my mouth, nervous, but as ready as I can be. I reach out to take him in my hand and he steps back. "Naughty, naughty. Rule number one, hands behind your back." Of course, I should have anticipated this. "Hold on. Hand me your belt first."

I pull the soft black fabric through the loops of my purple dress and hand it to him. Slowly, he walks behind me and binds my hands with it. "What's the safe word?"

"Red."

He returns to his place in front of me and strokes himself. A bead of pre-cum forms at the head of his manhood and he presses it against my lips. My tongue sweeps over him and I savor his taste. He groans. "Good girl. Wider."

The muscles in my jaw stretch as I grant him passage, taking him about two-thirds of the way. "That'a girl. Now relax," he says as he holds my head steady and gradually moves his hips forward. My throat expands and then my gag reflex kicks in. My instinct is to pull away, but his grip is firm, maintaining my position for several seconds. Finally, he pulls out, a trail of saliva connecting the two of us together still. I gasp for air and quickly note the small bursts of exhilaration and adrenaline that race through my body.

My grin is one of genuine enthusiasm. "Again. Please, Sir."

The pride glowing in his expression gives me immense pride in myself. "Well, aren't you an eager little minx."

"I can do better; I want you to be pleased with me." His pleasure is mine.

"Spoken like a true submissive. Beautiful. Trust me, love, we won't be stopping till your mascara runs down those rosy cheeks."

He picks up where he left off, and when I gag he draws out and thrusts in again, repeating the pattern too many times to count. I'm allowed to come up for air every so often. It's wild, filthy, being used like this, and I admittedly love every bit of it.

My eyes water as he continuously tests my limits, continuing to push deeper. I choke till tears trickle from my eyes like rain down a window. "Fuck. That's it, baby. You're doing so good." My bosom is more soaked than my face is as our deed becomes sloppier. We go on like this till Alexander's breath grows heavy and I can tell he's seconds away from climax. He quickens his pace, mercilessly pounding the back of my throat until he bursts, filling me with the warmth of his seed.

"Hold it," he huffs as he finishes, then crouches to my level. His hand clasps over my mouth. "Swallow." I watch him observe the way my throat moves as I ingest the product of his satisfaction. Then, his scorching gaze flits to mine once again. "That's how you cleanse a bad girl of her sins." He plants a kiss on my forehead before setting my mouth free.

From the bathroom he brings a warm, damp cloth and cleans off my face, ruined makeup and all, with such tenderness, it's bewildering to think he's the same man who's responsible for the mess. "What would you like for aftercare? A hot bath? Cuddle time? Perhaps something to eat?"

"All the above?"

He chuckles. "As you wish."

He moves behind me, crouching down once again to untie the bind. As he does, he leans in, trailing sweet kisses along my collar bone and beneath my ear. Then in a tone barely above a whisper he says, "Be mine." The way his voice travels through me is a soothing balm to my soul and, suddenly, it's as though I've been asleep all this time. For it's those two words, those two simple little words that wake me like blossoms on a tree when spring beckons.

However, along with the joy and relief that flushes through my system, comes fear to take root in their place. My eyes snap open. "Wait, you're serious?"

"I am. Let's make dating official."

I look over my shoulder at him. "Alex, this is too quick. You just lost—"

"Aralyn. Yeah. And it's because of her I'm choosing this."

The bind on my wrists drops away and I turn on my knees to face him. "What?"

"I have spent too long putting my own happiness on a shelf so I could be a savior, whether to those close to me, or as an attempt to protect myself from pain. Aralyn knew this about me. She knew I would never have allowed myself to be happy if I spent my time worrying about trying to get her better, which I absolutely would have done. I've only recently come to accept it as truth. And though that's to be expected from any partner, she also knew, for me, to have tried and failed would have sent me spiraling. I might as well have been buried alongside her, for the guilt I would have burdened myself with.

"I have been blinded by a self-imposed need to protect and hide and, in doing so, I had lost sight of what it is like to really live. That's all she wanted. It's why she did what she did, why she kept her struggles a secret. Aralyn wanted me to *live*, not for my business, not for my parents, not for her … for me.

"So you see, I have a dying wish to fulfill also. I have to grant myself permission to go after the things that will bring me joy. And I'm still working out what all of that looks like, but I know with absolute certainty that you bring me much of it." A tear descends from my eye, and with one fluid movement, his thumb sweeps it away. "I thought a lot about what you said, about fear being the real thief. I don't want to hide in it any more, letting precious moments slip through my grasp forever. I want to pursue a happy, full existence, and I'd love for you to be an important part of whatever comes next."

I throw my arms around him and sob with happiness. He rubs my back and I can hear the smile in his voice. "I take it that's a yes to being mine."

"Yes! A million times yes!"

After several minutes in each other's embrace, he says, "I'll start your bath." Then, he wraps his towel around his waist and rises, strutting to the bathroom like a proud peacock.

I sit where I am, in awe of how, at the most unexpected times, life can be gracious with her nectar, allowing us the taste we've craved, begged for. This night I am witness to such blessings, and overcome with gratitude. It's exactly what I needed before stepping into the black abyss of uncertainty that is the next few months. At least something is certain and good. Oh, so good.

Alex is the anchor to it all.

Journal,

There's sex, and then there's SEX! The kind of mind numbing, soul snatching, toe-curling sex that you don't have with just anyone. How is it that this man has completely diagnosed my needs and provided me the prescription all at once?

I've been sitting in this bed for two hours now, reflecting on what I thought I knew about pleasure and intimacy. I've come to the major realization that my perception of it all has been so skewed! I've been trying to find the words that explain what it is like to have someone not simply fuck me, but make love to me. To see my soul freefalling in the intense storm of passion and grab it, holding it tight, cradling it like it is the most precious thing in the universe. It is a feeling every woman should experience. When you've been through what I have, that kind of care means more than I could ever truly express.

It almost seemed like a dream, unreal, a figment of my imagination. But I pinched myself as we lay in bed after, breathless and dizzy with happiness, and I know it's far from it. He tucked me into him and held me for a solid hour. We didn't exchange a word, but we didn't need to. He said so much to me in how he made love to me. So much.

I've been trying hard not to entertain this man's advances. But there is no more running away. If this is but a mere taste of who he is, then I want the whole thing.

Journal,

Last night Alexander and I traveled south to Nice for a kink party at one of the underground clubs. It was my first time wearing the signature mask that lets guests know I'm off limits. I've never had a reason to wear it before. Actually, I never thought I'd ever have need to wear one. After all, I had sworn off partners. I was certain that I'd live a life free of commitment, free of what I thought at the time was limitation and restraint. I never again wanted to be shackled by anything or anyone. But Alex, there's something about him that makes it seem like those ideas and visions I developed for myself belonged to someone else entirely. He is the only person to ever make me feel as though commitment may not be as limiting as I perceived. I've never met a soul as beautiful as his.

He is a man who knows what he wants, but he does not take it with entitlement. He is, however, skilled in the art of persuasion, masterful at it. With patience, gentleness, care and tenderness, he can even convince stubborn me to kneel before him and submit to his will. And to my surprise, I love it. I love it because in his approach to obtain my submission, he's granted me the freedom to fall into it in a way that feels comfortable and right.

He has desired me as a lover from the moment we met, but he did not act desperately. He's a man who takes his time for those he believes are worthy of it, and his ambition in life echoes in his persistence for anything he seeks to have, including me. So, regardless of my reservations, I proudly wore the mask and allowed him to lead me through the club as his, and only his.

It's hard to say, Journal, but the feelings I'm developing for him are ones I'm not familiar with. They are foreign and frightening, yet exciting and joyful. Dare I say I'm in love?

Perhaps, he loves me too.

Seven months of devotion to his pursuit of me. Seven months of knowing, before I ever did, that there was something between us which deserved to be explored. Seven months of dealing with my messy life and family drama, and never once has he let it deter his affection for me. Seven months of calmly putting up with my continuous rejection because I was so afraid. He knew that. And through it all, he's remained.

Because he's remained, I shall too. I'm finally prepared to embark on a whole new journey with him. Prepared to be loved. Prepared to be his.

31

Alex and I stroll through the park, arms linked, while we wait for Luca's arrival. The setting sun glints through the trees, children's laughter can be heard in the distance, and many dogs are accompanying their owners on a leisurely walk. Statues glow as golden hour kisses them. It's a romantic setting, and I'm appreciative of the last bit of time together before Alex and I part ways once again.

"What would you like me to get you from Nebraska?" I tease.

"Haha, I'm afraid I'm not well versed on what one could desire from such a place."

"Hmm. I'll think of something."

His laughter is warm and honeyed. "Very well then. Gen must be thrilled to be getting her mate back for a spell."

"Oh, she's over the moon. She wouldn't stop squealing with excitement when I told her last night. She was going on and on about everything we'll get into. Don't worry, though, she's aware I still have to be cautious out there."

"You'll be well taken care of, I'm sure. Perhaps, when all this clears up, I'll come for a visit before you return, to see where you grew up."

I bounce with excitement. "Oh my god, yes. You could meet my parents! They will absolutely love you."

The smile he flashes is so wholesome. "It would be an honor to meet the two responsible for rearing such an incredible woman."

I fit perfectly beneath his arm as we continue our walk. "What about you? What will you do while I'm away, besides work, that is?"

"I think I shall take up pottery."

"Pottery? Why pottery?"

He shrugs one shoulder. "It's something new and unexpected. No one ever really foresees a billionaire taking an interest in clay. But for more personal reasons, I want to tap into my creative side more. What better way than to craft beautiful, delicate, intricate pieces with these hands." He raises them, turning them over as if examining their potential. I grab hold of one, entwining my fingers with his and kissing the back of it.

"Love it. I'm excited to see what these hands can do."

His grin is playful. "I'm sure you are. Naughty girl."

My phone chimes, alerting me to a text notification. "It's Luca. He says he's close and to meet him toward the east entrance of the park."

"Did he say how close? I don't want us to be delayed getting you to the airport. We're cutting it close on time already."

I text him to inquire how far out he is. I'd hate to have to leave without fulfilling his request for a goodbye, or getting the items Aralyn wanted Alex to have, but Alex is right, time is dwindling. We head toward the park's rear entrance and wait. A couple minutes pass, then a couple more. Then seven minutes turn to twenty, and the sun has almost completely disappeared below the horizon. The sounds of joyful people fade as the park empties.

Alex becomes visibly restless. "This is ridiculous. Why hasn't he responded by now? He does know you have a plane to catch, yeah?"

"He does. I texted him again a couple minutes ago to tell him we're waiting here, but still nothing. I hope he's alright."

The way the night creeps in causes the once scenic park to appear eerie, and a sense of foreboding quickly sets in. We are the only ones here, as far as we can see. "Something doesn't feel right about this. I'm giving Carmyn a ring. I'll tell her to have the car pick us up on the north side, it's a closer walk."

"Why not just have it pick us up at this entrance?"

He shakes his head. "I'm telling you, something about this isn't right. I don't like that we are in the dark, alone. I don't like that he's taking so long to get here. Something's up." I've never seen him so nervous and on guard. I question, momentarily, if this sudden anxiousness is because of all we've experienced lately, rightfully so. But I get the feeling he actually senses something very bad is about to happen, and I trust his intuition, so if he says we should go, we're going.

He takes my hand and we start down the path, "He'll have to make other arrangements at a later time. Sorry, Brown Eyes."

"I totally get it. Better safe than sorry."

A voice calls out, "I'm right here!"

We turn and watch a figure walking in from the entry gate. "Luca?" I ask.

"Yeah," he replies. As he approaches us, it's clear he's carrying something, but it's hard to make out what it is. Then, the park lamps turn on, providing some illumination, and what is revealed is a woman slumped in his arms. She looks like Sleeping Beauty, in an all black summer dress, with a coat of the same color, her feet bare. Pretty auburn waves fall across her face. Her pale skin and frail body are evidence of her sickly state.

I gasp as he draws closer, and Alexander stands paralyzed in shock as we both come to the jaw dropping realization that he carries Aralyn. "My god…" Alex utters.

"She's barely conscious," Luca casually says as he reaches us. "Doctor said she could pass any day now. It wasn't a good idea to travel so far with her, but I had no other choice."

"What is this? What is happening?" Alex asks in astonishment.

"*This* is your opportunity to pay me back, Marc. Jess won't stop going on about how much you love my sister. I'm still a skeptic, but for Aralyn's sake, I pray you can make me a believer. I've kept her away from our father for as long as I can, but he nearly found her. I can't allow it. I can't allow her last moments of life to be in the prison of his toxicity. You are my last resort. If she's with you, at least she won't suffer … at least she'll have peace. Hide her, and hide her well."

"Y-you told us she was dead." Alex attempts to choke back his emotions, though it's clearly difficult. "I've been mourning her for the past two weeks and this whole time … it was a lie you fabricated?"

"I had to," Luca replies with a stoic expression.

"WHAT THE BLOODY HELL FOR?"

"To come up with a reason to get Jess back to you while I went to collect Aralyn. But, it had to be in a way that would hold your trust enough to bring her to me today … to do this exchange." This can't be real.

Alex steps forward slowly. "*What* exchange?"

"Aralyn for Jess." He says it so nonchalantly, as if we are fucking trading cards. His eyes lock onto mine and he answers the flabbergasted expression on my face. "I never told my father we were dating. I knew he would not believe it. What I told him was that I was *pretending* to date you and that my doing so was a ploy to get you to trust me and hopefully open up to me about Aralyn's whereabouts. It worked for a little while, but he's grown impatient waiting for results and now wishes to speak to you himself. So, I had to come up with a plan to get you in front of him without Alexander interfering and, at the same time, ensuring my sister would be safe."

I shake my head in disbelief. "No, it can't be true. It's not true, Luca." Even with the evidence of his deception held in his arms, I still can't bring myself to believe the enormity of his betrayal.

"He's expecting you. I promised I'd get you to him, even if had to take you by force."

I'm at a loss for words. This whole time… This whole damn time he's been playing me for a fool, playing all of us for fools. How stupid I was to think he actually gave a shit about me. This wasn't some spontaneous decision. It was a well-developed plan. How long he's had it in play is unclear, but what is clear is that his sole intention was always to do whatever it took to keep his sister from their father's reach—even if it meant my sacrifice.

He moves forward again, slowly, and whispers things to Aralyn in Spanish as he kisses the top of her head. The mask he held onto cracks, and a tear slides over the scar on his cheek. It's as if he's saying goodbye, as if he expects that it could very well be the last time he sees her alive.

He stops directly in front of us, looking straight at Alex. "Come. Take her. Let's do this." Alex doesn't make a move; his face is marked by the emotional turmoil Luca has caused. The war waging within him is visible in his stormy glare.

Still, Luca persists. "What's with the hesitation? You owe me this, Marc."

"Are you completely mad? I'm not handing Jess over so you can play good boy for your fucking father!"

"Not even for the woman you claim to love? Or are you finally ready to admit your words never held true weight?"

"That's so unfair of you to ask him that and you know it," I yell, trembling with rage. "God, will you think about what you're doing? Aralyn would never want this, Luca!"

"She's on death's doorstep, Princesa, she doesn't have a say. I will act in her best interest until my last breath." One would think it would be desperation showing in his eyes, but it's not, it's certainty. In his mind, he's the hero, saving his sweet sister from torment. In his mind, he owes her this. In his mind, despite what we or anyone else may think, he's doing everything right. As long as she's okay, the rest of the world can burn, and he'll willingly throw himself into the flames, too, if it means she'd be kept from them in the end.

"Take her," Luca repeats.

Alex steps forward and looks at Aralyn, and his hand trembles as he sweeps strands of hair from her fair face. He sucks in a sharp breath, moved by emotion, taken aback by the reality that she is alive, although barely holding on. Then, in a surprising move, he steps back and stands in front of me, to keep me where I am. "No," he murmurs softly.

"What?"

"NO. The audacity to think you've remotely earned the right to make demands of me. If you want my help with Aralyn, fine. But there will be no exchange. Jess isn't going anywhere with you."

"Alex, this must be done. My father—"

"Oh, fuck your father! And fuck you!"

Luca shouts, enraged, "TAKE HER!" But Alex continues his lethal stare down. "Fine," he replies, then takes Aralyn to a bench a few feet away, gently laying her on it, along with a backpack I assume holds some of her belongings. As soon as he's finished, Alex takes large strides toward him and clocks him across the jaw with such force it knocks Luca to the ground. Then, without even a moment to collect himself, Alex grabs him by his shirt and yanks him to his feet, drawing his arm back to hit him again, but stopping as a raspy voice rings out from the darkness.

"I wouldn't, if I were you." Like the thing of nightmares, Emil emerges from the shadows, gun in hand. I gasp in fright as he points it right at the center of Alexander's forehead.

"Who the hell are you?" Alex frustratedly asks.

"Clearly, the man with the gun."

Luca pushes Alex off him and wipes the trickle of blood at the corner of his mouth. "I didn't want it to come to this," he remarks. "He is only here as backup. Do as I ask and it won't escalate. Like I said, I'm taking Jess with me, even if it's by force." They are working together? My heart drops to my stomach. How did I not see any of this coming? What did I miss?

In yet another unexpected twist, the barrel of Emil's gun shifts to me. Luca's eyes grow wide with shock. "Woah! What are you doing?" he asks Emil in French.

"Speeding things up." He pulls back the safety and every part of me goes numb. This has to be some insane fever dream. "She has two minutes to come with us or else. Two minutes." He glances at his wristwatch. "That is all the mercy my patience will allow."

"This wasn't part of the plan." Luca growls.

Emil is unphased. "Plans change. You should know all about that." He holds his position as his eyes study the fear in mine.

I can sense Alexander's mind working overtime to find a way to diffuse this situation. "You won't kill her if you need her."

"Who said anything about killing her? She can go with us, scathed or unscathed. What will it be?" Emil responds carelessly.

Glowering at Luca, Alex asks, "Did you ever bother to think what this would do to Aralyn when she wakes up to find you've done this?"

Luca shakes his head, frantically trying to make sense of Emil's actions while searching for an answer to Alexander's question. "She'll be alright. She'll be alright because she'll have you. She'll have the love of her life with her. All you have to do is keep her safe." Though concerned about what his partner might do, he speaks in a controlled tone. "Do you think you can manage that this time?"

"There's another way. I know there is," Alex replies.

"There isn't. I promised my father Jess, and I intend to deliver."

Alex quickly walks in my direction, coming to a stop in front of me, acting as a barrier between me and the weapon. "I won't let that happen."

A shot rings out. I scream as the bullet hits the ground, narrowly missing his foot. A bone chilling cold sweeps through my body. Emil glares at Alex. "That is my first and only warning." The look in his eyes is one of unwavering commitment to seeing out his mission … by *any* means necessary.

Aralyn stirs on the bench, still cloaked in sleep. Amidst these earth-shattering events, I think about her. I think about what she's had to endure from the moment she was born, the constant struggle to find her freedom from inside a cage, whether that cage was of Maxime's making or unknowingly her own. I think of how life has been so incredibly cruel to this woman, slighted her in so many ways. She didn't deserve the brutality of it then, and she doesn't deserve it now. Although Luca's actions are heartbreaking, I understand wanting to ensure her last moments of life aren't also riddled with the trauma she spent so long running from. So, as terrifying as it may be, I am willing to face her monster, if it will help bring her the one thing she does deserve, peace.

I grasp Alexander's arm tight, concerned about the turn this could take if a decision isn't made in a matter of seconds. "Alex, let me go. I can do this. I can face Maxime. I'm the last lead he has. We'll have a talk, and he'll realize I don't have the information he's after."

"That's what I'm worried about, what he might do if he doesn't find you useful."

"He won't hurt her, I swear it," Luca responds.

"I no longer trust you. Especially when you dare stand there, allowing your man to point a gun at her, like the fucking coward you are."

"Alex, I won't let you get hurt trying to protect me. Please, let me go with him. I'll be okay. I *will* find my way back to you. I always do." He glances at me, eyes pleading for me to stay. I reach up, cupping his cheek. "We'll see each other again, soon. I promise." It feels horrible making a promise I don't feel confident I'll be able to keep, but I'd do anything to stop this situation from escalating to the point that he'll get hurt—or worse. Before anything or anyone can change my mind, I step out from behind him. I notice his arm flex, though he resists stopping me. I know letting me do this is tearing him apart.

In an instant, another shot rings out. I screech as Alex pulls me against him. Hearts racing, we questioningly gaze at Emil and then Luca, whose skin turns pale as he looks past us and whispers, "Fuck."

"M-Mr. Marc?"

Alex and I whip our heads toward the whimpering voice that comes from behind us. "Oh my god," I gasp. I look on, horrified, as Carmyn stares at the bright red color that's rapidly blooming across the fabric of her pretty, light-blue blouse. For a moment, her body sways like a willow tree in a storm, then her legs fold beneath her as she collapses to the ground.

"CARMYN!" Alex screams out, taking a few panicked steps toward her.

Emil uses the distraction to grab hold of me. Completely caught off guard, Alex tries to reach for my arm, but it slips from his grasp. Emil walks backward, pressing the gun to my temple. My mind hasn't quite had time to process, but my emotions are a muddled mixture of sadness, rage, fear, and disappointment.

As I become attentive to the sensation of the cold steel, grave anxiety floods my being and I can see fear flashing across Alexander's features. On top of the concern for his friend, he's losing me, and he's terrified it could be forever. "Luca, stop this madness! Please, ju-just take me!" The desperation in his voice is gut-wrenching.

"Do the sensible thing for once and keep my sister safe. If he finds her, I swear, you'll never see Jess again." His threat makes my blood run ice cold.

The anger that rises from the depths of Alex's being is enough to override every other emotion tormenting him as he says in a sinister tone, "Worry about what will happen when *I* find *you*." The promise of hell on earth shines in his deadly gaze.

No more words are exchanged and the three of us back out of the park. My chest tightens more and more as the sight of Alex standing, enraged, between Aralyn and Carmyn's incapacitated bodies fades from view. My spirit is crushed. I am at a loss, what to do from here. With a gun still to my temple, I simply accept being dragged away to the danger I almost managed to flee.

Once we pass the entrance gate and make our way around the corner, Luca gets in Emil's face. "You idiot! I told you to stay back in case I needed you! Why the fuck would you do that?"

Emil looks at him, expressionless. "The need was clear when he had you on your ass."

"You didn't have to shoot that woman."

"It was a necessary sacrifice for our plans to move forward. You got the girl, didn't you? Let's go." He shoves me into Luca and leans in, waving the gun in front of me, "Try to run, try to scream, try to do anything to draw unwanted attention, and the next bullet is for you."

As I'm nudged forward, I can hardly see through the tears that fill my eyes. The sound of sirens are heard in the distance and they grow closer with each step. As we approach the getaway car, Luca quickly places me in the back seat and orders Emil to hurry and drive off.

As Luca gets into the back with me, anger finally finds its way through the muddled mixture that is my emotions. I'd never have guessed that after everything he and I had been through over the past few months, despite him being a pain in my ass most of the time, that this would be the scenario we'd end up in. I swing my fists repeatedly at the man I thought I knew. "Hey! Hey! Calm down, Jess! Stop!"

"You son of a bitch! You shot Carmyn!"

"Emil did! And that was never supposed to happen!"

I continue to wail on him, pouring all the hurt and rage I feel into each strike. He grabs my wrists and pins me back in my seat. "I hate you," I scream, sobbing.

The pain my words inflict disappears in his eyes as quickly as it shows. "You'll never hate me as much as I hate myself, Princesa." It's like a switch is flipped, and his features harden, "It may hurt to hear this, but I can't afford to care how you feel about me right now. What is done had to be done. It's like I told you before, I'll do anything to protect my sister. And although this might not be something you're used to, you're not the priority here."

His slight stings, but not as much as his betrayal. He's become simply one more man on my list of those I thought I could trust, but burned me in the end. "Whatever you have to tell yourself to make this all okay, right? That's always been your way, finding poor excuses for your treacherous behavior and actions."

He roars, "Christ, STOP TRYING TO DIAGNOSE ME! You're not my fucking therapist!" I sink back into my seat even more, startled and shaken. He releases his hold of me, surely seeing my terror. Then he faces forward, runs his hand over his face and yells, "Fuck!" A tear spills from his eye.

Oh, so, after all that, now he wants to cry? Now he wants to feel sorry? What is he sorry for? Does he even know? Well, I don't care about his feelings either. There's no erasing the damage he's caused. I have no sympathy for the devil.

The devil… The devil and the angel at war with each other—his tattoo. I wonder, how many times has this man been caught in a battle for his soul? How many times has he wrestled with what's right and wrong? What does he actually consider a win or a loss?

It's silent for a minute and then, with a trembling spirit and a firm voice, I ask, "Where are you taking me?"

He clears his throat in an attempt to choke back his emotions. "To Paris. It may seem like I'm trying to hurt you, Jess, but I'm not. You'll meet with my father, and it will sustain him long enough for me to come up with a plan to get you out of this."

"Right, because your plans have been working out *so* well."

"He's not going to do anything to you but have a conversation, figure out what you know."

I glare at him incredulously. "You don't know that! That raging lunatic is completely unpredictable. You can't promise me I'm going to be okay. And, news flash, I know a lot now!"

"NO, you don't. You know nothing. That's the story you stick with, no matter what. Don't worry, I won't let him hurt you, Jess."

I cackle, "Oh, really? So, I am a priority to at least some degree? Well, thank god for that!" My hand aggressively wipes my wet cheek and I twist in my seat, turning my back to him, and gaze somberly out the window.

Several moments pass before he attempts to say something else. "Jess, I—"

"You've said and done more than enough. Please … let me be heartbroken in peace."

32

There's a point where fear, anxiety and stress cease, replaced by an emptiness that's unprecedented in one's life. I've reached such a point, and at this time, it's hard to fathom when or how I'll return from it. My mind has chosen to detach from my body's experience, too overwhelmed by the effort to process, too exhausted by the cumbersome weight of emotion it bears. And who would know it? Who around me at present would care?

I am ushered into a large manor after about twelve hours on the road, and led to a grand living room. "Sit," Emil says, pointing to an armchair. I do what I'm told without response or reaction.

Luca squats beside me. "Jess, are you alright?" I don't look at him. I don't speak. I'm here and nowhere all at once, sheltered in a cocoon of my own making, harbored from the wretchedness of a situation I never asked to be in.

He says to Emil, "She's in shock. Pour a glass of that water over there." It's said so matter-of-factly, as though he actually has any idea what I'm going through. It makes me sick.

Emil hands him a half full glass of water and Luca holds it out to me. "Here, take a couple sips. You haven't eaten or drunk anything since we left Florence. This will help you feel better."

Without much thought, I aggressively snatch the glass and throw it across the room with all the strength I can muster. It shatters to pieces that scatter across the ground. Then, in a bitter yet controlled tone I reply, "Do you know what would *really* make me feel better? Never seeing you again, never hearing from you again, never hearing your name mentioned in my presence *ever* again. Erasing you from my existence would make me the happiest woman on earth."

He drops his head as the weight of my words settle on his shoulders. "Jess, listen, I—"

"Carmyn is like family to Alex. Can you imagine having two people you cherish ripped from you in a matter of seconds while reeling from having learned the love of your life, whom you were led to believe was dead, isn't? You may have obliterated Alexander's world, Luca. Congratulations. That's what you wanted, right?"

"Please, try to understand, this isn't about hurting anyone. It was never the intention. Aralyn is the only real family I have left. As long as she lives, I will always put her first. You hate me. Rightfully so. There aren't enough apologies in the world to make up for what I have put you through. I don't expect things between us to ever be okay again. The destruction of our connection was a sacrifice I had to make to protect her."

"You say that like you only recently came to the realization that it was what you would do. Except it wasn't, was it? You've known all along this would happen, didn't you?"

"Not the whole time, no. It was a plan I came up with the same day I left you to visit my father after his business card arrived on the doorstep."

I glare at him, disgusted. "And you came back to me as if everything was normal, pursued my interests, *kissed* me, *touched* me, all the while plotting to betray me."

"Enough of this," Emil interjects. "Luca, go inform Maxime we've arrived."

Luca cuts him an agitated look. "You get him. The walk might help you chill out."

Emil grumbles something out of earshot as he leaves the room. "I'm guessing you've been working with him all along too?" I ask Luca.

He takes the seat next to me. "No. He became part of the plan last minute, when Papa nearly found Aralyn a day or two before we fled Paris. This plan was never supposed to happen the way it did. It was much simpler; I would convince my father dating you was a setup to get information from you, and if I hadn't figured something else out by the time that no longer worked, I'd convince you to meet with him. But it was a last-resort option. I was doing everything I could to figure something else out before then. The problem was, time ran out.

"From what I learned, he recently posted flyers and ads around various cities in Europe, offering a large reward for anyone with information on where she was. Turns out the fucking gardener at the home she'd been hiding at had been going on for months to people he knew about the woman he worked for who he believed to be related to the infamous De la Rues. I'm sure you can envision how quickly calls poured in from the community. Thankfully, news reached me as quickly as it did my father, but it meant having to change my last-resort plan in a way I never anticipated.

"He sent a team of men to the area to figure out her exact location, and sent Emil for you as a backup, in case they ran into issues. I had to act fast. I contacted Alexander's assistant and told her Aralyn was dead and that you were about to be taken hostage if I didn't get you out of Paris. I then asked if I could bring you to them and, well, you know the rest."

"None of that explains how you ended up working with Emil."

His eyes dart around the room as if someone might hear us. Then, he lowers his voice. "After I left you on the train, I called Emil and had him meet me. We've known each other for years, and though he's one of my father's most trusted men, he has no real allegiance to him. He's a lackey like all the rest of us. I pleaded with him to help me, and in exchange I said I'd give him the one thing he really wants."

"What is that?"

"His freedom."

"How is that yours to grant?"

"It's not. Yet." He exhales an exasperated breath before continuing. "I told Emil that in exchange for his help—"

Realization dawns on me and a small gasp escapes my lips. "You're going to kill Maxime," I say quietly. It's the only method of "freeing" Emil that seems plausible.

There's a moment of silence as he considers his response. "It's like I said, I won't let him hurt you. I'm going to get you out of this. I'm going to get all of us out of this."

"N-no, Luca, you can't. Not like that. Think about the risk." Although he's not necessarily confirming it, I know it's what he's intending to do. I'm still so livid, and devastated by his choices and actions. But I'm also petrified by what his deal with Emil could mean for him. The murder of one's father has to taint the soul in some deep, immeasurable way, not to mention the target it might place on his back. Maxime is a madman, but is his blood worth the price in the end? I don't have that answer, and I don't want to find out what it is, either.

Emil strolls into the room. My heart skips a beat, expecting the man of the hour to be right behind him, but he's not. "He'll be down shortly," he says, more to Luca than to me. Then he plops down on the sofa across from us. I can't help but glower at him, irritated by his presence.

He snickers and asks in French, "Have something to say to me, girl?"

"Must feel really nice to sit down for a breather after shooting an innocent woman."

"It would feel a lot nicer if you stopped yapping."

"I guess congratulations are in order for finally doing something besides skulking around, stalking and waiting in the shadows. You can rest easy knowing you no longer have to hide behind guns and stupid notes like the coward you are!" I'm aware that nothing I say will phase him, but insulting him any way I can is a brings a small measure of joy to my soul.

He leans back in the couch and laughs. "Notes? What notes?"

"The stupid black notecards you or whoever is a part of your team keep sending, warning me to stay aw—"

"We don't send notes. As you can tell, we have other more … direct ways of delivering a message." Terror grips me. My biggest threat has now officially confirmed they aren't my only one, and suddenly I'm clueless. "I do know who's sending them, though. All that 'skulking' has given me ample opportunity to witness many things, including your special friend's deliveries."

My head whips toward Luca. "Have you known this too?"

"No. Emil, if you have the name, just tell her."

Emil gives me a fake pout. "You hurt my feelings." Then the side of his mouth draws into a sinister smirk. "Apologize, and I might find it within my cowardly heart to give you the answer to your mystery."

Before I can get a word out in response, I notice someone entering the room. He's a tall man, well into his fifties, dressed in a tailored light-blue suit. His salt-and-pepper hair is neatly styled, full at the top and slicked back to a fade at the nape of his neck, and his black beard is well groomed. His chestnut-colored eyes immediately assess me.

Luca and Emil rise to their feet in a flash, and I stand too, nervous about starting off on the wrong foot so soon. "Ah, you must be, Jess," he says as he approaches with a weird grin, extending his arms as he leans in to give me the French greeting of an air kiss to each cheek.

"Uh, oui. It's a pleasure to meet you, Monsieur De la Rue."

"Le plaisir est pour moi. Please, call me Maxime. It makes me feel less old." He laughs heartily, and I smile to not appear as unamused as I am. "It's good to finally meet the woman my son has told me much about."

Upon first sight, he doesn't strike me as the cruel man I've heard about, but then, he glances at Luca and dully asks, "She understands why she's here?"

"Yes."

"Good." In an instant, his eyes become void of light. "We can skip the uninteresting small talk. You, my dear, have information I need." He slips his hands into his pockets and steps closer. The scent of musk wafts from his body, and malice oozes from his aura.

"I just want to know one thing. One simple answer determines how you and I move forward." His eyes darken in a menacing way, calculated, cold and threatening. "Where is my daughter?"

My eyes dart to Luca, whose own are pleading with me to tread lightly with my response. But at this moment, I'm struck with exhaustion, tired of others dictating my course, so over depending on someone else to protect me. I'm done with lies, manipulation, and deception. It's time to take my life into my own hands. It's time to chart my own course out of this darkness.

I'm sorry, Luca. I won't wait for you to trace my fate in the shifting sands. I won't hold you to your faulty word.

Alex—please, forgive me… I'm about to risk it all.

"I'll take you to her."

<u>Acknowledgments</u>

Tierra Davis, my soul sister, though you'll never get to read this, I know you can hear my heart. You were like the warmth of sun in spring after the coldest winter. The light you projected while here was so brilliant and impactful that when you departed, the cold flooded in and color became duller, my world grew dimmer. But, my sweet friend, the embers of your memory are what keep me moving forward. I honor you by not holding back, by choosing to live with splendor and vigor, gratitude and love. My heart bled into the pages of this book, conceived and birthed through the hardest period of my life, the beginning of an era without you. I will love you forever and when forever ends, I will love you still. Rest in paradise.

Nicole Varela-Glass, my radiant motivator, thank you for being my Alpha reader. As an avid romance book lover, your feedback has been incredibly valuable. Not only have you made a large impact for my readers by helping gauge the flow of this book, you've continuously pushed me to keep going, especially during challenging times. Your enthusiasm for this series and the characters brings so much joy to my soul, and I'm incredibly grateful and honored to call you my friend.

Angel Velasquez, la princesa, thank you for not only being an Alpha reader and one of my closest friends, but for being one of the Red Souls Series' biggest fans. "Where's my book?" and "You better be writing my book!" hilariously plays in my head whenever I sit down to write, hahaha. Thank you for your continuous support and raw, un-sugarcoated feedback. You mean the absolute world to me and I can't imagine having gone through this journey as an author without you there, cheering me on.

Tabitha Saletri, the miracle worker, I can't thank you enough for the patience and kindness you've shown me. When everything in my world stood still, you empathized with my situation and patiently waited for it to spin again, all the while checking on me and encouraging me. You're one hell of an editor and an incredible human being. I will forever appreciate you and I'm so grateful for your hard work and commitment to making Black Hearts a beautifully polished work of fiction.

To all my friends and family who in some way or another provided support and assistance, and rooted for me. There aren't enough words in the world to express my gratitude. I thank you all from the depths of my soul. Know that you made a positive impact. You all have my love!

ABOUT THE AUTHOR

Besides her adoration for the world of romance novels, A. M. Darling is a lover of all things creative. A self-proclaimed Jill of trades, she lives for artistic expression in a variety of mediums- creative writing, fine art and photography being her favorites. She's also an avid traveler, a mentor and life path guide.

Her love for creative writing started at age ten. With her head often in the clouds, she spent a lot of time reading books and creating the characters she envisioned. Writing was her first and most profound form of self-expression and has remained one of the greatest constants throughout her life.

www.ingramcontent.com/pod-product-compliance
Lightning Source LLC
Chambersburg PA
CBHW022256310726
48973CB00001B/98